Dragoncharm

Graham Edwards was born in Shepton Mallett, Somerset, in 1965, and brought up in Bourne-mouth. He attended art school in London and now works as a designer. He lives in Nottingham with his wife Helen and their two children. *Dragoncharm* is his first novel.

ACKNOWLEDGMENTS

Special thanks to Jane Johnson and Joy Chamberlain, for your enthusiasm, support and relentless editing. And to Roger, for the song . . .

Voyager

GRAHAM EDWARDS

Dragoncharm

HarperCollins*Publishers*

Voyager
An Imprint of HarperCollins*Publishers*
77–85 Fulham Palace Road,
Hammersmith, London W6 8JB

www.voyager-books.com

This paperback edition 1997
9 8

Previously published as a paperback original by
HarperCollins Science Fiction & Fantasy 1995
Reprinted twice

Copyright © Graham Edwards 1995

The Author asserts the moral right to
be identified as the author of this work

ISBN 0 00 648021 7

Set in Meridien

Printed and bound in Great Britain by
Caledonian International Book Manufacturing Ltd, Glasgow

For Helen,
for all your love.
I couldn't fly
without you.

Prologue

A flat beach of rock lit by the distant stars.

On the beach a maze of boulders, each awaiting the morning tide. Each boulder was unique, a character in a crowd, and one was a dragon.

Welkin sat among his rocks and contemplated the dim stars, these days a blurred patchwork where once they had shone sharp and bright; to the old dragon the stars were growing more insubstantial year by year.

'Ah,' said Welkin to the waves, 'but there was more magic in the world then.' He chuckled. 'And perhaps my eyes are growing old.'

Stretching rough dragon wings he shifted a knob of driftwood away from the curve of his tail and settled more comfortably into his stone platter. Yellowed claws rested easily in the grooves they had worn over the years, and the rounded sides of what had become known as Welkin's Hollow embraced him as an old friend. The night sea nestled beneath a cool and distant horizon and the only sound was that of its waves lapping gently on the sloping shelf which formed the shore.

Old and at peace, Welkin dozed, then woke, then dozed again, waiting for the night dragons to fly.

A dragon many years his junior paused high on the cliff edge, momentarily confused by the puzzle of rocks laid out below him ... until one of the rocks coughed. His goal located, the youngster headed down towards the shore.

Welkin stirred afresh and glanced behind him as a clattering commotion descended the cliff. A shower of clay and sharp stones pattered around him as the young dragon scrambled down the shallow gully which split the high, brown cliff-face like a smile turned on its side; the intruder's eager panting was raucous over the swell of the ocean and he was calling out as his legs and flimsy wings danced and scuddered on the loose scree.

'Welkin!' he was calling. 'Sir . . . oops. Welkin, sir!'

The youngster caught his right wingtip in a great mound of dried seaweed and tumbled off balance, turning head over haunches until the cloud of debris which had accompanied his descent delivered him unceremoniously at Welkin's side.

'Wel . . .' was as far as he got before he realized that he was quite winded. He collapsed into a fit of coughing. Welkin grinned.

'Well what, young Wood?' he said, pleased with the sound of the phrases over the soft wash of the sea. 'Take your time now, son,' he went on as Wood offered a healthy splutter by way of reply, 'though I think I've guessed the news you bring so . . . spectacularly.'

Wood ducked as a late avalanche of pebbles scattered about them, then turned his young face up to the craggy features of the old dragon beside him. Welkin's eyes danced beneath the enclosing bony ridges which swept back along and then beyond his head to become a pair of chipped and twisted horns. Grey scales flexed, pulling back from the skin around his mouth, as he smiled, and Wood finally dispensed his news.

'It's Clarion, sir. She's . . . Welkin, you've got a son!'

Welkin closed his old dragon eyes as he heard the news for which he had waited so long. A son! At last, a son!

A storm of memories rolled through his mind – the swiftness of infancy, the release of flying free into the world, the years of study and training to join the Charmed . . . and the ultimate failure. The sombre return home, and failure. Failure in life, in love, old age sweeping him away like a flash flood . . . and then Clarion. Just when his life had seemed over . . . When all had seemed failure . . . Clarion.

She had arrived in South Point without drama one sudden autumn, old like him, her past a story untold to all but Welkin. Instantly friends, they had gradually found love as tender as that of the young couples who flew their courtships above them. They had become inseparable.

2

And now the egg that Clarion had borne, that all who scoffed had called sterile, ancient, impossible, that egg was hatched and Welkin knew his life at last had meaning.

If lives can turn on a moment, he thought, *then this moment is mine*.

And so he sat, comfortable and old and elated, listening to the sea caressing the shore. He closed his eyes, conscious of the rhythm of the world as it turned through the sky, carrying him and Wood and all dragons towards some distant, future light.

'Um, sir?'

Wood prodded Welkin's wrinkled, grey flank.

'Don't fall asleep, sir. Don't you want to see him?'

Welkin opened an eye and regarded the eager youngster.

'Clarion will call me when she is ready,' he replied. 'Have patience.'

Wood hopped from one rock to another, handling his infant wings clumsily, flight as yet an ineffectual flurry. He floundered back to the hollow and poked Welkin again, frustrated as the old dragon settled himself still further into his nest of stone.

'I'd never seen a hatching before,' he said, trying to gain Welkin's attention. 'It was all very slimy . . .'

'Ssh, young Wood,' murmured Welkin. 'Come and sit by me.'

Wood hopped up obediently and squatted by his elder's warm flank, absently curling his tail up and over his neck to where it brushed lazily against his cheek.

'You're right to be excited, Wood.'

Wood gazed wide-eyed at Welkin; a serious young dragon he was and it took something as important as a hatching to spark in him any kind of excitement. Welkin had often wondered what inner turmoil lent his childish features such adult expressions of concern. No doubt he still mourned his mother, but was it not deeper than that? The youngster's face was smooth, its scales still tight and glossy, but beneath . . . ?

And then another thought stole unbidden into Welkin's mind: *My son and this one will be friends*.

'Young Wood,' he continued. 'Every year on this night I come here to my hollow. Do you see where my claws

3

have worn the rock? We're comfortable together, the rock and I.'

He paused, then asked, 'Have you ever seen a night dragon?'

'One or two,' replied Wood, his gaze fixed intently on Welkin. Then he lowered his eyes and mumbled, 'My father says they're falling stars.'

'Well, whatever they may truly be, they appear in the night sky throughout the year, one here, two there. But there is one night, young Wood, when there appears not one, not two, but ten thousand!'

Welkin drew him even closer. The youngster was agog.

'They are the night dragons, flying high and fast over our world, too high for us ever to reach them. And as they fly they breathe a fire so hot that we see it as a white trail across the sky. They fly high and remote, these cousins of ours, and they are dragons we shall never in our lives meet; but still they fly, one here, two there. They fly.

'But on this one night, the night dragons meet and fly in a great celebration. Thousands meet and cross; they turn and swoop; they come together for the purest expression of life their souls can make – they fly. And as they fly, they breathe fire in the sky.

'On one night each year they do this. That night is tonight, young Wood, tonight!'

As Welkin finished speaking a star seemed to shoot across the speckled blackness of the heavens.

'A night dragon,' breathed Wood in awe.

'The first of many.'

And there they sat on that summer night, two dragons from the opposite ends of life, as the sky above them grew alive with threads of fire. There was magic in the air that night, and who is to say what those dragons truly saw in the sky? Wood scarcely knew himself. He gazed, transfixed, torn in his belief. His heart flew upwards with Welkin to the night dragons, but there was a voice in his mind, just one, and it was his father's, speaking of rocks falling through the sky, words scorning this glimpse of incandescent magic.

And though their light was not seen by the hidden eyes of the newly hatched infant tucked warm beneath the folds of his mother's wing, perhaps the presence of the night dragons was sensed there too, and a new dragon began to puzzle the workings of the world.

Whatever those lights may have been then, or may be now, they were wonderful to behold. They moved and played, then thinned and ceased, and dragons slept.

Wood awoke as the eastern sky began to grow pale. Beside him Welkin was breathing hoarsely, the tip of his bony tail flicking restlessly among the pebbles Wood had dislodged in his tumble down the cliff.

Careful not to disturb the old dragon, Wood crept from his side and made his way back up the gully. He reached the cliff-top and glanced back down to the shore, the frown he wore comfortable on his face.

Welkin was a rough, dark shape on a grey beach. All seemed lifeless. On the cliff-top the grass was washed with the day's early gold, but down on the shore there was no colour. He could just hear Welkin's guttural breaths rasping in time with the lapping waves; the old dragon seemed at one with the sea. Wood shivered and headed for home.

The sun rose further, lighting Welkin's grey face. A shadow danced across his back. Opening his eyes Welkin saw a hornless female crossing the sunlight as she alighted before him. In her mouth she carried a tiny, brown bundle of wings.

'I'm so tired, Clarion,' he sighed.

'I know, my darling,' she replied, placing her fragile load at his feet. 'Your son.'

Welkin's eyes filled with tears as he looked upon the small, folded shape. He reached forward and moved the baby dragon's crumpled wings away from its face. Shut tight the night before, the infant's eyes were now open and curious.

'His eyes are watery, like mine,' chuckled Welkin.

'I had to bring him, before . . .'

'I know. And he must be named.' Welkin coughed and stretched awkwardly. 'Last night I was so comfortable, but this morning . . .' He coughed again, his ribs pressing painfully against his thin flesh. The air was thin and damp; it, like the whole world around him now, seemed to have no taste.

'Hush, Welkin,' soothed Clarion.

Welkin touched the hatchling with his wrinkled muzzle. 'The world is turning, little one,' he whispered. 'Ordinal has told me that great change is happening. The Charmed know it – only too well . . .'

He coughed again, and then again. His son stared at him, still and calm.

'My son,' Welkin continued, although it seemed now that it was only his voice that went on, leaving the rest of him to drift further from the world and into the distant dawn. 'My son, seek the Charmed. There may be a way forward, a path to the future. Perhaps Ordinal knows. And yet, and yet . . .'

As he grew weaker, less coherent, he felt that heady separation between his voice and his soul widen immeasurably. He saw his son as if from a huge distance, from the cliff-top to the shore, or perhaps from above the stars. With an immense effort he stretched a claw across the chasm to touch the infant's face, and with a jolt their gazes locked and Welkin stared deep into his son's jet black eyes.

For that frozen instant, that endless age, Welkin saw in those eyes magic and nature, pain and suffering and inexpressible joy; he saw battle and birth, tasted anger and love; he felt the world shedding its skin.

And beyond it all and within it all he saw a great pathway of terrible complexity, a labyrinth both strange and familiar whose ending was shrouded in mist. On that pathway was his son, lost and alone, surrounded by dark turns and grasping shadows.

In the distant fog something moved with the power of the stars.

Welkin's lips breathed out . . .

'Fortune. Your name is Fortune.'

. . . and at last, in peace, Welkin died.

Clarion wept silently, drawing her son close as she covered Welkin's body with her grizzled wing. There they lay, one dead, one new born, one between, as the sun turned the beach to gold, spreading colour down from the sky to drive away the grey.

Far out to sea the tide turned and as the last of the stars deferred to the light a single night dragon flew clear upwards from behind the horizon, cutting a line of pure white through the cold morning air.

PART 1

SOUTH POINT

CHAPTER 1

Wood

Any young dragon basking on the grassy seaward slopes of
South Point, too lazy to fly anywhere, might easily find his
thoughts taking flight instead. He might gather his wandering mind and launch it out towards the smell of the salt and
the sound of the breaking waves, wings of thought pushed
skyward by the updraughts mounting the cliff edge. He
might then, in his mind, turn a spiral in the sky and look
down to see his own earthbound body pinned to the grass
below and gazing back up with the motionless ease of a
summer's afternoon.

Any young dragon might soar above himself so, cupping
imaginary winds with imaginary wings, his mind per-
forming the complex manoeuvres his inexperienced body
has not yet mastered.

Not so a young dragon called Wood.

Among his dreaming peers lay Wood.

Where his fellow dragons relaxed he lay tense; where
they yawned he fumed.

Amid a field of contentment, Wood was perfect, knotted
frustration.

The day had not begun well. He had woken early, restless
for no reason he could identify; perhaps a storm was building. But outside the nest the morning was like crystal. The
dragon settlement was clearly visible through the screen of
branches by his bed, and somehow minute in its detail. It
was summer still and yet winter seemed close enough to
smell.

Through this odd clarity of air Wood scanned the dragon
settlement. His own family nest, cold and lonely now of

course, was situated on top of the long, high ridge of chalk which defined the northern boundary of South Point, and to both his left and right along that ridge he could see the agglomeration of timber nests and linking structures which made up the primary living area of the colony. There was no movement of dragons through the wide thoroughfares between nests. South Point was still asleep on this brittle morning and Tongue had not yet opened up the aqueduct.

To the south of this great strip of habitation the land descended gently into a wooded valley, then rose again more steeply as the chalk downs met the surge of granite which had been thrust up in some ancient time to form the towering cliffs of the southernmost tip of the island of Torr. A naked crescent of the rock burst through the grass of the cliff approach to form a curved dam, and behind this dam was a small reservoir formed by the run-off water from the cliff slopes. This was the Sink, from which ran the spindly wooden aqueduct which spanned the valley. The aqueduct – the greatest work of dragon architect Tongue – soared over the roof of the densely wooded dale then split into a network of narrow waterways serving most of the dragon settlement.

Beyond the Sink were the broad slopes of the cliff-top and beyond those the sea and the sky and places far, far distant which Wood had no plan ever to see. Cold places, far in the south.

Before him, the jumbled timber of dragon nests had never looked so precise. Cloud shadows poured over the landscape like running water. The crazing of frost-cracks on the bare granite of the Sink was finely delineated and the world was sharp as a dragon's claw.

Many dragons might have found the scene invigorating, even uplifting, but not Wood.

Then his own name shattered the stillness.

His father, named Barker for the deafening power of his lungs, was calling him. Lately his words may have been few, but they were always loud.

Wood could remember a time when his father had been a talkative dragon, a warm, spark-eyed dragon who would speak into the night about the world, about dragons, about nature and magic, hunting and love. When he had truly been a *father*.

And then had come the year of storms. Wood's mother Eleken had been snatched from the sky by a sea so wild it was like a mountain range given life. Then Welkin, to whom Wood had turned as to an uncle when his father had shut himself away in his own storm of grief, had died quietly beside the same sea which had drowned his mother. The sea, whether at peace or storm, was no longer to be trusted. Terrible grief had followed death, and worse than grief – silence.

For eight years now silence had ruled the nest, prising its insidious way between Wood and Barker, throwing up barricades all the more impenetrable for their invisibility.

To begin with they had argued. In between the talkative Barker and the silent one there had been an argumentative Barker. Blame had flown at any convenient target, of which Wood had been the most convenient of all. Wood had fought back. He could remember with horrible clarity any number of nights when he had lain alone in the nest after yet another hysterical battle of words. Wood was not the daughter Eleken had always wanted; Barker should never have let her go fishing that day; Wood's disobedience had driven her to madness; Barker's obsession with Shatter and his cronies had driven her to despair.

Blame, always blame. Soon any conversation had merely inflamed passions; the endless, titanic arguments had left them drained, and so eventually they had fallen into silence. Father and son shared their nest in haunted emptiness; Wood blamed his mother for dying, Barker vanished every night to the sanctuary of his meetings, where he could fill his mind with other things and other blames; neither dragon helped the other to heal.

'Wood!' Barker was furious. He had just returned from another of his conferences at the Sink to find Wood gazing out into the morning. His son's body bore chipped scales and a long, red graze on the soft skin of his belly. 'I have forbidden you to fly! Either you obey me or . . .'

Wood's father thought him too young to fly. Most days he preached his usual warnings against going to the cliff gullies to practise; most days Wood went anyway and

13

returned home feverish with exhaustion, or covered with bruises, or both. To this defiance, these days, Barker had no response – he would simply draw in on himself, or more commonly skulk out of the nest and off to the Sink.

'Or what? What do you care what I do anyway!' retaliated Wood, lunging past his father and out into the transparent day.

As his backward glance met Barker's angry gaze, there was the briefest of pauses . . . filled with the familiar silence . . . and Wood swept away, stumbling off down the path which led through the wood and then up to the cliff.

There were tears in his eyes. Naturally, he assumed they were tears of rage. But he did not move from the cliff-top all day, least of all to defy his father and take to the air.

The chill of the morning was banished by a wave of hot, heavy air sweeping in from the sea and the space around Wood became as clammy as his own heart. Other youngsters came to bask on the grassy slopes. Later they began to drift back to their homes – their warm, friendly homes.

Presently Wood was alone and as the sky built around him he slept the shallow sleep of the uneasy.

When he awoke the sun was low in the sky and cloaked in scales of mist. The air was close and damp. If anything, the evening had grown hotter than had been the afternoon. Wood swiftly judged the time and jumped to his feet.

'Fortune,' he muttered under his breath, and tramped back towards the settlement.

Wood skirted west around the Sink. Apparently remote from the settlement proper, the Sink was nevertheless the centre of South Point. It was attractive both for the sweep of grassland which flanked its southern rim to form a broad, public drinking place, and for the hundreds of cracks and hollows in the shelter of the dry northern side of the dam wall: here were secret meeting places for any number of dragons from two to two hundred. For dragons eager to talk, to argue, to keep a lover's tryst, the Sink was meeting

14

place, arena, social forum . . . but for one kind of dragon only.

Barker would be there now with his cronies, perhaps grumbling about the youth of today, more likely grumbling about more pressing matters of dragon politics. Wood was anxious to avoid his father.

Behind him the sun was yielding to a blackness not entirely night, a massive darkness heavy with certainty; thunderclouds were swelling, great top-heavy shadows in the greater shadow which was the sky. Voices carried through the sultry air, voices from beneath the dam. Voices raised in passion.

He crouched, listened, but he could hear little. Phrases slipped past on the heated air . . .

'. . . by surprise . . .'

'. . . time has come . . .'

'. . . Volence cannot go on . . .'

And his father's unmistakable rumble: '. . . the Charmed.'

More plotting, thought Wood to himself. *He cares more about battling charmed dragons than he does about me.*

Wood was well aware of the depth of hatred felt towards the Charmed by many of the natural dragons of South Point, among them his father. The reasons for it he did not fully understand. Having never seen a charmed dragon – few did these days – he considered them, if they existed at all, to be figures from a colourful age in the past. Like their weak and outdated parliament, they had no real function in this world. Mythical and mysterious beings they were, for the wonder of a young dragon. He failed to see how they could rouse such loathing.

Although lately, of course, there had been the eggs . . .

Charmed dragons had inhabited South Point – and indeed much of Torr – for far longer than the Naturals who now prospered in their rude nests on the narrow ridge of chalk. Younger than the trolls, charmed dragons were still among the oldest of the charmed creatures who had flocked into the world when it was new. The skies were filled with gold and silver as thousands of the winged knights had moved through the sunlight in search of new homes in the burgeoning land.

Creation had clung to the world like the first fall of dew and everything had seemed possible. The time of the great migrations had been a golden age.

Even as they filled the skies and the lands the charmed dragons sought new frontiers and so they ventured underground, and here it was that they found their true destiny, or so they believed. Underground charm could be focused. Only underground could the mind truly be concentrated on magic, without the tiresome distractions of night and day and the constant confusion of the elements. So it was that the great Charmed cavern systems were established, and so it was that their magic was explored and refined until it was of unparalleled beauty, unheard-of complexity. The laws passed by their parliament were rigid and their morals were strict, and their magic was good. Among all the creatures of charm they were the most revered.

It was into this world of dragon knights that the Naturals gradually began to trickle. The first few Naturals who settled at South Point accepted the leadership of the Charmed readily enough. Powerful but gentle, charmed dragons cared for the land, and they were worshipped, for a time, by the Naturals.

But as the years passed, more and more natural dragons came to live at South Point and soon those magical days had melted into history; everything had changed, and the reasons for the changes were not told. The Charmed had long since retreated to their caverns in the west beyond the wood and the Naturals, great now in number, openly criticized their reclusive neighbours and made plans against them.

Various groups of subversive Naturals plotted time and again to attack the Charmed, but action was never taken. Though apparently weak and certainly reclusive the Charmed managed somehow to retain the one thread they needed to maintain control over the community — fear of the incredible powers they held in check. As young natural dragons grew to adulthood, so fear of charm grew within them. Over the years it was this fear that had held back the Naturals from striking the final blow.

But the fear was waning. Charmed dragons no longer travelled either in or out of the entrance to the caverns, and stories of the magical past were just stories to young dragons like Wood.

Barker belonged to a group of militant Naturals led by a dragon called Shatter. In the past Wood had often followed his father as he crept from the nest at night, eavesdropping on Barker's secret conversations with the other Naturals. Such conversations would reveal the familiar hatred of the Charmed and all seemed harmless. At those meetings dragons would relieve tensions and release aggression with words . . . but ultimately they would take no action.

The meeting this evening – if the fragments of conversation he had caught were anything to go by – was scarcely different to any of the countless meetings Wood had spied upon. But, despite the oppressive heat, he felt suddenly chilled. His lack of concern seemed entirely inappropriate. He had overheard little and yet he felt so much to be *wrong*. What were they plotting tonight? What did his father plan to do?

'. . . *by surprise* . . .'

'. . . *time has come* . . .'

'. . . *Volence cannot go on* . . .'

The voices of the arguing dragons receded into the accelerating wind but the phrases he had intercepted echoed through his mind, singing of doom and decision.

Behind him the storm loomed. Looking across the darkening treetops he felt as if he were about to be swallowed by darkness and spat into a world of shadow and fear. Thunderheads spread across the evening sky and the gathering wind whispered that the world was about to change. His world. Perhaps the whole world.

Looking down, Wood saw his own foreclaws clenched proud of the wing membranes they supported, their sharp tips grasping at the grass and fine soil which spread between them, defying his clutch. With an enormous effort of will he relaxed his muscles and hurried on to the path which led down beside the woods and west into South Point's old quarter.

The wood narrowed like a wedge to the west as it marched into the grip of the valley which shaped it. At the far western perimeter the trees thinned and disappeared, leaving the brief open meadow to end abruptly against a steep rock wall, drab and featureless but for a single opening. The wall marked the boundary between the two sides of South Point: the outside and the inside, the open air and the underground, the light and the dark. And here, also, was the single passage joining the two.

Wood's fear did not relent as he strode the steep path; indeed, the surroundings intensified it. Here many of the first natural settlers had made their homes. Here was an ancient forest laid flat — whole trees were stacked in great, oval nests, their branches woven into screens, their trunks bored out for food caches — nest upon nest. Where dragons had abandoned them, scrub and fungus thrived in their remains, the deeper parts of which had long since decayed to mush. The smell was foul.

What does Shatter plan for tonight? Why must things change?

For Wood, the concept of change was a monstrous one; it seemed that all the change he had ever known had been for the worse. He ran from the voices, from the Sink, from the storm. From the change.

As he ran through broken corridors he was aware of the hunched forms of the old dragons, just visible through slits in the walls, their grey, bark-like hides barely distinguishable from the coarse timbers which cloaked them. Those who still lived here refused steadfastly to permit clearance of the ancient site and it had thus become a kind of ghetto. Most of the dragons who lived up on the chalk ridge agreed that it was only a matter of time before the last of the old ones died and the entire quarter could be levelled and replanted. Until then it lingered, old and dying.

Dragons coughed and shifted in their ancient beds, the wood cracked and sighed, and the sounds merged in staccato harmony. Inhabitants and habitat were as one. Wood wove his way between the mighty nests, wishing he could fly well enough to reach the meeting place from the air.

With a growl the storm rolled closer and Wood ran faster, stumbling now in his panic.

Can't fly in a storm anyway!

Rushing blindly headlong through the passageways of the old quarter he pushed his fears down inside himself. Thrusting twigs thrashed at his flanks and the pain helped him suppress his growing terror; a dragon well practised in denying his emotions, Wood banished the terror from his mind to some interior place where it might trouble him no longer.

Just when it seemed the maze would go on forever he tumbled around a last corner, brushed past a last curtain of branches and there before him, seated comfortably against the rock wall which marked the edge of the old quarter, and indeed the western perimeter of South Point, cleaning his back teeth with a claw, was a dragon. Wood skidded to a halt, gasping for breath, legs flustered, tail sore from battering around the endless turns of the maze of nests.

The last rays of the dying sun cast a low shaft of light across the face of the rock wall in front of him, which was otherwise gloomy, and the light caught the features of the dragon sitting there. Young scales shone, a long, elegant snout lifted and Wood grunted as he dismissed the thought that this dragon was beautiful.

'Hello,' said Fortune. 'What kept you?'

CHAPTER 2

The Guide

It was Fortune who had come up with the idea of mounting a secret expedition to see the caverns of the Charmed.

He and Wood were lazing in the late summer sunshine, watching the older youths practising low hunting dives over the flat plain north of the settlement. The sun glittered off horns and spines as their pale brown forms arrowed in on the blackened tree stump which was the target in this traditional sport. A successful flight meant contact with the lightning-shattered stump, with a telltale flake of charcoal beneath the claw as proof. Neither Fortune nor Wood were yet old enough to compete, although Wood practised relentlessly on the nursery slopes, eager for his first taste of that charred and immobile quarry.

Three years older than Fortune, Wood had seen twelve summers and was now virtually of age, and indeed was closer in age to the youths rehearsing their hunting dives and courtship flights than he was to his younger friend. Where Fortune watched the aerobatics with an easy anticipation, Wood was tense and eager to join in.

Fortune glanced at his friend now with a knowing smile. Wood was crouched forward, his wings raised and trembling in the breeze, so obviously impatient to be up there with the other dragons. But today there was something else too: he seemed . . . sullen. Why was that?

Already bored with the flying display, Fortune sprawled back on the grass, his own unpractised wings folded at his sides. Unlike Wood he felt no need to exercise them. His body was young and fit enough, and when it was time to fly he would fly, not before. His mother had a name for him: 'Fortune, the Economical Dragon,' she would call him, and it was a name he liked.

His economy showed in so many ways, in his lightness of step, in his broad and easy smile, in his relaxed and unhurried approach to so much of his life. These qualities he recognized in himself and put them down to his mother. She loved him dearly and yet actively encouraged his independence. Had he grown up with a father he might, he fancied, have grown up more like his peers – competitive and brash. As it was, thanks to his mother's influence, he was little concerned with the typical male rivalry which dominated the lives of most of his fellow dragons.

Fortune's independence – what his mother called his 'economy' – also served to distance him somewhat from his peers. This was not something which bothered him; it suited him to be a loner, it suited his romantic nature. For he was a dreamer, prone to long meanderings through the northern meadows, dreaming of times past and times to come, but especially of times past. The times in which his father had lived.

His mother, Clarion, had spoken of his father, of course. Fortune had always listened eagerly to her stories of Welkin, of his humour, of his easy good nature and a little of his loneliness. But the tales had seemed always brief, their narratives sliding off into other stories, other realms. His mother's eye had never been able to meet his own; it seemed his father was not merely dead but elusive too.

He escapes me, Fortune would think, and the hole in his heart, a hole the shape of a dragon, would grow a little larger.

His mother's reticence he put down to simple sadness, and perhaps that was so. These days she seemed to yearn to be gone from South Point, gone to some distant place, and perhaps to talk of her mate was to tie herself back here somehow.

But there was something else, too. Whenever Clarion's tales of Welkin slipped aside it seemed that they slipped towards a realm of charm, of magic. Of the Charmed. His father and the Charmed?

She became remote and quiet when Fortune questioned his mother. She became remote from herself, as though she were trapped inside, where the past was. Fortune found it impossible to press her on the issue; he could only wait for the next tale and hope that a little more of Welkin might be revealed to him then.

To these tiny fragments of a dragon Fortune eagerly clung in his efforts to build a picture of his father which he could carry within him. But they were not enough, not nearly enough and so he was left with a permanent, gaping hole in his heart, a hole in the unknowable shape of a dragon he had never seen, never known, yet whom he missed terribly.

Most of Fortune's growing days were thus spent in peace and dreaming, in solitary thought and exploration, and it was during those days that his independence, his economy was firmly established.

But the hole in his heart remained, and worse, it grew bigger.

Then came the companionship of Wood.

Wood was a dragon he had always known a little, like a cousin, close in some ways and yet distant in so many others. Their paths had crossed frequently throughout their lives but only in this last year had they actually become friends. Why Wood had taken to him, Fortune was not entirely sure, but he suspected it had something to do with Wood's own sense of being tied to South Point — while Fortune spoke always of breaking free, of flight and adventure and leaving the nest. Wood, he suspected, would never do such a thing but for a while was able to find at least a taste of adventure in Fortune's dreaming.

For his own part the impetus for the friendship was simple enough: Wood had actually known Welkin.

Even though Wood said no more about his father than did his mother Clarion, Fortune discovered that merely by being with him he was able to absorb something of Welkin's spirit. Fortune could see the love they had shared: it shone from Wood's eyes like a charm.

So Welkin it was who locked these two young dragons together. For a whole year they laughed and explored and argued together and made up together, and grew up together. Fortune dreamed up ever more adventurous schemes along with which Wood tagged reluctantly until he found himself actually enjoying them. That year was full and fine for these two young dragons who seemed to be opposites and yet had found true friendship.

But it, as years do, was coming to an end, and Fortune was beginning to realize that growing up could also mean growing apart.

It showed in little things. Fortune recognized the signs and accepted them in his own quiet, economical way, for he saw no reason why he and Wood should not agree to differ on any number of issues and yet still remain friends. Up to now Wood seemed not to have detected the growing rift, but when he did Fortune feared that he would see things rather differently. And that was one difference Fortune did worry about.

We must always be friends, he said to himself, *wherever we are in the world, whatever our circumstances.*

He only hoped that Wood could see it that way when he too felt the rough edges their friendship was starting to display.

And so, seeing Wood's impatience to be in the air, somer-saulting, his friend's curious combination of excitement and sullenness, Fortune suggested the idea he had been mulling over now for many weeks: that they explore the caverns of the Charmed.

Wood, to Fortune's surprise, thought it a fabulous idea.

But then his attention was diverted by a shapely young female dragon swooping down though the cloud of males. He turned to Fortune and grinned, something he hardly ever did. 'Who knows what we'll see down there in the darkness, with all that magic.'

Fortune shook his head. 'I don't know exactly what we will see but it won't be what you're thinking.'

Wood grunted but the trace of a grin remained as he watched the young female drift off again into the clouds.

Anyway, it was settled.

And as if Fortune was not excited enough at the prospect of adventure and magic, later that evening, after he and Wood had parted, the strangest of seals was set on their agreement by an entirely unexpected and most unusual meeting. A meeting which thrilled Fortune to his very core and set him irrevocably on his fateful course towards the forbidden caverns of the Charmed.

He had felt hungry after saying goodbye to Wood and so diverted his path home to the outskirts of the woods low in the valley between the settlement and the Sink. Rabbits often gathered here in the evening, thinking themselves safe in the lee of the timber aqueduct. Few dragons hunted in the woods themselves, being wary of the trees which could easily rip a clumsy wing, and so the rabbits considered themselves to be out of harm's reach.

Not so the one Fortune spied and gave chase to.

It shot past him as it caught his scent and Fortune leaped towards it with a great bound, his wings unfurling instinctively as he turned his jump into a glide.

The rabbit sped over a low hillock and cut left into the trees. His hind legs scrabbling on the loose litter, Fortune crested the hillock and lurched upwards with a gasp, his wings flattening and crashing into the air as he braked to a sudden stop.

He alighted with a thud, squinting into the setting sun.

A shape was cut from the sun's disc: a creature poised on a second hillock a mere tree's length away.

It was a dragon, of course, but it looked odd. It was not *natural*.

Fortune held his breath as he craned his neck this way and that in a futile attempt to make out some detail in the strange silhouette. Then the silhouette spoke, its voice low and fast and compelling. 'Listen,' it said. And then all in one breath:

It said that it was Fortune's guide.

It said that it would meet him at a marked spot in the old quarter on the night of the next full moon.

It said that the world was turning.

And it said that its name was Cumber.

Then the sun moved from behind the dragon's strange contours, forcing Fortune to squint into the sudden halo. A confusion of shadows danced for an instant in the light, and when he had blinked away light-tears he saw that the strange creature had vanished.

That was all.

And Fortune knew that he had seen a charmed dragon.

He remained there on the outskirts of the woods until long after darkness fell. Before him, hidden at the western end of the valley, was the great rock wall, and in it the

24

tunnel by which he planned to enter the caverns. Though it was forbidden by tradition to all but the Charmed themselves (not that even they seemed to use it these days), nevertheless he intended to break the rules and go in. He wanted it, he yearned for it, he had dreamed it.

The valley receded to the west, narrowing to a near point as though drawing him inexorably forwards to the cavern entrance; for an instant it was as though he was moving there unbidden. The trees seemed to sweep past and the darkening clouds to boil away in his wake as some hidden force drew him into the waiting tunnels.

The illusion faded, leaving the merest hint of movement. Except now it was as though he were still and it was the world which was on the move, travelling towards him with frightening momentum while he remained locked in the same place.

The world moving towards him.

The world turning.

The waiting then was unbearable. Three days it was until full moon and during those days he avoided Wood completely. Though he knew it would undoubtedly throw his friend into deeper sulks, Fortune kept clear for fear of letting slip his secret, and thus causing the mission to abort. For he knew that if Wood even guessed that a charmed dragon had become involved in their expedition he would have nothing more to do with it. He gave Wood a time and a place and then made himself scarce. He was confident that Wood was curious enough to honour the meeting whether prompted further or not, and as to his ultimate reaction to Cumber . . . well, that would just have to wait until the moment.

Three days passed, the moon grew fat and full and a terrible storm massed off the coast and fell upon the land like a plague.

Despite the danger of the storm a dragon flew that night beneath the full moon, a dragon quite unlike the natural dragons who travelled and met and plotted in the landscape below her. A dragon to whom flight was less a task for the body than for the mind, less an effort than a thought.

Her name was Ordinal, and she was Charmed.

Amongst her other magic, Ordinal possessed the power to see emotion. Feelings were visible to her as beams of light and as she flew now she could clearly see one such beam emanating from the Sink. Its colour was that of anger, of aggression. Dragons were massing there, many dragons, and they were preparing for battle.

Shivering, she turned her attention from that ominous light and flew higher so as to catch the whole settlement in her subtle gaze.

Tiny pockets of light sparkled in the nests beneath her, the lights of argument, of love and of the numberless emotions which filled the wings of life. A vast field of stars was spread below for her eyes alone and each star was a dragon. A natural dragon.

Once those lights would all have been Charmed, she thought without bitterness. *Not now.*

Ordinal had seen the golden age of the charmed dragons, and she had lived it for many centuries, and now it was over and she found herself sad. But she would *not* be bitter.

But, oh, it was hard!

Turning her gaze west, she squinted hard into her miraculous second sight. There was anger deep underground within the caverns of the Charmed, too. Its light flickered over the magic of the entrance. Preparations for battle built there, as they were building in the Sink.

This night may be the end of it all. Oh, Mantle, is there any way our plans can succeed? Surely the task is too great!

But somewhere, in some hidden corner of her heart, she allowed herself to hope.

At last the storm met the headland. Lightning shattered the space between land and sky, the sound of thunder pulling Ordinal from her reverie as the two realms were joined by a brilliant web. Even for her the sky was becoming dangerous. She turned back towards the caverns from which she had come, and as she flew to rejoin her kin on this terrible night an immense sadness filled her heart.

She diverted over the nests of the old quarter, the blood loud in her head, scanning the land below as she permitted the fragment of hope to wrestle its way to the surface. Her second sight keen, she searched.

As she swooped over the nests the clouds paused and

then pulled momentarily apart, allowing a single beam of moonlight to blanch her shining hide.

There!

Her moon-shadow rippled over the skeletal framework of nests, a tiny patch of blackness flickering on the lattice, and as the wind rose, causing her wings to shake, there below her flared a sudden burst of the light that she alone could see. The explosion struck Ordinal an almost physical blow. She bucked in its sudden blast, the storm winds forgotten as its pulse swept through her, leaving her trembling in its wake . . . while it streaked out and upwards towards the moon, towards the stars.

For an instant the storm halted, the distant lightning checked by invisible powers. Then the clouds closed about the moon once more and the rain began to fall.

Ordinal flew on, her heart thundering, a place deep within her branded by the light she had just seen, for she knew what she had just witnessed. It was the very event she had for so long struggled to engineer.

In the old quarter on this darkest of nights a meeting of dragons had occurred which from a landscape of utter despair had fired a searing bolt of pure hope into the sky. The light of the explosion which only Ordinal had seen was fading now behind her, and the storm filled the void it had left. The storm and the fires of rage circled ever more fiercely about their twin centres of Sink and cavern.

But hope it was that Ordinal had sensed with her charmed sight – though its warmth was cooling now.

Wood had grown impatient. His sense of adventure had swiftly evaporated when Fortune, instead of setting off for the caverns straight away, had insisted instead on sitting and waiting for their 'guide'.

'Three's more likely to get into trouble than two,' Wood said. 'We didn't plan a guide last week,' he persisted.

'Things have changed since last week.'

Fortune went back to his vigil.

Above them the clouds moved as silent and invisible as deep sea creatures, an occasional flash of lightning whitening their undersides but somehow failing to illuminate their greater mass.

Then suddenly a rift appeared and there was the moon, full and brilliant, and silhouetted against its round light was a black shape, slowly traversing.

Wood knew that it was a dragon of course — the sky belonged to no other creature. But to fly in a storm! And the shape of its wings was somehow odd, its proportions disjointed. Wood wondered what kind of dragon would cast such a strange profile in flight.

A charmed dragon, of course!

Moonlight dimmed for an instant as the dragon's shadow slipped directly across them and then faded as the clouds bit once more.

Rain began to cascade out of the sky, thundering on Wood's unprotected head, and with a disgruntled shrug he moved closer to the sheer rock wall against which Fortune was huddled in the vain hope that it might offer at least a little shelter.

'Getting soaked now,' he grumbled, raising his wings to ward off the rain. Momentarily blind after the brief show of moonlight, he blinked and looked across to where Fortune was crouched. He gasped.

They were no longer alone.

A third dragon stood in the rain and shadow before Fortune, who rose now and greeted the stranger nervously, although, thought Wood, with some familiarity. Resigned now to being wet, Wood let his temper rise as he stamped over to them, still angry that Fortune had changed plans without first consulting him.

'Well, I suppose you'd better introduce me,' he announced gruffly, snorting as rain trickled down his muzzle and into his nostrils.

'Wood,' replied Fortune, 'meet Cumber.'

And Cumber turned to face him.

Wood was totally unprepared for this, his first encounter with a charmed dragon. That the Charmed were alien he knew well enough but to actually *see* one! He sat down abruptly in the mud, his jaw lolling.

Wood, along with Fortune and all of their natural kin, was a variation on one of nature's basic themes: his dull brown body bore four limbs and a long, tapering tail, his wings being light, tough membranes stretched from wrist to waist; his rear legs were short and muscular. It was fundamental knowledge to a dragon like Wood that natural dragons, like all natural creatures bar the grubs and fish, shared this order of four limbs: four legs for the rabbit, two legs and two arms for the bear, two legs and two wings for the dragon.

It was different for the Charmed, and of course Wood knew this. What else did the old stories tell if not that the Charmed wielded mighty powers, powers with which they changed their bodies, powers with which they reshaped both themselves and the world in which they lived?

Wood's head reeled as he stared with a stupid, open mouth at Cumber.

Dragon? It was surely a monster, defying nature itself as it squatted heavily on its four legs *but with a pair of wings tucked also at its side!* Something deep inside Wood was sickened by this six-limbed slander on the natural order and though on the surface he remained icy calm inside he was as revolted as he would have been had he met a flying rabbit or a fish with fur. As far as he was concerned things were either right or wrong . . . and Cumber was definitely *wrong*.

Where natural hides were brown and dull, Cumber's was golden. Horns were meant to be rough and strong but this interloper's looked spindly, too thin to support even their own weight. Wood's own wings, and Fortune's, were massive, efficient flight surfaces rooted with powerful muscles, and yet here was a charmed dragon with wings like golden leaves, surely too tiny to be anything but vain decoration.

And to top it all this monster was actually smiling at him. No, not smiling, *grinning!*

And so Wood stared, silent, at this metallic thing around which the rain seemed to hesitate as though repelled.

Repelled. That's how I feel. More than repelled – insulted!

Fortune on the other hand thought Cumber quite the most wonderful dragon he had ever seen, and was busy telling Wood so.

'You see,' he was blurting, 'they colour their scales. All the old stories are true. Cumber's gold, but he could just as easily be green or red, and they can change the shape of their bodies at will . . .'

29

'Not quite "at will" to be truthful,' corrected Cumber. 'Actually, you see, it takes a lot of practise.'

'I'll bet,' murmured Wood, dumb struck.

'How do you do?' said Cumber, nodding a greeting. 'You're the second Natural I've met face to face so I should be getting used to it although I daresay I'll never understand how you manage with all that flapping and *why* you should want to live in the open air quite defeats me . . .'

'Cumber never pauses for breath, by the way,' interrupted Fortune with a delighted grin. 'Isn't he splendid?'

They both stared expectantly at Wood, awaiting his reply, and although all he wanted to do was spit his repulsion into the dirt and grind it away, curiosity proved his master and he said, 'You're a Charmed.'

Cumber smiled and said, 'I'm a dragon.' And then, 'So, now we've met, what are we all waiting for? Let's go!'

Without any further ceremony he whirled around and marched off along the base of the rock wall. Fortune scurried after him, leaving a sulky Wood with no choice but to bring up the rear. Cumber led them along a narrow track which hugged the base of the rock wall until they reached a large tunnel entrance, partly obscured by a great sweep of ivy.

'This will be where you were planning to enter the caverns of the Charmed.' It was a statement, not a question.

'Well, yes . . .' began Fortune, only to be interrupted by the busy young charmed dragon.

'Wrong, of course, because you see *this* entrance is just a decoy – the real entrance is over *here*. No Natural could ever find it.'

Cumber lifted one of his absurdly small, gold wings and there, behind it in the rock, was a second entrance which had not been there before.

'How did you . . . ?' blurted Wood.

'I'm a Charmed.'

He turned as if to enter the tunnel and then frowned.

'What's the matter?' asked Fortune as he pressed close behind, eager to follow his new companion into the caverns.

'Ah,' came Cumber's reply, his voice muffled until he withdrew it from the darkness. 'Wrong one.'

Chattering to himself he trotted off into the rain, his legs throwing themselves in all directions as if driven by some manic engine inside his skinny body.

Raindrops shattered on the ground all around the two Naturals as they watched Cumber sniffing and prodding at the rock. They had left the nests of the old quarter behind and even the distant woods were no longer visible behind them. Only the oppressive storm and the sheer, uncompromising rock wall existed, and it seemed to Fortune that they were trapped between the two, exposed and defenceless before powers they could not control. He watched Cumber search and hoped that this strange, charmed dragon was the friend he seemed to be.

Wood huddled next to him and shivered.

'Guide!' he spat. 'Where did you find that freak?'

'He's not a freak,' retorted Fortune. 'He's a Charmed. They're all like that, he says — sort of. Well, they *change* themselves. It's all to do with tradition and honour. Isn't it fantastic?'

But Wood was unimpressed.

'You're even beginning to talk like him,' he said. 'I thought this was our expedition.'

'It is. But Cumber knows ways, routes. And besides . . .' And although no spy could possibly have overheard him over the crushing sound of the rainstorm, Fortune glanced suspiciously over his shoulder and huddled forward as he went on, 'Something's going to happen tonight. Here, in the caverns.'

'What do you mean?' said Wood, feigning a surprise he did not feel. He could not let Fortune see he was scared. Not Wood.

'Haven't you sensed it?' persisted Fortune. 'Haven't you heard the rumours?'

But Wood could not bring himself to tell of what he had heard; for reasons he could not define he needed for the moment to keep that information buried inside.

'What rumours?' he replied evasively.

'They're going to confront the Council,' Fortune explained. 'Shatter wants to oust Volence and . . .'

A flurry of legs appeared through a curtain of water.

'Are you two coming or are you going to discuss community affairs all night, hmm?' demanded Cumber, dancing excitedly on the spot, his tiny, gold wings flapped comically at his sides. 'Come on, come on. Sentries will be posted soon if they're not already since there's no doubt tonight will be one to remember. Now, here's the entrance!'

'But that's the tunnel Wood and I were going to use in the first place,' said Fortune with surprise as Cumber gestured grandly towards a familiar, overgrown hole in the rock.

'Ah, yes,' came Cumber's embarrassed reply. 'It appears they have made it real, although why such a thing should be done I cannot imagine since it means that any Natural could just walk in and . . .'

'Are *we* going in or what?' cried Wood in frustration. 'Because I'm getting soaked!'

'Mm,' responded Cumber, distracted and staring at the opening with obvious concern. 'How strange . . .'

As they entered the tunnel it seemed to Fortune that it widened a little and somewhere deep in its throat came a faint, dry gasp of sound, perhaps a whisper of wind, perhaps a dragon moving unseen in the deep caverns. They exchanged the night without for the night within and travelled down into the underworld of the Charmed.

CHAPTER 3

Underground

The Sink dam loomed like a giant of myth over the natural dragons huddled in its shadow. Before the rain began to fall tiny whirlwinds spun around the sheer rock face, lifting dust and sand high into the air. A fine wet spray hung like a shroud over the assembly as the baying wind peeled water from the great lake held back by the immense wall of granite above the dragons. The water level in the reservoir was high; it squatted at the dragons' backs like a waiting monster.

Moonlight was spare, stolen by the gathering clouds. The air felt thick, tasted hot.

Architect Tongue spoke eloquently about the great heritage of the Charmed, advocating peaceful confrontation rather than outright war, but even he could not stem the deep and swelling hatred building as the night wore on.

'You would defend them!' jeered Tumely, a hot-headed young dragon more than ready for a fight, and more representative of the group as a whole than the venerable Tongue. 'They helped you build your waterways, so it's said.'

'That is true,' acknowledged Tongue, his voice betraying an unexpected edge of malice. 'But I will not defend dragons who practise infanticide! For that I condemn them utterly!'

And so it went on. Tempers flared and subsided until at last it seemed that a crucial moment had come.

It was only then that Shatter spoke.

He was the eye of the storm. He seemed to have no age; neither youth nor infirmity troubled his brow, he simply was. His heavily-plated back glistened dark with moisture and deep within his red eyes glinted a spark of madness.

'You might think I hate them,' he rumbled, after a

33

moment's deliberation, 'but that is not the case. No, they are old. They are weak. They have none of the strength we fear. Their time is over, my friends, and that is our strength. This is our time. They have no power over us any longer. I do not hate them. I pity them!'

His red eyes scanned the crowd as he told his skilful lies. Wide dragon eyes stared back at him. Names he knew — there Peal, and that was Tongue, whom they all called Great Tongue . . . but for names he did not care. It was the power of the mob which was his concern. And in turn his own power over them.

'Yes, I pity them!' he thundered, his voice battering through the sound of the wind. 'They are ancient. They are not of this time. They are of history!

'And we are not. We are of now!'

A chorus of 'aye's rippled through the circle of the audience. These were the words they wanted to hear. But still there was something . . .

Their fear of the Charmed still holds them back, thought Shatter. *Very well.*

Shatter breathed deeply, the claws of his hind legs clenched tight as if on some invisible prey. He shifted his wings to ensure that the objects he had concealed beneath them remained hidden. It was almost time. He nearly had them: the boulder was primed to topple, but not quite yet, not quite . . . for reasons of his own he waited for the rain to fall.

Shatter had emerged fully grown from the caves in the far eastern cliffs of South Point. His parents had kept him trapped in their tiny, crazed world for all his growing years, during which time Shatter had known only the feel of rock — and the breathing silence of the two dragons that brought him food.

On that incredible day of revelation Shatter had finally thrown down the walls of stone which had held him underground for so long. The slitted eye of the entrance admitted him into the shocking expanse of the world outside and his own eyes, burning red beneath the unexpected sun, turned instinctively back towards the rock which had been his egg until this long-delayed emergence. Confused, in pain, he swayed in the sand, fearful of the brilliant space around him yet anxious to explore its boundless possibilities. His parents – whom he now knew to have been his gaolers – moved like restless shadows in the depths of the cave, and as his aching eyes touched them he discovered hatred.

His first act as a denizen of the big world had been to kill.

His father, a huge bull of a dragon, had not died easily, but the landslide Shatter had manufactured eventually did the job; it took several days before the old, mad warrior breathed his last. His simple-minded mother Shatter simply ripped to pieces.

These acts he did not consider to be wrong because these dragons had not been real – only the rock was real, the dark, enclosing rock. The rock, and Shatter, who came from the rock.

The discovery then that other dragons – and more, an entire dragon *community* – resided a mere short flight away was almost too much for the young Shatter to bear. However, the way of life of these 'new' dragons was so bizarre to his senses that he was intrigued. He acquired by stealthy observation a grasp of the dragon language which had always been denied him beyond a few curt words. In secret he managed to incorporate the settlement of natural dragons into his distorted perceptions, and after many years he made the crucial move from hidden cave to dark, sombre nest: a tall brooding structure of his own creation on the eastern perimeter of South Point.

Natural dragons, he had decided, were harmless. Garrulous, dependent on each other, natural dragons lived only for the joy – a strange word to Shatter – of hunting and mating, and they paid no attention to the rock beneath their scaly feet. The rock, and Shatter, were not threatened by them. The Charmed were another matter.

Now they were a puzzle, and eventually a worry. His frequent return visits to the familiar cave system on the east shore reassured him that the rocks which had borne him were still there, still real. But these Charmed, they lived in caves, too, they lived in the rock. And this disturbed Shatter.

Surely only he was worthy of the rock's embrace? The Charmed were an infestation and a danger, and furthermore their *unnatural* powers were an affront. The idea dawned on Shatter that the empty-headed Naturals were a gift to him, a *resource* thrown up on the surface of the world especially for his use: against the Charmed.

It was not hard to find sympathetic support for his campaign against the Charmed, for the Naturals were growing tired of the once-proud leaders who had abandoned them and retreated into their caves. Tithes were no longer paid; ceremonies and rituals were no longer held; the Charmed no longer showed any interest in their Natural cousins. They never even came above ground any more.

But they were still down there somewhere, no dragon doubted that, and there was still the occasional demonstration of their control over the Naturals. The nest of an outspoken anti-Charmed protester might mysteriously catch fire, and troublesome dragons had even been known to disappear altogether on occasion. It was generally thought ominous that lately strange lights had begun to flicker in the west, in the vicinity of the one known cavern entrance.

It was into this atmosphere of rebellion that Shatter introduced his own arguments for change, and he found to his astonishment that he was listened to. As he reached his middle years, Shatter discovered that these strange, social dragons seemed . . . attracted to him. Their gazes told him they were wary of him – the Loner, he was called – but other words were used too: *charisma*, and even *handsome*.

Dragons listened to him, they clung to him, they welcomed his ideas and took him into their lives. Even among the small number of Naturals eager to rouse relaxed, easygoing dragons from their lethargy his sense of purpose was unique. The novelty of conversation and eventually the thrill of leadership, of control, became a drug to Shatter. The unreality of these other dragons – what he perceived as their lack of solidity in this curious world outside the cave – became less important, became subordinated to the heady realization that this was a world he could manipulate.

The rebellion was already formed and poised to fall upon the Charmed, but it took Shatter to find the way that its power might at last be unleashed.

The storm had been his cue. The weather loomed and it was during the days of gathering tension and oppressive heat that he brought South Point to the brink.

All the old arguments had been worn to dust – the abandonment of the old ceremonies, the Charmed as a forgotten race, the Charmed as evil bureaucrats or twisted spellweavers. So many dragons agreed with everything he and others said but none of them would actually do anything. They were afraid, ultimately afraid of the Charmed, of their legendary magic.

But Shatter had a dream which allowed him to deal with their magic, and perhaps this dream held a little magic of its own.

He saw himself vividly in the warped landscape of his mind, climbing a mountain to discover at its peak a great boulder perched on a cairn of small stones. These stones he gradually removed. An assembly here and the boulder settled imperceptibly towards the edge, a rumour there and it rolled a fraction nearer the precipice.

The boulder was revolt and the cairn was fear, fear of the wrath of the Charmed. With the cairn removed the boulder would fall. And the aftermath? From that one dragon would rise, his wings spread like mighty clouds, sole guardian of the rock and of all dragons who crawled before him.

That he was powerful enough to achieve this without aid he had no doubt, but to enlist these other creatures, these apparent dragons, was a choice he had long ago made. He enjoyed his dominion over them; it, like the boulder in his dream, seemed elegant.

The rock would fall. Only the cairn of stones held it back and this week Shatter had all but destroyed that cairn.

He had stolen two eggs and a single baby dragon from a careless young mother and carried them in secret to the entrance of the Charmed caverns. There, in full view of the watching stars but unseen by dragon, Shatter had broken the neck of the helpless infant and crushed the eggs over its broken body. Next to the carnage he had placed with infinite care a treasure he had kept – apparently for this very day: four gold scales he had discovered one day many years before, half buried in the marsh near the cave, his home. As an afterthought, he removed one of the golden scales and put it back in its secret place within the cave where he was hatched.

He had surveyed the awful scene and felt proud of what he had done.

Shatter stared beyond the eyes of the watching dragons and caressed the secrets he held hidden in his claws. The storm was about to break.

'Yes, my friends,' he bellowed, 'all those things which the Charmed promise they do not do. Nothing of their leadership remains, nothing of their honour, their wisdom . . . their charm. They have no magic now. If they had such powers as they claim would they resort to THIS?'

Now! This is the time!

Shatter pulled back his wings and held aloft a single fragment of white eggshell. Its edges were pale and ragged. On it, clearly visible even in the failing moonlight, were stains of dried blood and gore. And he held up the last golden dragon scale.

A great roar erupted from the crowd. As the rain began to fall Shatter prepared his final words.

But he had no need for them. Thunder bit into the sky and suddenly dragons were moving, clawing, whipping themselves into motion, clambering past and even over each other in their frenzy. Individuals were lost in the greater organism which was the mob, a great writhing beast which surged down the slope from the dam wall and crashed its way along the perimeter of the woods towards the entrance of the caverns of the Charmed, an entrance which up until this very night had been nothing but a decoy. Its voice was a mass of voices, its wing a mass of wings; it moved and surged and thrust its way from the turbulent shadow of the dam and out into the towering night.

Shatter slipped back into the darkness as the mob swept past him. Blurred and nameless faces rushed through his field of vision; in his eyes they became rocks, a landslide of dragons demolishing all before them. Close by, the thunder mixed its bass with the bellowing of the crowd. Shatter's malformed heart rejoiced, for the power had been his to command.

Doubt was destroyed; whatever last uncertainties the throng may have held were vanquished. The boulder rocked forward and then pitched itself unerringly on to the slopes below. Behind Shatter's red eyes an avalanche enveloped the world.

The young adventurers entered the caverns of the Charmed as if by magic. 'How else?' whispered Fortune to himself as he passed through the boundary between the world outside and the world within.

Behind him the rain fell heavily into the muddy clay. As he paused in the entrance itself, Fortune's combined senses reported nothing but blurred images, distorted sounds, unlikely smells, as though some subtle membrane protected this strange limbo from the realities outside.

'Move up — I'm getting drenched out here!'

Wood bullied him forward. Then Cumber was back, appearing from the darkness of the tunnel into which he had swiftly vanished.

'We must be quiet from hereon in,' he whispered. Then he looked pointedly over Fortune's shoulder at Wood. 'Although something tells me not all of us are capable of it. I imagine you'll be uneasy in the tunnels, being Naturals, although *why* you should I can't imagine, after all, at least the storm won't bother us any more.'

Cumber turned to go and Fortune made to follow him, then stopped as he saw Wood squatting doggedly in the entrance.

'Come on, Wood,' he urged.

'Not until you tell me exactly what's going on,' came the retort.

'But you *know*. It's what we planned — we're going to explore the caverns. It's just that . . . well, by *coincidence*, tonight's going to be something special.'

But Wood was not convinced. Ignoring Cumber, who was beginning to pace restlessly to and fro in the rock corridor ahead, he half spoke, half whispered to Fortune.

'What we planned was to dodge in, watch them do whatever it is they do in there, then get out quick. We never reckoned on tonight being *special*, as in *especially dangerous*. And we never reckoned on a guide.'

This last word was spat out with some venom, but Cumber chose to ignore it.

'And after what happened last week . . .' Wood continued.

At this, Cumber inhaled sharply, and was about to speak when Fortune surprised them both by announcing, 'I don't believe a charmed dragon was responsible for that.'

Pleased to have an ally, Cumber calmed himself. 'Of course not,' he said. 'We certainly don't slaughter infants outside our own caves.'

'Where do you do it then?' sneered Wood.

Cumber was about to turn on him when Fortune intervened once more.

'Listen to me, Wood,' he said. In the half-light Wood saw again the handsome dragon his friend would soon become. 'We made our plans for this expedition lightly but we've been overtaken by events. Cumber, whatever his reasons, has chosen to join us and for one I'm glad he has. We need his knowledge of the cave system and of the Charmed. And we need you too, Wood. We may need your strength. Terrible things may happen tonight. Please stay with us, if not for Cumber then at least for me.'

Fortune's words touched Wood in a way that quite shamed him, for in them he heard something of Welkin. He had been so afraid recently that their friendship was coming to an end, that Fortune would finally go off on some great adventure and leave him, simple, plain Wood in South Point, where he would surely live out his days.

But now, in Fortune's eyes, he saw a light which was entirely new to him, not the hot light that sparked between dragons at sport in the sky, but a light from the soul: the love of a friend.

Embarrassed and uncertain how to respond, he sought refuge from the intensity of Fortune's gaze and instead found Cumber's. He saw that the charmed dragon recognized the look that had passed between him and Fortune and he felt . . . exposed. He felt naked to this creature he found so offensive and he did not like it one bit.

In his confusion of embarrassment and anger, he failed to see that Cumber's gaze upon him was wholly sympathetic.

'Well,' he said gruffly, 'come on then, if we're going.'

The tunnels were weird and frightening to the two Naturals. An eerie suggestion of light enabled them to see where they were going . . . just. But other than where their eyes were directed there was total blackness inside the earth. Even the maze of the old quarter was nothing compared to this. The ceiling crowded down on them, as though the sky had fallen in. They felt clumsy in the confined space and with good reason — their wings were large and ungainly, spread as they were from foreclaw to flank, and their claws and elbows and long, branching fingers snagged on every outcrop in the narrow corridors. Their normal wide-stretched gait, no handicap in the open air, now hampered them to the point of distraction and even Wood began grudgingly to envy Cumber's narrow, small-winged physique.

Both Naturals were experiencing a new sensation — claustrophobia.

'Take care,' whispered Cumber from ahead, 'it's narrow along here.'

'It's narrow everywhere,' responded Wood acidly.

The darkness swallowed his voice and Fortune groaned as the rough ceiling clubbed against his head. Pulling his wing-arms and membranes as tight into his chest as possible, he shuffled awkwardly through an invisible chicane and came up short against a solid rock wall.

'This way,' came a muffled call from his right.

Gingerly Fortune crept to the side. The tunnel underwent a series of sharp turns, all of which caught both him, and behind him the eternally grumbling Wood, quite by surprise, until the final twist brought them doubling back completely to find themselves at last in a small chamber in which they could suddenly see again.

The cave, which was nearly full with only the three of them in it, was flooded with a strange, slightly pink light, the source of which floated seemingly unsupported near the low ceiling. Fortune stared rapt at the gentle fire — to him it looked like a slice of rainbow.

'Magic?' he asked cautiously.

Cumber nodded and pointed out the several exits to the chamber.

'These two we must not use, the one we have travelled leads only to the surface, but the fourth, this one here, well, we shouldn't really but I don't think there's much option.'

He became more agitated as Wood approached the fourth and narrowest slot and peered in.

'Great. Another black hole,' he grunted. 'What is this place anyway?'

'Guardroom,' replied Cumber quickly.

'Why that tunnel?' asked Fortune. 'You don't seem very sure about it.'

Cumber was hopping nervously again as he replied, 'It's forbidden, but the other two will be guarded, you see — even now. It's the only clear route to the Great Chamber so if we want to get further we have to take it, although I'm not so sure that . . .'

'This guardroom's deserted,' Wood butted in impatiently. 'Do the other tunnels go to this Great Chamber, then?'

'All tunnels go to the Great Chamber.'

'Then what are we waiting for?' said Wood, lunging for the nearer of the two larger tunnels.

'STOP!'

Fortune's heartbeat stopped and restarted twice over before he realized that the awesome voice which had stopped Wood dead and temporarily frozen his own blood had issued from Cumber's scrawny throat. In that voice the two innocent Naturals heard undertones of a world of which they had neither knowledge nor experience; they heard the harmonies of magic, the voice of bewitching command. Cumber had literally charmed them both to a standstill.

'You would not survive an encounter with a guard of the Charmed,' he warned by way of explanation, his voice still echoing with strange sub-vocals.

So it was that Wood found himself compelled to follow Fortune, who had followed Cumber into the narrowest of the three tunnels, squashing his oversized, natural body into the blackness. Twice now Cumber had made him feel foolish. He followed them, and as he battled his way into the hole it was as though he were being consumed.

Whereas the first and larger surface tunnel had been rough, with broken walls and floors, this one was smooth-sided and almost round in section. Cumber explained that there were easier routes a dragon could take to the Great Chamber but that tonight this one-time water course was the safest.

'You said it was forbidden,' called Fortune in a hoarse whisper. 'Why?'

'You'll understand when you see the Great Chamber,' replied Cumber unhelpfully.

The troop fell into silence until the end of the tunnel drew into sight, a pale circle now visible, now invisible to Wood as it was alternately revealed and eclipsed by his companions' shifting forms. A tree's length short of the opening Cumber stopped.

'The Great Chamber, I presume?' muttered Wood, and saw their guide's silhouette nod affirmation against the disc of light. The play of shapes brought to mind another silhouette, another disc – the strange dragon he had seen earlier against the moon, and he demanded, 'Were you flying tonight?'

Cumber snorted. 'In a storm? I may be Charmed, but I'm not mad! Tell me, what did you see, Wood?'

The stocky Natural said nothing.

'What did you see? You must tell me!'

Cumber's voice quivered dangerously, magical undertones poised again behind his words. Wood ground his teeth in fury as he felt the vast potential of the control this dragon might wield over him, but eventually he gave in.

'Oh, all right,' he said sulkily. 'I saw a dragon, that's all, just before we met you. It flew in front of the moon. It looked . . . weird. Weirder than you, even.'

'Ordinal,' breathed Cumber, ignoring the gibe. 'If Ordinal is flying then the time has truly come.'

All of this, of course, was new to Fortune.

'Ordinal? What "time"?' he demanded. Ordinal was the charmed dragon his mother spoke of more than any other.

'I think,' said Cumber, beginning to move forward again, 'we had best enter the Great Chamber. Follow me.'

He led them cautiously into the light and, waving them low, out on to a narrow ledge overlooking the cavern. Fortune stepped out eagerly, tense with anticipation, his breath motionless in his throat.

The Great Chamber that his mother, Clarion, had conjured for him in childhood stories had been vast, flooded with magical light, resounding with the heavy wingbeats of the knightly charmed dragons. At one end of the huge cave

43

sat the mighty Council of the Charmed – wise, good, passing sage judgement on great matters of state.

Here in the Great Chamber itself Fortune found only a fragment of the wonder of those stories, for it seemed a place in utter ruin.

To be sure, the cavern was huge. Shining stone plunged away from the ledge beneath them, gradually curving outwards in complex folds to form a glistening floor far, far below. The ceiling flared out close to their heads, its surface coarse with suspended fronds of rock reflecting the pink light of the rainbow floating in the chamber's centre.

But apart from the light source itself and the baleful glow it cast over the tremendous cave, there was little to illuminate the Great Chamber. It was filled with ghosts and blackness, dead.

The far wall rose much less steeply, much of it sculpted with loose boulders set free by some ancient collapse. As Fortune gazed at them it began to dawn on him what those boulders were, or once had been.

'Those rocks,' he whispered to Cumber, 'are they . . . ?'

'The Council Seats? Yes – twenty-four hollows in twenty-four boulders, each one a seat for a Council member, although they've toppled now, every one, and there, above them all, the High Seat.'

Wood snorted in disgust at Cumber's wistful yet reverent tone. Fortune ignored him, craning forward with Cumber towards the edge of the shelf of rock on which they crouched. Both dragons were quite unaware of the hard and angry look which had filled their companion's eyes, and of the way his gaze flickered from the broken seats to Cumber and then back into the cavern again.

Squinting past the thin glare of the floating rainbow, Fortune could just make out the great monolith rising from amid the Council Seats, seemingly the only structure still intact among the debris of this once-proud chamber. His viewpoint was such that the scintillating colours of the magical light all but obscured its peak, but there at the top a shadowy form was just visible.

'Is that Volence?' he asked nervously.

'Yes.'

'Hmph!' sniffed Wood, his unfriendly gaze fixed firmly now on Cumber.

Fortune was about to ask where the rest of the Council was when a distant rumbling echoed through the cavern. The three young dragons froze on the ledge as they strained to make sense of the faint sound.

'The mob is coming,' said Cumber, disbelieving. 'They must have been right behind us, but they've come straight through the guardroom and not followed our way up here. Why have they been admitted?' His eyes rose to the ceiling in a gesture of helplessness. 'Well, we should be safe enough up here on the forbidden ledge,' he managed to say. 'But be warned: we must not be seen. I don't know what they'll do when they find out . . . perhaps nothing, although I fear the worst, and perhaps . . .'

But his words of panic were cut off. Wood, his eyes flaring now, suddenly wheeled around, turning on Cumber and pinning his seemingly frail body up against the smooth stone wall beside where the tunnel opened on to the ledge. He demanded in a furious undertone, 'Now look, freak! I've been soaked, squashed, ignored, insulted . . . I don't care for you, and I don't care for your so-called charm. As far as I'm concerned you've got none! Answers, that's what I want from you, not these ramblings about mobs and magic! What's going on?'

Fortune tried to pull him back but Wood stood his ground, stopping his friend short with a wild look. Fortune reeled, unnerved by the fury in Wood's eye. So much anger, and beneath it . . . grief?

'Why is this ledge forbidden?' Wood ranted. 'What'll happen if we're found here? Why are we here at all? And where's this so-called Council of yours? Great Volence! *Where* are all the dragons he's going to lead?'

Wood was breathing heavily now, anger releasing itself in short bursts. His grip on Cumber was powerful but the charmed dragon flicked his head *so* and turned his shoulders *thus* and he was free on the opposite side of the ledge, leaving Wood grasping hopelessly at empty air. Eyes fixed on his surprised adversary, Cumber began to speak, quickly and efficiently.

'This ledge and the tunnel we have come down are

forbidden because they create a vantage point within the Chamber higher than the top of the High Seat, and since no dragon is above the Leader, only the Leader may use them. The reason we are here is that whatever happens here tonight must be witnessed, and believe me, Wood, you will be safer up here than anywhere else in the Great Chamber.'

In some deep tunnel the sound of claw on rock and booming voice grew louder and closer.

'Safer?' glowered Wood, pacing dangerously on the ledge. 'Why should we feel safe at all in the company of dragons who steal eggs, slaughter infants? Charmed scales were found! Your kind are not knights – they're murderers!'

Fortune shook his head in dismay as his oldest and newest friends fought before him, and with the dismay came disappointment. His high expectations of the Great Chamber had been totally unfulfilled – grey it was where it should have been white, rugged instead of refined, shadowed where light should have blazed in glory. His friends in conflict, Natural pitched against Charmed on a narrow ledge of rock in a dead cavern made from broken dreams.

Having carried his sense of wonder out on to the ledge and into the Chamber, Fortune was now facing the hard wall of reality it had struck there. A tear left his eye and fell to the distant floor.

Waves of sound from the tunnel doubled and redoubled in strength and bounced off rock pillars and turns of stone.

Dragons came.

The mob burst chanting and calling into the Great Chamber, stamping with wing and claw to fill the cave with the cries and echoes of the promise of war. His heart filled with horror, Fortune froze; both Wood and Cumber halted in the midst of their raging and stared in disbelief at the crowd of dragons surging in below. Tails whipped and wings lashed across the floor of the cavern and the jarring voice of the mob broke into the lifeless air, a deafening vent of anger and uprising, of retribution and a misguided craving for justice.

In the feeble magic light of the cavern, the voice of death.

CHAPTER 4

In the Great Chamber

Only now did Fortune see the true shape of the hole in his heart, now as the light of sudden knowledge illuminated it from within. While he had wandered dreaming over meadows, the meaning of his mother's gentle juxtaposition of Welkin's name with those of the great Charmed — Ordinal, Destater and old, old Halcyon — was ignored, unconsidered. He had not understood how the stories of glorious knights of old could have any relevance to a young natural dragon getting on with his life in the open air.

Now he could see her purpose, the hidden clue. *To know my father, I must know the Charmed!*

But the Charmed themselves, where were they? Gone!

Too late, he understood. His heart ached within him. He had always been fascinated by the Charmed but only now did he know why — now the Charmed could no longer help him.

'What has happened here?' he whispered to himself, turning his back on the mob, turning away from the dim shape of Volence crouched on top of his stark pinnacle of rock. He stared into the tunnel entrance at the back of the ledge. It was a black hole which echoed the void in his own heart. Behind him Naturals clamoured on the floor of the cavern: still he sought the dragons of his dreams, the elusive shadows which might be moving in the depths of the tunnel . . . and yet might not.

The void of the tunnel expanded to claim him and Fortune was suddenly alone with his father's shade, a blank dragon spirit which wavered ever just out of reach, trapped as it was in an unattainable past. He trembled as though winter had fallen on him . . . and though he did not realize it, so surrounded was he by his own thoughts and fears, at his side Cumber trembled as well.

Cumber too had retreated into the past, although for him the memories were clear. He conjured an image of Ordinal in his mind, recalling their last meeting and the fear it had impressed into his young heart, for now was the climax of the task with which Ordinal had entrusted him. *They must believe what I tell them*, he thought desperately, *though I find it near impossible to believe it all myself. Where shall I find my conviction?*

He had not seen Ordinal since she had spoken to him the words he was now preparing to pass on to Fortune and Wood. He feared she had deserted him, and perhaps South Point, but Wood's claim that he had seen a charmed dragon in the storm reassured him that she might still be here.

She had spoken of the world into which Cumber must venture, and of the dreadful, hunting pressure of time. She had sent him in search of Fortune. 'My own destiny binds me here, but South Point will no longer be a place for you nor the Natural you must take with you to Halcyon.

'The world is turning, Cumber. The bones of the trolls are on the move.'

Then it was Halcyon of whom she spoke, great and wise dragon who presided at Covamere, the citadel far to the south. There it was that all worldly dragon affairs were conducted and there, perhaps, was the cure to the plague which had destroyed the Charmed of South Point – even before the lies and schemes of Shatter could bring them down. If any dragon could intervene it was Halcyon and if he could, she swore, he would.

Yet her words were tainted with resignation and defeat, and this frightened Cumber. His youthful exuberance fought against it and he told her so. Ordinal sighed.

'That is why I must charge you with this great task,' she explained weakly.

'But what can Halcyon do? He's only a dragon, after all.'

'Nothing for South Point, I fear. You must bear witness to the fate of South Point so that you may tell Halcyon of the fate of dragons here. But our settlement is just one of many, and despite our differences we – Charmed and Natural – we are all dragons. Only Halcyon's power can prevent the final downfall.'

But even as Ordinal said this she looked away into the darkest corner of her cave.

'What else?' her student demanded. 'There's something else, isn't there?'

'There is nothing more. You must find your companion and go with him to Halcyon. Your destiny demands it.'

She looked suddenly very old to Cumber.

He knew in his heart that Ordinal had kept back more than she had told and this knowledge weighed heavy within him as he tried to muster conviction with which to pass on the story he must tell to Fortune and Wood. He too would be concealing a greater truth – though he had no idea what it might be – and his conscience told him that he had begun to play a dangerous game.

He was concerned also that two Naturals had presented themselves to him where Ordinal had foretold only one, and the inevitable question raised itself like a spectre. *Which one will I leave behind?*

At first Wood had been thrilled to see such a display of force, of Natural force in this bastion of the Charmed, for here was an army to wage on a grand scale the war he himself was fighting with Cumber on the ledge. Here at last would be justice.

But then he swayed, and the thrill became tainted with fear as he saw the set of the Naturals' faces, the bloodlust which had driven them here. Some dragons registered fear of their own as they gazed up and around the awesome chamber but most remained resolute, jostling and chanting as their fellow rebels forced their way in behind them. An army it was to be sure, one which would not leave before Charmed blood had been shed upon these ancient stones.

However, just when he began to doubt, just when he began to edge closer to Cumber, who crouched wide-eyed and open-mouthed at his side, in the midst of the army he recognized a face.

That face, which had once floated smiling over his own, whispering lullabies on the night wind, or rested content against the warmth of his mother's flank. That same face, once kind, now contorted with rage as it twisted in and out of sight among the shouting vigilantes.

Wood's loyalties lurched back to the mob, but even as they did so he identified what it was that fuelled his father's rage: not revenge for murder, not hatred of the Charmed, but grief for his lost Eleken. His father cared — at last Wood saw that he cared!

He had to be alongside his father, and he had to make his stand against the Charmed, but he recognized too the falseness behind Barker's anger, and it was that recognition which held him back, in conflict with himself, unable to decide what action to take.

Below, two massive dragons had taken up station at each of the four entrance passages to the Great Chamber; the rest milled restlessly, packed across the floor wing to wing. The shouting had reduced itself to a murmuring as they waited for their leader to take charge, and yet the murmuring was uneasy as some in their number began to register the fact that Shatter was not there.

Taking advantage of the lull in the noise of natural dragons, Cumber hissed at Fortune and Wood and eventually succeeded in attracting their attention. Giving them no time to question him and ignoring Wood's constant glances over the ledge to the shifting crowd below, he began to speak fast, in a low, level voice.

'Listen to me,' he started and when Fortune at once tried to interrupt he raised a wing and hushed him down. 'No, please, just listen. I have a lot to say and I must say it all at once and before that lot down there really start to make trouble.'

Wood shuffled a few paces away from the young charmed dragon, although it was obvious that he was listening intently. Both he and Fortune were frowning, one a frown of conflict, the other a frown of anticipation, and perhaps of hope.

He's going to explain everything, thought Fortune with desperation. *He's going to explain it all and everything will be all right!*

The muttering of the mob began to build again as several dragons called out unanswered to Shatter, and Cumber began.

'There isn't much time now and there is too much, far too much for me to say, but I'll try all the same. Now, I am a charmed dragon just like those you know from legend – at least as I understand your legends to be – and we *live* by charm, that is to say, by *magic*, by ways you can never understand or experience. Once your kind and mine lived in harmony – there were even those of your kind who aspired to become Charmed like us – but no longer. Natural dragons have lost all respect for the Charmed way. And now we Charmed are sick! Once there were two thousand charmed dragons living here in these caverns but in recent times our number has halved. At the same time, those in power here saw how you dull, invading Naturals thrived – and despite themselves they grew bitter.'

'Scared more like,' growled Wood.

Below in the chamber an argument had broken out and the young observers watched briefly. At length, two burly male dragons were despatched down the main entrance tunnel, evidently to see if Shatter might be following on, perhaps rallying extra support along the way.

'Hold fast, dragons,' called an anonymous voice from the throng. 'He won't let us down.'

'But what made it happen?' asked Fortune, anxious for Cumber to go on. 'Why are the Charmed in decline?'

Cumber shifted his weight uncomfortably. Although he knew they were invisible up here in the shadows he felt exposed and uneasy.

'Forces are at work greater than any dragon, Charmed or otherwise, can hope to understand.' Cumber shivered. Ordinal's words were jumbled together in his memory.

'You say your numbers halved,' protested Fortune, 'but even a thousand Charmed is still more than, what, seven hundred Naturals here at South Point. You still outnumber us. Why don't you ever come out? There doesn't need to be fighting, not if you come out and talk with Naturals again. Perhaps it won't be like it was but . . .'

'Fortune,' interrupted Cumber, 'you're right only when you say it won't be like it was, because you see it can't be. There *were* a thousand dragons here, quite recently, but now . . . now there are far fewer.'

'But that doesn't matter,' urged Fortune, almost pleading.

'A thousand, a few hundred – however many you are . . .'

'Fortune, Fortune.' Cumber hushed him, fearful that their voices might carry now the mob had temporarily quietened. 'I'm afraid we are not merely few: we are all but wiped out!'

'Twenty-four Council Members,' responded Fortune doggedly as though reciting a list learned by rote, 'and the Leader the twenty-fifth. Below them the fifty administrators and then . . .'

And for one, final time Cumber silenced his Natural companion.

'Seven,' he said, his face expressionless. 'We are seven now.'

With a roar the two dragons who had disappeared into the tunnel emerged again into the Great Chamber.

'Shatter is nowhere to be found!' the first of them shouted furiously. 'The Charmed have taken him!'

'The tunnels seemed *different*,' added his comrade with panic in his voice. 'Like it was further to the surface. We weren't sure of the way.'

The familiar voice of Tongue boomed out from the crush of bodies. 'Our so-called leader had abandoned us, as I predicted. So, brothers and sisters, now that we are here, let us *talk* with the Charmed, if we can.'

Fortune and Wood ignored the barrage of protests that erupted against Tongue, their attention wholly captured by Cumber's revelation.

'Seven?!' they exclaimed as one.

Cumber sighed the sigh of a dragon charged with too great a task. How could he go on with this? Why had Ordinal chosen him of all dragons?

Because there was none other left. He despaired.

Fortune was lost for words but Wood reacted strangely, huddling intimately against Cumber in a way the charmed dragon found threatening.

'The numbers are good,' he whispered. 'How many natural dragons are down there, do you think, Cumber? Seventy? Seven hundred counting those outside? And you are seven? Poor odds, Cumber, poor odds!'

At this something in Cumber snapped.

'Poor odds indeed, Wood!' he hissed. 'But not in the favour of Naturals, I can assure you. Oh, they are many, of course, and we are few, but believe me, the Charmed will fight with terrible powers, charm the like of which you would hope never to see in your life!'

'Seven against seventy?' scoffed Wood. 'Against seven hundred?'

'Neither I nor Ordinal will fight,' responded Cumber icily, 'so you might say the numbers of the Charmed are not seven but five. However,' he pressed on regardless as Wood rolled his head in disbelief, 'those five could destroy seven hundred natural dragons as easily as you might crush a line of insects.

'Believe me when I say that, Wood, for it is true!'

'We'll take some of you with us,' grated Wood, his eyes hot and confused. Was this dragon working some magic on him?

'Have a care before you commit yourself,' came Cumber's cold reply. 'Charmed dragons will die in such a battle but the point is that all dragons will die. Wood, this battle will happen, and it will destroy the entire dragon population of South Point, Charmed and Natural alike. There will be no victors; there may not even be survivors!'

Except us, I hope! But only if they accept my words, only if they believe me!

'Listen to me closely now, both of you, closer than you have ever listened to anything before,' he went on, heedless of the cacophony rising now from the army of Naturals. Some had even begun to leave by various of the exit tunnels, but whether they sought to confront the Charmed or simply return to the surface was not clear. 'South Point is lost. Simple, awful . . . but true. Every dragon here is doomed.

'And the coming battle is just part of a great war which could wipe all dragons from the face of the world!'

Hurriedly he told them of the plague of madness which had first reduced the numbers of the Charmed and finally all but decimated them. Disease, hysteria — whatever the madness was it swept through the Charmed population like a forest fire leaving few dragons untouched. Dragons grew stupid, dragons grew paranoid, dragons fought with their friends and murdered their families. The blood ran thick in the caverns of the Charmed and the mad dragons laughed as they waded through it.

Cumber's father, then his mother had slipped into insanity and finally both had died in one of the many lethal scuffles which were forever breaking out in the labyrinthine tunnels and caverns. His friends, his family, all were consumed by the madness which had descended upon the South Point Charmed.

Ordinal it was who had protected him through these terrible times, who had gathered the distraught Cumber in her wings and talked him back to a world of reason.

The Council had swiftly collapsed, its members too claimed by the plague, although Cumber, ever astute, noted that it had been in decline for many years before the arrival of the madness, as though the plague were an indication of some breaking point which had at last been reached.

A breaking point or, perhaps, a turning point.

Both Fortune and Wood were staring at him wide-eyed, but how much of this they were taking in he could not judge.

I can scarcely take it in myself, he thought frantically.

'But,' he continued, rapidly now as the unrest in the chamber below rose to a fever. Something would happen very soon now, some spark which would start the fire. He had to be quick. 'But there may be a hope. South across the sea lies ancient Covamere, once the world capital of all dragon affairs. There presides great Halcyon, Dragon Supreme, and though even his power is diminished still he might stop the war, he might make the peace.

'But only if he is brought the news.

'It is our task to observe and remember what happens here tonight and then we must race the tide of war across the world to bring the news to Halcyon. If we come to him as one, Charmed and Natural together, and tell of the horror of the destruction of South Point, then he will intercede.'

Before either Fortune or Wood could respond, let alone determine their own reactions to Cumber's words, before Cumber himself could even draw breath from his tirade, a voice exploded through the Great Chamber, a voice of such colossal power that at first the watching youngsters thought it was a voice of charm. But no, it was that of a natural dragon and it was Wood who first recognized it as being that of his own father.

'VOLENCE!' Barker bellowed like an earthquake, and by the time he had called the name a second and a third time the Great Chamber had fallen utterly silent.

'Father,' whispered Wood.

Dragons moved back as Barker shouldered his way roughly to the foot of the High Seat, the great stone monolith which dominated the far end of the cavern. They followed his gaze to its peak and there was a collective gasp as to a dragon they all saw what none of them had yet seen: Volence, Charmed Leader of South Point was here in their presence.

The Charmed premier was curled at the top of the pinnacle of rock, craggy, bronze, motionless. Light reflected from the large, metallic wings he had folded around himself as if to shut out the world.

'VOLENCE!' thundered Barker one last time, then, his cries eliciting no response, he turned back to the mob and shouted, 'How can you hold back now? Would you rather dither like Tongue? I can't weave words like Shatter – but I feel what we all feel. We must rescue Shatter. The time for talking is over and the time for action has come – the time for attack!' And once more he filled his mighty lungs and the Great Chamber reverberated with the sound of his battle cry. 'ATTACK!'

Eyes lifted with him as he leaped up the sheer face of the High Seat, powerful wings battering the air, half-flying, half-climbing up the precipitous tower until finally he lunged at the summit and landed there, his spread wings poised over the hunched form of Volence whom, they could all now see, he dwarfed.

Wood alone saw the slight frown which flashed across his face before he drew back his wings and cried,

'DEATH TO THE CHARMED!'

With a massive blow he struck Volence from the tower.

Below, dragons surged forward, hungry for the kill . . . but Volence's body did not fall.

Instead, as Barker struggled to regain his balance, it exploded with a soundless concussion. A cloud of metallic dust flew outwards, glittering and sparkling as it slowly drifted up on to the ceiling of the Great Chamber where it clung, a wondrous, weightless veil.

On the secret ledge Fortune flinched, then gaped in wonder.

'Volence was already dead!' he gasped.

Cumber merely shook his head and said, 'That's done it!'

Barker clung awkwardly to the Leader's empty perch, looking suddenly exposed and defenceless. His fellow rebels retreated from the base of the tower.

A gust of icy wind swept through the chamber, scattering Volence's remains and sending them dancing through the air towards the spies cowering on the ledge; before the bronze dust reached them it had dissolved into nothing. With a sharp crack a section of rock behind the Council seats snapped aside to reveal a dragon looming – glimmering – in the darkness beyond.

'Volence is dead,' announced the dragon, stepping into the light. 'But I am not.'

Cumber's heart lurched. Sublime relief swept through him to see Ordinal alive, magnificent – but she was facing death!

Her voice knocked him into a swoon, and for a time he drifted in the memories which poured from the countless cracks in the stone his mind seemed to have become.

'I think even the bones of long-dead trolls are on the move,' echoed Ordinal's voice in his mind, which had become Ordinal's cavern . . . a favourite place of Cumber's, an almost spherical cavity cratered with thousands of irregular holes. Two rivers entered at one side, joined, and left as one river from the other. And Cumber heard in the turmoil of his mind the constant roar of the waterfall by which the river ultimately emptied itself into the sea.

Ordinal had explained that her cave was a trolls' burial chamber. Those giants of old had long since vanished but once they had thrived here on Torr, and evidence of their rituals was plain in the holes which littered the inside of the round chamber.

They were full of bones.

'Trolls were charmed – in those days all creatures were charmed – and born as they were from rock, they returned their bones to rock after death.'

Upon examining the bones more closely Cumber had discovered that they were somehow fused into the rock walls.

He imagined one of those legendary giants pressing the skull of an ancestor into the very fabric of the rock itself, slipping the two solid materials into one another with a subtlety of charm which belied the troll's oafish appearance.

'Do the bones just stay there then, forever?'

'Yes. At least, in the past that has always been our belief, that they would. But it seems the future will prey on them like everything else. The world is turning.'

Cumber wrenched his senses back to the present.

The world is turning.

Old though she was, Ordinal gleamed. Metallic blues and greens shimmered beneath her skin and the scales on her back and tail were scarlet. A fronded crest ran down her spine and merged into her wings, and as she opened her mouth to speak again fire glowed deep in her throat.

Against the drab, muscular bodies of the natural dragons Ordinal's slender frame flashed like a jewel among coals. The Naturals knew this and they were afraid.

'Hey, freak!' yelled one, braver than the rest. 'Colourful you may be but you don't have it where it counts!'

A coarse chuckle rose from the joker's neighbours.

Ordinal cocked her head strangely and blood gushed from the nose of the dragon who had insulted her. He screamed in panic and lashed out at his fellows, spraying blood in their astonished faces as they backed away in horror.

Then Ordinal blinked and the jet of blood stopped as quickly as it had begun. The dragon dabbed at his muzzle tenderly, suddenly embarrassed.

'I have no wish for blood to be shed,' Ordinal said in her steady, penetrating tone, 'but have no doubt that I will defend myself if need be.'

On the ledge Cumber grasped Wood's elbow with his claws and whispered, 'Take note, Wood, of the power of charm. Bloody noses are just the beginning.'

While Wood angrily shook off Cumber's grip Fortune was fighting to gain perspective on these unprecedented scenes.

He found himself alternately trusting Cumber and doubting him, unable to reconcile the nervousness and certainty he saw combined in this one charmed dragon. All his young life he had dreamed of adventure but now it was being offered to him he found that he was terrified.

57

The world is turning, he thought. *But am I ready to turn with it?*

Ordinal was speaking again.

'I urge you to leave peacefully,' she said. 'No harm will come to you if you go now, but if you stay . . .'

'We will stay!' bellowed Barker from his perch. 'The murder of our young will be avenged!'

Ordinal appraised him coldly.

'Consider where you stand before you speak of vengeance, dragon,' she murmured. 'The greatest of our leaders have occupied that seat. Are you as great as they?'

'Your great leaders are turned to dust!' spat Barker. 'Give us the charmed dragon who killed our young and we may not slaughter you all.'

'No Charmed killed your young.'

Ordinal's flat statement begged no argument, and though her gentle voice was almost drowned by Barker's her words echoed around the Great Chamber long after his had died away.

Meanwhile, Wood had crept forward into the light and now clung to the edge of the rock pulpit, tendons corded on his limbs, wing membranes rippling, eager for action.

In the arena the two dragons faced each other, Barker and Ordinal, Natural and Charmed.

The mob was hushed.

'Murderer!' bellowed Barker.

He launched himself from the High Seat, thick wings drinking great draughts of air as he hurled himself at the old charmed dragon. All his pain surfaced then as he attacked and for an instant he saw not Ordinal but Eleken, his own, beautiful Eleken, drowning offshore in a terrible summer storm. As if he had summoned it the distant cracking of thunder signalled that the storm outside had mustered enough power to punch its way into even these ancient depths.

Ordinal stepped lightly to one side and gaped.

A shaft of fire sprang from her mouth and Wood saw his father's wings enveloped in an orange flame which seemed to flow about his body like running water. Light pierced holes in his wing membranes as the fire consumed him and his cries of pain filled the Great Chamber with a sound more terrible than even the thunder which infiltrated from above.

'Father!' shouted Wood.

With a cry of anguish he leaped from the ledge and spread his wings into the air. His target was no burnt tree stump now but his father's killer, it was the force which had taken his mother from him, it was the cold-blooded killer of infants . . . it was the terrible, terrible Charmed.

For the first time in his life his course of action was clear to him. All of his frustrations and indecisions were swept away by the rush of air across his skin and blood through his veins. His father was dying and the solution was simple.

Attack!

Action pulsed through the mob. Dragons scrambled up the tiered rock benches towards Ordinal, dragons took to the wing, dragons clustered around the fallen Barker, trying to smother the flames which were feeding on him.

And down into the bedlam swept Wood, cutting through the air with the confidence in flight he had long hoped to achieve. He had but one target now: Ordinal.

The old charmed dragon looked up as he swooped on her and her mouth opened. He flinched, expecting a gush of fire, but she simply closed her eyes and lowered her head.

Before Wood even reached her the natural dragons had swarmed over her surrendered body and were tearing it to pieces. Glistening scales flashed in the air, turning to dust and flame. Distant thunder boomed down the tunnels but it could not mask the dreadful sounds of death.

Fortune looked on horrified as Wood vanished into the frenzy, and for him too the future was now a cold certainty. To see all that the Charmed believed in, all their code and honour swept aside by brute force, was repulsive to him. Disgusted by the actions of his natural kin he turned to Cumber for support, and only just grabbed his companion in time to prevent him from hurling himself off the ledge as had Wood.

'They killed her! They killed her!' Cumber was howling, his eyes red and wild. Tiny licks of flame lanced from the corners of his mouth and Fortune almost drew away in horror.

He's a monster! Like the rest of them!

But as quickly as the panic had come it left, reason slamming down like a great block of stone and he held on, grappling and hauling Cumber back from the edge.

'Let me GO!' screamed Cumber. Fortune lowered his horns and butted him back against the far wall hard enough to knock the wind from him. Cumber sprawled there digging for breath.

'It's started,' he panted. His gaze cleared. 'We have to get out of here, Fortune – now!'

Fortune risked a look below. Ordinal's remains had vanished and the marauding Naturals were beginning to disperse into the tunnels in search of the rest of the Charmed. If they found their way up here both he and Cumber would be killed without hesitation.

Wood was nowhere to be seen.

'Where to, Cumber?'

But he had drifted away again. Fortune shook him.

'Where to?' he repeated.

'The guardroom. Back to the guardroom.'

'Right!'

Fortune pushed Cumber back into the tunnel – he was remarkably light – and pummelled him along without ceremony. Before long Cumber had had enough of this treatment and decided that propelling himself was a better proposition.

'Where to from the guardroom? Back to the surface?'

Fortune jabbed Cumber in the rump to prompt a reply.

'Excuse me, but do you think you could cut out all this roughness, which isn't entirely necessary in my opinion – you Naturals are all the same, you know,' came the grumble from over Cumber's shoulder.

Fortune allowed himself a brief smile – that was more like Cumber!

They emerged breathless into the guardroom with an unexpected splash – mercifully empty of dragons it was however half full of water. Storm floods had breached the surface tunnel and were pouring into the small cave. The water crashed about their breastbones as it whirled around and around before exiting through the two passages which led down to the lower levels.

'Well, that settles that,' said Fortune unhappily, looking

at the tunnel by which they had entered earlier. 'We can't get to the surface that way. Now where?'

'Down.'

Fortune looked doubtfully at the two equally waterlogged tunnels. Water splashed into his mouth and he spat it out with a grimace.

'I knew you were going to say that,' he muttered.

But before they could move a strange sound invaded the cave.

It came from the tunnel on the left. To Fortune it sounded like the rumble of a great fire, but somehow it seemed . . . alive.

Cumber knew exactly what it was.

'They have opened the Realm,' he said 'The remaining five Charmed have come out of hiding and joined battle with your friends.'

'They're not my friends,' retorted Fortune.

'My apologies. Greater forces are at work than dragons . . .'

'. . . can hope to comprehend, yes, yes, I know all that. But what are you talking about, Cumber? The Realm, what's . . . ?'

'No time! I'll tell you about it another day – if we see another day. Come on, it's heading this way!'

As they slipped into the other tunnel the rainbow light which floated in the centre of the guardroom flickered out, its magic spent. The chamber was dark now, lit only occasionally by a clawtip of lightning probing its way through the waters from the surface, more frequently by the darker colours of magic which sparkled and blew on subtle winds from the bowels of the caverns of the Charmed.

The battle was already raging in those underground passageways, a hidden battle, the details of which would remain hidden forever but the effects of which would soon light up the world as they now lit that one, tiny cave.

As Fortune and Cumber fled the battle so the battle pursued them.

As Cumber had told so it began.

CHAPTER 5

Flight

Their flight through the underground caverns would not easily be forgotten. When the way ahead was blocked by battle or bodies they had to double back. They had to run from lethal rock falls that were the result of the thunder and noise or the magic infused in the rock, or both. Thunder assailed them at every breath and not all of it came from the storm.

Sight blurred upon sight of skirmishing dragons and hideous cries of agony echoed from all directions in the tunnels to assault their ears.

They crouched in a shadowy corner while a Charmed dragon held ten Naturals at bay with a jet of fire; they passed a natural dragon turned to stone, a look of puzzlement etched incongruously on her face; they found another turned to ice. This latter victim was melting before them into the flood waters and Fortune thought he saw tears in the dragon's dissolving eyes.

At every turn Fortune expected to meet Wood, to confront him, berate him, plead with him to rejoin them. But in his heart he knew his friend must either be dead or following the battle as at last it started to move back towards the surface. Either way he was quite lost to them.

They had counted some thirty bodies on their journey. Wood had not been among them. And not one had been that of a Charmed.

They were deep inside the ground now, inside the cliffs of South Point, and when they had slowed enough to realize it above the rattle of their passing, there was silence. And a noise — the constant rush of water about their claws in a flood which was growing stronger all the time and soon threatened to wash them both along with it.

Five against seventy! Fire charm! The Realm!

Fortune's fear now was less for their own safety than for that of those above ground. His mother, Clarion, old and frail, lived alone in a nest some distance inland from the massed nests of the settlement itself. He hoped desperately that she was far enough away from the fighting to be safe, and that she might flee inland if threatened, perhaps even to the mountains of Torr island's western peninsula, for it was said by some that there were still dragons there.

As they paused to catch breath Fortune panted, 'My mother . . . she lives on the other side of South Point. Do you think . . . ?'

Cumber seemed not to hear him.

Fortune suddenly thought what it might be like, to see a loved one torn to pieces.

'Not all Naturals are brutes,' he offered lamely, touching Cumber's shoulder.

Cumber looked at him, curious. And Fortune was forced to wonder how it felt to witness your whole race reduced to madness and persecution.

Enigmatic, Cumber, that's what you are, thought Fortune. It was a word his mother used.

But he must wait until later to think of his mother.

'Where are we going?' he asked.

By way of reply Cumber ushered him into a narrow slit which broke the left side wall ahead. A roaring came from the blackness and after a short wade through the constricting space they emerged into a cauldron: Ordinal's chamber, almost completely awash.

The two incoming rivers, bloated by storm water, were gushing into the cavern in torrents which ripped stone from the walls. Whirlpools danced through the lake which was inexorably filling the chamber. The exit hole was out of sight, drowned beneath the new water level, a level which was rising even as they watched. A rainbow charm cast a pale light over the bubbling water, a light which dipped and bobbed as the charm struggled to stay alive.

The noise was deafening.

Fortune strained to see over the roaring torrent, to locate

some other exit, then realized that Cumber had frozen and was staring open-mouthed at the roof of the chamber.

A monster stared back down.

Its silvery body clung to the broken ceiling, claws biting deep into the bone-filled cavities cut from the rock. A shiny scale dropped from its back and was swept away by the foam; a single wing twitched miserably, its twin a bloody stump.

A charmed dragon, mortally wounded.

'Pander,' breathed Cumber.

The dragon slowly uncoiled its neck. Fortune flinched as he realized that its eyes were in fact mere empty sockets — yet they *stared* at him. Cumber remained motionless at his side.

The dragon opened its mouth. The air around it rippled with heat but no flame emerged. It hissed wretchedly, 'Help me, Cumber!'

The broken dragon scrabbled across the ceiling in defiance of gravity, chipped claws tapping out a nightmare rhythm as they gripped and released the rock. A terrible leer broke its face while blood ran from its eye sockets into the lake.

Cumber still did not move.

'Your skin, Cumber.' The words forced themselves through the guttering fire in its throat. It gained strength suddenly. Something rippled beneath its hide like a worm under soil and it covered the remaining distance to the watching pair in the blink of an eye.

Then Cumber spoke. 'NO!'

But his skin rippled in waves which matched those on the back of the wounded dragon and he stood like stone in the rising water though it beat against his chest; his eyes had filmed over.

A red glow shimmered in the empty eye sockets of the monster looming over him, and underneath its torn skin, and as it glowed so Cumber grew dull.

'Stop it!' howled Fortune as he bared his teeth at the evil creature. He was powerless; whatever this monster was doing to Cumber was utterly beyond his understanding.

His shout carried through the chamber and its service tunnels and he heard a gruff voice return a call from the far end of the entrance passage.

'Down here,' it growled, its words followed at once by the sounds of several dragons on the move.

The wounded dragon started in fear and let out a wail of infinite sorrow. Fortune acted.

'This way!' he shouted, then coiling his limbs he reared back and butted Cumber into the water. The icy torrent instantly brought the young Charmed to his senses and he started thrashing to stay afloat.

The light died in the wounded dragon and for an instant Fortune felt sorry for it. Then he had jumped and the coldness of the water struck all breath from him. It snorted up his nostrils and into his ears and the powerful current tore him away from the scene of the confrontation.

Half afloat, half drowning, floundering beside Cumber as the raging flood waters dragged them towards the invisible exit tunnel, Fortune saw only glimpses of the fight which ensued. Bobbing above the waves he saw a Natural dissolve like salt. Through a film of angry water he saw the legs chewed from the charmed dragon. He sank and rose again to see another Natural peeled like a fruit, but screaming still.

This he saw, and worse. Then, as he surfaced for the final time before being sucked down into the submerged tunnel, he saw the charmed dragon in pieces, and four Naturals dead around it.

A fifth Natural stood panting over the carnage, blood trickling from a dozen wounds. A young dragon, stocky and proud.

Wood!

Fortune tried to call his name but the waves closed over his mouth and the world was eclipsed.

A current gripped him in the underground river.

He floated in the void, robbed of his senses. Instinctively he tried to open his wings, a young dragon who had never flown more than a hesitant tree's length trying to glide through white water.

His breath tightened in his lungs, his head felt starved and light, the pounding of blood filled his ears. He opened his eyes into the liquid storm – and there was light ahead, the dullest of glows. It slipped behind him and then it was ahead again. Before long Fortune realized that the light was stationary and it was he who was doing the tumbling.

Not stationary. It was approaching, or rather he was approaching it.

The light of death, he thought as the last bubbles of breath were snatched from his mouth by the wicked current.

With a strangled cry he opened his mouth to fill his lungs with what he knew would be a killing blow of ice water . . . and inhaled the sweetest air he could ever have hoped to taste.

The river exploded around him into a million droplets of spray, hurling him clear as it was blasted out into the night air.

His wings, already partly unfurled, peeled open with a will all their own and lifted him free. Some ancient will to live gave him the knowledge of flight his experience had failed to provide and he flapped higher, turning in the air to look back at what had so nearly been his grave.

Half the cliff was gone.

Where once had hung a waterfall there now stretched a great arch of flood water firing out from the broken land in a mighty jet of spray. Rubble was piled in the sea beneath it; it was like an ocean in flight.

Before he realized it Fortune had been flying for hundreds of wingbeats. His mind caught up with his body and his wings faltered. As he floundered a shadow passed over him and Cumber was at his side.

'So you're flying! Don't worry about it, don't think about it, just do it!'

Fortune was observing that Cumber made only one wing-beat to his three when he realized that there was light all around them, though it was night.

He choked as he looked beyond the shattered cliffs to the source of the light, a light which reflected off the undersides of the storm clouds and illuminated the night with a fierce orange glow.

South Point was on fire.

Together they rode the wind and flew nearer. The rain had all but stopped now but Fortune sensed that even the earlier downpour could not have tamed this fire. Timbers buried deep and dry, untouched by the storm, had been plundered and set ferociously alight. The great ridge of nests was a line of flame stretching as far as they could see; the woodland was an inferno.

The old quarter was burning with flames as big as oaks and within it tortured shapes curled and charred: the bodies of the elder Naturals, indistinguishable in death as in life from their timber home.

Fortune followed Cumber through the hot air which rose in vicious eddies from the burning nests. Cumber was exercising some kind of protective charm which kept away the sparks and embers leaping endlessly into their path.

For the moment the enormity of the destruction below him was failing to register and Fortune found himself dwelling on the nightmare encounter in Ordinal's cave. 'That dragon, in the chamber, what did he *want*?' he asked.

'He wanted me!' Cumber shivered in distaste. They were flying over Tongue's mighty aqueduct now; as they passed overhead a jet of fire raced along its length. The timber structure exploded in splinters and the two dragons wove to the side as a huge cloud of steam and smoke enveloped them.

'He was so badly wounded,' coughed Cumber. 'His only chance of escape, well, of survival at all, was to take over the body of another charmed dragon. That's a rather special charm, by the way.'

'I don't doubt it,' replied Fortune, repulsed. 'But what would have happened to you?'

'I would have entered his dying body and perished. Pander was one of the five dragons left, insane like the others. Look below, Fortune — see what damage just a few charmed dragons can do . . .'

They were flying over the Sink now, or what remained of it. The great granite cup which had held South Point's drinking water for ages past was utterly smashed, a mountain of rubble through which the water had already drained away to join the swollen rivers which had flooded the caverns.

When he saw the Sink destroyed Fortune finally knew that South Point had died.

The fires burned high and hard illuminating the end of his world, but it seemed to Fortune that as they consumed they also cleansed, erasing the hatred which had fuelled

67

them. The storm was moving inland now, its power spent, and a strange and unexpected peace was falling over the settlement.

Cumber saw Ordinal's prophecy laid out before him, as clear in its truth as a drop of dew. South Point was no longer a place for dragons. *Halcyon must know of South Point. We must succeed*, he urged himself. *We must reach him!*

'Covamere lies south over the sea,' he called to Fortune, who was beginning to drift north, following the storm.

'My mother . . .' protested Fortune.

'We have no time – *no time!*'

Fortune did not reply but flew doggedly north, growing smaller in Cumber's vision.

Cumber hovered there a while, considering their collective loss. Between them they had lost more than any dragon deserved, and they were young, scarcely grown. Now Fortune feared for his own mother and Cumber was in danger of being left without his one friend and companion.

He decided.

The flames crawled dying among the dead.

Neither Fortune nor Cumber had seen survivors but survivors there were. Few and weak, but alive, and they came slowly together amid the muddy remains of the Sink.

'My children,' whispered Shatter to the six who crouched before him. 'If only I could have shared in your triumph.'

He limped badly and was caked in blood. His whole demeanour spoke of a dragon who had fought to the very brink of death and barely clawed his way back.

The illusion was faultless.

Little of the blood was his own and none was the result of conflict. His only genuine wound, a cut to his left hind leg, was superficial and self-inflicted for effect. His pained hobbling belied its falseness and the tales he wove convinced his onlookers of his valour in battle.

He had in truth seen out much of the fighting in hiding in a secret cavity below the Sink wall. When the Sink was destroyed he suffered a few minor scrapes and bruises but otherwise emerged unharmed. By then the battle was all but over and it was easy to dodge the few remaining skirmishes.

Within the safety of the rock he had even found time to

sleep. The granite of the tiny cave was sharp and it crowded him — but with love. It soothed him, it lulled him, and in its cold embrace he dreamed of the boulder.

Only now the boulder was greater than he had ever seen it before. It was not the rock he had unleashed upon South Point, this, but a mighty deadfall, poised above the land upon a single claw of stone and ready to fall, awaiting only the one dragon who would recognize its power and send it tumbling to destruction. The end result of such a fall? Why, the ultimate extermination of the Charmed, of course — not just the Charmed of South Point but of the world.

In his dream the deadfall was proud and mighty and awaiting only his instructions. He saw it vividly, in agonizing detail: behind it a mountain, behind that the low winter sun, all around it ice. And in the detail he saw that it, like him, was real. He thought, *It lies south of here!*

There were six other survivors. Shatter's gaze alighted on each of them in turn. Their names he had been told but those he would soon forget; to him they were just dragons. Poon, a heavy, slow-witted dragon whose hide was charred and cracked; Torque and . . . Tumely? — brothers who had fought side by side and between them reduced a charmed dragon to dust; the fourth, whose name he had already forgotten, a sharp-eyed thief who had stolen his way through the fighting, avoiding the battle as Shatter had done.

At least two of these four were his, he knew, and the fifth too: Barker. Barker's body was burned almost beyond recognition, his wings crumpled autumn leaves, his face terribly scarred, but somehow he had survived to report to his beloved leader. Now he looked up at Shatter with complete and uncompromising loyalty.

The sixth dragon was Wood.

He stood foursquare beside his father. His body seemed to have gained maturity over the long hours of fighting, numerous cuts and bruises lending it a weather-beaten appearance years older than the young dragon who looked out from within. Of the six he was the only dragon in whose eye Shatter saw a spark of independence.

Wood, thought Shatter, for some reason the name brighter in his mind's eye. *I must watch this one.*

'Our community has suffered devastating loss,' he said, his words well-planned and carefully spoken. These weak, ghost-dragons would not understand his need to find the deadfall. 'Each of us has lost loved ones, and it is the Charmed who are responsible. It is the Charmed who must pay. We will form the core of a conquering army; we will seek them out in every corner of the world. Only then can we truly settle again.'

But even as he spoke he saw that these dragons were beyond his rhetoric. They needed sleep. Better to leave them to recover.

'Brothers,' he said, feigning the same weariness he saw in them, 'we are brave warriors all. Let us close our ranks and sleep, for tonight we have rid South Point of evil. Soon our energies will be renewed and we shall begin our travels. We will bring peace to a world without the Charmed.'

His thoughts came back to Wood as the bone-weary warriors settled gladly to sleep. The young dragon was not yet fully grown but his wide shoulders and broad muzzle promised a formidable adult to come. Shatter decided then that at the first hint of mutiny he would kill Wood. Until such a time, however, his obvious talent for combat might prove a valuable asset.

His future begun, Shatter settled back with his cohorts to sleep through what little remained of the night. They curled up in the open air, the storm over now, the wind fresh and gentle. Stars showed again in the south, unveiled by the passing clouds.

Shatter gazed about him: all around was devastation. His imaginary boulder had flattened the settlement utterly and, thinking back to the infant dragons he had sacrificed, he savoured the way in which that tiny act of violence had been magnified into such spectacular carnage.

Death was his bedfellow that night and he believed that as long as he showed it his loyalty he would live forever.

Wood was numb; he knew only that he was with his father again and it was good. Shatter, he knew, was quite mad and very dangerous . . . but that was a problem for tomorrow. Something nagged at him though, denying him sleep. In the caverns, after his troop had fought to the death with the wounded dragon in that waterlogged cave, he had glanced across to where the river was sucking itself into a whirlpool.

What had he seen?

A dragon floundering in the torrent? A familiar face straining to breathe above the waves before being dragged under?

Fortune? Or was it his mother's ghost, her own drowning replaying itself before him in that underground grave?

He shook his head, unable to deal with the possibilities. Better to forget, better to stay now with his father. They had rediscovered their family at last and nothing in the world would see Wood lose it again. *Too much loss*, he thought.

And so a young dragon older than his years banished doubt to the hidden corners of his heart and held his poor father close. Of the seven he was the last to fall asleep.

When the Charmed are wiped from the world, he thought as he drifted into sleep, *then my father and I will know peace*.

For the moment, at least, he believed it.

Cumber found Fortune squatting beside a pile of blackened ash some distance from the main settlement. The young Natural did not look up as Cumber landed at his side.

'My home,' he explained, indicating the debris which had once been a dragon's nest.

'I know,' replied Cumber.

'She's not here; there's no body.'

'She could be anywhere. We could search but . . .' Cumber's voice trailed away. The smoking desert South Point had become was eloquent enough.

'. . . but we have a mission.' Fortune completed the sentence for him. He looked up at Cumber, eyes filled with tears. 'She's alive. I can feel it.'

His certainty impressed Cumber. Such conviction was unusual in a Natural. Flickering embers sent up strange reflections in Fortune's eyes and Cumber caught a depth of glance which made him wonder just who had chosen whom for this great journey.

Fortune sighed heavily.

'I'll see her again. One day I shall,' he said. 'But now we must go.'

He frowned, puzzled, as though hearing some distant sound. A gust of wind blew past them, gathering up the remains of the nest and carrying them off into the night.

'I've lost Wood,' added Fortune as they turned into the freshening wind. Cumber could think of nothing to say in consolation and simply patted Fortune on the flank with his wing.

Something exploded in the distant valley, showering sparks into the sky and as if that were a signal the two dragons launched themselves upwards once more to fly back across the smouldering nests of South Point, out over the cliffs and across the sea.

Towards Covamere; towards Halcyon.

Orange light clung to them as they traversed the battle-field, turning Fortune's dull brown hide to a deep red and sparkling off Cumber's dusty gold scales with a thousand tiny flames. Glowing wreckage popped and sparked in the smoking remains of South Point and it seemed to Fortune that there was great colour in the devastation below them, that the orange and the red of the fires against the blackness of the debris spoke of life against death, of light against dark and of hope against despair.

The heat baked them again as they flew deliberately low over the battlefield, searching in vain for survivors, then as they passed out over the cliffs the air cooled suddenly with a great blast of wind from the sea. Their own fires fuelled with purpose they quickly left the remains of South Point behind and soon became specks against the night sky, specks which dwindled and then vanished.

PART 2
AETHER'S CROSS

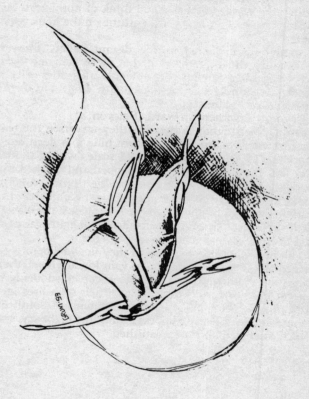

CHAPTER 6

Gossamer

Aether's Cross was a place with more than one history.

The first told how a huge ravine had been cut through the Low Mountains by a mighty troll lord many ages past to afford a route from the great Injured Mountains of the south, from whence all trolls came, to the northern seas and thence to their final sanctuary, the cold land of Chaemen. Giant Aether had scooped out the channel over many days, it was said, in the time when nature was a mere rumour and other, older powers held sway. The rock which he excavated step by laborious step he crushed to powder in his craggy hands and blew away to the north, where it eventually fell to rest to form the fine, grey beaches of the Heartland's northern coast. It was charm he wielded, and over that charm he had awesome control.

Through the ravine which Aether had carved there journeyed trolls. They were tireless travellers, those ancient wayfarers, and thanks to Aether's Cross and a thousand passes like it they moved over the world and became its masters.

But aeons were brief in those ancient times and even then the world was beginning to turn. As the mountains from which they had been born were worn away by the passing of years so were the trolls; to frigid Chaemen they fled and abandoned the fire which had once filled their veins. Behind them they left only bones and the scars which marked their work upon the land. Scars like the Cross. In their place other travellers came and went, and then the dragons came and soon the dragons settled and the citadel of Aether's Cross was reborn.

Thus did the charmed dragons of Aether's Cross tell its history.

The Naturals of the Cross knew a little of this history, but the stories they told were different. They told not of a troll but of a tremendous river which had carved a way through the softer rock of the Cross over the course of countless years, opening a natural pathway through the mountains. Weather, not trolls, had broken open the fissures and caves, and some even claimed that a massive river of ice had once rolled down from the north to smooth the lower reaches of the canyon. These were dragons unconvinced by stories of troll and fire but seduced instead by different heroes: storm and flood, weather and time.

Neither story could be proven and so both lived on.

Quite simply, Aether's Cross was a wide place in the deep, narrow gorge which split the Low Mountains from north to south. Contrary to the promise of their name, the mountains were in fact steep and treacherous – and very high – and even dragons found passage through the gorge preferable to struggling on the wing through the cold and rarefied air above the peaks.

This wide safe place, this welcome broadening of the meandering, snakelike slot of the ravine, was home to a dragon community divided somewhat like that of South Point, for here too there existed the domain of the Natural and that of the Charmed. But whereas South Point had always seen at least some interaction between the two domains here they were – and always had been – quite separate.

The charmed dragons inhabited the network of tunnels their ancestors had cut from the rock of the ravine's east wall. The wall was sheer and uninviting, marked only by the melt-water cascades, the countless cracks and ridges of the rock and the seven black holes by which the Charmed entered and exited the cave system. In the manner of many of their kin across the world they were reclusive, and they took little notice of their neighbours, the natural dragons of the west wall.

This other wall, in contrast, sloped more gently in a series of flat terraces and on these terraces the Naturals had settled, building for themselves a tight community of interlocking nests. As the nests relied upon each other for support so did the dragons: the Naturals of the Cross were close and loyal, well aware of the vulnerability of their perch on this great, grey cliff and as committed to the welfare of the community as a whole as to that of their own individual families and selves.

In the earliest times, when all dragons were Charmed, the Cross had been a single Charmed colony, a welcome waystation for all those travellers who crossed the Heart-land. Here the noble Charmed of old had held court in their golden age, before the coming of the Naturals.

The invasion was subtle. Strange dragons would arrive, plain and dull, to settle among the rocks of the west cliff. Charmed eggs suddenly bore infants with the same dullness, the same deformities. To raise them in magic proved difficult and eventually impossible and these charmless youngsters were banished in ever increasing numbers to their kin on the opposite cliff. The Naturals accepted these infants without judgement, raising them as their own, and soon the Natural population grew and the Charmed were few.

The world was turning.

And like the Charmed of South Point, the Charmed of the Cross understood it was turning away from them.

They retreated to the depths of the tunnels which honey-combed the eastern ramparts of the treacherous canyon which was Aether's Cross and for a long time, in the calm, simple way of all dragons of the Cross, they stoically embraced the horrifying threat of extinction. But then, as the years stretched by, a strange madness began to creep through the tunnels, and whether it was a disease or a prod-uct of their suppressed fears no dragon could say. Under-ground, once noble knights became paranoid and aggressive, while outside the Naturals thrived and all but forgot their elusive neighbours. Underground, the tensions mounted, for a growing swell of Charmed opinion said that it was the Naturals who had brought the madness to the Cross, that these interlopers, these cripples without magic were to blame for the destruction of their glorious heritage.

That the only way they could turn their path back to the destiny they deserved was to destroy the Naturals.

This they plotted and thus did something of the story of South Point threaten to retell itself at the Cross, and who can say in how many other dragon settlements that story was replayed?

But not here.

Fate had something quite different planned for the Cross.

The river which ran through the Cross, named Aether for the troll who may or may not have released it, was high and angry with snow-melt. From the sheer mountain faces which rose high above the torrent waterfalls large and small were cascading into the depths, loud and shining drapes on walls of grey stone.

Higher up, above the spray and the constant roaring, lived dragons. Here was the west cliff which held the nests and paths and landing platforms of an entire Natural community, and there the east showing only empty entrances to seemingly abandoned tunnels, black sockets in a vertical wall which looked more like bone than rock. Where the west side danced with life, the east seemed quite dead.

But most of the Naturals of the Cross paid little attention to the comings and goings of their neighbours. When it seemed they had disappeared altogether, many Naturals began to forget that they had even been there at all. They had more important concerns.

While life for the Charmed was comparatively easy – one cave was much like another and magic allowed for miracles quite out of the reach of natural dragons – for the Naturals the Cross was an inhospitable place. Plant life and cover were scarce: the north wind which sliced through the ravine moved unchecked across the tight nests of the western terraces. Food was almost exclusively fish, plucked perilously from the mountain torrent far below by the highly trained fisher dragons who rightly enjoyed great status in the close-knit community. The cliff itself was unstable and landslides would often damage or even destroy nests – and occasionally kill dragons.

A hostile place then, and yet the natural dragons remained. A few departed each year, those dragons too old or too fearful for the Cross, but the majority stayed: the air was fresh and clear and rich with the scent of the mountain and the spray of the river; to some dragons the Cross itself seemed alive.

And even the perils themselves were good, for had they not created a dragon community superior to any other in health, resourcefulness and closeness of spirit? Was this not truly a community which coped and cared? Which *loved*?

For the natural dragons loyal to the Cross this was the only home; this was truly the centre of the world.

Many dragons were typical of the Cross, few more so than Gossamer — on the surface, at least. A brief excursion into her private thoughts might have revealed broader interests than sheer survival at the Cross warranted. For Gossamer had a secret.

That she was interested in charm she did not hide; indeed it was something of a standing joke amongst her friends that she was fascinated by all things magical. But a dream haunted her, a dream in which she would fly across the canyon and into one of the seven tunnel entrances. She would search in the darkness for what seemed like days and find nothing. And then she would wake, tantalized yet frustrated.

An unspoken taboo prevented natural dragons from flying over to the tunnel entrances. Most dragons were not interested, of course, but a few, especially the youngsters and *especially* Gossamer, found that those gaping black holes held a talismanic attraction. They watched the openings as though hypnotized, waiting and watching for the merest glimpse of what lay within: charmed dragons.

And so an unofficial pastime had come into being. Hole-watching.

Evening was a favourite time, after lessons and before supper, when the sky was receding and the sun was gone. They would line up along one of the many stony terraces of the west cliff, and sit, and stare. Usually they would see nothing but occasionally, just occasionally . . .

Regular — if not champion — hole-watchers were Gossamer and her younger brother Brace.

That they were brother and sister was a fact not easily

deduced. Brace maintained that he was 'well-built' but in truth he was fat. His mother delighted in telling her friends what a large hatchling he had been and seemed determined, by incessant feeding, to prove what a large adult he could therefore become. By contrast Gossamer was as slender and light as her name. Already Brace could see in her the beautiful dragon she would soon become and recognition of her beauty tore him between love and jealousy, for while he would have fought to the death to protect her he envied her easy grace and lightness of touch. It was Brace on whom their mother doted but he suspected that her deeper affections were reserved for her daughter alone.

As for Gossamer, she loved her younger brother with the simple directness with which she led her whole life. If any dragon were kin to the pure mountain air which tumbled into the Cross from the peaks above, that dragon was Gossamer. Pretty of face and already swift of wing, she turned many heads with a hide uncommonly colourful for a Natural, her back and wings being patterned with ochres and reds, earth colours quite unlike the garish extravagances of the Charmed.

That summer evening, in the dying light, she shone.

Subtle as it was, this colouring, Gossamer fancied, gave her a natural affinity with charmed creatures. As she squatted in her favourite hole-watching spot she glanced down over the precipice at one of the numerous waterfalls spouting out over the river hidden far below in the mist.

Silver forms darted back and forth in the spray: water sprites at play, daring each other in the airborne stream. She recognized Ant and Gnoll among them, for although she could not exactly speak their language she at least knew some faces and names, and it seemed to her that they understood most of what she said to them. Her encounters with them were always brief and frustrating however, since they were so tiny and moved so fast that she could barely follow their actions, let alone hear their high-pitched, whistling voices.

Charmed you may be, she thought, *but why do you have do be such fidgets?*

Their charms, like those of their fellow earth creatures, were gentle. They could swim without breathing, sing to the rocks and weave curative spells. The magic they knew was earth magic, kind and cool, very different to the magic of charmed dragons.

The charm of fire.

'There are four different kinds of charm,' Gossamer's mother had once told a rapt audience of infants during a teaching period. Gossamer had been fascinated; Brace had snored quietly. 'However, those four are really only two. The first three are earth, air and water, all of which are really earth. Earth magic is the charm of the land, of our world, of giants and sprites and nymphs and all the creatures of earth. It is strong and gentle, and rarely does harm.

'The fourth charm is fire. This is the magic of our cousins, the charmed dragons. It is different because while it can be used for good, unlike earth magic it can also do terrible wrongs. And unlike earth magic it is not of this world; fire charm is the magic of the Realm.'

'What's the Realm?' asked Gossamer. Her mother's eyes had grown misty.

All the small dragons waited patiently for Gossamer's mother to answer her. All except Brace, who had complained it was late, very late . . . and the class broke up.

Later, in their home nest, Gossamer had asked her mother, 'Are dragons the only creatures who can use fire charms?'

'There were others once,' had been the reply, 'but it seems they are all gone now. The trolls were the first, it is said, for they were born of fire and killed by the ice. I fancy there were others before even them, but they were not of this world.'

'The Realm, then?' hazarded Gossamer. Her mother looked at her, knowing what was coming. Gossamer took this as an encouraging sign and promptly asked, 'What's the Realm?'

'So many questions,' her mother had sighed. And the same glazed look came into her eyes as it had earlier, before Brace had so rudely ended their lessons. She seemed to shake herself. 'You're more inquisitive than your brother is, that much I know,' she said with effort. 'The Realm? Well, none of us can know that – Naturals, I mean. The best that I can say is that it's a place, a place that we can't get

81

to but charmed dragons can. And it's the place where the fire is.'

'The fire that makes the fire charm?'

'I think so, yes.'

And with a vague shake of her head she had left Gossamer to wonder who those other ancient wielders of fire charm might have been, and what sort of a place this Realm might be. After that day thoughts of the lesson filled her young life and so she devoted herself even more to her hole-watching until it became an obsession. She would see in the tunnel entrances of the east cliff a flash of gold, a flicker of silver, and that alone would be enough to fix her to her perch for a whole day. Brace would quickly be bored. He stayed because Gossamer stayed. Gossamer could wait for days in order to see the tiniest of motions in the gloom, proof that the charmed dragons were indeed still there within the earth. Close to the Realm. That charmed dragons should forsake the wonders of the great outside for the darkness within the earth could only mean that there were wonders far greater close to the Realm. In the Realm!

On one, thrilling day recently the river had been turbulent, and the mist high in the canyon, and Gossamer had for a moment believed she could see a creature, pale and ghost-like . . . beautiful, a long, elegant female with pure white wings, sheer as a spider's web, perhaps barely older than Gossamer's ten years . . .

'I could fly across,' she had whispered to herself, 'and we could talk and play, and we could each find out the other's name!'

But the mist thinned and her new friend vanished into the blackness of the tunnel, not a charmed dragon but a phantom.

But still Gossamer dreamed of the day when Charmed and Natural would fly together, however briefly. Her secret dream.

Then, that same summer, on another evening, Gossamer watched the shadows flee up the east cliff, trailing dusk high above them. The water sprites had vanished upstream like salmon and night was collecting in the depths of the canyon. Brace fidgeted beside her. 'I'm hungry,' he moaned.

'You're bored,' corrected Gossamer. 'You only think you're hungry because you're bored.'

'Let's go home.'

'Just a little while longer,' she urged. 'We might see something.'

'Hah! If we see something I'll . . .'

Brace's scornful voice hesitated as he looked up into the sky. Where the sky plunged into the darkness of the east, the mountain seemed to have grown an extra peak.

As they watched, part of the east cliff detached itself from the paler, ragged summit and dropped down towards them, a shadow made solid, slicing through the twilight, a chunk of night falling on them from the sky. Instead, the apparition alighted soundlessly on the ledge outside the largest of the Charmed tunnels. And Gossamer realized that it was a dragon.

Only with the greatest difficulty could she make out its shape. It had massive wings and seemed to have too many legs. Like a spider.

And it was black. Utterly black.

And it was *beautiful*.

A head like a claw flexed and turned their way. The dragon looked across at them with featureless yellow eyes, the only points of colour on a form as black as midnight. Gossamer shrank back against the rock and glanced at Brace. He was transfixed, terrified. She heard the dragon's breath, smooth and deep, and felt it suck the heat from her like a sheet of ice.

When she looked back the black dragon had turned to enter the tunnel. For a brief moment it held its wings wide against the rock face and it looked for all the world as though it *were* the tunnel. Then those awesome wings folded themselves away and the dragon vanished into the mountain.

Gossamer, realizing that she had been holding her breath, sucked in air with a gasp. Her heart slowed its pounding and she gathered Brace to her. They were both trembling, but Gossamer was forced to smile as she observed her brother struggling to put up a brave front.

'Was that . . . ?' he blurted.

'A charmed dragon? Yes.'

'It was . . .' he stammered, 'it was . . . big!'

'They don't all look like that,' Gossamer replied. 'There's no need to be frightened.'

But they could all look like that if they wanted too, Gossamer thought. *Charmed dragons can look any way they want to. Even like that: frightening yet . . . wonderful!*

'I'm not frightened,' blustered Brace, pushing her away with a great show of independence. 'They're just dragons after all. I'm not afraid of them.'

Gossamer slapped him playfully.

'You'll protect me, won't you, Brace?'

'Of course!' came his automatic response. As he puffed out his chest and marched off back towards home Gossamer saw in him the curious mix of loyalty and jealousy which made her love him so much. But even as the love warmed her so an icicle stabbed into her heart. *What was that dragon? A stranger, a traveller Charmed coming here. Why?*

Gossamer would talk to her mother and father about the strange newcomer the next morning. She left her perch and wandered back along the winding shallow trench towards the complex structure of woven branches which was her home. The new starlight was dim and defined the world only in a series of blocks and shapes, shadows within shadows. It seemed to Gossamer that all detail, all precision had fled the scene leaving instead mere approximations of things. Dragons moved within her vision but they were rough-hewn, clumsy shapes, unrecognizable as though pressed crudely from clay and not yet given names. The wind had died, stilling the air and closing the oppression in on her even further.

The settlement seemed terrifyingly dull. Almost unreal.

Like it's turning to stone.

Suddenly, Gossamer was convinced that something dreadful was going to happen, something she could not articulate but of which dragons had to be informed. But even as she passed into the warmth of her home nest a little of the urgency drifted away as she realized her parents would not be back until later and Brace seemed to be already asleep. Heart thumping with the same, dull vagueness she sensed in the world outside she resolved to voice her fears first thing in the morning.

But before morning could come, the night became day

and the fire blew from the seven tunnels of the Charmed, and the Naturals of Aether's Cross knew that the horror was upon them all.

They knew that the Black Dragon had come.

CHAPTER 7

Heartland

It was mid-morning, the sea below them was vast and Fortune's body ached. Already the events of the previous night seemed remote and unreal.

What a strange pair we make, he thought.

Natural and Charmed, dragons both, they were as different from each other as day and night. Where Fortune's body was lithe and streamlined Cumber's was angular and awkward; where Fortune's wings were massive, built for power, Cumber's seemed impossibly small; where Fortune flew with his body, Cumber flew with his mind.

Cumber told him of the magic he had had to learn in order to change his body to the traditional Charmed shape.

'We learn to grow new legs and move our wings on to our backs,' he explained. 'Later we bring metal to our skins and scales – the range of colours is endless.'

'So if it wasn't for the charms you'd look like me?' asked Fortune, intrigued.

'Pretty much, but you see this is all part of what's going on. Once upon a time a charmed dragon was *born* a charmed dragon. Lately we've had to struggle to maintain our forms. And our charms are less powerful now, you see – we have to work harder to make the simplest magic function.'

'Magic still made a sorry mess of South Point.'

'It's easy to destroy with charm, especially fire charm, but constructive magic grows harder day by day, and soon it may be impossible. Even the Realm is shrinking, Ordinal said.'

'The *Realm*, what is it? And why is this happening?'

Cumber frowned.

'Ordinal once said, "The world is shedding its skin." Perhaps charmed dragons are the skin.'

'Very enlightening. But what about this "Realm"? That's what I want to know?'

'I'm not the dragon to ask,' answered Cumber abruptly. There was pain in his voice. Then silence but for the movement of air through their wings. Fortune resisted his need to press the point.

Presently a thin line of grey appeared, balanced on the blue horizon, its promise of landfall giving new strength to aching muscles. It drew near with agonizing slowness.

Behind them the narrow stripe which was their homeland had long since vanished; ahead was the future and the future was a curve of sandy beach a thousand painful wing-beats away. The closer it came the more it seemed to Fortune that South Point no longer existed.

Later that day they lay together on the lower slopes of a shallow, sparsely-wooded river valley. Fortune's muscles were tightening up as he rested and he began to resign himself to spending the night there.

'We shan't be travelling any further today,' he said. His spirits felt light and he could not understand why. His companion was sprawled on his side gazing up at the clouds racing past in a deep blue sky. A wind had risen since they had landed and Fortune hoped there would not be another storm.

'What's this place called?' he asked. 'Is it another island like Torr?'

'Well,' replied Cumber, 'the local name I don't know but Ordinal used to refer to it as the Heartland. It's big – much bigger than Torr – a continent we must cross in order to reach Covamere. Not an easy journey, you realize.'

'How far?'

'Maybe eight or nine days of good flying, if the winds are favourable, but the land around Covamere is barren and cold, so it's said. We're lucky to be travelling in the summer.'

As if to contradict him the wind whipped the surrounding trees until a flurry of leaves scattered past them and danced off down the valley.

'Autumn's coming. Maybe even winter's on the way,'

commented Fortune. 'Anyway, we should find some food before nightfall.'

Cumber yawned and stretched.

'Which would you rather do?' he asked. 'Hunt or make camp?'

'Do they have rabbits in the Heartland?'

'Rabbits and much more,' replied Cumber inscrutably. 'Race you. I'll have a shelter built before you've got a sniff of dinner.'

With that he bounded into the undergrowth, leaving Fortune to rouse his weary body and scout off up the hillside in search of prey.

The valley was gently curved and bounded at one end by a conspicuously large hill. He paid the view little attention; he only noticed the hill at all because its shape seemed odd – long and stretched somehow. He concentrated instead on trying to pick up a scent.

The air was different here. On the valley slopes of South Point, beneath the scent of mouse and rabbit and heather, was the ever-present mix of salt and dragon, the characteristic aroma which seeped from the settlement like perfume. It was a smell, barely noticed it was so familiar, that Fortune missed terribly now as he crouched on this foreign hillside breathing in air with no taint of dragon to lend it life.

No life, he thought, trying to summon his grief.

But all he could smell was empty woodland, all he could see was green hills – his memories of the battle remained obstinately misty and far away.

What has happened to me? Where is my pain?

A flash of brown fur raced through his vision and he leaped after it with the instinctive reflex of a hunter, disappearing into a thicket, his mind gratefully filled with the thought of food.

A short while later he had caught five rabbits. *Five will do for tonight*, he thought as he loped down the hill, his stomach gurgling with anticipation. Rounding a bend in the track which led back to the riverside he stopped, then slipped behind a bush to observe the scene on the bank.

Cumber had built a stack of timber on an open patch of ground and was standing before it, head cocked. Then without warning, he spread his jaws and spat a ball of yellow flame deep into the woodpile. The branches jumped and popped as the fire swarmed and presently the whole mound was burning, sending sparks skywards and cloaking Cumber in a shroud of smoke.

For an instant, Fortune thought Cumber quite the most alien creature he had ever seen, but the moment swiftly passed and he was just Cumber again, stood before a bonfire. Fortune emerged from behind his bush feeling a little foolish and trotted down to where his friend was waiting.

'Why the fire?' he asked good-naturedly as he proudly laid his catches on the ground.

'If you're travelling with me, Fortune, you'll learn the pleasures of cooked meat!'

Fortune watched fascinated as Cumber lifted the first rabbit with his teeth and, with a flick of his head, tossed it into the air. When he caught it again it was skinned. With a 'plop' its pelt dropped at Fortune's claws.

'Cooking charm,' Cumber explained. 'One of the first you learn. Of course, throwing them about's a bit extravagant but then that's what cooking is all about if you ask me.'

Presently all five rabbits had been skinned and staked over the fire. Amazed, Fortune inhaled for the first time the aroma of cooking meat and decided that charms may be alien but they certainly smelt good.

'Do you always do this – burn your food, I mean?'

'Usually,' replied Cumber. 'I think you'll approve.'

He did. The texture and flavour of the meat was so exquisite that it was all Fortune could do not to devour his portions whole. But Cumber convinced him to eat slowly and savour the taste and Fortune reluctantly agreed that it was worth it. They ate well, meat washed down with fresh river water, and at last they lay comfortably on the soft grass at the water's edge.

Night fell, bringing chill air into the valley, and now Fortune recognized the strange virtue of fire for, although his kind regarded fire with superstitious awe, the warmth and flames brought him the comfort he needed. When he least expected it, and from a source he had always feared, he found comfort.

Cumber had built two nests – a shallow, open dish for Fortune and an enclosing shell for himself – but for the moment they lay together by the fire, unable to sleep. They began to talk about South Point, trying to conjure up the world they had lost, but that world was elusive. Both found themselves unable to focus their minds on that terrible night. Memories blurred and slipped aside, and they became easily side-tracked. Conversation turned instead to the subject of their quest. Fortune wondered why Cumber had chosen him for a companion.

'It wasn't really my doing,' confessed Cumber. 'Ordinal told me to go to a certain spot on a certain day and wait for the first dragon I saw, and that dragon was you. I was to bring you to the Great Chamber on the night of the full moon and, well, the rest you know. I was surprised when two of you turned up but . . . well, Wood saw to that I suppose.'

'But how did she know?'

'Ordinal could see things other dragons, even other charmed dragons, could not see. I think she could even see a little of the future.'

'Did she tell you anything about the Heartland?'

'She said it was stronger in magic than our own tiny island. That's why Covamere is still our ultimate goal – the decay hasn't reached it yet, or so she believed.'

Insects buzzed in the chill night and Fortune shivered.

'Do you mean there will be more charmed dragons here?' he asked nervously. His innate trust of the Charmed had suffered severe blows of late.

'Undoubtedly. And other charmed ones too.'

Cumber yawned and began to amble up to his cocoon but Fortune was not to be left hanging.

'What do you mean, "other charmed ones"?'

'You have your legends,' said Cumber, stifling another yawn. 'Once upon a time on Torr those legends were true, but no more. But here in the Heartland, here they are all still true. Probably. At least, I hope, over here, magic is still very much alive.'

And having thus thoroughly frustrated Fortune he disappeared into his makeshift wooden cave.

Fortune cast a final look around the valley. He noted the oddly shaped hill, still just visible now in the starlight; it seemed to have changed – a contour was different, or perhaps a treeline had altered. He shook his head wearily and collapsed into his nest.

'The land doesn't move,' he mumbled to himself, and then sleep claimed him.

It was the middle of the night when Cumber shook him awake.

'Wha . . . ?' Fortune started to say before a gold wing slapped him quiet.

'Ssh!'

A mist had settled during the night and the moon had risen, and Cumber's body looked insubstantial in the eerie light. Wiping bleary eyes, Fortune reluctantly followed him down to the river.

'This had better be worth it,' he grumbled.

'Oh, it is,' smiled Cumber. 'You remember what I said, you know, about other charmed ones?'

'Oh, that. Yes, and while I'm about it, why . . . ?'

'Hush. And look.'

Cumber pointed up the valley.

The hill was gone.

Fortune blinked, unable to believe what he saw. The valley seemed twice as long as it had been, ending in a line of distant mountains almost invisible in the hazy night. His strange hill had utterly disappeared.

'A charmed hill?' he gasped.

'In a way.'

The ground beneath them vibrated suddenly, sending up a deep pulse which drummed at their teeth. Ripples disturbed the surface of the river and the trees trembled in sympathy.

'Come on,' whispered Cumber, ushering Fortune up the hillside.

The night was cold, the dragons' moon-shadows long and faint as they crept past the belt of trees halfway up the incline.

'What's happening?' Fortune asked.

'I don't know. I'm only guessing. It's just that Ordinal told me a little about this sort of thing. Earth magic she called it. There's nothing like it on Torr now but over here . . .'

Another shock rumbled through the ground. Rough grass

replaced leaf litter and the dragons left the trees behind, approaching the heath at the crest of the ridge which flanked the valley.

'Keep low,' warned Cumber.

'Is it dangerous?'

Another powerful thump, properly audible this time. A thin layer of soil leaped from the ground and settled again.

They crouched together just below the brow of the hill. The thudding noise came at regular intervals. Wavering just above the broken ridge was the pale disc of the moon, casting what to Fortune seemed a magical glow over the landscape. Moonbeams flickered in the haze like frozen flames.

The ridge dropped from their vision as they crawled their way to the very top. Beyond was another valley, a flat river plain stretched taut beneath them; the ghosts of far hills floated in the mist. The moon, ringed with a shining aura, looked upon them like a vast eye.

In the centre of the long-dried plain stood a pale-skinned earth giant. Ten trees high it stood, as near as Fortune could judge, trunk-like legs planted firm in the haze, feet obscured, massive shoulders straining as it bent down to lift a great rock from the pile of boulders next to it.

A stranger creature Fortune could not imagine. He wondered what Wood would have made of this charmed colossus. Cumber, despite his bizarre appearance, was at least recognizably *dragon*, but this earth giant, balanced precariously on its hind legs, its skin naked but for the mane of brown hair which ran from its head down its spine, this was quite different. Its face, flat like the moon, grimaced as it hefted the rock on to its shoulder.

With a prodigious effort the gleaming giant hurled the boulder up into the sky. The dragons watched agape as the granite slab, itself larger than ten dragons without any doubt, turned end over end with ponderous ease and finally came to earth with a crashing thud both recognized as the source of the vibrations which had drawn them here.

Around the giant, in a broad quarter-circle, similar boulders lay embedded in the ground and it was clear that by the time it had completed its task a complete ring of stones would have been created. A massive paw wiped a brow like a cliff face and sweat rained into the mist.

92

Cumber rolled his eyes as Fortune asked the inevitable question.

'What's it doing?'

Fortune's endless questions simultaneously flattered Cumber and made him feel inadequate; none of Ordinal's training had prepared him for this role of oracle. But, at the same time, Charmed pride obliged him to keep up appearances.

'It's, er, throwing rocks in a circle,' he explained.

The giant lifted its head as though listening. Mist silently embraced the two spies as they shrank into the heather.

'Do you think it heard us?' was Fortune's next question.

Cumber weighed up pride and honesty and decided that, on balance, honesty was by far an easier path to tread.

'To be frank, Fortune, although I hate to admit it, I know less about earth giants' ears than I do about earth giants themselves. The only thing I can judge for certain is where it's come from.'

'The hill!' exclaimed Fortune, suddenly inspired.

'Fortune, it *is* the hill.'

And that was when the shock truly hit Fortune.

A month earlier his days had drifted by in a dreamy, adolescent haze, his thoughts blown on the wind. He had still been travelling with his eyes closed through a world of harsh and unseen light.

Meeting Cumber had been his first hint of that unseen light, but it was in the Great Chamber that Fortune's eyes had been opened fully . . . and brutally.

Many of the tales his mother had told him about the ancient Charmed revolved around a great knight known as Destater. He was a dragon born for the sky; legend told how he had hatched from above the clouds, his new-born body learning to fly within three beats of its wings. He never touched the ground thereafter, and refused ever to die. A permanent member of the Charmed Council, he attended every meeting, hovering over his seat with lazy beats of his vast, silver wings.

Few dragons were greater than Destater, immortal so long as he refused to touch the earth, wise beyond limit.

When Fortune had first entered the Great Chamber on the

night of the battle one of the many things he had expected to see was Destater.

But there had been no such dragon.

That same night he had seen Volence turned to dust, his friend Wood transformed into a fighting demon, familiar dragons torn apart by dark magic.

His birthplace was burned, his whole life wiped clean in an instant, dragon Fortune reduced to a blank statue. *Choose a feeling*, he thought, *and stamp it on my face.*

Destater is dead, he thought. *He has touched the earth. Perhaps he never lived at all.*

My father is dead, he thought, *and I never knew him.*

My mother is gone, but I will find her.

But that last irrational certainty was a seed blown in a storm. The battle returned to Fortune then in all its horror. With each *thump* of a giant stone hurled on the distant river plain a new memory triggered itself.

Thump!

Wood screamed, 'Father!' and hurled himself into a writhing mass of spines and teeth which bore more resemblance to some distorted, many-limbed monster than to the group of doomed, clamouring dragons it was.

Thump!

A headless charmed dragon, neck pumping blood and flame, danced like a tornado in an underground chasm while its slayers fought to hold it down.

THUMP!

Fortune's home burned furiously and he wept at last, crying for all those dragons he had known and lost, for all the dreams reality had destroyed.

And then, Fortune's tears a catalyst, Cumber's grief surfaced too.

And so Fortune and Cumber held each other at last, weeping for their collective loss, for their dead. Shock banished, they gave in to their sorrow but as the dreadful memories unravelled themselves so the dragons' resolve grew. And though outwardly they seemed weak that night they became strong within, light dawning inside them even as the moon set, casting a web of darkness across the world.

Under cover of that darkness their sobs gradually subsided and they drifted into deep, dreamless sleep.

Its night's work complete, the giant slapped its dusty paws together with a sound like thunder and plodded back into its valley. When dawn stretched an exploratory claw into the sky it had already settled itself down and closed the lakes of its eyes.

The transformation was as subtle as a fall of dew – like a reflection caught in a pool of water a ripple passed across its sleeping form and it became again Fortune's hill, its thigh riddled with rabbit warrens, its hair a dense patch of thicket. Its breathing halted and, for another day at least, it became the land again.

As daylight stroked the two dragons they awoke with slow ease, to find themselves still in the heather where they had hidden beneath the moon. Cumber recalled the ancient Charmed word for 'morning', which really meant 'beginning'.

Well, he decided, *today certainly feels like a beginning, sure enough*.

He exchanged a secret smile with Fortune. Together they had flown the storm of their sorrow and emerged scarred but intact at the other side. They would carry their pain in their quest, to be sure, but they were *alive*.

Together they ambled down the hill towards the camp, intending to clear it away and begin their first day of travel into the Heartland. But there, rummaging through the smouldering remains of the camp fire, stood a dragon!

The stranger watched their approach. He was a charmed dragon, that much was clear. His body was a plain, metallic green and relatively unadorned, but the real splendour was in his wings: much larger than Cumber's, they were supremely ornate, delicately patterned with a mosaic of coloured scales which shimmered in the fresh sunlight.

'I hope he's friendly,' whispered Fortune to Cumber as they swaggered down towards the stranger with a confidence neither one of them felt. Of the charmed dragons Fortune had encountered so far only Cumber and Ordinal had been friendly, and uncomfortable memories of the roof-walking beast which had tried to suck the life from Cumber fuelled his caution.

The air was tense as they drew together. *We were three before*, thought Cumber, *and that was not meant to be*.

The stranger nodded slowly as they halted on the opposite side of the embers of the camp fire. Then he frowned, screwed up his face and assumed an expression of extreme discomfort. The moment dragged itself out; Fortune and Cumber looked on agog as this jewel-winged creature balanced in front of them as if poised for some dreadful outburst.

'Aaaat-shoo!'

The almighty sneeze simultaneously rocked the stranger back on his haunches and scattered charcoal over Fortune. *Praise be*, he thought, *that charmed dragons don't sneeze fire as well!*

'Sorry about that,' said the stranger sheepishly. 'Sucked up too much smoke. Never did go in for that fire business. Scoff.'

'I'm sorry?' said Fortune.

'No, *I'm* sorry. And I'm Scoff,' repeated the dragon. 'My name,' he explained.

'Oh, I see,' joined in Cumber, relieved that the dragon at least seemed amicable enough. 'I'm Cumber and this is my good friend, Fortune.'

'Pleasure. You're not from these parts.'

Scoff, as they would discover, was a dragon who liked to get straight to the point.

'We're from Torr, over the sea,' explained Cumber, gesturing vaguely behind him with a wing which felt suddenly inadequate in the shadow of Scoff's splendid sails.

'Right,' nodded Scoff as though the answer were acceptable but of no particular interest. 'Well, you don't seem mad. Where are you going?'

'Who says we're going anywhere?' responded Fortune, still cautious.

'If they're not mad they're suspicious,' muttered Scoff under his breath. 'Temporary camp,' he went on, indicating their makeshift nests. 'Bags under the eyes. You're travelling. Am I wrong?'

Cumber found himself warming to this dragon. Although age was difficult to judge with the Charmed he guessed Scoff to be considerably older than himself or Fortune — thoroughly middle-aged. Maybe the assistance of experience would not go amiss at this early stage of their journey.

Fortune too could not help but like Scoff, despite his natural caution. There was something friendly in the wrinkles around his eyes, something inherently trustworthy in the easy line of his broad mouth. Nevertheless, this was the Heartland, where things were not always what they seemed.

'. . . breath of fresh air,' Scoff was saying, pacing up and down the river bank. 'Mad they are, every last one. Glad to be shot of the lot of 'em, that's me. I'll say again, where are you going?'

'South,' said Fortune, still reluctant to give too much away despite Scoff's easy charm.

'Hmm. Not much there. I'd head north. Have to pass the Cross to go south.'

'The Cross?'

'Aether's Cross. Don't you know anything?'

'Is that where you're from, Aether's Cross?' ventured Cumber.

'Was from. All mad now. Head north.'

Fortune was beginning to wonder if Scoff was not a little mad himself when Cumber spoke again.

'We have to reach Covamere.'

Scoff's eyes widened and his pacing ceased.

'Covamere, eh? Well, now, there's a journey and more. Over and beyond the Low Mountains, no less. What's in Covamere for a pair like you?'

Fortune nudged Cumber in an effort to prevent him from blurting out their story, but once the words started to flow he found it impossible not to join in. The tale seemed almost to tell itself, and as it was told its weight left their backs like melting snow. Scoff listened carefully and spoke only when the words ran out.

'Quite a tale,' he agreed. 'Like I thought — madness everywhere. All Charmed mad. We're the lucky ones, Comber, you and I . . .'

'That's Cumber, actually.'

'Whatever. At least our minds are still our own.'

Scoff looked over at Fortune and added, 'You'd better watch yourself. Naturals aren't popular round here. Take my advice, both of you — head back north. Go as far as the ice for all I care but forget Covamere. If Halcyon's still alive he's mad as the rest of 'em.'

'Scoff, you say there's madness here . . .' began Cumber, hoping desperately that it not be true, that here in the Heartland the disease had not taken hold.

'What happened at your South Point,' interrupted Scoff, 'is happening at the Cross. Magic's weak, Charmed are mad, Naturals are taken captive. Same thing.'

Cumber groaned at the news.

'Even here,' he said. 'Even here.'

'Eh?' said Scoff, losing his train of thought.

'It's become a race then,' said Cumber. 'That's what it's become. I thought we'd beaten it out of South Point, you see, but it's reached the Heartland already – it's spreading like a plague.'

'What're you babbling about?' grumbled Scoff, but Cumber was turning away from him to address Fortune.

'Our quest is a race against time and the awful thing is that I've always known it – you see, whatever it is that's setting dragon against dragon, that force has been travelling faster than I thought. *And faster than us*! Ordinal said, "The stone has been cast into the water and you must race the ripples to the shore," and she was right. Fortune, we have no time to waste!'

Cumber spread his golden wings and leaped into the waiting air.

'Wait!' cried Scoff as Fortune too unfolded his wings. 'Don't go through the Cross. Go around at least. More days to your journey but . . .'

'We don't have days!' Cumber shouted, angrily wheeling over Scoff's upturned head. Fortune beat his way strenuously into the air beside him.

'Listen to me,' called Scoff as they rose away from him. 'Go north, go home!'

'We have no home,' retorted Cumber. 'Come on, Fortune, let's leave this, this pessimist to his madness!'

As they circled up from the camp site Fortune wondered if, to Cumber, the word 'pessimist' might have been the most dreadful insult imaginable. After all, who but an optimist of the highest order would race a tide of insanity across the world to seek a dragon who perhaps no longer even existed, if indeed he ever had?

Have faith, Fortune, have faith, said his mother's voice.

Scoff had one last gambit to keep them there, and it almost worked.

'Don't ignore me like the other one did!' he shouted.

Fortune fanned his wings forward and managed to hover clumsily over the charmed dragon, the effort pulling angrily at the muscles of his back and breast; perhaps one day he would learn to fly properly.

'What other one?' he demanded, his spine tingling.

'Old dragon,' responded Scoff at once. 'Female. Natural, like you. Ignored me. Don't think she even saw me. Went south too, like you.'

Cumber saw Fortune's hesitation and called to him desperately.

'You can't know it's her, Fortune. It could have been any dragon.'

Fortune hovered there for a moment more, looking down at Scoff. Then he peeled away to the south and led Cumber off towards the mountains.

'All the more reason for me to go this way too, now,' he muttered between clenched teeth.

Even as they left him by the riverside Scoff cried after them, a tiny gem of a dragon set in the lush green valley.

'Keep to the west wall! Avoid the tunnels! The Black . . . !'

But the rest was lost as Scoff, the smouldering fire and empty nests fell behind them and vanished.

Ahead, the heavy silhouette of the Low Mountains squatted on the horizon, a vertical slash which could only be Aether's Cross just visible in the otherwise unbroken cliff, and Fortune wondered if, like the hill, those distant mountains concealed a secret identity.

What magic might reveal itself were he to blink and open his eyes to find the mountains gone?

CHAPTER 8

The Cross

Had Scoff stayed beside the river for the remainder of the day he would almost certainly have encountered the other group of dragons flying south towards Aether's Cross, but stay he did not. Had their paths crossed, Scoff may sooner have found the strength he needed to play his part in the struggle; but perhaps other matters would then have turned out differently too, and not necessarily for the better.

He watched the space Fortune and Cumber had left in the sky for a long time after they had vanished. Finally, as the sun rose high, he turned and carefully cleared away the remains of the fire and the makeshift nests.

'Youngsters!' he grumbled as he flicked sand over the last of the ashes with one of his glorious wings. 'Don't know the first thing about journey-making!'

He took to the air and flew up over the same ridge which Fortune and Cumber had scaled the night before. He paid little attention to the newly-formed stone circle as the plain opened up before him, taking instead a direct line north along the opposite flank of the ridge until a short time later he reached the small, unremarkable cave in which he himself had been camped for the last two nights. Into the cramped space he slipped and there he lay for the rest of the day, compressing charm into the wounds on his legs. He dozed and woke and dozed again. Night fell.

Scoff had to admit that in recent years he had become lazy. Posted to Aether's Cross by Halcyon many years before, he had performed his duties well enough at first, when the envoy dragons flew up from Covamere on a regular basis. He would entertain the envoy for a day or two, at the end of which he would deliver his report and despatch his visitor on his — or frequently, to Scoff's satisfaction, her — way. The news the envoy brought would be his to distribute throughout the caverns of the Cross. Dragons were always glad to see him; as Halcyon's ambassador, Scoff was generally liked and respected by the Charmed of the Cross and he in turn liked them. He felt comfortable there. And that, he had to admit, was the root of the problem: he became *too* comfortable. The work, frankly, was easy.

For as long as he could remember the work had been easy, until his jaded senses took in the rumours that foreshadowed plague, and he woke to the terrible possibility of change. Thinking about it, he calculated he had not heard from Covamere for . . . well over a year. But no matter — he was comfortable.

Then dragons at the Cross had started to rumble about extinction, about rebellion, about teaching the Naturals a lesson. Of these topics Scoff listened only to the first, for it was indeed apparent that Charmed numbers were in decline the world over — the most recent of Halcyon's envoys had said as much — as well as here in the Cross. What could a simple dragon such as Scoff do about that? Nothing, of course. Better to relax into his own life and enjoy his own time in this world. Better not to worry that mountain rivers once brimming with water sprites were now almost barren, that hornless unicorns now roamed the great plains of the south, that even charmed dragons were going the same way as the trolls.

Better to be *comfortable*.

But then the Black Dragon came and the fire poured from the tunnels and the rumblings became focused into cries of rage, and worse than that — into action!

When he realized what was happening Scoff was at first angry that his repose should have been disturbed. But when he saw the first of the Naturals dragged into the caverns his outrage — to his later shame — turned to fear. Terrified of his one-time companions, and in particular of the Black Dragon himself, unable to make a stand (for how could one dragon make a stand against a whole army?) he fled north. He charmed his way through a brief scuffle with one of the more alert guards who had been posted at either end of the Cross to prevent the escape of the Naturals and finally hid

101

away in the tiny, anonymous cave in the far north of his native Heartland.

Two nights ago that had been and this night the third, and the outrage remained.

They have gone mad! All of them! To take the Naturals prisoner!

His friends and hosts of so many years had at a stroke become a tearing, cold-hearted army which had wiped the west cliff clean of life. For that Scoff found it hard to forgive them, but deep in his heart – and here lay the real terror – he knew that it was the Black Dragon who had set the spark to the fire.

Without the Black Dragon perhaps Scoff might have remained comfortable for at least a few years more.

Before he dozed again he looked around the spartan cave. *I'll go north again tomorrow*, he decided. *Or perhaps I'll be comfortable here*, was his last thought before he drifted into a shallow, troubled sleep.

Fortune and Cumber reached the foothills of the Low Mountains early on their second day of travel from the camp, unaware, like Scoff, that another group of dragons was following in their path. They had paused in their journey only briefly to eat and drink, and had slept the previous night beside a quiet lake surrounded by fir trees. They had met no other dragons since leaving Scoff behind, and the only thing out of the ordinary had been their occasional sighting of a circle or part-circle of boulders embedded in the ground, more evidence of giants at work. Since they were no obvious threat they had paid them little attention.

The air cooled noticeably as they flew higher. All of a sudden the Low Mountains did not look so low and their confident plan to avoid the pass at Aether's Cross and simply fly right over the top collapsed with frightening ease. The mountains looked solid and deadly in their sparkling armour of ice and snow. Deadly, too, in the bitter cold they promised.

Across their path the peaks marched with massive authority, meeting sea mist in the far west and rising ominously in the east to meet the ghostly, half-seen giants which Cumber identified as the great mountains of the Spine.

'Be thankful we're not headed there,' he said with a

shiver. 'Even Ordinal never ventured along the Spine. It's said that if you follow them east and then north, you'll reach the crest of the world. These so-called Low Mountains are too high for me!'

'And cold,' added Fortune. 'Can't you use your magic?'

'Difficult. I might be able to contain us in a ball of warm air for a while but I couldn't keep it up because what you Naturals don't seem to understand is that charm takes energy, you see, and it would inhibit my flight charm so we'd be slowed down too, and then there's . . .'

'Okay, okay. Just asking. Well, Aether's Cross it is, then.'

They picked up the line of a broad river which thundered from the great gash of the mountain pass in a mighty cataract. The entrance to the ravine soared into an empty sky, defying them to penetrate its depths, and it was with trepidation that they battled their way through the crashing spray and finally passed up into the lowest reaches of the Cross.

Sheer rock walls dwarfed the dragons. They felt belittled under the majestic gaze of the grey mountains. The gorge twisted its way south, the river rising below them and growing narrower as they gradually approached its source. The ragged walls closed in on them and they began to fly in single file.

The sun flashed briefly overhead, high and harsh in the thread of sky trapped between the ice at the canyon's remote crown, and painted tiny dragon shadows on the water far, far below. The air felt thin and cold despite the midday sun and Fortune's muscles protested at the extra effort he needed to buoy his body in the rarefied atmosphere.

What had Scoff said as they parted? Keep west? Well, west was a wall of rock to their right, east its twin to their left — there was nothing to choose between the two.

Did you fly this way, Clarion? Or shall I lose my mother too?

The noon sun disappeared from the gap of sky above them and the temperature dropped sharply. Ahead was a tight turn, the way forward concealed by a jagged corner of rock, and a new chill joined the tingle of coldness in Fortune's spine: fear.

The walls clamped even tighter as the two dragons negotiated what turned out to be a sharp double bend in the ravine. Way below them the river churned and hammered its way through rapids, the snake shape mirrored in the slit of openness high over their heads.

Fortune's left wingtip grazed the canyon wall as, mesmerized by the awesome scale of the geography, he drifted too far from the safe, central course. Scree scattered from a narrow ledge and tumbled down into the water, the splashes quite lost in the boiling foam, and he juddered back to the middle.

'Steady!' called Cumber, seeing Fortune's near-miss. 'There's no room for error in here, that's for certain.'

'I was going to try flying higher!' shouted Fortune over the crash of the river. 'But it gets even narrower up there. And I'm not sure my wings would hold the air, it's so thin.'

'You'd be surprised how high a dragon can fly.'

'I hope I never have to find out; this is high enough, thank you very much!'

The gorge squeezed them tight until it seemed they could go on no further. Ahead was a featureless grey chicane which they entered in fear for their lives. The river raced hungrily; the sky watched, impassive; they disappeared from each other's line of sight and were, for a breath or two, in limbo.

Then rock lips peeled apart and spat the dragons out. Behind them the passage they had just traversed was a mere crack in a steep cliff which opened out into the comparatively wide gorge through which they now flew. In truth it was barely as wide as the initial stages of the pass back at the junction of foothill and mountain but to the two young adventurers it was literally a breath of fresh air.

Fortune laughed with relief while Cumber swooped drunkenly behind him. *We need to rest*, he thought, appalled by his own fatigue. He angled towards the western heights and away from Cumber, who was virtually looping the loop in delight. *Rest and gather our thoughts.*

'Nests!' cried Cumber, banking swiftly above Fortune's head, his slipstream buffeting the young Natural as he swept past.

Sure enough there on the west cliff, clinging to the ragged rock face like limpets, were nests. The nests of the natural dragons of Aether's Cross.

And they were empty. All of them.

* * *

It took Fortune several passes before he was able to alight next to Cumber on the tiny ledge his friend had chosen. While Cumber had wielded a flight charm to aid his landing Fortune had to battle with the treacherous draughts and eddies which whipped around the canyon wall, and it was with growing respect for the dragons of the Cross — wherever they may have been — that he finally managed the tricky stall and lunge necessary to touch down on the outcrop.

There they clung panting, recovering their composure as they surveyed what had once been a thriving dragon settlement. The west cliff sloped back at a steep angle and boasted a vast network of cracks and ledges on which dragons had woven the fabric of a community.

Nests sprawled over the side of the gorge in every direction, the brushwood from which they were constructed light and economical. But an aura of threat seemed to hover over them. They looked scruffy and unkempt as though abandoned suddenly. Though there was no evidence of violence, no bodies, no signs of war or fire, the two young dragons felt an undeniable need to stay alert.

Across the canyon the opposite cliff was much steeper, almost vertical, and flawed by a single ledge which described a meandering line along its face. Immediately above this ledge were spaced seven holes of varying size, all roughly circular, all uncompromisingly black . . . dangerous cyclops' eyes staring blindly. The entrances to the caverns of the Charmed!

What happened here?

'We shouldn't stay here too long,' blurted Cumber. 'I mean, Scoff did warn us and it feels . . . it feels creepy.' He eyed Fortune suspiciously and added, 'Whatever happened here, we can't do anything about it. Fortune, we have to keep moving. We can't afford to interfere.'

Can he read my mind? thought Fortune. *Can he*?

'And no,' continued Cumber, 'I can't read your mind if that's what you're thinking. You want to investigate — it's obvious by the look on your face. All right, so you're curious about what's happened here, well, so am I, but unlike you I don't believe we can do anything about it.'

'What makes you think I . . . ?'

105

'You want proof that these Naturals are safe because you don't want to believe that all Charmed are evil. Well, they're not all evil . . . just insane.'

It was with bitterness that Cumber intoned these last words and Fortune saw briefly the depth of his despair. He realized that the sinister tunnel entrances must beckon Cumber as well as scare him. After all, for him they represented home.

But then Fortune looked around at the deserted nests again. Something terrible had happened here, he *knew* it. And also . . .

'And I know you think your mother might be here,' continued Cumber more gently, 'but there's nothing we can do.'

Fortune shuddered, for it seemed that Cumber could follow his thoughts more clearly than he could himself. 'This is a dangerous place for Naturals,' he said. 'If she came this way she might have been taken; *we* might be taken.'

'All the more reason to fly straight through,' urged Cumber. 'If Halcyon can be roused then he'll put a stop to this and they'll *all* be freed, or should I suppose that you're thinking of flying straight into those tunnels and flying back out again with a wingful of dragons you've rescued from the clutches of the evil Charmed, among them your mother?'

Fortune could only sigh.

'I just thought there might be more to this adventure than just flying south and telling our tale to this Halcyon of yours. I just thought we might be able to do something to help, just something, somewhere, for some dragon. Instead of running away all the time.'

'But this is for *all* dragons! And besides, Fortune, if you want adventure you'll have to pick some other companion because I'm not here for the adventure, oh no — I'm here to do what Ordinal wanted me to do, and I'm afraid that "adventure" — which by the look in your eyes means "danger" — is the last thing I want to have to deal with. Fighting every dragon we meet and freeing prisoners is not my idea of carrying out our mission in the most efficient way possible, in fact I might even go so far as to say that . . .'

'Shut up!'

'What?!'

'Shut up, Cumber, and listen.'

Cumber shut his mouth with a clack, his nerves instantly tingling, but he could hear nothing over the din of the river.

'What?' he hissed. 'You'll be seeing ghosts next.'

'I thought I did,' whispered Fortune. 'Over there, on the other side of the canyon, by the tunnels.'

Cumber squinted through the haze, tuning his tired senses as he probed for magic in the air.

'There's a lot of charm in that cliff,' he murmured. 'Makes it hard to . . . wait!' He sniffed the air then shook his head.

'Just ghosts!' he proclaimed loudly, turning back to Fortune. 'Now, are you coming with me?'

Fortune stared at his companion, then looked back at the tunnel entrances. The air moved like a heat haze in front of them.

Ghosts?

'No,' he replied carefully. 'There's something we must do here.'

'Oh, Fortune!' exclaimed Cumber, exasperated. 'And what precisely would that be, do you think?'

'I don't know! I just know there's something. Why were the Naturals captured and not just killed like they were at South Point? Cumber, there hasn't been a battle here. The natural dragons have just disappeared. Why?'

'I don't know and I don't care! All I know, Fortune, and you would be as well to remember this, is that we've got to get to Covamere before this madness overtakes us or before we're captured ourselves, and the longer we stay here the more likely that is! Now come on!'

'No,' said Fortune quietly as Cumber opened his wings and ventured to the edge of the terrace.

They gazed hard at each other, each testing the other, but the argument was never resolved for it was at that moment that the sky burst open.

The air boiled as four charmed dragons leaped from their magic cloaks of dimness and into visibility. Their rutted, metallic hides glittered with the blue sparks of the flight charms which kept them aloft; their wingbeats were utterly silent. They crashed on to Fortune and Cumber with the ferocity of a firestorm.

Polished talons grabbed Fortune as Cumber struggled to break away, spitting orange fire at his attackers until one of them knocked him unconscious with a blow of its heavy wing.

The charms which the approaching dragons had employed to render themselves all but invisible to their unsuspecting prey flickered in and out of existence as if forgotten by their makers. Thus Fortune caught only glimpses of his captors: a half-cloaked talon, the far cliff dimly visible through its hazy form, a pair of forelimbs, viciously serrated along their whole length, a malevolent red eye.

Then he was scooped up and flying, or rather being flown, across the gorge. Broken shards of charm cascaded from the dragons who had so brutally seized them, gradually revealing their true shapes, although even those seemed to melt and shift before his eyes. Spines stretched and fangs bent and he heard a name hissed across the rushing wind. 'Brutace!'

One of the tunnel entrances approached like an avalanche and engulfed them all. As the dragons passed from light to dark an outcrop of rock struck Fortune a heavy blow on the side of his head. In the darkness he saw a sudden explosion of light and then the world slipped away from him.

The sun had scarcely moved in the sky before a second, ragged band of dragons flew unchallenged through the Cross. Into the wide place they swept and out again into the southern pass, their wings taking them swiftly and efficiently past the remains of the Naturals' nests without slowing, without noticing the strangeness of the nests' abandonment.

Shatter it was who set the pace, while behind him flew Torque and Tumely. Wood brought up the rear, urging and reassuring his father who slapped his burnt and broken wings in agonizing rhythm, determined yet to follow the dragon he still idolized. The sixth dragon, the thief, had already abandoned the party.

Through the Cross they passed, ignorant of the drama which had unfolded there scant breaths before.

Except perhaps Wood who, as he entered the narrow gap

of the southern pass, whispered Fortune's name, unsure of what had brought his friend to mind.

But Fortune was surely dead, killed in the battle if not drowned in the caves below ground.

Fortune, too, thought himself dead. He was in the void. Circles turned lazily somewhere behind his eyes.

You are travelling.

The voice was in his mind but it was not his own.

There is a place where lost dragons can be found.

Vision flowered, watery and distorted. Circles came, and spirals, complex patterns spinning about each other in an endless parade, a wheel completing another turn, the world revolving.

The images settled and coalesced to form a single image: a ring made up of tiny, irregular shapes – pale islands in a dark sea.

The other voice he suddenly recognized.

It was his mother's.

He was floating above a ring of islands in the sea. At the centre was a reef. He floated higher, taking the whole scene within his gaze.

This place has always been here, said his mother's voice. *It is Haven and you can be safe here. Here the lost are found* . . .

The voice drifted away. Either into the past – was that where Fortune had heard his mother say these words? – or because a new sound, a steady drumming, took its place. He drifted higher above the ring of islands with the reef at its centre until they had vanished into the black ocean.

The drumming grew unbearably loud, hammering at the void in which he floated, and he recognized it for what it was.

Wingbeats.

The stroke of wings greater than the world, the beat of some mighty dragon through the void itself. The beat of doom.

Fortune's view expanded still further and the ocean was now a shadow in a vast, yellow eye. The eye blinked slowly, tears tumbling about its lids as they closed, opened, and a new voice resounded in the jaundiced light.

I know you are there, Natural, it said.

It can't see me, thought Fortune, repressing panic. *It wants me but it can't see me.*

And he knew that it was the enemy.

The eye exploded towards him, its fruitless search abandoned in a storm of rage.

A tantrum, thought Fortune.

Dragons were hurled past him, natural and charmed alike, all either dressed for or mutilated by war. Limbs tore and dissolved, wings ripped and burned, faces screamed and shattered. Dragons pleaded for help as they writhed past in agony but Fortune closed his mind against the vision, for to reach out would be to expose himself to the enemy.

He can smell me, but he can't see me!

With a supreme effort he turned into a strange *sideways* direction and fled the carnage.

A soothing glow appeared, a pink glow Fortune found oddly familiar. Rainbow colours flashed across his vision and he returned to the world he knew.

The rainbow hovered just out of reach. A charm, shining in the air like those in the caverns at South Point, the pink light it radiated glancing off the walls of the cave . . .

Cave?

'Cumber!' he cried, sitting up then instantly regretting it as a spear of pain thrust its way through his head. Groaning, he flopped back on to the cold, hard floor.

'Ssh,' came a gentle, female voice. 'Don't try to move.'

Mother?

Fortune turned his head to see a young female Natural smiling anxiously down at him. Worry painted her features with a beauty that would have been lost on any other face and Fortune's heart leaped up to greet her.

'Hello,' she said, brushing his face softly with her wingtip. 'I'm Gossamer.'

CHAPTER 9

The Mad Dragons

Cumber ungummed his eyes to see a parade of teeth.

The teeth were yellow, looked very sharp and framed a smile which all but split in two the face of the charmed dragon who wore it. Hot, stale breath lingered in the air and Cumber sneezed heavily. A lazy claw cuffed him over the head with astonishing force. His head was hurt already by the heavy blow he had received from the rock.

'All right, Snot,' the dragon rumbled, 'who are you?'

'Cum . . .' said Cumber then, thinking better of revealing his true name, began again. 'Cummion.'

'Think I'll call you "Snot" anyway,' the dragon laughed.

He turned clumsily away and lunged at a line of shadows on the cave wall behind him. Cumber could just make out . . . something, hanging there . . . but what the shapes were he could not guess. His vision was blurred.

Just as Cumber had begun to identify the shapes as being brown and round a crunching sound came from the other dragon's jaws. The dragon turned back, smiling even more extravagantly, champing indelicately on the object he had snatched from the wall. Fur and bones danced between his teeth as he gulped back what Cumber now realized to be one of several thousand dead rats suspended by their tails all around the small cave.

A food store, he thought, trying to gather his wits. The smiling dragon belched in his face.

'You're thinking you're in the pantry,' said the dragon, picking chunks of rat flesh from between his teeth with a claw as sharp as frost. 'Too right, Snot. Food's what we keep down here and you'll do just as well as the rats when you've been, ah, tenderized! There's not enough of you for four, mind; I'll have you all to myself.'

Cumber shrank back against the wall as the foul-breathed dragon loomed over him, claws extended to grasp his body. A tiny eyeball hung from the tip of one of his yellow fangs like water off an icicle. Cumber prepared to bolt for an exit he had not yet even located.

'Hex!' bellowed a new voice. 'Guard duty, prison level. NOW!'

The effect of this voice on Hex was startling. Dorsal spines cringed against his back, eyes dulled and his mouth shut with a snap. He retreated from Cumber instantly, head bowed, shuffling sideways out of the cave and skirting respectfully around the dark, gleaming dragon who had entered so quietly behind him.

'Just teasing the little one. Just a joke, just a tease, Brutace.'

'Shut up, Hex,' intoned Brutace. 'Now get out of here before I string you up by the tail along with all the other rats.'

'Yes, Brutace. Sorry, Brutace.'

Hex lunged backwards into the tunnel outside, eyes fixed on the floor until he was out of Brutace's sight, whereupon he glanced back up at Cumber and flashed him a dangerous look. Then he was gone.

Cumber thought fast. *I may not be a Natural but I was caught with one. Still, they haven't killed me yet.*

'Speak!' barked Brutace.

For a moment Cumber could not speak. He needed to think. If Scoff's warnings were true then Fortune was probably still alive, held prisoner in the Charmed caverns with the other Naturals. And where had Hex just been sent? Prison level!

His task was clear enough: find Fortune and escape. But how?

He began to speak. Where the inspiration came from he had no idea, and as he spoke he felt the pressure of impending doom crushing the fortitude he had managed to find within himself. This Brutace was overwhelming, a chieftain among dragons; how could he, Cumber, possibly outwit this warlord?

Well, I can try!

And the inspiration came.

'My lord,' he began, bowing his head enough to suggest the traditional acknowledgement of a charmed dragon meeting a superior, but not so much as to suggest that Brutace was all *that* superior. 'My master will be most pleased with the way you have handled this situation.'

And he realized that he had said exactly the right thing.

Before he could even begin to tell the lie of how he been sent forth from South Point with Fortune (a charmed dragon who had altered his body so as to disguise himself as a Natural) to test the defences of Aether's Cross, Brutace's jaw was already dropping wide with astonishment.

'The Master?' exclaimed Brutace. 'He has sent you?'

Although he no longer felt entirely in control of the conversation Cumber felt confident enough to improvise upon his bluff.

'The Master has sent me,' he agreed, wondering desperately who 'the Master' might be. 'The dragon who was with me is not a Natural . . .'

And so he proceeded to spin his tale, filling it with oblique references to this unknown 'Master'. Fear masked Brutace's face to begin with, although as he let Cumber ramble on that was replaced in part by suspicion. That he was afraid of 'the Master' was obvious but Cumber began to realize that it would take more than clever words to convince him of the veracity of his story. Brutace, undoubtedly of high rank and able to dispense his own justice, was suspicious enough to take nothing at face value.

Cumber finished his tale and Brutace nodded thoughtfully, scrutinizing his captive storyteller with a keen gaze. *Don't shiver*, thought Cumber as he stared back.

But it was not easy. Brutace stood solidly before him, a coil of muscle studded with bony blades. His tough hide was silver-grey, shining beneath the glow of the cave's floating light charm. Unlike Cumber's his wings were large and thick, glittering with stored flight charm. The wide face which topped a long, sinuous neck was coated with backward-facing spines and was now quite without expression.

Here is a dragon of power, thought Cumber. *Here is a dragon of war.*

'An interesting story,' said Brutace at length. 'If it is true your friend will be freed. You have earned your own freedom for now but only within these caves. If you attempt to leave or free your friend yourself you will both die. I have much to do now. Tomorrow night you will prove your story. If you cannot I will kill you both.'

He spun his massive bulk out of the cave with oily grace and slipped away into the gloom of the tunnel beyond.

Cumber began to shake uncontrollably, shock and relief seizing his muscles. Rats swung around him like rotten fruits as he flopped against the hard wall, quite exhausted. Little by little the tremors abated and he began to consider Brutace's parting words.

'Tomorrow night,' the charmed commander had said. A glance at the floating charm confirmed that it was already approaching midnight (like South Point this system seemed to operate a colour sequence in its light charms and, if he was not mistaken, the blue fringe around the otherwise pink globe indicated that today was just turning to tomorrow).

I have less than a day, then.

Brutace had at least confirmed that Fortune was still alive – presumably imprisoned somewhere within the cave system. *And what did Hex say? 'There's not enough of you for four . . .'* So the Charmed garrison here was small.

Even so, two against four. Poor odds, but perhaps if they had surprise on their side . . .

He laughed despite himself, a dry chuckle. Fighting dragons and freeing prisoners! Well, Fortune had dragged him into the adventure after all!

Still, at least the situation was plain enough. *If I fail to get us out we're both dead.*

The only cloud obscuring his otherwise clear view of their predicament was his memory of Brutace's initial look of terror when he had innocently referred to 'the Master'.

Such a look of terror on a dragon as powerful as the fearsome Brutace?

Who – or what – was the Master?

As she spoke Fortune drank in her words, was himself swallowed by her eyes, jumped at her every gesture. He was entirely captivated and even though he listened closely to

114

her terrible story, absorbing every detail of it, he felt distanced too, as if he were there only in part; she was his focus, for now the centre of his world. Gossamer.

So these are the feelings Wood tried to tell me of. Fortune recalled a rare moment of poetry in Wood. They had been lazing together on the practise slopes of South Point; the young males had finished their jousting in the low skies and now it was the turn of the females to swoop over the burnt tree stump.

One female in particular, a slim, long-winged dragon called Caprice, had captured Wood's attention. Unlike her competitors, who tended to swoop in dramatic dives from which they pulled out only at the last possible moment, she would instead hover over the stump, motionless but for the steady, languid beats of her wings holding her in position. Then she would pluck delicately at the target with an outstretched claw, hold her proud head high aloft and drift away as if on a breeze.

To Fortune she was just a show-off but now, watching Gossamer, he understood how Wood had been moved by Caprice, who was, Wood said, 'the most wondrous creature'.

Gossamer was just that. She was his most wondrous creature. She spoke, and he listened as he had never listened before.

'It all started the night we saw the Black Dragon. He — I suppose it was a he — dropped out of the sky. He was terrifying . . . but he was beautiful too, somehow . . .'

She frowned, a little puzzled it seemed as she remembered the contradiction of that moment: the dragon's darkness, his lack of form, his strange, ethereal beauty.

'I could almost have believed he was a saviour; instead he ravaged the Cross.'

Fortune listened aghast as Gossamer described the sudden plumes of fire which had jetted from the seven tunnels later that night. The flames had been hard and short, extending barely halfway across the canyon and not even touching the nests of the Naturals. Not for Aether's Cross the conflagration of South Point. But something even worse!

Charmed dragons had poured forth in the wake of the fire; they had fallen upon their natural neighbours and bound the fit and the young Naturals with cords made from liquid flame, transporting them limp across the ravine and into the tunnels as though they were bundles of dead leaves. Only when dawn had finally begun to threaten the night were the infants and elderly taken. Among them Gossamer and Brace.

'We watched them take our family and friends,' sobbed Gossamer, breaking down. 'I'm s-sorry, F-Fortune. I haven't even admitted to myself yet what has happened at Aether's Cross . . .'

'It's all right,' blurted Fortune, draping his wing tentatively around her and feeling startled by the feelings aroused in him as he did so. She pressed close to him, hitching in her breath in great gulps until gradually the tears subsided.

'I'm okay,' she sniffed. 'I can't even remember how long ago it happened — I can't keep track of the time down here.'

'Was it many days ago?' prompted Fortune.

'Not many. Five or six maybe.'

Fortune expected her to pull away from him as she recovered her composure but she did not. Instead she nuzzled closer into his flank and continued her story.

'Brace and I were hiding by then, of course. There aren't really caves on our side of the Cross, just a few hollows and scrapes. We were huddled at the back of one of the deeper ones, just waiting to be captured. The Charmed were patrolling everywhere . . .'

They shrank together as two huge charmed dragons glided towards them. As they landed an elderly, tottering Natural named Thant stumbled into their path. The larger of the charmed dragons sidestepped around the old Natural and headed straight for Gossamer while his comrade landed and arrogantly considered his choice.

'I've never seen Brace so distressed,' shivered Gossamer. 'He's proud, you see. He was angry that they hadn't considered him worth picking off in the first wave, and when that second dragon hesitated before choosing between him and Thant — he just went mad!'

'He *wanted* to be caught?'

'Of course not. But he didn't want to be overlooked. So he rushed them.'

The first dragon had already bound and lifted Gossamer when Brace sprang out on to the ledge in front of Thant, only to be cuffed to one side by the charmed dragon waiting there. Before he could even shout out his defiance the dragon had gathered up Thant and sped off in his colleague's slipstream.

'We'll pick up fatty later,' he called ahead.

'But of course the words must have floated back to Brace,' concluded Gossamer. 'The last I saw of him he was taking to the air behind us. He looked so angry . . . and so *crushed*. I imagine they must have taken him shortly afterwards.'

She stopped, as though a chapter of her tale were over. Fortune breathed in her silence; it intoxicated him. There they remained for a space of time, warm and comfortable in each other's embrace.

'This Black Dragon,' said Fortune at length. 'Did you see any more of him?'

'No. But I knew he was controlling the Charmed. Charmed dragons are not bad dragons, Fortune, but if a bad dragon takes control then terrible things will happen. Have happened.'

Fortune nodded. He had already told Gossamer of the fall of South Point and of Cumber and their mission to reach Covamere. There seemed little point in being secretive and besides, was Gossamer not on their side, on the side of unity and peace? Was she not . . . *beautiful!*

'We'd better move away from the wall,' she sighed, raising herself away from his side with a graceful, fluid movement. 'The water will be coming through soon.'

Fortune followed her to the other side of the cave. The cell they shared was twice as long as it was broad and boasted uncannily smooth walls. A small patch of rock in the ceiling glowed, casting a flat light over the milky-white walls. The walls themselves were featureless. Seamless.

'How did we get in here?' asked Fortune, amazed as for the first time he realized the impossibility of their predicament. 'How can we *breathe*.'

'Oh, that's charm,' replied Gossamer airily. 'Either there's a hole in the wall which we can't see, disguised by earth charm or some such magic, or else there isn't really an entrance and they just push us through as needed.'

She spoke so authoritatively that Fortune was forced to smile.

'You seem to know a lot about charm,' he commented.

'I'm interested,' came her warm reply.

'Me too.'

Another comfortable pause, another gaze shared, a deeper heat than simple warmth bringing them comfort in the confines of their prison.

'Where I come from,' stammered Fortune, overwhelmed by his response to this beautiful young dragon, 'there's very little magic, you see. I've always wanted to know more about it. Here in the Heartland it all seems more *real*. It's as if legends are springing to life before my eyes.'

'Charm is a wonder,' agreed Gossamer. 'I only wish you could meet Ant.'

'Ant?' asked Fortune suspiciously, his heart doubling and sinking inside him. 'Who's he?'

She regarded him with a solemn face and then laughed a delightful, flirtatious laugh.

'Oh, Fortune! We've known each other no time at all and already you're jealous! Ant's a sprite. He's tiny; you've nothing to fear from him!'

Fortune ducked his head, painfully embarrassed. A sprite! How stupid of him!

'Then I suppose he's . . .'

But he got no further. As if in response to this talk of charm the cave seemed to tense around them. A brilliant point of light stabbed from the far wall and expanded into a network of lines and spirals. From the web of light a crackling sound emerged and the air thickened with the smell of lightning.

The web solidified with a great, wounded *crack* and for the briefest of intervals Fortune was looking through the rock wall and into a corridor beyond.

Then the rock snapped shut — as though the rock were just a pattern etched into the weave of some greater fabric which had somehow been folded out of sight — returning the wall to its rightful place in this world.

Except now it was punctured in two places, one high and one low, a narrow stream trickling between the two.

'That happens twice a day, as near as I can judge,' said Gossamer. 'Drinking water!'

'Race you!' cried Fortune and, their worries temporarily

forgotten, they scrambled over each other to get to the fall of crystal water which played gently against the milky-white wall of their cell.

Cumber had stumbled upon the guardroom in his attempt to follow Brutace. He had straightaway left the smelly food-store and its festoons of rats and ventured into the corridor. The commander had vanished however, as had the sly Hex, and now Cumber was to encounter the other two charmed dragons who acted as gaolers in this forsaken place.

Had circumstances been otherwise the sight that con-fronted him when he first entered the guardroom would have reduced him to helpless laughter.

The rock inside Aether's Cross was quite unlike anything Cumber was used to. Familiar shale and granite were absent here, replaced by white limestone, its surfaces translucent as frozen milk beneath the glow of the floating light charms.

Against this pale backdrop were poised two dark dragon shapes locked in a furious tug of war, two sets of metallic grey jaws hauling on opposite halves of the object of their desire — a single rat.

The two dragons differed in appearance so greatly as to be comical: where the one was running distinctly to fat the other was skinny to the point of emaciation. And yet, despite his vast weight advantage, the larger of them was having enormous difficulty even standing his ground, let alone win-ning the rat from his opponent's jaws.

Blue sparks showered from the thin dragon's back as he spent charm frantically, locking his wiry body into immobil-ity; the fat dragon seemed to be relying entirely on brute force. The rat was remarkably durable.

Cumber cleared his throat and both dragons rolled their eyes towards him, mute surprise distracting them utterly from their contest. Thin jaws relaxed before fat ones and the larger dragon somersaulted backwards, propelled entirely by his own bulk until a nest of dry branches broke his fall, scattering everywhere like autumn leaves in a whirlwind.

Silence.

Then the thin dragon cackled with laughter while stray magic rippled out from his body and lifted dust from the floor in tiny thunderstorms.

The rat dangled lifeless between the fat dragon's teeth until presently he threw his head back and gulped it down whole. A satisfied smile broke across his cavernous mouth.

'Hahaha!' The thin dragon continued to laugh, then the grin which split his skeletal face suddenly disappeared, exchanged instantly for a dangerous snarl.

'Could kill him, Rite,' he said, 'but Brutace says not. What do you say, Cummion?'

This last question was directed at Cumber and it was several blinks before he remembered the name he had given to Hex. Knowledge that his deceit was working at least in part restored his confidence and he puffed out his chest. In silence Cumber turned his eyes to the battle spurs and razor scales which decorated the bodies of this strange pair and he recognized them as two of the four dragons who had attacked him and Fortune the previous day.

The fat dragon sat mute, frowning in his nest of broken branches, staring intently at the floor as if trying to solve some vast problem. He was motionless but for the tip of his heavy tail, which described precise circles in the air behind him. When he made as if to speak, the thin one's expression switched again from aggression back to glee.

'Brutace says not to tell him anything,' he rasped. 'Well, Rite, you shouldn't tell him that Brutace says not to tell, should you? Fat rat! Fat rat! Hahaahaha!'

When Scoff said they were mad he meant it, Cumber realized. This disease, whatever it was, that had rendered the Charmed of South Point slow and bitter had turned these dragons into dribbling idiots.

As if to prove his point, fat Rite began slowly to blow bubbles.

He looked at these two wide-eyed dragons and for a moment felt sorry for them. Then he took a deep breath and said, 'Well, dragons, are you hungry?'

Suddenly docile, they stared at him. And so he taught them to cook.

That they had never learned such elementary charm astonished him but the enthusiasm with which they tore into the steaming rat flesh he had grilled over a gentle fire was proof enough of their ignorance. Before long they had filled their bellies and even the thin dragon, whose name was Stition, was showing a remarkable paunch on his otherwise scrawny frame.

For his part Cumber ate enough of the foul-tasting meat to fuel his stomach, for it had been a whole day and more since his last meal, and he learned that Hex was on guard duty all day while Brutace was scouring a far flank of the colony to check for any last Naturals hidden there. But he could not persuade Stition to divulge Fortune's whereabouts.

Full with rat meat, Stition and Rite fell asleep, leaving Cumber marginally the wiser and free to explore the rest of the cave system.

Small triumph this proved to be. Aether's Cross boasted a peculiarly complex system of tunnels.

At first, Cumber felt rewarded for his cunning in putting Rite and Stition out of action by a layout relatively easy to map. A single, wide corridor leading from the surface ran far back into the mountain, the only way in or out of the deep tunnels where the Charmed of the Cross had actually lived. Crucial to navigation in these tunnels was a broad, round cave where the single corridor divided into three smaller ways. From the first of these ways – down which lay the guardroom, the foodstore and most of the living quarters – Cumber now emerged, and was faced with a choice.

He took one of the other smaller tunnels and found that it led to a Great Chamber much larger than that of South Point – but just as deserted. Though here the Council Seats were still intact, still it felt cold and broken to Cumber; he did not linger there, leaving this dead end to its gloom and desolation and returning to the main junction cave.

The third way beckoned, but something prevented him from taking it. He scented the air. *Natural dragons!* He could smell them. This was the way to the prison cells. And Hex. Fortune would be here, somewhere, too. But how would he find Fortune and rescue him? *I could go back to the guardroom, kill them now while they're sleeping,* he thought suddenly. *And then maybe kill Hex too, and rescue Fortune . . . and the other Naturals.*

Brutace would return to find the captured dragons freed and ready to face him. An army of dragons.

121

Of natural dragons . . .

Dragons who would almost certainly kill the first Charmed they laid eyes upon, even if it were the very dragon who had set them free. Fortune, as a fellow Natural, might convince them to let Cumber live but which cell held Fortune? None of the four guards had let that secret slip and without that knowledge Cumber would as likely open a cell on a murderous vigilante as on his dearest friend.

But he knew this logic concealed a deeper truth: he could not kill another dragon in cold blood. Perhaps not at all.

Some adventurer!

Escape was the thing. Before he rescued Fortune in a blaze of newly acquired charm he must find a way out of the caverns – along the main tunnel then out through one of the seven holes in the east cliff. It was then he discovered how treacherous the cave system really was.

Those seven mouths which opened into the tunnels inside the Cross were lined up in a regimented formation with one purpose only – confusion. Aether's Cross was a strategically placed settlement which had once been one of the greatest journeyways in the Heartland, and it was defended with care. Its first gambit was to make no one entrance superior to any other so that there was no such thing as a main route into the caverns. Immediately inside each cave mouth the tunnel split into two, then each of those into two again, and again and again until each entrance had spawned sixteen passageways. The tunnels rose and fell, twisted and deceived so that all sense of direction would quickly be lost. As a deterrent to entry it was unparalleled.

Having confidently travelled the single deep tunnel to the point where it met this writhing maze, Cumber swiftly became bogged down by the outer system's complexity. He could locate only three of the seven exits; each lay beyond a part of the confusing labyrinth – and, worse, each was guarded by a powerful charm that denied him passage. The first two were blocked by invisible walls, but as he neared the third exit, a narrow triangle of light beckoned Cumber into the world outside.

He crept forward hesitantly, nerves armed against the slightest hint of danger, wings and limbs clenched tight to his sides where they pulsed with the beating of his heart.

The air here was still and heavy, as though the very rock were stagnant. A smell like marsh gas reached his nostrils.

This is wrong.

And indeed it was. This close to one of the cave's exits there should have been an appreciable draught. This high in the mountains it should have been cold too.

The air was motionless.

The air was hot.

Cumber thought he knew why.

Reaching cautiously in front of him he probed the air with a tentative claw. Nothing happened.

'It's there somewhere,' he muttered under his breath and slithered forward cautiously. Now his claws encountered a slight resistance, a sponginess in the air ahead. The rank, marshy smell was stronger, turning his stomach over. He closed his nostrils against it and pushed his outstretched claws gently into the invisible barrier.

For an instant the odour disappeared utterly and the air was clear and true, as though whatever force were generating the smell had momentarily turned its attention elsewhere. Then it returned, redoubled . . . and took shape.

Cumber, his reflexes charged to capacity, had already snatched his claws away and was leaping back down the corridor away from the daylight when the floor ahead began to flex and bubble like the waters of an angry lake. Great, swelling globes heaved upwards from the vibrating rock, glowing with a terrible, internal light, and as he scrambled even further away they started to rupture. Dark, half-seen shapes struggled within, eager to escape the yellow light which imprisoned them.

But then a sigh swept down the tunnel. The huge bubbles of rock which dwarfed the fleeing Cumber paused in their moment of birth . . . and subsided, the cracks which had begun to craze their glistening surfaces closing over.

As Cumber retreated still further they sagged reluctantly back, losing power and light as they finally flattened back down to become again the smooth white floor on to which, had he not been so cautious, he would innocently have walked.

The sigh faded away, the breath of a frustrated monster.

Cumber hitched in a great breath of his own – from back

here the smell of gas and swamp was at least bearable – and leaned heavily against the tunnel wall.

Just as he had suspected, Brutace had sealed the system against escape.

He considered those giant bubbles of rock as he made his way back down the deep tunnel. Fire charm he had seen before but this was different – more *alive*.

This is the Heartland, he thought. *Magic is stronger here. And to defeat it I must take on the Realm. For the first time in my life I must become a true wielder of fire charm!*

What was inside those bubbles? *Parched, yellow shadows moving in broken light!*

He was definitely out of his depth. Escape was a different proposition now. Even if he did manage to release Fortune before tonight could they evade the charms guarding the exits? He might be able to set up a countering charm to combat the defences but would it be strong enough? It would have to be. But he still had no idea where Fortune was being held.

Cumber hurried back towards the deep system, terribly anxious now. He heard snores from the guardroom and decided to check on Rite and Stition. Entering, he cast his gaze around, scanning the pale, shimmering limestone for any clue, any lever he might use to set a plan moving.

Blank walls. Sleeping guards. A narrow channel set halfway up the far wall to carry drinking water through the chamber.

Nothing.

The chattering water called Cumber over and he drank gratefully, glad to get rid of the cloying, marshy smell which still clung to his nostrils. He splashed his snout into the water, the coldness refreshing, its taste clean and pure.

He stopped, held his breath.

Tiny, silver shapes were darting about beneath the surface of the stream. He squinted, virtually crossing his eyes in order to focus on their small, glistening forms.

Minute creatures they were, each barely the size of a tadpole, each bearing a silver fishtail and a slender body with mobile, finned arms and crowned with a delicate, pointed head. Silver hair framed them like auras of light.

The water sprites regarded Cumber with gentle, intelligent eyes.

Fascinated, he watched them dance their underwater ballet. He had heard of such creatures, of course, but the Heartland had granted him his first sight of them. He was overwhelmed by their pristine beauty.

Water ran indelicately out of his nose as he gazed upon them enraptured.

'. . . em . . . ba . . .'

A high, sweet sound pierced the air. Even as he glanced around him Cumber realized its source.

'Em . . . ba . . .'

This time he bent close to the laughing water, trying to separate the splash of the wavelets from the strange words of the sprites. One of them broke surface briefly, fighting against the water tension like a dragon caught in a downdraught.

'K . . . em . . . ba,' it whispered in its loudest cry.

K . . . em . . . ba. Kemba. Cumber?

Cumber!

'Yes,' said Cumber at once. The sprites turned and rolled in their glassy sky, fighting the current.

'K . . . em . . . ba . . . go.'

Go. Go where?

'. . . go . . . wa . . . teh . . . ful.'

Waterfall?

A violent wave swept through the channel, tumbling the sprites in its wake. They struggled to hold their position as they were tossed roughly around.

'. . . rok . . .' came a faint cry, then suddenly the water stopped flowing and the sprites were carried away down the length of the trough. Cumber stumbled after them but could only watch as the last of the icy water disappeared into a black cleft in the wall.

Drinking time was over.

Cumber's heart pounded in his chest. At last he had a clue, a goal. The message was from Fortune, of that he had not the slightest doubt. His goal was a waterfall – find that and he would find his friend.

Colours scanned the rainbow overhead as the afternoon sped on. Stition and Rite slept alone in the guardroom. And Cumber performed his first serious act of charm.

CHAPTER 10

Fire Charm

Perhaps it was better that Cumber did not appreciate the extent of the damage his rockfall would cause or else he might have despaired.

The large round chamber where the main corridor divided into three Cumber had dubbed the Switchcave. He stood there now, staring towards their difficult escape route – the only way out of the system short of excavating a mountain's worth of solid limestone. A charmed dragon could do that, of course, given a year or two . . .

Behind him the dust was still settling in the left-side of the three deep tunnels, fallout from the havoc he had just wreaked down there. As the two guards had slept he had brought down the roof in the entrance to the guardroom, trapping them inside. As far as he could tell they had not even woken up.

That'll keep Rite and Stition quiet for a while at least.

Brutace, Rite had informed him grandly, was touring the canyon today in a last search for Naturals, and would not be back until sundown.

Which left Hex.

The right-side tunnel beckoned then, the way to the prison level, down which lay Hex and, Cumber hoped, Fortune.

If only I can find this waterfall!

No sound of water emerged from the tunnel, nor any hint of life. It was brightly lit by floating charms but curved gradually away to the right so that he could see only three or four tree-lengths into its depths. Cumber stood there in the Switchcave, trying to prepare himself for what he knew must lie before him but which he had dreaded for so long. He shook himself, but the motion failed to dislodge the buzzing sensation that disturbed him.

The rockfall by which he had imprisoned the sleeping Rite and Stition within the guardroom he had initiated entirely by judicious use of earth charm but as he had done so, for the first time in his life, he had been aware of an itching sensation deep inside his mind. It was like a stinging at the base of his tail where he could not reach, a buzzing he could barely hear but which insisted on being heard. It worried away at him as he brought down the rock, and it worried away at him still as he gazed down the prison tunnel, wondering what awaited him there.

Call it adventure, call it conflict. Cumber called it the Realm.

Earth charm and fire charm: charmed dragons practised both. Earth charm was gentle and easy, and all that Cumber had so far wielded. Even the fire he could spit from his mouth was simply a kind of lightning, a heating of the air and a concentration of natural elements into unnatural forms.

But fire charm was very, very different; of fire charm he had always been afraid, and as a dragon who yearned to understand the world, to comprehend the detail of things, to analyse and ponder, Cumber especially feared the Realm. The Realm had always before seemed to avoid him and so he had long ago determined to avoid it.

But though he had never experienced the buzzing sensation before he recognized it for exactly what it was: the Realm. *The source of the fire. Another world beyond our own.* It sensed his need for its power and was scratching away at his consciousness, eager for the release he could allow it, hungry for the freedom he could bestow.

'We use the Realm,' Ordinal had once told him, 'but unless we are wary it will not hesitate to use us. Its powers, once unleashed, are not easily controlled.'

Cumber carried fear with him as he stepped from the Switchcave into the gradual curve of the deep prison tunnel.

Without realizing it Cumber had crushed several of the charm webs used by Brutace and his guards to control the various services to the cells. Networks of charm impressed

127

into a section of the guardroom wall operated most of the automatic systems which had been introduced into the prison and now Cumber had wrecked at least half of them, with the result that many of the prisoners were now in danger of their lives.

The ragged hole through which water exited the cave where Fortune and Gossamer were held was growing smaller – even as they watched it was growing smaller. Its perimeter vibrated as it shrank.

And it was gone.

Fortune had been drowsy from the pain of his bruised head but he suddenly felt very alert.

Only one hole now violated the cell, and through it was pouring a constant stream of cold water. This hole showed no sign of shrinking, and the water it was disgorging had nowhere to go.

'I think we're in trouble,' commented Fortune.

Amid the silence of charm, none knowing the predicament of any other beyond the limestone walls of their own cells, water rose through the prison. With random shudderings which cried of weakness and decay, of a system breaking down, charm shrank and withdrew. For some there was no more air to breathe; many had lost all light; one cell had shrunk to half its original size and was still getting smaller. And six cells away from where Fortune and Gossamer were trapped another young Natural was fighting for his life.

Brace's cell was small and had flooded quickly. He swam near the ceiling now, his head pressed up against the rock as the water rose higher and higher. Within a few breaths he would drown.

So cold!

Hope had left him but his anger remained. The Charmed had placed him here to die and it seemed now that that was what would happen. They had ignored him, taken ancient Thant instead and only returned at the end; one of the last Naturals to be captured, he was still furious.

'If I ever get out of here,' he spluttered, throwing his words like blows against the ceiling as though they might somehow breach the rock, 'no dragon will ever overlook me again!'

And mixed in with his anger was his guilt.

I let them take Gossamer. She is my sister, and I should have protected her!

The water pressed him up against the white rock. One of his horns sliced into the light charm which was bobbing on the waves and it expired, leaving him in total blackness. Higher rose the icy water and with it rose his panic. He thrashed frantically and only when sanity caught hold of his wings again did he realize that he was completely enveloped by the coldness and that if he breathed in now he would be taking the last, liquid breath of his life.

Despite his anger, despite his guilt, something within him decided that Brace was not quite ready for that yet. He held his wings tight against him and flicked the tips outwards so as to thrust himself down into the water. Opening his eyes into the ice he searched for some means of escape.

'I'm scared, Fortune,' said Gossamer, her voice trembling.

'You know something?' confessed Fortune. 'So am I.'

They clung to each other, sharing their warmth in the icy liquid. It seemed to Fortune that the looming threat of death had sharpened his mind – no, his heart – like a claw. His choices were so narrow now that only the truest of them had any reality and the truest of them was this – that he loved Gossamer.

To Gossamer it seemed that the warmth they made together in the freezing water was greater than a merely physical heat and she found herself thinking of charm. There was something more between them than could possibly be generated by the natural world – not fire charm of course but a subtle magic all their own, perhaps the nearest a natural creature could come to knowing the wonder of charm.

But they say that once upon a time there were Naturals who became Charmed, she thought. *Is it possible, even for dragons like us? Or was that only ever a story, a dream for another age?*

She clung to Fortune and knew that he loved her already, and she knew that very soon she would love him.

The tunnel slowly curved, always to the right, descending gradually in a deep spiral. The walls were smooth and white with a milky shine which looked wet but which, when he

129

touched it, he found to be quite dry. The place was utterly quiet but for the click-click of his claws upon the floor.

Surely I would hear a waterfall, Cumber worried. He was concerned too that the smell of natural dragon was gone, completely gone. He had found not a single prison cell, nor any evidence that dragons were down here at all, though he knew there *must* be, beneath a layer of charm he could not even detect. The light charms bobbed inscrutably and the walls they illuminated were bare.

Where is Hex?

As he thought of his adversary he felt again that strange prickling sensation, more insistent and quite impossible to ignore.

'Very well,' he muttered. 'If I can't ignore it then at least I can show it who's the boss!'

He stopped, listened carefully for a moment to check that no dragon was approaching around the corner and then sat back on his haunches. All he had to go on was a brief speech of Ordinal's, spoken to him what seemed like a lifetime ago.

'The only safe way to the Realm,' she had explained, 'is from within yourself. You form the gate, you open it, you control it. All inside your mind. If you do not do it this way you will be consumed. It is not difficult but it is dangerous; accuracy is needed. As for how you open the gate, well, that is up to you. I myself imagine a claw in my mind, a claw that can rip and then mend in the blink of an eye. The membrane is fragile but it will obey you – if you make it clear from the outset that you are capable of the level of control which is necessary.'

Cumber thought back over those words now, thought very hard. At the time they had merely confused him but now it was different: now he could feel the Realm close by. He could sense its proximity to this world and as he focused his thoughts fully on it a vision opened up in his head.

A skin, a bulging, rippling, steaming skin stretching away from him in every direction. It was livid red, stained and soiled in some places and glowing with brilliant and unbearably sweet colours in others. Like some world-sized sac it writhed with the life it contained – no, not life, charm. Shapes pressed against it from inside, contorting its outer surface into forms sometimes unrecognizable, occasionally

130

horribly familiar; some were like gigantic deformed heads; many bore teeth; all seemed desperate to escape.

The membrane between this world and the Realm, thought Cumber, his mouth dry. *All I have to do is break it.*

In his mind he held up a claw.

He concentrated on the claw intently, seeing it, shaping it before his mind's eye. It was long and black and sharp as winter and with infinite care he pushed it forward until it touched the undulating surface of the membrane.

At once the shapes beneath swarmed to the point of contact. The writhing became a hurricane of motion, a terrible snapping orgy which lunged at the tip of his imaginary claw, the trapped charms working together with but one intent — to impale the skin of the Realm on the weapon of this interloper and release their powers into the real world. The membrane buckled and stretched, pink lines of stress gathering about the point where Cumber's claw was pressing deeper and deeper into its thickness; another fraction of a breath and the skin would rip open and release its clamouring contents.

Cumber withdrew the claw, dissolving it instantly and destroying what tenuous existence it had possessed. A great shudder shook the Realm across its entire rolling surface and the shapes within subsided, their motion much calmer now as if they understood that this particular chance had passed. They moved still, however, a background dance. Ready for the next time.

Drawing a deep, cold breath Cumber turned his mind away from the unreal spectacle of the Realm and fixed his eyes back on the line of the corridor which swept away from him into the pale and milky distance. His pace steady and deliberate he moved off again in search of friend and enemy.

The lightning vaporized the water as it coruscated through its icy waves, creating a searing storm of bubbles which expanded and fled through the wrenching hole which had been torn in the wall. A vast, gasping rush, a release of pressure so fast as to create its own shock wave through the sudden air. An impact that was less of a splash than an explosion. The cell wall collapsed, dumping its load of liquid and dragon into the tunnel outside, fire still flickering across the surface of the liquid and flashing it to steam before it could run away into the secret channels in the rock.

Brace coughed mightily, expelling a watery cloud from his lungs. With a prodigious effort he heaved himself up on to his wings and then collapsed again into the vanishing pool.

Something hard and metallic clicked out a monotonous rhythm on the floor behind him.

There was the sound of an extravagant yawn. Jaws creaked and a voice said, 'Got some water trouble, have we? Still – at least you're a fat one!'

Brace whirled round. Before him was the dragon who had rejected him in favour of Thant, the one who had called him fatty. He did not know the dragon's name but, of course, it was Hex. Panting still he narrowed his eyes and coiled his body back on his haunches, at which Hex let out an almighty laugh.

'Oh, stay there, little rat!' he commanded. As though the mere effort was tiresome he cocked his head back and spat a tiny ball of fire into what was left of the puddle of water evaporating from around Brace's body. The liquid turned brilliant orange and snapped into a band which crossed over Brace's back, trapping his wings against his sides and pinning him helplessly to the floor, half suffocated.

Hex smiled and tiny sparks leaped between his yellow teeth. Fire roiled in his throat and his smile widened immeasurably until it filled Brace's entire vision, and whether Hex had simply leaned close or had used charm to turn his mouth into this wide, gaping maw Brace could not tell, for he had fainted dead away.

There was a sudden, rumbling splash and a flickering in the distance.

Cumber crouched and slunk along the tunnel, towards the flashing light. He found himself in luck: a pile of rubble was leaning against the wall, rivulets of water still trickling between the boulders. No waterfall this, but at least it was cover.

Reaching the wedge of rubble he pressed himself against it and craned his neck cautiously up and over the top. The Realm scratched at the inside of his head. The scene beyond the rockfall chilled him and for an instant he feared that panic would take control of him . . . but the fear subsided swiftly leaving in its place a strange calm.

Beyond the boulders lay a plump natural dragon, unconscious and trapped by some kind of charm. Over him loomed Hex. Somewhere in the core of his mind, Cumber was aware that the Realm had been breached, but he tried to concentrate on what was before his eyes.

Hex thrust his right foreleg out towards his prisoner. Blue light rippled over it like a living spider's web and it doubled its length in the time it took Cumber to take a breath. It stretched and warped, claws fused together, tendons plaited themselves into a single strand, anatomy danced in the brutal clutch of fire charm. Sparks and sweat dripped from the end of the horribly changed limb.

Now Hex lurched towards the Natural, moving awkwardly on three legs. The fourth had become a giant, lashing tongue, its underside set with vicious spines – a fat, purple serpent reaching out for its prey with fascinating delicacy. He raised it high above his head, paused it there briefly and finally brought it lashing down in a blow designed to decapitate his helpless victim.

Cumber's mind was filled with the Realm. Without thought, he recreated the imaginary claw with which he had previously tested its defences – and drew a great slash across the surface of the Realm. The sides of the wound peeled apart – they boiled and writhed – and he reached in.

He grasped fire. He grasped ice. In the fraction of an eyeblink it took him to find what he was looking for Cumber touched a million forces, a million living charms clambering over each other in their vain attempts to gain purchase into the real world. His claw groped in the brilliant darkness for its single goal while his mind prevented the invasion of the world by a flood of chaotic magic.

There!

His claw locked on to the charm he sought and wrenched it, dripping with creation, into this world. At the insistence of his mind, the gash in the membrane of the Realm snapped shut behind it with the concussion of a felled forest.

And when Hex's writhing limb lashed out towards the Natural it struck instead the sheet of blue Realm fire Cumber had thrown into its path.

133

This fire, a vertical mosaic of tiny, individual flames, each burning from apparent nothingness with volcanic heat, solidified instantly, slicing the limb neatly from its owner and charring the cut end with awesome precision.

Hex screeched as the sheet of fire collapsed over him, slamming the stump of his mutilated limb against his chest and ripping his wings apart as it gathered him bodily into the air.

The charm, now a bulging sack of fire, paused briefly as Cumber emerged from behind the rock which had concealed him. Hex glared at him through pain and flame. To the side the Natural was hunched in oblivion, the lifeless worm of Hex's severed limb oozing across his neck.

Then the fire moved sideways and plunged into the rock of the tunnel wall. Hex cried out as though from a great distance, then his voice was cut off abruptly as dead stone enveloped him.

Stillness.

Inside Cumber's mind the scratching wind had stopped. Delicately he probed the interface between the world and the Realm: it was shut tight, scarless. Its work was done.

Shaking, both horrified and ecstatic at what he had managed to do, Cumber bent over the dragon Hex had been about to kill and willed the binding orange charm to release him. It did so, sliding into the floor and vanishing away into the Realm as if it had never existed – and Cumber scarcely recognized that he had cut a tiny slit in the Realm membrane to achieve this. With an odd mixture of horror and triumph, Cumber remarked to himself, *You'll make an adventurer yet!*

But the magic was not over. The corridor wall swelled, and a gigantic, grossly elongated dragon's foreleg forced its way out. It seemed made of rock; he could see hot, white magma coursing within it like shining blood and its outer skin cracked and split as it twisted towards him.

Stone talons closed painfully around his neck and dragged him across the floor. The wall sped towards him and all his triumph gave way to the horror as he realized that Hex was still alive.

Suddenly everything was overlapping, interlocking; Cumber sensed massive charm at work as Hex fought to regain a clawhold in the real world.

White stone filled Cumber's vision and his claws squealed across the floor as Hex hauled him towards and finally into the wall.

Before he even knew it Cumber had opened a way into the Realm again. This time it was different — instead of pulling magic out he pushed himself in. Charms lunged at him, jealous of his hold on the real world, desperate to escape their prison, but he held them back.

Hex's hold was weaker within the Realm and Cumber suddenly realized that the dragon was dying. This attack was a final act, a death-rattle, deadly if uncountered but feeble nonetheless. With an easy twist of his body he slipped free of Hex's grip and slithered away through the Realm. Hex followed sluggishly, batting hopelessly at Cumber's ghostly form as it danced away through spaces in the rock which did not exist. Hex floundered in a Realm which had suddenly become his enemy, which at last sucked every vestige of magic from him and ejected him back into the rock.

The rock claimed him, stilling his heart, locking his blood forever in his veins and freezing his mind into a lifeless cast of hatred. Hex became stone and would taste the air no more until the mountains had worn down to expose the echo of his corpse, many aeons hence.

An instant later Cumber reawakened the solidity of his body and dropped lightly into the corridor, the air he occupied feeling thin and insubstantial. He felt powerful, as though he had aged without tiring, grown more aware without learning. The Realm sat restlessly at the limits of his mind, eager for its charm to be summoned once more.

Not yet, thought Cumber. *Nor ever again, had I the choice.*

The power he felt moved his thoughts on swiftly and he turned his attention back to the dragon he had rescued and who was stirring now. Behind the fallen dragon was a great, jagged hole in the corridor wall, evidently the means Hex had used to break this prisoner out of his cell, only to attack him.

At least now Cumber knew why he had not found any cells along the way: they were hidden behind the walls, the entrances created solely by the use of charm.

He watched Brace awaken . . . and scream, his eyes mad!

He was staring over Cumber's shoulder, and when Cumber turned he saw that the wall was milky white like the rest of the tunnel but there was a peculiar shadow across it. As he shifted his head, he realized he was seeing inside the rock. The shadow was Hex, locked into the mountain. The expression of his face was one of utter agony. Cumber was again face to face with Hex . . . or what was left of him.

He shuddered and took a step back. His eyes widened. He took another step back.

The rock formation in which Hex was trapped was like a crystal in which his corpse was the flaw. No, not a crystal!

For what Cumber saw in the magical glow of the light charm which floated behind his head was a towering edifice of limestone, a mass of sculptured deposits moulded into tubes and globes and long, running channels which shone with creamy translucency. Here was a memory of water, its ancient passage, a column of lime more beautiful than anything Cumber had ever seen.

A waterfall made of stone.

CHAPTER 11

Race to the Light

Brutace rushed at the entrance tunnels, iron wings pumping the air as he bullied his way through the sky.

Urgency had fallen upon him this afternoon. His sweep of the Cross, as he had hoped, proved fruitless. No natural dragons remained now, of that he was certain, and no new dragons had dared to shelter in the deserted ruins of the colony. The settlement of natural dragons at Aether's Cross had been extinguished.

But these visitors – the Charmed and the Natural – were a strange pair indeed. Brutace did not for one moment believe the story of the charmed one (Cummion, was it, if that was his real name?) but he had mentioned the Master and so care needed to be taken lest even a part of his tale might be true.

Brutace was cold and unimaginative – in fact these were the qualities on which he specifically prided himself, for while he had seen many of the other charmed dragons of Aether's Cross degenerate into madness he himself had remained strong and alert. And when the Master had arrived Brutace had been the first to support his desire to conquer the Naturals, the undoubted cause of Charmed decline.

Exactly one hundred dragons had been gathered in the Great Chamber that night, of whom perhaps only half were wholly sane. Paranoia characterized the madness which had taken the other half and they had split into uneasy factions; suspicious glances abounded and the air was thick with tension. They had no Leader now, old Wast having died in delirium a moon or more before; no dragon had taken her place.

The Master's arrival had been heralded several days earlier

by an alert, wiry dragon who called himself Insiss. His affect on the Charmed community had been odd, for while all those who encountered this lieutenant swore that he was not to be trusted as a dragon, they nevertheless believed every word he said about his great Master who would shortly be paying them a visit.

'He will give you the purpose you seek,' Insiss had crooned in his soft, sly voice, and not one dragon there had understood the true wit of the Black Dragon in sending so suspect a herald, for in mistrusting Insiss the dragons of Aether's Cross became strangely prepared for receiving a dragon they *could* trust; Insiss's very dubiousness opened the way for his master with a subtlety no dragon could have guessed.

It was into this throng of suspicious, hopeful, divided dragons that the Black Dragon had swept. He entered their midst not through tunnels but through the Realm, a blinding light behind him to throw his monstrous form into an even greater shadow. Without exception the dragons of his audience in the Great Chamber had gasped, astonished, and with the ease of experience − for he had done exactly this in many Charmed communities before he came to Aether's Cross − he had placed himself on the empty Leader's Dais and proclaimed himself their new Master. All had bowed to him, for not only was he formidable but he also delivered exactly what they craved − unity, common purpose, and the promise of action against the dragons towards whom they had grown so bitter: the Naturals of the western cliff.

'This night,' the Black Dragon had intoned. 'No other will suffice.'

The attack had been launched before the night was out and in that one, devastating sweep the Naturals, just as the Black Dragon had promised, had been conquered

Had Brutace had his way 'conquered' would have meant 'destroyed'. The Black Dragon's decree that none should be killed but all imprisoned was the only one with which he personally did not hold, but the Master's word was law − indeed his apparent leniency was what had swayed many of the less belligerent dragons − and Brutace had sufficient faith that some greater plan would see the Naturals' ultimate destruction. Until then, confident in his own powers and respectful of his master's authority, he was content to be chief gaoler of Aether's Cross.

The majority of the Charmed population the Master had taken south with him two nights later, leaving Brutace with three dragons under his command – Hex, Stition and Rite – a poor selection in intellect but efficient and cruel enough nonetheless. However, all three had drifted further into insanity whilst guarding the Naturals. Brutace was aware that only Hex was even partly reliable – unless madness had claimed even him whilst Brutace had been absent. Brutace was unconcerned, even so; the Master had promised him a place high in his command chain when eventually he was summoned to the new citadel in the south, where the Master had led the rest of the charmed dragons of Aether's Cross . . . there was the future for the Charmed.

I shall have to kill those three soon, mused Brutace as he neared the cavern entrances. *I can survive on my own until the Master sends new orders.*

But these new dragons, these two travellers, they smelled of trouble. He had no doubt that he could deal with them easily enough, miserable youngsters that they were, but still there was something, something which made him . . . afraid.

Afraid?! Brutace has no place for fear in his heart!

Something was very wrong. A scent of death was seeping from the tunnel mouths and Brutace channelled his fear into anger. He had been away too long.

His claws snapped shut on the air and in fury he flexed them, ready for whatever might await him. Lethal spines sprang angrily from his back and his wings sharpened with barbed charm.

Urgent now, with growing wrath, he swooped into the darkness of the caverns.

'A waterfall made of stone!' whispered Cumber, entranced. 'And I might have strolled right past it!'

He turned his back on the glossy construction – his foray through the Realm had already indicated to him that there were no cells on that side of the tunnel – and probed into the rock on the opposite wall. It was hard work, for the web of charm which had been laced through the rock was dense and complex, and something seemed to be dulling his charmed senses, blurring the images he was forming in his mind. A cell was there behind the wall, to be sure, but how deep was it, and why was the image so indistinct? It seemed murky, as though he were seeing it . . .

'Under water!'

The cell was flooded! Of course. Cumber cast a panic-stricken glance at the wreckage strewn around the entrance to the cell of the dragon he had saved from Hex's vile charm. The young Natural was picking himself up and staring at Cumber with undisguised malice – and fear, which at least prevented him from attacking Cumber. Cumber had no time for him now. In his mind he meshed the signals he was receiving from the waterlogged space behind the rock with the details he picked up from the debris in the corridor – faults in the rock, thickness of the wall between cell and tunnel, fragmentation patterns. Without drawing breath he sliced deep and struck a bolt of energy into the wall of the tunnel, hauling a cylinder of limestone out of the mountain and ejecting it far into the waiting Realm where it was consumed even as it entered. The Realm belched and smoked and again Cumber drew shut the wound he had made in its skin.

Each time it gets easier; I wish that it wouldn't!

For that instant the scene was frozen in time: a circular hole pierced the rock to the exact depth of the cell, revealing a wall of water poised and ready for release. Then the natural world caught up with the charm which had been unleashed upon it and the water gushed out of the cell in a single blast, pouring over Cumber and Brace and spinning off down the sloping floor into the depths of the mountain. At the head of the flow came foam and fragments of rock while on its tail rode two dragons, cold and bedraggled but gasping for joy as they realized that they were still alive.

'Cumber!' shouted Fortune as he crashed into his friend. The two of them rolled over together and came up against the stone waterfall with a great thud. They spluttered and coughed, and then laughed and butted heads. Around them the waters receded and they looked back at the hole Cumber had made in the wall. 'I bet that's the first time you've ever spun a charm like that!' exclaimed Fortune with gusto.

140

They laughed again and embraced, whirling around in the water, only gradually drawing breath and pulling a little apart again, panting and gasping in disbelief that they should finally be back together.

'Not quite,' was Cumber's breathless reply, but his wry smile told Fortune nothing. Yet Cumber seemed to have grown somehow and for the moment at least Fortune was quite overwhelmed.

He can get us out, he thought with conviction. *Cumber has the power!*

'I'll tell you later,' added Cumber as he saw that his friend was preparing to unleash the inevitable barrage of questions, 'but until then we simply must . . .'

'Brace!'

'Gossamer!'

And so Fortune and Cumber turned again to see a second reunion as Gossamer embraced her trembling brother so hard that his eyes bulged and his short legs were lifted off the floor. The two Naturals spun around in a whirlwind dance and then eventually staggered to a halt in front of the others, breathless and ecstatic.

'Fortune!' gasped Gossamer, 'he's all right. Is this . . . ?'

'This is Cumber,' confirmed Fortune, watching Brace closely. From the look the young Natural gave Cumber it was clear he had no love for the Charmed – not this particular Charmed nor any of their race. Cumber for his part seemed oblivious to Brace's animosity however for already he was trying to hurry the others off up the corridor.

'Introductions will have to wait, but if you'll please just keep moving in this direction we can find out who we all are as we go along. But we have to hurry, we have to keep moving. Please hurry, everyone, there isn't any time to waste.'

His excitement was infectious and before they knew it Fortune and Gossamer were being bustled along ahead of him. It was only when they heard Brace's call that they paused and looked back.

'We're not going without the others!' he cried. He had not moved from the waterfall.

As one Cumber, Fortune and Gossamer came to a halt.

'He's right,' said Gossamer at once. 'What was I thinking?

Our parents, our friends . . . Fortune, you said you thought your mother might be here . . .'

At this Cumber threw Fortune a quizzical glance but his friend shook his head. *Later*, the gesture seemed to say, *don't worry about me*.

'Cumber?' prompted Fortune, his tone at once informing his companion that he would abide by whatever decision he might make.

Fortune's trust touched Cumber and for an instant he was uncertain of what he would say, but his innate sense of reason took control and he found himself not speaking but acting.

He stepped over to the cell-side wall and pressed his head against it. Inside the rock he could feel jagged remnants of charm still working — and only now did he realize what damage he had caused the system when he had trapped Rite and Stition in the guardroom. The network of charm was too complex for him to absorb in a hurry so he did the only thing he could think of: he shut down the entire system. At the same time he found a charm in the Realm which punched several million tiny holes through the walls all around them, not enough to weaken the rock but sufficient, he hoped, to admit air into the cells which they pierced; he prayed they pierced them all.

'Listen to me,' he barked as he whirled around. 'I've stopped the flooding and your friends have got air. That's all I can do for now, although I'm sure you would dearly love me to free all the rest. But you must believe me when I say there is no time — if we stay here now I might get a few out but we'll all be trapped like rats when Brutace gets back, and believe me it wouldn't matter how many were freed — he would kill us all. Mind you, I'm not sure a lot of your friends wouldn't lynch me on sight, bearing in mind what the Charmed have done to them.'

'Frightened, are you?' taunted Brace.

'Brace!' hissed Gossamer. 'He could be right. Fortune said . . .'

'And this is Fortune, is it?' responded her brother in a bitter tone which spoke volumes. He glared at Fortune with obvious dislike.

'In answer to your question,' persisted Cumber, 'yes, I *am*

142

scared. And so should you be – of Brutace, and what he will do to you if he has you cornered down here, because I'm quite sure it will be worse than anything Hex could have thought up.'

He finished by gesturing angrily at the shadow in the waterfall. Fortune and Gossamer both frowned, then inhaled sharply as they realized they were looking at the agonized face of a dragon frozen in rock. Brace simply shuddered when he saw his attacker imprisoned there forever.

'What . . . ?' began Fortune but Cumber interrupted him.

'I'll tell you about that later too. Now come on, we have to get out now, there's no time to lose!'

'Story of our lives,' shrugged Fortune. He looked into Gossamer's eyes and found trust there, and for an instant his heart missed its beat.

She trusts me in this, she will come with me! Does she love me too, can it possibly be?

And somewhere inside her gaze he began to see the answer, and it gave him the courage he needed.

'Come on then,' he said, his gaze not leaving hers. 'If we get out now we might stand a chance of freeing the others later. They'll be safe for a while – it's us this Brutace will want first. Gossamer?'

She closed her eyes and nodded.

'Brace?' demanded Cumber.

The plump young dragon shifted from one wing to the other and finally, with the greatest of effort, said in a sullen voice, 'I'll come with you, Gossamer, if only to protect you from these two creeps. But I'll come back – I swear it!'

'Your manners make me wish I hadn't saved your life,' retorted Cumber with obvious ill-humour, 'let alone been lumbered with you as a travelling companion!'

'Cumber, if you want us out of here now I suggest you stop bickering and start leading!' snapped Gossamer.

Cumber actually stepped back a couple of paces and shook his head as though he had been slapped. Gossamer glared back at him.

His composure shaken but rapidly regained he scuttled off up the corridor at a pace the three Naturals found difficult to match. Fortune smiled to himself, delighted to be back in Cumber's company despite the obvious peril they were in. Hoping to win over Gossamer's brother he turned to share his smile but Brace, who was loping along at the rear, showed only a sullen scowl.

They caught up with Cumber at the entrance to the Switchcave.

There Cumber turned to face Gossamer and Brace. He pitched his voice low. 'I'm Charmed but I'm your friend, believe me,' he said with urgency. 'We have only one adversary now but I suspect he's stronger than the four of us put together; stronger than all the Naturals down here for that matter.'

'But what about the other guards?' began Fortune.

'There were only three others. I have killed Hex,' explained Cumber, surprised at the lack of emotion he felt when he acknowledged the fact. 'The other two — Stition and Rite — are asleep in the guardroom and I've barricaded them in; there's solid rock all around them now. I think Brutace will go to the guardroom first and spend time trying to get in — at least, that's my hope. That should place him *behind* us while we make our escape past . . .'

Cumber hesitated. 'Past what?' asked Fortune.

'Nothing,' he lied, shuddering as he remembered the charms which guarded the exits. 'I'll deal with it when we get there.'

Gossamer had observed the doubt in his voice. *Why, he's just a dragon*, she thought. 'How did you find us?' she asked hurriedly. Cumber's combined charm and ordinariness intrigued her and she discovered that she liked this young dragon.

'The sprites told me,' responded Cumber. 'Did you give them the message?'

Gossamer exchanged a glance with Fortune but shook her head.

'No. We saw sprites in the drinking water, just briefly, but then they were gone. They can't have been there for more than a few moments.'

'Well, it was enough, and it meant that I was able to find you.'

'Too bad about all the others,' put in Brace angrily.

'We've been through all that,' retorted Cumber, 'and I

don't like it any more than you do, believe me. Now, be quiet everybody. I need to determine whether or not Brutace has returned yet.'

He signalled his companions to remain in the corridor while he ventured out into the Switchcave. A dry breeze blew from the wide surface tunnel carrying the scent of flowers incongruously into the otherwise lifeless chamber. The pale walls shone beneath the glowing charm which was embedded in the low ceiling.

All was still.

The tunnel which had brought them up from the prison level was silent and empty.

The other two tunnels leading back into the mountain were black holes.

Darkness shrouded the depths of the surface tunnel.

Where was Brutace?

'I think . . .' began Cumber, when the breeze became a blast of air pressing with sudden fury into the chamber. Skittering back beneath the low ceiling of the prison tunnel he forced his fellow dragons back against the wall. The scent of flowers was overlaid with a rankness that was mingled with the stench of sweat and fire. What had been simple air pressure became a blast of wind, then a gale, howling around the cave. Echoes tumbled over themselves in a reverberating crescendo.

The four fugitives shrank back into the shadows as the oncoming force gathered itself into a single wedge of dust-choked air that swept past them with a dizzying, consuming roar and Brutace erupted into the chamber. Heat pulsed, the threat of fire storm.

But in an instant he was gone again, a hurricane passing, vanishing into the tunnel which led to the guardroom. The vision of that instant would remain with them all for the rest of their lives: Brutace was flying. His huge wings were fully spread, thrashing in blind rage, and where they should have struck the inhibiting walls and ceiling the blue fire which sheathed them was crushing the rock to powder. In his path he left the surface tunnel hot and scarred, great waves of rock scooped out of its walls in smoking testament to his passage.

And (though he could not possibly have known it yet)

there was imprinted on his face the sure knowledge that his latest prisoners had escaped.

The only thing which saved Cumber, Fortune, Gossamer and Brace was the blindness of Brutace's rage. He flashed through the chamber without seeing them!

'Come on!' hissed Cumber, and as one they fled their hiding place and half-ran, half-flew up the broad exit tunnel, now even broader in the aftermath of Brutace's incredible flight through air and rock. Cumber flew ahead while behind him hurried Fortune and Gossamer. Between leaps and flurries Fortune somehow found time to marvel at the rich reds and ochres which patterned Gossamer's wings.

Brace brought up the rear, sick to be fleeing, terrified.

Daylight floated at the limits of vision, a promise of escape far ahead. All around them the tunnel walls had been scarred and torn in Brutace's wake; cracks split the floor like grinning mouths. The rock groaned and shook as the mountains pressed down on it from above.

For the Naturals it was a perilous passage, for where Cumber was able to steer a safe central course through the wrecked tunnel, balanced as he was on a flight charm, they could not properly spread their wings and were forced instead to scramble and lunge, relishing the occasional glide and cursing the constant blows they received from the jagged remains of the tunnel walls. The light brightened slowly, very slowly.

Behind them came a roar. Brutace had turned.

At last they reached the maze. Here their enemy's brutal passage worked to their advantage for rather than traverse the complex turns of the protecting labyrinth Brutace had simply plunged through it, carving a new tunnel for himself as though the rock were but a sea sponge. This new passageway stretched out before them, its heat baking their skins but a welcome sight nonetheless.

And a splinter of light ahead was the day outside!

Cumber glanced back at his lagging companions and listened hard to the deafening howls of rage approaching them rapidly from behind, borne on the wind of Brutace's flight. Against those howls he gauged the distance to the daylight.

The comparison was not good.

146

He slowed, then stopped abruptly, hovering on a charm with not a single beat of his wings. His colleagues blundered up behind him, forced to perch painfully on the glowing rock as Cumber held his wings wide to block their passage.

'What the . . . ?!' blurted Brace, clutching hurriedly at a smoking outcrop with extended claws. Hot wind pressed at their rear.

'Down there!' ordered Cumber, indicating a side tunnel. Then to Fortune he said, 'First right, first left, second left, first left, first left. Then wait at the turn before the exit. Do *not* under *any* circumstances try to go out without me. Repeat!'

Fortune repeated this word for word. Cumber had grown since they had argued among the abandoned nests of Aether's Cross and he did not even think of challenging his commands; this was Cumber's adventure now.

'But we can see the light,' protested Gossamer, pointing ahead.

'We must trust him,' responded Fortune, bundling her and Brace into the side tunnel. 'Have a care,' he added to his Charmed friend.

Cumber nodded silently – and vanished.

Fortune shook his head. It was as though Cumber had suddenly realized his true potential and the idea that his friend might be as powerful as any of the charmed dragons he had seen yet filled him with a kind of dread. Then his own words returned to him: 'We must trust him.'

'I trust you, Cumber,' he whispered.

Blue light swelled in the passageway and for the second time Fortune shrank back as Brutace thundered past. This time the Charmed commander flew more slowly, deliberately and with infinitely more threat. He was sniffing the air in great draughts and Fortune could only hope that the smouldering of the charm-torn rock was enough to mask the scent of their fear. Into the ruptured maze they retreated, silent as night.

These tunnels were smaller again and blessedly cool. Fortune led the way, following Cumber's directions precisely until the daylight grew from a glow into a brilliance which filled the air.

'We mustn't go out yet,' cautioned Fortune, pausing at

what had to be the final turn in the corridor, but Brace, overcome by the prospect of escape, rushed impetuously past him and around the corner. Gossamer lunged after him and barely missed grabbing his tail with her outstretched claws.

'No!' she cried.

The blinding light bled around Brace's disappearing form.

'It's all right, Gossamer!' came Brace's shout from around the corner. 'There's nothing to be . . .'

But his words were cut off by a harsh yelp and an unearthly groaning sound which Cumber would have recognized only too well. A stagnant smell enveloped Fortune and Gossamer as they hurried round the corner, terrified of what they might be about to see.

Spreadeagled, silhouetted against a triangle of sunlight so bright that their eyes watered, Brace hung whimpering in a net of fire as though trapped in a spider's web, while all about him the rock bubbled with sickly yellow light as if it were about to give birth to some volcanic abomination.

'Help me!' screamed Brace.

They looked on, helpless.

Cumber had pulled himself into the Realm.

After a brief flight through a nightmare of clamouring charm he emerged at the far end of the tunnel Brutace had carved, just short of the exit.

With breathless ease he de-activated the guard charm.

Here the weapon had been ice: any dragon trying to pass would have been flash-frozen and then consumed by the tooth-lined mouth the corridor would have become. A countering charm plucked from the Realm reversed the freezing effect and rendered the guard charm quite inert.

His most feared obstacle had been destroyed with ease.

'Have a care, Cumber,' he muttered to himself, 'over-confidence could kill you yet.'

Then, from the adjacent entrance, he heard Brace's cry.

'Help me!'

Damn, thought Cumber, *must I always be rescuing that one?*

Cumber threw himself to the side towards the source of the cry – just as Brutace erupted out of the tunnel Cumber had emerged from.

Flailing claws clutched at Cumber's left wing and found it, ripping great tears down the delicate membrane. Cumber howled in agony as his blood splashed into the air like a rain of golden mercury. He wheeled in the sky, charm heating his body unbearably as he fought to regain control.

Brutace's claws bit deeper as his own wings pumped the air. Cumber turned to face his opponent, who seemed all tooth and spine, and delivered a devastating blast of Realm fire into his face. Lilac flame lit the canyon with a brightness which rivalled even the sun and Brutace relinquished his grip, allowing Cumber to retreat into the sky above.

But even as the fire dissipated Brutace's snarl appeared through its vestiges and the powerful dragon sped upwards towards his weakened opponent, wings pounding, charm showering sparks from his legs as claws lengthened, teeth sharpened. His neck bloated and grew rows of vicious, serrated hooks which jabbed at the air. Cumber watched aghast as Brutace changed shape before his eyes.

Yet still he thought of the others.

From the corner of his eye he saw movement in one of the entranceways. Light flashed there and a rumbling was shaking the cliff face; a guard charm had been activated.

With a groan Cumber turned in the air and arrowed his body down towards the yellow glow which was flickering in the tunnel mouth. Brutace veered to a new course and intercepted him just short of the ledge, falling upon him with mouth agape, flames bubbling in his throat in hungry expectation.

This time Cumber was ready. He opened a doorway into the Realm which sucked the flame into harmless oblivion.

Brutace growled with rage and lashed his wings around Cumber; only his own flight charm now kept them both aloft. Cumber's jaws clamped down on his wingtips, locking them in their tight embrace, and together they tumbled away from the ledge in a strange, windblown dance, neither one relinquishing his grip on the other, a ball of shining leathery skin within which two dragons battled for their lives. Tumbling in the air, their struggle was totally hidden by Brutace's enormous wings which enclosed them both like an eggshell. Occasional flashes of light illuminated those wings from within, veins standing in a dark network against glowing, orange skin.

Inside the tunnel entrance Brace had fallen unconscious. The web of light which trapped him was closed tight about his neck and the flesh around his throat raged purple. Every so often his body twitched as great concussions shook the whole tunnel.

Gossamer watched helplessly as a bubble of rock swelled on the floor and burst open with a wet gasp, squirting yellow light on to her brother's inert form and revealing its terrible contents. Countless spidery creatures, transparent as water, fangs sweating venom, swarmed from their breeding ground and spread a living floor across the tunnel. As she watched their bodies began to join, merging into each other as if to commence the creation of some greater beast, the form of which she could not begin to conceive.

She could only look on in horror at this obscene birth. Then shadows filled the slot of sky beyond Brace's motionless form. The crashing light of charm dulled the sun as Brutace intercepted Cumber just beyond the ledge outside. Nothing in her life had prepared her for this – and yet she realized that she had foreseen this instant when she and Brace had witnessed the coming of the Black Dragon. She could do nothing to help her brother.

Looking around at Fortune she saw the same question burning in his eyes: *Are we so weak that charm will always defeat us? Is there nothing we can do?*

She thought of the sprites but their magic was of the water and the earth. She thought of her love for her brother but that could not rescue him now. She thought of the Black Dragon and felt numb.

In the fraction of time it took her to think of these things, Fortune moved.

The unburst bubbles of rock were subsiding now, as though the first to unleash its cargo had won some unearthly race and forced its competitors into submission. Ten thousand or more crystal spiders were assembling themselves into a larger creature, the outline of which was indistinct, rippling with yellow sparks and pulsing with deadly life.

As the defeated bubbles retreated the extent of the damage they and the spiders from the Realm had caused to the entranceway was finally revealed. Cracks had completely shredded the floor and walls; the curved ceiling looked like a dried lake bed turned upside down and as Fortune looked towards the ledge outside he saw huge chunks of rock peel away from the tunnel mouth and disappear on their journey to the river below, allowing daylight to lance in with fat, dusty beams. Above, the mountain creaked.

The entire tunnel gyrated as the cliff began to tear itself apart.

But Fortune felt calm.

As if in a dream he watched the spiders coalesce into a vast, chitinous mass. Teeth clambered over each other in its emerging mouth, a continual battle for supremacy. But even as this monstrosity closed in on the motionless Brace, Fortune understood a new truth about it.

Even as it was being spawned *it was losing its magic.*

It was created of charm but it was not itself charmed. The more it grew the further it emerged into this world from whatever world had bred it, and therefore the less true magic it held.

Every spark which flew from it was a loss of power; it shed charm like sweat; with every movement it grew less magical. More real.

And I am real too!

He did not stop to consider his reasoning. Instinct would not withstand analysis, that he knew. But perhaps he had discovered a crucial truth about the power of charm – and its weakness.

If he was right . . .

With a howl of fearful hope he launched himself not at the monster but upwards towards the crumbling ceiling. The giant, blurred spider monster turned towards him with a sluggishness which betrayed its dimness. Fortune tucked his head in at the last possible moment and felt pain blossom across his back as he slammed into the teetering ceiling. A sharp crack told him he had shattered one or more of his spinal plates. No matter. The creature grunted its confusion.

His course took him ricocheting straight into the web

which held Brace but by now the collision had started the whole tunnel collapsing. The web's individual strands of light broke apart and clutched at him, but their strokes were feeble as though some other force were pulling them away. He grabbed Brace with his hind legs and held him close to his body as they fell together towards their monstrous adversary.

'Get out!' he yelled to Gossamer, who had frozen in terror. As he shouted he swept his tail and shattered the insect's face. It broke into pieces and each piece turned instantly into a spidery shard which melted away as it hurtled through the air.

The ceiling transformed itself into a hail of rock as the cliff began to collapse above them. Fortune kicked away from the writhing, headless monster, his wings straining to keep himself and Brace aloft in the confined space, his claws scraping more spiders loose from the monster's slippery hide and to their deaths. Muscles protesting, Brace weighing heavy in his embrace, he dodged his way through the raining boulders towards the light.

Gossamer!

He threw a look behind. She was just visible, scrambling over the remains of the monster, which were now consuming themselves among the strands of the magical web, vanishing from this world in a series of tiny explosions. Dropping the unconscious Brace on the ledge outside he turned and swooped back through the falling debris until he swung around behind her, pummelling her along as the tunnel tumbled around them.

'I can't . . .' she gasped.

'You must!' ordered Fortune. 'Look, we're nearly there!' A curtain of rock fell just behind them and with a last, desperate shove Fortune ejected Gossamer outside, following her barely in time as the whole corridor succumbed to the weight of the mountain and closed its one, blind eye forever.

Dust exploded past them and the ledge shook, threatening to give way. Deep, deafening concussions resounded through the rock as the six neighbouring tunnels slammed shut. They were lifted bodily from the ledge. It seemed as though the entire gorge were breaking apart, but the cliff face held together, and their ledge, sloping dangerously, stayed beneath them.

The cloud of dust billowed out over the gorge, filling the air and darkening the sky, and gradually — so gradually — the shaking began to die away. Fortune scanned the distance below, seeking out . . . there they were!

His heart stopped. The dust obscured all detail but the large shadow looming over a helpless form could only be Brutace, and his friend was motionless, held limp in the air by some invisible magic. Brutace hovered, considering a fitting torment for his prey no doubt — and his body changed shape.

He meant the kill to be spectacular.

But even as his ghostly silhouette opened its jaws wide for its final lunge the dust cloud rippled and Fortune's sensation of being in a dream returned.

A dark shape disturbed the dust. It arrowed down from above in eerie silence and was gone again, swallowed by the depths of the cloud.

In its wake it left salvation.

Brutace's head dropped from his body like a stone. His mighty wings beat the air feebly, once, twice, then faltered and folded, leaving his body, blood showering from its neck, to plummet into the obscurity of the dust.

It all happened without a sound.

As Brutace perished so did his magic, and Cumber fell with Brutace. For an instant Fortune thought his friend had woken when he saw his wings unfurl, but it was only the pressure of the air which had moved them apart. They fluttered uselessly as he too vanished in the dust. Cumber was gone.

Silence still.

They lay on the ledge, waiting for the dust cloud to settle. Gossamer held her unconscious brother and Fortune in turn held her. Tears would not flow.

What had happened? What had killed Brutace?

How can I go on without Cumber?

A grey shadow startled Fortune as it crossed at the limit of his vision. He glanced about. Nothing.

And then he heard a voice.

'Bloody heavy . . . for a skinny runt,' the voice, incredibly, was saying, its words punctuated by grunts and pants. 'Warned you . . . didn't I? Should've gone . . . back home. Covamere . . . indeed!'

There, through a veil of parting dust, rose Scoff. Cumber was held firmly in his grip as his rainbow wings beat the air with determined thrusts.

Cumber woke then and looked up bewildered as Scoff placed him with unexpected delicacy on the ledge beside Fortune before alighting himself and folding away his colourful wings.

'This is the east wall,' said Scoff. 'I said keep to the west wall. Youngsters! Pah! Never listen. I suppose I'll have to show you the way myself.'

He wrinkled his nose uncomfortably.

'What is it about you,' he began, 'that always makes me want to . . . aat-shooo!?'

Dust and fear fled from Scoff's titanic sneeze. It woke Brace. He and his sister looked on in amazement as Fortune and Cumber exchanged a look and began laughing in great, bellowing waves. The ledge shook again, but this time with love and relief.

They had survived and in strength they had grown – and also in number.

For now they were five.

CHAPTER 12

The Message

The bones of the Plated Mountain groaned in protest as a new mood twisted their ancient marrow. As it had done so long before the Plated Mountain was beginning to move.

Cocooned within the mountain, Mantle moved too.

Of all the Injured Mountains only this one, the greatest of them all, moved still. Sudden tremors shook old wounds even though the land was tired and nearly spent of its fire. Cracks gaped and closed again.

As the shock wave left the Plated Mountain and travelled outwards into the world, Mantle worked his charm.

At last he had a messenger.

For such an earthquake he had waited long and now he harnessed to it his message. Outwards the waves of energy spread and northwards. In its path the land trembled. Lakes dampened the vibrations, down gullies they accelerated, Mantle's will directing them north, ever north.

His seismic messenger reached the southernmost tip of the Low Mountains and plunged underground, deep rock shaking in its path. Narrow the shock wave was now and focused, its target the gorge, the canyon.

The Cross.

The deep rock parted in welcome then deflected until Mantle's messenger-earthquake struck the dragons of Aether's Cross.

The day following their escape was a day of tranquillity. Numb with shock, the five dragons had struggled across to the west cliff and collapsed there among the abandoned nests. The dust from the collapsed tunnels had gradually settled into the depths of the canyon where it was snatched away by the river. A great peace descended in its place. The dragons slept long and woke late and first to wake were Fortune and Gossamer. They stole away together into the late morning light, Gossamer leading her new companion to her favourite place – her hole-watching perch.

They sat there together gazing across the ravine at the scarred and broken east wall where once the tunnels had been. They shivered, for it was cold. Far below in the clean, clear air the river was just visible, the constant spray disturbed and thinned by a sudden north wind. Strangely, its waters looked brown and sluggish.

'I think it's covered with leaves!' exclaimed Gossamer as they craned their necks downwards in an effort to make out what had turned the waters to mud. 'Autumn leaves!'

'But summer's not over,' whispered Fortune.

The two dragons exchanged a glance and shivered again, this time not just with the cold. The wind blew past them and in it they felt the promise of ice and snow and a long, long winter.

'Gossamer,' blurted Fortune, 'I think I love you!'

She did not reply but simply rose without a word, nuzzling softly at his neck as she did so. He smiled at her and leaned forward, then started back in surprise as she took to the air, the draught from her wings forcing the cold morning air into his upturned face.

High she flew, lifting herself up towards the slit of sky which capped the gorge of the Cross, the subtle colours of her wings glowing against the pale grey rock as she described a strange and seductive path through the sky. She hovered, then swooped, air buzzing as she swept low over Fortune's head.

He snatched playfully at her then launched himself outwards in pursuit. She filled his vision as they danced between the two opposing cliff walls and up towards the sky again.

Her tail brushed his face and a bank of wispy cloud rolled into view, drifting lazily down into the ravine from the sky above. Fortune lunged at her but she was gone. Puzzled, he flew on – until she broke free of the concealing cloud and butted his chest with her head, swerving away and vanishing again behind him. Fortune laughed dizzily, inspired by her command of the air, heated by her beauty.

Now she was a distant mote, dark red against the pale cliff. Vapour streamed from her wingtips as she dived in the thin air then looped close over Fortune's head. Laughing out loud he finally took her lead and tipped on to his back to follow her in her dive towards the leaf-bound river. They accelerated downwards, pulling out and speeding together a claw's width above the brown water then gained altitude again, their wings brushing, darting and weaving in perfect unison, each one's move the other's reply, every turn a harmony, every wingbeat a duet.

Closer still they flew and faster. Fortune's head grew light. He was no longer aware of the cliffs around him, nor even of the air which held them. He was aware only of Gossamer, of her lithe, ochre body flashing in and out of sight, of the perfect wind as she darted by, of the smell of her. Closer yet they flew until at last he embraced her and held them both. His heart pounded but his body suddenly had the strength of ten, a thousand. It seemed that with his wings he might lift the world itself and that his dearest Gossamer was but a breath in comparison.

Into the swelling cloud he pulled them both and as the world grew brilliant white he cried out for the very joy of living, that he had survived the ordeals of Aether's Cross and that his new love was with him. His bellow filled the skies as they disappeared from the view of earthbound creatures and into a private realm of their own.

One dragon watched them vanish.

Devoted to his sister, Brace watched stone-faced with jealousy as Gossamer shared the heavens with this interloper, this Fortune. He closed his eyes to await their return, but he did not sleep.

By the time the young lovers returned to the west cliff their companions were awake and deep in debate. At least, Scoff and Cumber were deep in debate – Brace was sulking some way off, picking through the ruins of the nests as though searching for something. They landed somewhat sheepishly

157

next to their Charmed companions. Scoff greeted them with a quick nod.

'Nice couple,' he commented.

Cumber simply grunted; to Fortune he looked distracted, even irritable, but for what reason he could not judge.

'Cumber?' he began, only to be interrupted by Scoff.

'Found something interesting,' the charmed dragon announced, flexing his colourful wings. 'Caves might not be destroyed.'

Fortune gestured across the canyon to the opposite cliff. 'But . . . it all collapsed!'

'Might be intact,' repeated Scoff. 'Might be, mind you. Can't be certain.'

'But how?' asked Fortune.

'Charm,' replied Cumber with uncharacteristic brevity. Fortune wondered if something of Scoff's terseness was rubbing off on his friend.

'Look,' he said, exasperated, 'if there's something we can do to help those dragons you've got to tell us.'

This time it was Brace who interrupted him, bounding over to where they stood. It was quite obvious that he had been listening all along.

'If there is,' he demanded, striking an aggressive pose upon a chunk of rock, 'then we've got to do something about it! And we've got to do it now, while we've got the advantage over these Charmed monsters!'

Scoff and Cumber both turned their heads slightly towards the young Natural and glared at him. Brace stepped back a couple of paces but maintained his bravado nonetheless.

'I'll forget I heard that!' intoned Cumber. Fortune frowned: there was definitely something wrong with his friend. The fight with Brutace, he decided, but he was not convinced that was the whole story.

Throughout this debate Gossamer had listened without comment but now she spoke.

'Scoff, Cumber,' she said softly, 'just tell us what you've found. Then we can discuss whether or not there's anything we can do about it.'

Cumber seemed to respond a little to this, releasing a great sigh and explaining, 'We've probed into the mountainside and there's still charm in there – a lot of charm. It's possible there's enough charm locked around the prison cells to have protected them from the collapse of the cliff.'

'But won't they all starve, or suffocate?' questioned Gossamer.

'Maybe not.' Scoff took up the story. 'Charm may create a stasis. Or may not. Hard to say.'

'*Hard to say!*' exclaimed Brace. 'Then do something. Find out! Can we save them or can't we?'

Neither of the charmed dragons responded to this.

'Surely we can afford to spend a few more days here?' suggested Fortune. He could not understand Cumber's melancholy mood. His friend, normally so garrulous, had become a silent, sullen ghost of his former self.

What has happened to him?

As if to confirm Fortune's fears Cumber chose that moment to lose his temper.

'We don't have *days*, Fortune, and well you know it! We have to go. We have to get to Covamere, as we always planned. Nothing has changed that!'

'I know, but . . .'

'But nothing! We go!'

Now Fortune was growing angry, for he found himself back in the same argument in which he and Cumber had been embroiled when Brutace and his dragons had first pounced upon them days before. Had they come through so much only to go round in circles again?

And what of the poor Naturals – surely hundreds of them – trapped inside the rock of the east cliff? What of them? If there was any possibility that they were still alive then surely some kind of rescue attempt had to be mounted.

But only charm can get them out now. And that means Scoff and Cumber.

Cumber.

He thought of his friend, and of what they had been through so far together, and of what unknowable future events they must surely be destined to share, and he began to wonder if Cumber might not be right.

Maybe there isn't the time.

South Point destroyed, Aether's Cross ravaged.

The Black Dragon!

The world, turning.

He looked around at his companions, for it seemed that they had reached an impasse.

Cumber, his expression blank and cold – incomprehensible.

Scoff, inscrutable, shrewd, and clearly in agreement with Cumber. But could he be swayed?

Brace. His jealousy of Fortune was plain to see, but so was his depth of feeling for his kin. He would surely do anything to see these wretched dragons freed from their prison of stone.

And Gossamer, his own, dear Gossamer, who had entered his life so swiftly, so completely, with whom he had crossed the void into adulthood in the single blink of an eye. What did she really want?

And they all seemed to be looking at him for an answer.

Go or stay?

'I . . .' he began.

And then Mantle's message came crashing into their midst.

The ledge beneath them trembled for the last time and a hard, metallic groan issued from the very bowels of the mountain. With blinding speed a vast array of cracks fled the cavern entrances and sprayed themselves up the cliff face opposite. High above, sheets of rock peeled away and turned end over end as they fell in a deadly aerial dance.

The land writhed.

The dragons leaped to the air as one and the sky shrank as it became filled with broken rock and falling debris.

What's happening? Where can we go?

The cliffs began to close about them.

Slowly at first, seductively, then fast, the slot by which Fortune and Cumber had entered the wide gorge from the north of Aether's Cross shut tight. So Fortune had his direction: he turned south and the others fled with him. Behind them the cliffs continued to fall and the walls of the Cross itself began to grind together; they were clamping shut in the dragons' wake like the jaws of the land.

It was no longer possible to distinguish between the mountain and the sky; whether rock filled the air or they flew through air-filled rock Fortune could not tell. *Is something guiding us?* The thought flashed through his mind but he had no time to consider it. The southern exit from the Cross loomed ten tree-lengths away, five . . .

The narrow gash of the exit claimed them with scant breaths to spare. The gorge finally closed, punching a great blast of air which sent them crashing and rolling through their cramped refuge. There was a *slam*.

Aether's Cross was gone.

It was gone!

'Well!' shouted Scoff over the colossal noise. 'That settles it. We couldn't get them out now even if we wanted to!'

'South, then,' murmured Fortune.

'We have no choice,' whispered Gossamer, flying close enough by his side for him to hear her every breath, and she was right: the decision was made.

Slowly they recovered, flying on all the time, desperate to be free of the confining tunnel of rock which led them ever away from the closed wound which had once been the Cross. The silence which held them was broken only once more in that long, sullen flight out of the mountains, and that was by Brace.

'They're alive,' he called suddenly, then added more quietly. 'You'll all be free again. Someday I'll return, I swear.'

They flew south towards the winter.

Towards Covamere.

Around Mantle the Plated Mountain was still again, its power spent for now. He had sent his message and now they were coming.

Mantle closed his eyes and contemplated what lay beneath his chamber.

PART 3

INTO THE MOUNTAIN

CHAPTER 13

The Black Dragon

A single peak stood proud and high among the Injured Mountains.

It was in these very mountains that the trolls had been born, erupting from the primal fire which had torn the land in the most ancient times. The flat plains of the southern Heartland had trembled then shattered as raw charm had burst through from deep underground, searing the air and lifting a new mountain range into the world. Again and again these mountains had spewed forth their fire; with each new eruption more rock had hardened across their ever-rising peaks.

And with each new eruption a troll had been born.

Black they were, like the rock which spawned them, slow of thought yet mighty of deed ... and charmed. Like the liquid stone which crawled through their veins they crawled out across the land, carving it into shapes which suited their purpose: to travel. For the trolls were restless wayfarers, and over the course of an aeon they spread from their birthplace until the whole world was their domain. Until there was nowhere left for them to go.

Then it was that they returned to the mountains which had given them life, powerless to resist the inscrutable instinct which drew them together again ... and pitched them against each other in a series of titanic battles. During those long and dreadful days they unleashed fire charm the like of which the world had never seen, breaking the mountains and so giving them the name by which they would be remembered: the Injured Mountains.

Those few trolls who survived retreated into the north and were seen no more. Of the mountain peaks one alone remained to pierce the sky. Isolated it stood, the one, barren alp from which no troll had ever been spawned. The lava it had once thrown out had long since solidified into towers and spires and coated its slopes with frozen rivers of rock, rivers which over the years grew flat and ragged until they resembled scales laid across a dragon's back. Plated it was and hence its name – the Plated Mountain.

Then dragons came.

The passing of the trolls a mere legend for their story-tellers, the charmed dragons arrived, attracted to the mountain for many reasons: the wealth of tunnels and caverns which lay beneath it, the lushness of the evergreen forest which girdled its conical form . . . and more. Here it was that they built Covamere.

A huge puzzle of caverns and chambers, open areas and roofed passages, Covamere swiftly became the capital of the growing dragon world. A complex government established itself – the Great Council – whose envoys kept dragons in touch the world over, whose laws and tenets kept the peace for many, many years.

Most of the members of the Great Council claimed to have been among the first dragons in the world. Their enormous age and wisdom could not be doubted but only one of their number was truly believed to be so ancient: Halcyon, Leader of the Great Council. Ever respected, always obeyed, Halcyon was guardian of the hidden knowledge which his position had brought him. He alone knew the secret of what lay below the Plated Mountain, he alone knew the truth behind the turning of the world.

And now that the time of the Turning was near he retreated into his caves in order to work the charm he knew he must. His retreat was necessary, vital to achieve the total concentration needed, but it left him – for the first time in his long and magnificent rule – vulnerable to attack.

And a dragon came with the power to exploit his weakness. The Black Dragon.

Halcyon owed his position as Leader to one thing: he was the first charmed dragon to survive the challenge of the Maze of Covamere. The Maze lay beneath the Plated Mountain and because of it Covamere was the spiritual as well as

166

the administrative centre of the dragon world. Few dragons knew what actually lay beyond the threshold of the Maze, but all dragons had their own ideas . . .

There, the Realm meets our world . . .
There, our world meets all worlds . . .
There, within the Maze, is the power of the stars . . .

Halcyon would not speak of what he had witnessed in the mysterious depths of the Maze and so its secrets were kept, but for many young dragons curiosity – and ambition – proved too much, and they dared to challenge their venerable Leader. Such challenges were accepted with due respect, for the constitution of Covamere stated that any dragon had the right to attempt to unseat Halcyon. Indeed, a strictly regulated academy had been established which schooled and prepared such dragons for their one, formal attempt at the challenge of the Maze.

Each graduate was invited to enter the Maze and only if that dragon – as Halcyon himself had done ages past – emerged again unscarred would he or she be accepted as Leader of the Great Council. By Halcyon's own pledge, such a dragon would be worthy of the title Leader, and Halcyon would step down.

And though many, many dragons had tried, in all those years no charmed dragon had ever succeeded. The challenges had failed, every one. And in the Maze of Covamere, failure meant death.

Except once. Dragons spoke for many years about the day when not one but two dragons had returned from the Maze. But the circumstances were so unusual, so bizarre, that neither of the emerging dragons could possibly be accepted as Leader.

The first had emerged to be held in the deepest respect, although he could never lead; the second had emerged into shame and ridicule. Neither of the two dragons had remained in Covamere and so Halcyon reigned on.

And even that great tale soon became lost, buried in the many great tales of Halcyon's glorious history. Lost and buried beneath the Plated Mountain.

A mote of black moved in the dawning sky above the Plated Mountain. High over the northern slopes this mote, this dragon flew. The rays of the rising sun struck the dragon's wings and were trapped beneath their skin, heating the flesh until heat became fire and fire became charm. The charm filled his body with a glow all its own, a black light which scintillated at the limits of vision and seemed to make this dragon a creature lit not in this world, not by this sun but by some other, internal flame. A dragon black to many eyes yet rich with a deeper, darker light.

This mote: the Black Dragon. Wraith. Called by his legions 'The Master'.

Since conquering Covamere Wraith had taken many such solitary flights over the Plated Mountain. It was familiar to him, for here he had flown as a young dragon a hundred or more years before, and now that he had returned to the flying grounds of his distant youth he felt the strengthening of old ambitions, old desires. Old memories.

Then his colour had not been black. As a lean, tawny youth he had soared high above his peers in the academy of the Maze of Covamere, and of all the candidates of his generation it was Wraith, they said, who had the strength and the wit to conquer the Maze. Even Halcyon seemed to recognize his potential, wishing him fortune as he passed through into the hidden spaces beneath the Plated Mountain. Wraith entered . . . and emerged! But not into glory.

For Wraith was the second of the two dragons who had emerged that fateful day – and he had been rescued by the first. Even now, as he stroked the air above that same mountain, he recalled with vivid pain the horror of his failure inside the Maze and the awful, numbing humiliation of his rescue by the dragon who had followed him in. That dragon's name he never learned, for Wraith had fled Covamere the same night while his saviour had been exalted by the very dragons who had once supported Wraith in his quest.

But though Wraith did not know his rescuer's name, that dragon he would never forget. His face, the set of his wings and particularly his scent would be always in his memory.

When the Maze had finally gripped Wraith and started to tear him apart, when a dragon had appeared from the void and dragged him clear, in the sudden reversal of his fortune, one thing had focused Wraith's mind. It was his saviour's uniqueness in the midst of the agony of the Maze – the same uniqueness which meant that even though he survived the challenge of the Maze he could never become Leader of the Charmed.

For he had been a Natural.

Much had changed in the world since then and it seemed to Wraith, now that he had returned to Covamere, that the flow of time itself had stretched, that those hundred years had become a thousand or even a million. Charm had begun to fail and now the ring of forest around the mountain was full of natural dragons.

The world was changing, and Wraith had changed. During those years he had radically altered his appearance. His wings grew dark with the infinite colours he layered into them, deep red joining his original tawny colour, then gold and moon blue and evergreen and the orange of the deepest fire . . . year after year, each new camouflage was absorbed into the one before. Until at last he held all possible colours inside him and their total was dazzling, priceless black.

Only one thing had not changed. Wraith's exile had been long and bitter and the memories of his failure had rooted deep: his single ambition had grown relentlessly. His task here was unchanged, although now his motivation was so much greater, his determination quite unshakeable. No dragon but he remembered that young, tawny exile, so old was the tale in these later times. He knew that this time he would conquer the Maze. This time he could take up the challenge on his own terms.

He flew high and fast through the mountain dawn, his eyes drinking in the subtle snow of the peak, his stranger senses probing at the deep patterns of magic which lay under the land. Probing at the Maze.

Behind his speeding shadow lay Covamere – only now Covamere was his. In exile he had assembled a mobile army, recruiting over many years and from many lands. With the help of his lieutenant Insiss he had sharpened the army's claws until he had surrounded himself with a mighty engine of destruction, so loyal that it was virtually an extension of his own body. That the loyalty was born of fear of their commander was of no concern to Wraith. His lust for power

169

drove the fear, and that fear reciprocated and forced him to prove himself ever more powerful. Then, when word reached him that Halcyon had retreated into the Plated Mountain he knew the time had come to unleash his power.

The attack on Covamere had been devastating. Wraith's legions had crushed completely Halcyon's pitifully neglected defences. It had been rumoured the Black Dragon was poised to take on the Maze itself and most of the survivors from Halcyon's routed army had swiftly changed allegiance and pledged their loyalty to the Black Dragon. Those few who rebelled against the invader, though they banded together and dared to call themselves Wraith's Hardship, were judged by Wraith to be wholly without power or influence. He dismissed them from his mind, tolerating their existence though others advised against it.

Having captured Covamere Wraith had felt compelled to build his army back up to strength, for despite his over-whelming success a number of his warriors had died in the caves beneath Covamere. In addition, the settlement itself needed considerable rebuilding after the battle, and Wraith was determined that his Covamere would be a citadel beyond compare. Several moons had passed while the reconstruction proceeded, and during that time Wraith had conducted recruiting campaigns in settlements across the Heartland — among them Aether's Cross — while he con-sidered the timing of his final assault against Halcyon him-self. Now the time was right . . . now it felt right. Before the moon grew full again.

Before the world turns.

But he had returned from Aether's Cross to find that Wraith's Hardship had grown. Now they were no longer few — now they numbered in the hundreds!

'They speak of possibilities, my lord,' Insiss explained to him after a night's spying on one of their rallies. 'In your absence they have been asking questions. They ask if Wraith's way is the only way. They ask if violence is the only way. They even ask if charm is the only way. They should be crushed, my lord.'

'Charm?' mused Wraith, intrigued. 'They speak to natural dragons?'

'I think not, my lord. But they wonder. And their influence is spreading through the army. You cannot tolerate them. They must be destroyed.'

'I do not kill, Insiss. I prevail.'

Naturals!

Sunlight struck Wraith's body as the mountain lightened below. He gazed deeper at the lines of force hidden in the land and sensed their convergence, and his convergence with them. Events and histories were drawing to a point and that point was here beneath the Plated Mountain, and his history was drawing here too. This time he would prevail.

This time Wraith would be the one to emerge triumphant.

But as he probed so he scented, and it seemed to him that something was travelling here on the air, some smell he had once fled. *The Natural!* he thought with familiar venom. The scent was thin and fleeting but it seemed that he recognized it nonetheless. Then it filtered away, leaving Wraith wondering if he had simply imagined it as he had so often in the past. No matter — if he were destined to confront the Natural again along with old, feeble Halcyon then so much the better. It would be so much more . . . symmetrical.

The moment passed and he returned his attention to the mountain itself, for something was happening here and now which prompted him to tuck his thoughts of revenge away to wait for another day.

The land cracked.

The movement was in many ways slight — and certainly unexpected, for earthquakes were rare here these days. The northern slope shook, just once, cracking the ice on its upper reaches into a random patchwork of lines and angles. A single, enormous crack sprinted down from the summit and vanished into the forest; it did not reappear at the opposite side.

The movement stopped but the sound came close behind. The concussion crashed in Wraith's ears and only gradually died to a distant rumble, fleeing north. Wraith tracked its passage with unnaturally acute ears, squinting far into the distance as he followed it into far-off silence. He was curious, for it seemed to him this was not simply an earthquake, nor even merely a flexing of one of the Maze's inscrutable muscles.

Something about the receding tremor, about its taste, made Wraith believe that the earthquake was being directed on its journey north. Directed by a dragon.

Halcyon?

It was an obvious thought but Wraith dismissed it. The magic did not taste right. Some other dragon?

Then he recognized the taste.

Mantle! Is he still alive?

Excellent, another foe of old to be dealt with at last. The Keeper of the Maze himself!

It was largely thanks to Mantle that the Plated Mountain, though it stood above the Maze of Covamere, had never let loose any of the fire beneath it, although tiny leaks from the Maze's vast reservoir of charm did occur from time to time, restricted to the broad belt of forest which encircled the mountain. Here, occasionally, the Maze breached the surface and manifested its powers in the outside world. Only in the forest did it expose its tentative claws for only here, in the constant shadow of the enormous pine canopy, could it rely on the seclusion it need for its unfathomable experiments.

Great tracts of the forest were filled with magic and unexplored by dragons; tales of those dragons who had strayed into the forbidden zones were lurid and horrifying. Dragons spoke in quavering voices of manifestations both beautiful and terrible: winged creatures robed in liquid metal floating through the trees and dissolving back into the ground; spaces where the air seemed compressed and busy with motion as though it had taken on a life of its own; black spears firing up through the soil and snapping at the trees, releasing red blood from the severed trunks.

Wraith had never seen such things but now, as the earthquake died away, he knew he had seen something.

Maintaining his height but focusing in with his gaze, Wraith watched breathless as a new clearing opened up among the trees. Tremendous cracking and splintering sounds filtered up through the clear sky as some force was pressed from the ground, turning mature pines instantly to dust. A cloud grew above the widening arena, obscuring the view.

Putting caution aside, Wraith flew lower.

172

He entered the cloud as the splintering sound reached its climax. For a short time all around him tasted of broken wood but presently he burst through into clear air again to find himself flying low into a huge new clearing which had been carved from the forest. The ground still trembled here but his charmed senses told him that the Maze had subsided again, leaving the remains of its experiment here on the surface for him to see.

It was an isolated place. Cliffs rose high all around, closing in on the forest and making it inaccessible other than from the air. Like a prison. Beyond the southernmost cliff the Plated Mountain towered but Wraith was more interested in the vast, oval swathe which had been cut from the forest.

The trees which had once stood here had not just been felled, they had been decimated. The land was stripped bare; only a fine, powdery soil covered the site all the way up to its sharply-defined perimeter.

More interesting was what the Maze had put here in place of the trees.

In the middle of the clearing were hundreds of blue, flickering globes, each about twice the size of an average dragon, each floating a little above the ground and anchored by a thin, fiery tendril. Wraith made swift calculations and reckoned there to be four hundred of them. They flashed and sparked, ribbons of energy leaping between them and racing across the group with the speed of lightning. They were hot. They were made from pure charm.

Wraith wandered up to the nearest of them, confident of his dominion here now that the Maze had retreated, and peered into it.

Spheres of charm, he pondered. *Ancient charm, the oldest I have encountered. Now, how might they be of use to the Black Dragon?*

As he walked among the glowing spheres it seemed that here might be an answer to his most pressing problem. He smiled, then spread his great, black wings and soared off into the brightening sky, a new and splendid plan building itself inside his head.

Wraith's Hardship will be defeated. Soon no dragon will dare to swear allegiance to that sad and misguided cult, for they will see the consequences of such disloyalty.

The Black Dragon flew back to Covamere with the means to deal with the rebels. Now nothing would prevent him defeating Halcyon and, after so many years, the Maze. Behind him the globes of charm flickered, abandoned by the Maze which had created them but with the power still to be harnessed by a dragon with the vision so to do.

CHAPTER 14

Realmshock

For as far as he could see there stretched nothing but black, porous rock. It dipped and surged as its jagged contours led it away towards the distant mountain that dominated the horizon – the Plated Mountain! – barren but for the spare groves of large-leaved plants which clung to the more sheltered slopes. At the base of the mountain Fortune could make out what appeared to be a huge band of forest but the promise of even that did little to raise his spirits. All about him was dead, black desert and ahead was surely danger.

They had flown hard out of the Low Mountains, punishing their wings relentlessly for fear the whole gorge and not just the wide place which had once been the Cross might close upon them. Even when they emerged on to the wide southern plains of the Heartland they kept their speed up: the landscape below was featureless and drab and there was nothing else for them to do but fly.

The first three days of the journey followed much the same tedious pattern of hard flight during the day and deep and exhausted sleep at night. Camps were makeshift and uncomfortable but there were no complaints; they were so tired. Food was scarce and gathered largely by Scoff, who seemed to have a knack for seeking out well-stocked burrows or rivers full of fish. He also cooked for the others – except Brace who insisted on taking his food raw – since Cumber showed little interest in eating other than for nutrition's sake, and even then made little enough effort.

The party soon split into three groups: Fortune and Gossamer had become distinctly a couple; Scoff and Cumber as fellow Charmed; and Brace, the odd one. It was in these divisions that they flew and ate and slept and only Fortune and Gossamer seemed to be communicating. Scoff and Cumber, while keeping close, said little to each other and Brace, in self-imposed isolation, had scarcely a word to say to any of his companions.

On the morning of the fourth day the ill-humour and mounting tension which underlay the first part of the journey was finally released in an inevitable explosion.

They had spent the night camped on the shores of a great inland sea which Scoff — with characteristic brevity — announced as being named Heldwater.

'Old water,' he had proclaimed to nobody in particular. 'Good night.'

The one positive thing which Heldwater did for the dragons that evening was to offer them fresh colour, for most of the vegetation they had seen on their journey this far had been dying. There had been no green. Autumn colours abounded everywhere, despite the fact that it was surely still late summer. So it was with lighter hearts that the dragons had landed here among the green foliage of the lakeside woodland. Great, gnarled oaks reached out to dwarf the shy willows which leaned over the water's edge as if trying to embrace their own crystalline reflections. Even the soil smelled fragrant. It was a beautiful, warming place.

Until morning.

Brace it was who woke first into the new, damp light. He looked bleary-eyed around the camp and stumbled most of the way to the water before he fully took in what had happened to his surroundings. For as he bent down to drink he realized that his claws were completely covered by leaves. Dead, brown leaves.

He snapped his head up, quite awake now, to observe the scene.

Every tree had lost its leaves. Bare-branched they stood except for a few hardy conifers away in the distance, and all about their roots the leaves were piled, dead and brown. Brace moved his claws and they did not rustle, so damp were they. There was no glory of autumn red or yellow in them — they were just brown. Dead and brown.

The sight struck Brace as sad, pitiful, so that it was as

much as he could do not to burst into tears where he stood. Everything about the journey so far had been this way — mournful, over a dead landscape. It was as though some evil, spiralling down-draught were dragging them all down into some dreadful abyss. He sniffled, and might yet have wept had he not heard someone moving towards him through the blanket of fallen leaves. Swiftly composing himself he turned to find his sister there and his face set hard.

'Oh, Brace!' exclaimed Gossamer as she waded towards him. 'What is happening to the world?'

Brace softened his expression a little when he saw the depth of Gossamer's distress but still could not bring himself to reach out to her. Instead they stood awkwardly at an uncomfortable distance, staring at the ground and shivering in the damp air.

'Charm's to blame!' he blurted suddenly. 'You'll see.'

Gossamer sighed and moved past him to drink delicately from the gently lapping water. He watched as she did so, and nearly reached out a wing to embrace her, but she stood back from the water again before he could do so and the moment passed. Gossamer turned back to face him, her gaze intense and appraising; he squirmed beneath it.

'I know you don't like Fortune, Brace,' she said softly. 'But that's only because you won't let yourself get to know him.'

'Don't be stupid,' Brace retorted. 'I've got nothing against him.'

'He saved your life,' Gossamer reminded him. 'And mine.'

But I should have saved your life, Brace thought desperately, trapped inside his own perverse logic. *Not him. I should be the one to protect you!*

'I suppose so,' he grated, obviously uncomfortable with the admission. 'But I don't have to like him.'

'And the others . . .'

'They're Charmed!' he snapped before she could finish. 'And that's an end to it. You know what they did to us!'

'Not these dragons,' whispered Gossamer sadly, for she could see no way to get through to her brother. 'Come on, eat with us this morning at least.'

'I'll be all right here for a while,' he replied, turning his back on her and staring out across the misty water. She touched him gently on the flank and moved away back to where Fortune was stirring, her worry for her brother compounded by the devastation around her, the endless expanse of dead, damp leaves which had fallen all in a single night.

Charm at work, she thought with a shiver. *Winter's coming, coming fast. But why?*

But that she could not answer, so instead she shuffled back through the mounds of leaves to where her lover was waking, while about her the stripped trees raised their empty branches to the sky as if echoing her question.

Fortune nuzzled her as she reached his side.

'Like the leaves in the river,' he commented sadly, pointing at the devastation. Gossamer nodded her reply. 'I was thinking,' he went on. 'Would you have come with me if you'd had a choice?'

Gossamer looked down at him in surprise and he smiled bashfully.

'Well,' she replied, 'that's a very direct question for so early in the morning.'

'Well, would you?'

Gossamer tipped her head to a coy angle and narrowed her eyes. Slowly and deliberately she ran her gaze along the length of Fortune's body from his own eyes along his flanks and folded wings to the flattened tip of his long, coiled tail, then brought them on a return journey back to reach his face again. Throughout the examination Fortune's discomfort rose until by the time she was looking into his eyes again it was all he could do not to leap up or take to the air — anything to be rid of that awful, wonderful scrutiny.

'Hmm,' pondered Gossamer, enjoying the power she was wielding. 'I'll have to think about it.'

'You . . . !' exclaimed Fortune. He threw his wings about her body, rolling them both over and over through the blanket of leaves until they came to a breathless halt just short of the lakeside. In the distance Brace turned his back in disgust and wandered off into the trees in search of breakfast.

There they lay, panting and giggling, whispering nonsense.

'Sorry to break in,' came Scoff's familiar rumble from behind them. 'Need to talk.'

The two young Naturals clumsily untangled themselves from each other, fully aware of Scoff's discreet inspection of the distant landscape and also of the wry smile on his wrinkled face.

'Autumn's come,' Scoff observed as they finished brushing themselves clean of the damp and clinging leaves. 'Winter next. Soon. Need to talk.'

'So you said,' acknowledged Fortune. 'What did you want to talk about?'

'I think it's high time we all talked,' put in Gossamer.

Scoff nodded his head in agreement.

'We three are all right,' he said. 'Your brother, though . . .' he added, nodding towards the trees where Brace could be seen rummaging through the litter of leaves. 'Still very angry. And Cumber . . .'

'What about Cumber?' asked Fortune at once. His fears about Cumber's well-being had not eased at all during the course of the journey so far, indeed they had grown worse. His friend, having been affected in some way Fortune could not understand by the events at Aether's Cross, had become slowly more and more introverted so that now he spoke not at all, not even to Scoff, who had remained at his side almost constantly for the last three days. His expression remained blank, his eyes dull; none of the vivacity which had previously characterized him was in evidence.

It's as though autumn has come to poor Cumber too, thought Fortune gloomily. *If only there were something I could do for him.*

'Tried to help Cumber,' continued Scoff, his voice breaking back into Fortune's thoughts with a jolt. 'Couldn't. Maybe you could.'

'But what's wrong with him?' blurted Fortune, and as he said it an explosion went off in his head.

Oh no! Oh, please, no, don't let it be that!

'He's not . . . please don't tell me he's . . . ?'

Luckily Scoff was perceptive enough to see where Fortune's thoughts were leading him.

'The madness?' he responded. 'No. Not as bad as that. But bad enough, in its own way.'

'What then?' Gossamer pleaded, as anxious in her own way as Fortune, for during her short acquaintance with Cumber she had grown to like and respect the young Charmed immensely, even though she had hardly seen him at his best. 'What's wrong with him?'

Scoff sighed heavily and squatted down, inviting his companions to do the same.

'Simple really,' he began. 'This is something all charmed dragons experience. I did; we all do. We call it Realmshock.'

'The Realm!' whispered Gossamer.

'Is this the Realm Cumber talked about?' demanded Fortune. 'Because if it is then I want to know exactly what it is. Please, Scoff, if we're going to help Cumber then you have to share some of your secrets with us.'

And so Scoff told Fortune and Gossamer about the Realm, about the world beyond this world where fire charm was forged. He told them about his own experiences of the fire, of its powers of good as well as evil, and of the way it was alive. And he told of Realmshock.

'Hit me hard,' he said, his eyes misty with memory. 'Took many days to come to terms with it. Like Cumber. Frightening, you see — the power, the responsibility for the power. Could destroy the world if misused.'

'No exaggeration?' quavered Gossamer, knowing the answer. Scoff shook his head silently.

'You begin to understand,' he commented drily. 'Most dragons get through Realmshock. A few don't: they go mad. Cumber will be all right, but will be better with your help. He needs you, Fortune. More than me, I think.'

Fortune smiled sadly and felt Gossamer's wingtip brushing against his face; with surprise he found there were tears on his cheek.

'Go to your friend,' she whispered, pointing to the distant break in the trees where Scoff and Cumber had spent the night. The young Charmed lay there still, curled up against the cold, his gold scales decked with dew and glistening in the damp air.

Fortune shivered, for although the early sun was beginning to burn its way through the thin mist still he felt chilled. Shaking the last of the leaves from his wings he walked off up the gentle slope to where Cumber lay not asleep, as

Fortune discovered, but awake and watching his friend's approach with dull, disinterested eyes. Unsure of what to say, Fortune loitered there for a moment, watching his breath clouding about him. Finally he summoned the courage to speak.

'We were worried about you,' he offered lamely.

'No need to be,' came Cumber's brisk reply. The charmed dragon promptly closed his eyes. Fortune glanced back down the slope towards the lakeside where the others were waiting and watching. Brace, he saw, had emerged from the woods and was stood a little to the side of the other two, looking first across towards Gossamer and then up the hill to where he himself stood before Cumber.

What can I say to him? he thought desperately.

'I understand what you've gone through,' he began, only to be cut off by his charmed companion's sudden cry.

'Understand?!' shouted Cumber, rising to his feet in a fast, fluid move. The suddenness of the motion scattered leaves to every side and Fortune took a couple of steps back as Cumber marched angrily towards him, droplets of dew cascading from the scales of his back and hissing as they left his body. Blue trails of charm snaked over his flanks, vaporizing the water. His eyes were wide and mad.

He's insane! thought Fortune, horrified. *Just like all the others. The madness has taken him! Scoff was wrong!*

'Understand?!' repeated Cumber, his voice like thunder. 'How can you possibly understand, Natural?! How can you understand what I've seen, what I've experienced? Do you understand what the fire is? Do you understand this?!'

Fortune leaped to the side as Cumber spread his jaws wide and exhaled into the ground. At the limits of his hearing it seemed that there was a tremendous ripping sound, as though a flap of skin had been torn from some giant creature of doom. Then the ground trembled and lightning raced through the soil. Fire vaulted up in front of him . . .

He was about to take to the air when he heard Scoff's cry, 'Stand your ground! All of you – don't move!'

Terrified, yet fascinated too, Fortune forced himself to remain where he was.

Cumber did not move either. He was standing with his legs planted firm and wide and his neck angled low so that the fire which streamed from his mouth was directed into the ground, where it seemed to vanish. But all around it was breaking free again. Plumes and jets of blue fire charm burst from the soil in every direction right down to the water's edge and away deep into the woods, and wherever it appeared it turned the fallen leaves to cinders. Only where the dragons stood did the ground remain cold; everywhere else it boiled.

The Naturals looked on astonished; Scoff's face was grim. There Cumber stood, his expression now one of agony as he poured unimaginable energies into this massive release of charm. The mist thickened as the dew boiled away from the leaves and then it became smoke as the leaves themselves charred. Soon the damp blanket had become a thin, black skin which even now began to fragment and scatter before a growing breeze from the north.

Presently the fire grew thin in Cumber's throat and his legs began to tremble. Then, without further warning, they buckled altogether, the flames subsided and he tumbled on to his side, rolling a tree's length or more down the slope until he crashed against an old oak stump. There he lay inert as his friends rushed over to tend to him, their flailing wings beating down the coarse veil of ash and mist which was begining to move with the cold wind.

Brace watched through the clearing air, still at a distance. still unable to participate in the group. Uncertain of his role here he squatted by the water and contemplated the feelings which drove him on — and those which held him back.

No dragon will overlook me again, he thought. *And the Charmed will pay for what they did to the Cross.*

He watched closely as his sister leaned over Cumber's prone body, aware that her presence here prevented him from doing what he really yearned to do, namely abandoning the group altogether and striking out on his own. There had to be dragons, natural dragons who had as much reason as he to hate the Charmed.

But he could not leave his sister, not to this other dragon, this Fortune who was a friend of the Charmed and who claimed the power of love over her.

She'll come to her senses soon enough, he thought. *Then she'll need me with her again. And then we can both make our stand against the Charmed.*

And maybe some day go back to the Cross.

Some day.

Maybe.

Cumber's outburst had indeed broken the tension for all but Brace. Three more days and three more nights had passed since Cumber's breakdown and now, at last, after six weary days of hard travel they had come within sight of their destination – the Plated Mountain.

Cumber had still hardly spoken since that morning, but he had seemed less introverted.

Squatting alone on the uncomfortable mound of jagged, black rock, with nothing before him but the wasteland of the Injured Mountains and the brooding, threatening shadow of the Plated Mountain itself, Fortune found himself missing Cumber very badly indeed. Despite the new joy he had discovered in Gossamer he realized that he needed his friends just as much as he ever had.

I miss Wood too, he mourned.

Taking one final look at the bleak sea of rock which stretched before him he turned back towards the camp where they had settled for the night. He could just make out three bodies nestled in the hollow of porous rock: there Gossamer and Scoff, with Brace off to the side . . .

Where's Cumber?

Without disturbing the others, he clambered to the top of a low peak and scanned the bleak landscape.

Behind: the sandy grey of the desert which had dominated the final day of flight across the Heartland. Water had been scarce there and they had been glad to find streams flowing through the broken, black hills of the Injured Ones.

Ahead and to the sides: the Injured Mountains.

And ahead, of course, the Mountain.

But no Cumber.

He scanned again, sweeping his gaze nearer the camp this time. Suddenly he spotted a flash of gold in the low dawn light – there he was! Cumber was perched on a high outcrop of rock a short flight away. He was too distant for Fortune to be able to make out what he was doing, but the air around him seemed to be shimmering, as though some local heat haze were distorting the view.

Don't tell me he's using fire charm again, thought Fortune with a heavy heart as he lunged into the air. His wings ached terribly from the arduous flight and he could almost hear his muscles creaking as he glided the few tree-lengths to where his friend was crouched. He alighted quietly behind him, and was about to speak when it occurred to him that Cumber might not have heard him arrive. He peered over the young Charmed's wing and stared into . . .

. . . magic!

A dragon floated in the air before them, a fraction of its true size. It was contained within a globe of air the size of a pumpkin, the perimeter of which was defined by a glistening skin of sparks. As Cumber moved his head so the charm moved with him. The dragon inside it – a large warrior Charmed – was stood at attention and looked pale and flat as though it were some tremendous distance away, which of course it was. It was evidently quite unaware that it was being observed.

'It's a magnifying charm,' announced Cumber, his voice startling Fortune, all the more so after the days of silence. 'You see, I was beginning to wonder if we shouldn't be a little more careful as we approach the mountain and Covamere and so I've been observing the outposts a little, and I must say I'm beginning to wonder if everything is as it's supposed to be down here in the south, because the dragons I've seen all look more like the sort of dragon we encountered at Aether's Cross rather than the sort Halcyon would want on his guard duties, although I suppose if . . .'

'Cumber!' interrupted Fortune.

Cumber blinked and dragged his attention with obvious reluctance away from his magical sphere of air.

'What?' he inquired innocently.

And Fortune could only grin like a fool, for there in front of him was Cumber – the real Cumber whom he loved, and not the grim, closed dragon of previous days. His heart bounded in his chest and he began haltingly,

'Cumber, I . . .'

'Don't tell me,' Cumber said, raising a wing to silence his friend. 'I know I've behaved abominably and you deserve an explanation, although I imagine Scoff's told you more or less what's been going on in my head since he went through it too, in his day – in fact, I suppose it's something every charmed dragon experiences sooner or . . .'

'Cumber!' cried Fortune, laughing now for it seemed that Cumber was determined to make up for six days' worth of silence in just a couple of sentences. 'It's all right, I underst—no, I'm sorry – I don't understand what you've been going through, not fully at least, but I do understand that it's been bad for you. If there's anything I can do . . .'

'It's okay, my friend,' replied Cumber, dissolving the magnifying charm and turning to his friend with a wistful smile. 'It's enough that you didn't give up on me.'

'Do you want to talk about it?'

Cumber shook his head.

'I have killed,' he sighed. 'Fire charm works on a dragon's soul, Fortune – it stains it somehow – I can't explain.'

'Hex would have killed you,' offered Fortune.

'I know. But the Realm makes things taste . . . bitter. It can do good too, you must remember that, but in these times it is so hard to make good magic, so hard . . .'

Cumber smiled again, a sad, knowing smile, and it was then that Fortune knew that his friend was going to be all right again – perhaps not today, nor tomorrow, but he would heal.

But there's something else, isn't there?

'What aren't you telling me, Cumber?' he asked now, certain that the time had come for them to be entirely open with each other. He draped his wing across his friend's back and patted him. Cumber pulled away, a little embarrassed.

'I'll always be here to help you, Cumber,' pressed Fortune. 'Remember that next time you need a dragon. But we've got to be straight with each other, especially now, now that we're here, in sight of the Plated Mountain. There's something you're not telling me, isn't there?'

Cumber looked over Fortune's shoulder towards the camp, craning his neck in an exaggerated fashion.

'The others are waking up,' he said, his attempts at diversion so transparent as to make Fortune smile.

You are such an infuriating dragon! he laughed to himself. *Maybe that's why you make such a good friend.*

185

'Just tell me, Cumber,' he said, exasperated. 'Whatever it is, just spit it out.'

'Oh, well, yes, all right then,' grumbled Cumber, pacing about on the rock outcrop. 'But it's nothing really.'

'Well, we'll see.'

'All right. It's nothing I can really define, you see, it's just that I don't think Ordinal was entirely honest with me.'

'What do you mean?'

'Well, when she laid out the details of the quest, you know, observe the fall of South Point – which she had foreseen – and then race the madness to reach Halcyon first and inform him of the danger, get his help . . . well, there was something she wasn't telling me. And that's the same thing I'm not telling you.'

'But what is it, Cumber?' Fortune could happily have throttled his friend at this point.

'I don't know – she never told me!'

'Oh, Cumber!'

'But,' Cumber added, his tone more serious now, 'I have wondered for a long time what it might have been, and now that we are near our destination I am beginning to get a sense of it. Not its true shape but, you might say, its colour.'

'Cumber, what are you talking ab—?'

But then Cumber's words struck Fortune true.

Colour!

'Something else Ordinal had foreseen but which she didn't tell you about?'

Cumber nodded.

'Something bad?'

Cumber nodded again.

Fortune breathed out noisily. He knew Cumber's fears for he shared them himself. There was one thing for them all to fear, Charmed and Natural alike. One thing which, had they known of it before they left South Point, might have prevented them from ever leaving at all on their quest to reach Halcyon.

That thing, that dragon.

The Black Dragon!

Fortune exhaled the words rather than actually speaking them. 'Do you really think Ordinal knew about him before she sent us on this mission?'

Cumber shook his head not in negation but uncertainty.

'I don't know,' he replied, 'and I won't ever know. But I'm convinced she knew more about what's going on than she let on — and that there was *another* reason she didn't tell me about the Black Dragon.'

Cumber went silent.

Alarmed that his friend was becoming morose once more, Fortune started nodding encouragement for him to continue but frightened to say a single word.

Cumber recovered. But he had obviously changed his mind about discussing whatever it was that was bothering him.

'Or perhaps it's something else altogether,' he finished lamely.

'Hmm. Do you think he's here? The Black Dragon?'

Cumber looked back over his shoulder towards the distant mountain. The coldness of the air, the bleak lie of the land, the empty sky — he felt certain that something was wrong here. Something — if not the Charmed madness then something equally as terrible — had beaten them here. Somewhere unseen was the dragon guard he had been observing before Fortune had interrupted him. That dragon had been large and powerful but also . . . dark, dull.

'I'm sure of it,' he announced in response to Fortune's question. 'And I'm sure his wings are spread between us and the mountain. But mark this, Fortune — however complex our quest may have become its primary purpose remains the same: we have to reach Covamere and speak to Halcyon, because that is what, despite everything, Ordinal wanted from us, and that is what I for one am going to do!'

Cumber looked so proud, so indomitable that Fortune was quite taken aback. Here again he saw how his friend had grown since Aether's Cross and he found himself grateful that he had the young Charmed as an ally and not as an enemy. Now he could wield the fire too and that made him all the more formidable. As Wood had done the instant he had leaped from the forbidden ledge, Cumber had at last come of age.

Which just leaves me, Fortune thought a little mournfully.

'If any dragon can lead us to Halcyon, it's you, Cumber,'

he proclaimed fondly. Then he turned to the wind and thrust himself into the air.

And as he led Cumber back to the warmth of the camp he did not see the doubt which had stolen across his friend's anxious face, for it seemed to Cumber that much was unresolved about this place.

The sun rose a little further but remained low for the rest of the day, its light spare and cool. The sky remained clear, the day cold but without the bite of ice; it surrounded the Injured Mountains with the temperature of gathering snow.

If the summer had been short then the autumn would be shorter still, and from its grip and into the marching winter flew the dragons.

CHAPTER 15

The Eve of the New

If a dragon had been dropped blinded into the heart of Cova-mere and then granted again the gift of sight, he would no doubt have proclaimed the citadel to be a disaster of planning, a place entirely without form or structure.

At close quarters this did indeed appear to be true, for Covamere was a maze of intersecting thoroughfares and vast spans of awkward roof, a fussy, over-developed labyrinth, an exaggerated network of screens and towers, tunnels and tracks, bridges and hollows and huge, open arenas, all made from the rock or from the products of the endless forest which embraced the Plated Mountain. It would have taken any one dragon a lifetime to map.

A crazy construction it was, built and rebuilt over the ages so that now Covamere had no true foundation, only a dipping, dancing system of levels and sub-levels and soaring spires which took a dragon first high then low in his tortuous passage across the city. Even Wraith's recent reconstruction had failed to bring it any apparent order.

And yet, if a dragon were to take to the air instead, to spread his wings and fly – which so many Charmed in these times abhorred doing – he might to see Covamere in a rather different way. Instead of the texture he might see the shape and the true pattern emerge.

That dragon would see Covamere as a great, pointed fang reaching up the mountain, its root lost in the rolling forest but its tip clearly visible as it narrowed to a point one quarter of the way up the western slopes of the Plated Mountain. All Covamere conformed to the thrust of this single tooth, this inexorable direction which led the eye and the dragon up, up to the place where once all dragons of the world had thought to journey at one or another time in their lives. To the Portal.

A tear in the mountain itself. A wide, beckoning slot framed with black stone teeth. The mouth of the Plated Mountain.

In fact the Portal was one of seven entrances to the underground caverns of Covamere (which were not to be confused with the meagre tunnels which lay beneath the city itself). The other lesser portals were spaced equally around the mountain, all of them inconspicuous and rarely used. The Portal was the primary route into the mountain, into its caverns and ultimately into the very deepest, most distant chambers where the first stirrings of the Maze itself could be felt. And beyond that? Only the Maze knew.

But the Portal was the only way in for a dragon of power and a dragon of ambition. A dragon like Wraith.

And it, like the six lesser doorways, had been sealed against attack by a dragon quite unlike Wraith yet perhaps his equal in strength. Halcyon.

The moon carved a low, tenuous crescent in the bright sky. By tomorrow night it would not be there at all, having closed its one eye on the world at the end of its wane.

The night of the new moon will be dark indeed.

Wraith was bothered by the ache of nostalgia which had kept him from rest and brought him into the air as the failing moon tracked the morning. For he felt with growing intensity that the past, that constant companion, had moved closer in recent days than he had realized. And might move closer still.

Following his mood he found himself at the very lowest edge of Covamere, among the trees of the forest that ringed the mountain.

Not without regret he acknowledged that the forest was almost empty of life. He wandered through the now barren spaces where once life and charm had thronged, and could still imagine the creatures that once had lived there.

Little life now, he pondered. *Even less charm.*

The dragons of Covamere had kept herds down here in the golden times, herds of tall, slender zirafae. These elegant charmed creatures, their limbs impossibly flimsy yet braced

190

by the gentle magic which had filled their veins, had wandered among the trees, passing through the fabric of the trunks themselves where gaps between were too narrow even for them, scaring the hamadryads from the boughs with their soft hooting song

But Wraith had returned to Covamere to find them gone, the zirafae, and whether they had finally fled their herdmasters, or died away into extinction, or simply changed into something new, he could not judge, nor could any dragons tell him; they had simply vanished.

And their charm? Had that vanished too, or changed to something new?

Changed, or *turned*?

Was all charm leaving the world?

'No,' whispered Wraith in answer to his own question, 'for where I see charm fail in the world I see it grown within me. Charm is not failing; if it seems to leak from the world that is because it leaks into *me*.'

He smiled a thin, moonlike smile and imagined the zirafae grazing high among the treetops. Some day he would perhaps recreate them. It was within his power.

He absorbed the morning sunlight greedily and as he did so a little magic left the world, and a little more entered Wraith.

'. . . lost dragon!' a voice cried behind him. He whirled around to see a small, wiry dragon floating a claw's width above the ground, just beyond the tip of his tail.

Insiss!

'What did you say?' he growled dangerously.

'The last dragon, my lord,' responded his lieutenant at once. His bleached, white scales flashed in the sunlight, their appearance thin and sickly. 'I was notifying you of the deployment. That dragon,' he explained, pointing out a lashing tail at a dragon disappearing round a distant corner, 'is the last one.'

'The last one?'

'Of the deployment, my lord,' repeated Insiss, making the most of his exasperation by tilting his head back and adopting the trace of a sneer.

'You would do well to show me a little more respect, Insiss,' rumbled Wraith, clearly unimpressed by his lieutenant's hint of insubordination — not that it was anything but in character. 'Walk with me a while. We will speak of the attack.'

Insiss floated in Wraith's shadow like a snowflake in a thunderstorm. Insiss it was who had found the ways to build his master's reputation through those long, demanding years. He had joined Wraith perhaps halfway through his campaign, appearing at his side one night in some far eastern land filled with white deserts and terrible mountains. A dragon of the desert, Insiss had at once proved his worth by betraying those few dragons in Wraith's ranks who spoke ill of their leader, and by suggesting several subtle ways by which the Black Dragon might strengthen his hold upon his troops.

He had spread rumours of Wraith's outrageous powers, some of them true, some false; he had shaped his own reputation as a dragon devoted to the destruction of traitors, and his mere appearance in the ranks of a resting platoon was enough to whip into line any dragon whatever.

Tiny by comparison to his great master, his bleached scales hugged a spare, sharp frame and an equally sharp wit. Insiss was a genius among dragons. He was, dragons knew, like his master, a dragon to be feared.

His intellect explained his confidence in the presence of his master. He could manipulate Wraith with ease, the ease of long years of practice. It was not that Wraith was not quick, for he was fearsomely intelligent and ruthlessly decisive — it was just that Insiss was quicker.

He had never made Wraith look a fool, but he often came close . . . very close.

A game-player, Insiss.

But a very dangerous game, he thought as he floated behind Wraith, dwarfed by his master's spread wings.

Wraith's great size was enough to explain much of his strength. His chest was huge; dragons swore they could hear even from a distance the heart which thundered within. His body was dark and undecorated — except for the wide carapace which sprouted from the back of his long, tapering head. This armour protected his back and neck when he was in flight and created a black crown which followed his gaze when at rest. His wings were of phenomenal size, glittering with hidden metals and stored charm. Wraith was clearly capable of flight either with or without magic; he preferred to use both.

But what above all set Wraith apart was his hold on the Realm.

Most dragons entered the Realm only when they needed to, considering it too dangerous to remain in there for anything but the briefest of times.

Not so Wraith. He was there *all* the time.

And to this end he had twisted his body into a form which allowed him to maintain constant access to the Realm and grown two additional limbs from his distorted shoulders. These arms extended out from either side of his backbone at the base of his sinuous neck, long, thin rods so fleshless as to be virtual bones. Each bent twice at a rough, knobbed joint and ended . . . nowhere.

Or rather, ended in the Realm.

Alone among dragons, Wraith had made solid the imaginary claws most other Charmed use to break the Realm membrane. As his extra limbs left this world, fading from the view of ordinary eyes like melting snow, so they reappeared in that seething pit which was the source of all fire charm. The power needed to maintain the integrity of this junction between the worlds was colossal, but then Wraith too was colossal and such power was his to command.

And that is what makes him a monster, thought Insiss. Every time he moved into Wraith's presence he deliberately took the time to appraise his master's prodigious strength. One look at those long, probing claws, the ends of which simply evaporated into the air, was enough to give him caution and remind him yet again of what a dangerous game it was indeed that he played.

'Tell me of the deployment,' commanded Wraith.

'As you wish, my lord. As you know, the majority of our strength will be retained within Covamere itself, for the Portal is the main focus of the initial thrust. Ten dragons only have been despatched to each of the lesser portals, and I feel . . .'

'Ten? That is too many.'

'My lord?'

'Halcyon will not try to escape. Those bolt-holes are of no

consequence. I need the strength here. Two dragons at each of the lesser portals will suffice. See to it.'

'As you wish, my lord.'

Wraith pondered this decision for a moment, then added, 'However, see to it that they are strong dragons, Insiss. You know the sort I like.'

'Of course, my lord.'

Dragons pulled away from this formidable pair as they marched up through the arenas and corridors of Covamere; some even fled before the Black Dragon. At intervals Wraith stopped to inspect troops or to brief lesser commanders, but nothing impeded his inexorable progress up towards the narrowing slopes of the steep approach to the Portal itself. At his head dragons were frantic, busy with preparation and eager to impress; in his wake they sat back and exchanged pensive smiles, for to a dragon they realized that they were at last ready, fully prepared for the greatest dragon offensive of all time.

The attack on the mountain.

Wraith spoke to many dragons on his march through Covamere and with every new exchange he was reassured of his power here. Covamere, the place he had once left in disgrace, the place to which he had at last returned with the army of dragons he had gathered from across the world. The place which would finally, gloriously, be his.

I am fortunate among dragons, he mused as he paused to look back over the span of a mighty bridge of rock, *for I have a second chance. It was for this moment that I was allowed to survive the Maze once. I shall now claim my rightful victory. This time I have the power; this time I am the charm!*

The approach to the Portal was wide and grand enough for ten dragons to march abreast up its steep slope. Wraith, his wings spread almost to their limit, filled it from one side to the other, forcing Insiss to coast behind him, supported on his constant cushion of charm.

The slope of the approach was far steeper than that of the mountain itself so that only afternoon sky was visible ahead as they ascended. When they reached the top, the pathway would level out, affording them a spectacular view of the soaring blackness of the Portal framed by the grey wedge of the Plated Mountain.

As they neared the top, Wraith stopped and turned to look back over Covamere.

Tomorrow night the attack on the Portal will begin.

A junior officer scurried nervously up to Insiss and whispered something to him. The thin, white dragon nodded briefly and then, motioning to the officer to wait, addressed himself to Wraith.

'My lord,' he announced. 'It is reported that the last of the Hardship has been rounded up. Nine dragons in all, captive in the Round Arena. Your judgement upon them?'

'The same as their treacherous comrades,' murmured Wraith, still looking out over the citadel and appearing quite disinterested in these latest proceedings.

Three days it had taken to break Wraith's Hardship, and now it would be wiped out. For on the very day he had determined to deal with the Hardship, the earth tremor had struck the mountain and revealed to him the forest clearing and the globes of blue fire. He was forced to wonder for the first time in his life if he was not being manipulated by some higher power.

The Maze had given him his solution.

Gone was Wraith's Hardship, into the globes of fire.

'My lord,' said Insiss with feigned hesitance, 'is that wise? There is so much we do not yet know. Much could be learned from these dragons.'

'Nothing that is not known already or which cannot be learned tomorrow night, Insiss,' growled Wraith, eyeing his lieutenant balefully.

Insiss glanced at the officer squirming at his side, obviously uncomfortable to be present at such a high-level exchange.

'But my lord, the Portal is sealed against attack, that much we know. What lies behind? We do not know. Where is Halcyon hiding? We do not know. What forces does he still command? We do not know.'

'Your suggestion, Insiss?'

'Read their minds, my lord.'

Damn you, Insiss! This time you go too far!

Wraith's alleged ability to read a dragon's mind was one of the more powerful weapons in his own arsenal of fear. It was, of course, Insiss who had spread the false rumour of this unheard-of power, and now few of Wraith's dragons doubted that their commander could, at will, determine their thoughts and their loyalties and deal with them accordingly. Instant trial, and instant sentence. A terrifying weapon.

In fact, and this even Insiss did not suspect, Wraith did possess a fragment of this legendary talent, the full manifestation of which was now entirely lost to the world. Wraith could not read a mind as such, but he could steal some of the thoughts of a dying dragon. At the point of death, when a dragon's spirit leaves its body and undertakes the next great journey, something of its mind is laid open to any creature with the wit and speed to pounce.

Wraith, with his constant access to the Realm, was such a creature.

He had done it only once before, but tomorrow night he planned to do it many times over . . .

As Insiss goaded him before their embarrassed witness, he wondered if he should not simply kill his lieutenant here and now and steal his thoughts, so that he might understand the true nature of this thin, bleached dragon who thought he could outsmart his master, the Master, Wraith – Black Dragon.

'Listen to me, Insiss,' he intoned. 'These traitors know nothing of worth. I already know more than you or any dragon can conceive. And I know you, Insiss; I know you better than you guess.

'Tomorrow night the moon will be new, and after tomorrow night many more things will be new. Consider that, Insiss, as you leave my presence now; consider it very carefully indeed.'

Insiss held his master's gaze for as long as he was able, until finally he was forced to lower his eyes. His thoughts boiled as he absorbed the fact that Wraith seemed suddenly impervious to his taunts.

The Black Dragon is changing, he thought with something akin to dread. *How long can the game continue now?*

'Then kill them, my lord,' he replied abruptly, hoping to provoke Wraith into a simple temper.

But the Black Dragon would not be pushed. Instead he looked out over Covamere with a serene, yellow gaze.

'I do not kill, Insiss,' he responded coolly. 'I prevail. Go.'
'As you wish.'

Insiss spun around angrily, ushering the trembling officer
down the slope before him. Wraith ignored them, drinking
in instead the panorama of the citadel.

*Tomorrow night many things will be reborn. A new moon, a
new age.*

As his body sucked at the failing sunlight he opened his
wings to the darkness of the Portal, their membranes sensing
the massive barriers of charm which Halcyon had woven
across and within the towering entrance. The magic felt
strong and old — very old — and Wraith forced himself to
consider his adversary's immense age and power . . . but
briefly.

Halcyon's age is over, he thought, swiftly banishing any
traces of doubt. *The new age approaches.*

With the ghost of a smile he sent a filament of charm into
the space before the Portal. It heated and coloured the air
and formed the shape of one of the ancient zirafae, galloping
elegantly between trees of pure magic. The projected image
danced swiftly into the black entrance where it began at
once to fade.

You shall be renewed, thought Wraith. *You and others shall
live again; the past shall return.*

But on Wraith's terms.

A lick of fire sliced through the shadows as Wraith's magic
met that of Halcyon. The image of the zirafa vanished
abruptly. The fire died.

The sun set and night claimed Covamere. Wraith, black
in the darkness, did not sleep.

CHAPTER 16

The Forest

It was agreed that they would walk the remaining distance to the Plated Mountain. Cumber had spied out too many sentry posts in the distant hills for them to risk approach from the air, and despite the fact that this decision would slow them up considerably they all reluctantly conceded that safety was more important than speed.

'It's not far now anyway,' Cumber said in an effort to raise his companions' spirits. 'And we'll be safe enough once we reach the cover of the forest and from there it's only a short jump on to Covamere.'

The broken land moved past with agonizing slowness over the course of the day. In fact they made better progress by night, beneath the sliver of light cast by the waning moon, so that by the morning of the second day in the Injured Mountains they had descended into the final river valley beyond which the steadily rising slopes of the Plated Mountain itself began to assert themselves at last.

On the lower stretches of this valley the crazed black rock gave way to areas of smoother, dusty ground separated by groves of low, broad-leaved shrubs. Movement across the smooth soil was easier and morale slowly improved as the sanctuary of the forest drew near. When Scoff discovered that the strange shrubs bore odd, elongated fruits with green skins and a soft, sweet core, spirits rose even more. By mid-day they had crossed the river which struggled through the dusty vale and soon they were ascending, stealthily now, into the foothills of the Plated Mountain.

While Brace pushed excitedly ahead, and Scoff and Cumber marched deep in conversation behind him, Fortune and Gossamer dropped to the back of the group. Fortune scuffed the ground as they walked, kicking up black dust and tiny flakes of pumice. He felt a melancholy cloud settle over his heart. His face was drawn.

'What's wrong?' asked Gossamer at last.

For a while Fortune said nothing. Gossamer knew this young dragon well enough by now to give him time to think his words through and so she left the question to hang while she considered the mountain looming ahead.

It ached with magic. She could sense the charm pouring off it as a palpable force, a life-force which swam through the rock just as the sprites swam through water. To her Natural senses the charm was barely a smell, a mere reflection of the power it truly held, but it was there, all around her, calling her.

'It's calling me, Gossamer,' said Fortune, and somehow she was not surprised that his thoughts mirrored hers. She felt her love for him burst through like a break in the clouds and hugged him tight, stopping them short in their tracks.

'What was that for?' laughed Fortune when they finally parted.

'I don't want to lose you,' Gossamer replied, looking earnestly into his eyes.

'You're not going to lose me,' came Fortune's reply, but even as his words emerged a current of cold air came rolling down the mountain and enveloped them. They shivered in the sudden draught and held each other close. Winter air, despite the season.

'It's just a breeze,' said Fortune but the wind – although it was not a wind, more a voice – grew strong and surrounded them with its icy grip. The others continued ahead unaware.

Fortune squinted into the cold and braced himself against Gossamer. An image of Wood came to mind, of Wood diving from the ledge and vanishing into a sea of flashing teeth; Wood carried along by the war against the Charmed. Wood lost to him. Cold and sorrow, cold and loss.

He missed Wood terribly.

Cold and loss, whispered the Plated Mountain, *these will be yours again if you proceed further*.

Fortune held Gossamer tight as the breath of the mountain thundered past them, freezing their hearts.

The mountain speaking? Or something else?

'Let us pass!' he cried defiantly.

The wind faltered, then died, although as it evaporated Fortune fancied he heard the voice become a chuckle and finally a dark, empty sigh. In his mind that sigh went on for the rest of the day.

He turned back to Gossamer then and looked at her fondly.

'Yes,' she said unexpectedly. He frowned, not understanding. 'You asked me if I would have come with you anyway,' she went on. 'Oh, Fortune, don't you know the answer to that question? Even if Aether's Cross still existed I would still be here. The first time I took a breath in your presence I left my home. I've been with you ever since, and will be with you always.'

In the warmth after the cold they were close and tender, and for that instant nothing existed but the two of them, and their love for one another.

'We've had so little time together,' he sighed.

'You speak as though we have little left,' replied Gossamer, trembling in his embrace.

'No,' smiled Fortune. 'We'll have all the time in the world.'

'I hope so,' shivered Gossamer, looking up the mountainside towards the snow-covered peak. 'I truly do.'

'Come on, you two!' called Scoff from high above them. 'Time for that later!'

Their hearts bound together but weighing heavy with the awareness of a winter which had not yet come, they began again a climb which had become suddenly arduous and full of dark premonition. The Plated Mountain sat like a predatory beast, quiet and cold, as they mounted its back.

The pine forest closed in around them, and with the gloom came a surprise: all around were signs of dragon. Natural dragon.

Old nests sheltered in the lee of the larger rocks and great belts of the tall, wiry trees had been cleared for camp sites which by the look of them were temporary.

'Nomadic,' explained Scoff. 'Not much food. Dragons have to keep on the move.'

'Naturals live here!' gasped Fortune in wonder.

'I thought this was a Charmed place,' said Brace excitedly as they entered a clearing. The sun filtered through the canopy of needles and threw a patchwork of light and shade over the forest floor. The ground was hard, the soil black and coarse, thin over the omnipresent porous rock. This was evidently a place where life was hard, especially for natural creatures; here the Heartland supported only with reluctance those lacking in charm.

'Once it was,' confirmed Cumber, smiling at Fortune and Gossamer as they finally caught up again, 'but natural dragons have reached even here it would seem.'

Brace's eyes were shining as he rummaged around in the abandoned camp.

'Maybe we'll meet up with these dragons,' he said.

'They're probably watching us already,' responded Fortune, eyeing with some suspicion the deeper belts of forest where foliage hugged elaborate waves of rock, creating gullies and canyons where a whole army could hide. He felt vulnerable and added abruptly, 'Come on, I'd prefer to be through this forest before nightfall.'

The terrain was steeper now and the paucity of wildlife meant that there were few trails through the forest. Progress grew slow again as the dragons toiled ever upwards. For Cumber and Scoff it was easier but for the wing-bound natural dragons the going became very difficult. Sharp pumice threatened constantly to tear delicate wing membranes, as did the outreaching limbs of the trees.

'Naturals! It all looks very un-natural to me,' grumbled Scoff to Cumber as their companions fell further behind. They waited until they had caught up again.

'We must be nearly through it,' panted Fortune to Cumber, suddenly jealous of his charmed friend's four-legged gait which allowed him to tuck his redundant wings safely away. The forest closed in ahead so densely that he found it hard to judge what time of day it was, but the general murk suggested that the sun was gradually going down. The forest unnerved him; it smelt cold.

'We should rest, my love,' whispered Gossamer. 'We're all so tired.'

'We ought to press on,' said Fortune pensively. 'What do you think, Cumber? There's no telling what . . .'

A rustle came from behind them.

Nothing stirred in the dimness. The dragons loitered, their nerves stretched taut.

'Come out where we can see you!' called Brace suddenly. 'We're not afraid!'

'Speak for yourself,' muttered Scoff.

'Ssh!' warned Gossamer.

Fortune squinted into the twilight. Slate grey trunks soared into a dull suggestion of sky leaving random shapes between their dark stripes. The air was still and pregnant and nothing stirred.

'Where are you?' cried Brace.

Fortune was just about to warn him against calling out further when something scuttled sideways between two of the trees and was absorbed into the darkness of the foliage. Faint and broken voices whispered close on the breeze.

Even bolder now, Brace stepped forward and was about to shout again when one of the voices raised itself to a hoarse whisper.

'For the Mountain's sake, young dragon, keep quiet!'

And shadows transformed themselves into two dragons slowly emerging. Naturals they were but their wings were stubby, obviously adapted to the forest environment. Both were old and wrinkled, with chipped horns and missing scales.

'Come over here quickly,' urged the larger of the two, beckoning with a stained claw.

'Why?' responded Brace belligerently.

The dragon rolled his eyes at his female companion.

'Look around you, young imp,' he said impatiently.

Upon doing so, Fortune and the others were surprised to find that they had strayed into a ring of small stones, hardly more than pebbles, spaced meticulously in their hundreds to form a large circle on the ground.

'You ain't in any danger,' said the female dragon, 'but we don't want to offend no-one now, do we? Come along now, all of you — strange ones as well if they must.'

Her tone was warm and accommodating and although Fortune's nerves were still tugging at him he relaxed at least a little when he saw Gossamer smile and step out of the circle. Taking care not to disturb any of the stones, she stepped over the perimeter and the others followed. The gloom was thickening towards night.

'I'm Tillery and this is my mate, Loom,' said the female dragon as they met. Fortune introduced himself and his companions as dragons journeying through the region after the river which had served their home settlement had run dry, a story by which the forest-dwellers were clearly unconvinced, casting as they did suspicious looks at Cumber and Scoff. However they remained genial enough and took the weary travellers a short distance into the darkened forest to a small camp, where roughly-woven screens of branches sectioned off a clearing into several private areas. Snores drifted up from behind most of the screens and as they entered the camp both of the elderly Naturals urged their guests to make as little noise as possible.

'You're welcome to stay a day or two,' whispered Tillery to Fortune. Then she looked pointedly at Cumber and Scoff and added, 'After that you'll no doubt be on your way.'

'You're very kind,' replied Fortune. 'We'll be little trouble, I assure you. But tell me, why did you urge us out of that ring of stones? Whom might we have offended?'

'Them as built it,' replied Loom unhelpfully.

'Best not to ask too much,' explained Tillery, winking in a most unenlightening way.

'Stay out of their way . . .' added Loom.

'. . . and they'll stay out of yours,' concluded Tillery.

Fortune caught Gossamer's eye and felt their thoughts collide. *How I love her*, he thought. He knew she was remembering his description of the giant circles he and Cumber had seen in their early days in the Heartland. But this circle was so much smaller . . .

'Sprites, perhaps?' she ventured to the group in general.

'Perhaps,' agreed Loom with a shrug.

'We have food, if you would like to eat,' said Tillery, changing the subject.

'This is fascinating,' whispered Cumber to Fortune. 'These are Naturals living right next to the very centre of Charmed affairs and yet they have absolutely no interest in charm.'

No, thought Fortune. *It's not that they have no interest, it's that they are actively disinterested in charm.*

When Fortune caught up with the others, Scoff was

already living up to his name and eating heartily, although both Loom and his mate studiously ignored him.

As they ate, Loom and Tillery explained a little about their small band. They were twenty, it seemed, and today marked the end of a particularly strenuous migration from a distant part of the forest.

'Four days without sleep we've travelled,' explained Tillery with a proud sigh. 'No wonder most of us 'ave been asleep all day! Nomads we are, the lot of us – it's not a bad life, as lives go.'

Conversation on both sides continued in polite fashion until eventually, as the slow night settled on the woods, Loom cleared his throat and asked Fortune if they really intended to continue up the mountain. Fortune, aware that some useful information might be forthcoming, replied innocently,

'Is there any reason why we shouldn't?'

Loom and Tillery exchanged a look and tutted to themselves.

'Go back to the river, I should,' advised Loom. 'You'll not get far higher up, I'll tell you that much.'

'Why not?' asked Brace.

'Too rough,' replied Loom quickly.

'Too steep,' added Tillery.

'No food.'

'Very cold. Not a place for dragons.'

'But there are dragons up there,' countered Fortune.

Tillery rolled her eyes at Loom in what was becoming a familiar gesture. Fortune had to suppress a smile: despite their irritating evasiveness he could not help but like these two comfortable old dragons.

'Always impetuous, the young. Take our advice and . . .'

'We want to go on,' interrupted Fortune briskly. 'Tell us why we shouldn't.'

Now their hosts began to look quite uncomfortable. Their faces, dark and shadowed in what little starlight penetrated the forest, grew both suspicious and wary.

'There's been terrible stories lately. Terrible,' Tillery blurted.

'What stories?' Fortune urged.

Tillery shook her head.

'It's dangerous up there,' agreed Loom, making a great show of shuffling himself and his mate off towards their sleeping area. 'Dragons like us might go up there but none'll come back. We'll be sleeping now. You'll be gone in the morning, I daresay.'

When they had disappeared Cumber spoke.

'Few Naturals have ever been allowed to enter Covamere,' he said. 'Should the Black Dragon be there already, it will be a more dangerous place than ever a Natural has been . . .'

He breathed deeply and felt, there at the perimeter of his mind, the itch which was the Realm. All of a sudden the night seemed darker, if that was possible. *The Black Dragon's wing is darker even than this*, he thought with a shiver.

'What should we do, Cumber?' whispered Fortune, hugging Gossamer close to him,

'Well, I suggest a scouting trip straight away, tonight. It's new moon. Darkness is on our side.'

'But why tonight?' groaned Gossamer. 'I'm so tired already.'

'If we wait until tomorrow night we'll have lost a whole day, so tonight it is. But we won't all go — only Scoff and I need go for the moment, since being Charmed we'll be more likely to talk our way out of any trouble and there's always . . .'

'I'm coming too,' interrupted Fortune before he could think. The blood thundered in his ears as he blurted out the words. He could not look at Gossamer.

Brace frowned, a sneer twisting his face. Gossamer flinched as if she had been struck, but said nothing.

'Well,' stuttered Cumber, switching his gaze between Fortune and the obviously unimpressed Gossamer, 'I'm not sure that . . . I mean, I don't know if . . .'

'Cumber, I'm going with you,' repeated Fortune. 'I started this journey with you and I'm going to finish it with you. It's as much my quest as it is yours.'

And still he could not look at Gossamer. He felt her trembling at his side.

'But it's only a scouting trip,' suggested Cumber. 'There's really no need . . .'

'There's every need. I'm coming, and that's final.'

'But you're too conspicuous,' protested Cumber, looking desperately at Gossamer for support.

'You can disguise me,' came Fortune's prompt reply. 'I imagine you can do that. Scoff? You can work a charm to disguise me?'

'Of course,' rumbled Scoff.

'Then that's settled,' Fortune sighed. Only now, with the decision made, did he turn at last to his love. He found her with tears on her face. 'We shan't be apart for long,' he soothed, only half-believing it himself. 'We'll find out where Halcyon is and how best to get to him, then come back and make proper plans. Don't worry – I'll be back before you know it.'

He stopped as his own tears sprang suddenly to his eyes. She stared back at him with a terrible intensity.

'Brace,' he said, nearly choking with his tumbling emotion, 'you must take care of your sister. Will you do that for me?'

And of course Brace could only agree, angry that Fortune could manipulate him so easily but secretly relieved that he would not be required to face the Black Dragon again . . . or at least, not yet.

'He's right, Gossamer,' he muttered. 'Let him go with his charmed friends.'

His statement was cold and bitter. Once it was said he turned and forced his way past Fortune to a distant corner of the camp where he curled up against a heap of pine needles. 'We have little time,' warned Cumber gently as he and Scoff withdrew also. 'We must leave right away.'

Fortune nodded. Once again he could not bring himself to look at Gossamer; he just stood in the dark, head bowed. A fragment of a dream floated in the front of his mind . . . stone circles rotating in space . . . a mountain opening like an eye . . . shadows searching for him inside the egg.

Haven!

The stars turned imperceptibly, like islands in a vast, lost sea. The thought broke Fortune's dream.

'Haven,' he whispered. Gossamer frowned. 'Have you heard of it?' he went on, but she shook her head, puzzled.

And so he told her of his dream, of a circle of islands in

a distant sea; of how his mother's voice had told him that this was Haven, a place where he could be safe.

'If a time should ever come when we are truly parted,' he said carefully, 'meet me there. Haven is our place, our sanctuary. Our safety.'

'But . . .'

'I know it's folly!' Fortune grasped her tight, his eyes suddenly wild. 'I don't even know where it is, let alone if it exists at all. Just promise me, Gossamer, promise me you'll go there if . . . if you should ever be lost!'

Scared by his intensity Gossamer nodded shakily.

'I promise,' she said, then as she regained her composure she found a miraculous smile. 'I'll be there. Wherever it may be, I'll be there.'

The trees, black against the deep, blue starlit heavens, towered over them like prison guards eager to prevent their love spilling out on to the mountain. Voices whispered in the heights of the pine giants, but they were the voices of the dryads and sylphs, and to the natural ones below they were but the stirrings of the midnight breeze.

We'll be gone a day at most, he thought. *I'll be back with her tomorrow night, perhaps the next morning.*

He looked back at Gossamer and smiled, but she could not meet his eye. With difficulty he pulled his gaze away and joined his colleagues.

'There are two ways we can disguise you,' explained Cumber, launching straight in without any ceremony.

'Force-growing your body's the first,' elaborated Scoff. 'Make you look like us. Painful though. Tiring for us too. Not recommended.'

'A cloaking charm is a better idea,' concluded Cumber. 'We can make you, well, not invisible as such, but . . . you remember how Brutace and his thugs appeared when they first attacked us at Aether's Cross? When they just appeared out of the air?'

'Yes. They were sort of . . . vague. It was as though my eyes slipped away whenever I tried to look at them, even when they were carrying us back to the caverns. It was like trying to grasp a fish.'

'That's exactly it!' cried Cumber triumphantly. 'Just like trying to grasp a slippery fish: every time you think you've

207

got it, it just wriggles its tail and slips through your claws. We'll make you slip through their claws, Fortune, you'll see!'

Gossamer looked on mournfully as the three dragons fell deep into discussion. She knew Fortune was as true to his word as any dragon, but the thought of their parting tore at her heart and for a brief, agonizing breath she wished that she had never met him.

But then she saw him laugh and clap Cumber on the flank, and saw his easy smile.

Never apart, she thought. *Wherever we may be, however far the distances between us. Never apart.*

'Gossamer,' said Cumber. 'If we're gone any longer than a day you must assume the worst and put yourselves under Loom and Tillery's wings. They'll take you in.'

'I wish this wasn't happening,' said Gossamer eventually, her voice tight.

But as they parted, she whispered, 'Haven.' Then she turned and joined her brother, tears still coursing down her face. Fortune watched the broken starlight caress her body and fixed an image of her beauty in his memory.

Surprisingly calm, Fortune followed his charmed friends in a steady march out of the clearing. He forced himself not to look back until they were right at the edge of the waiting forest, then he cast a single glance behind.

Gossamer and Brace stood close together, watching their companions leave. The meagre light continued to pattern their bodies, colouring Gossamer with a pale and magical glow.

Haven, he thought. *She is my Haven.*

The trees enveloped them.

It seemed no time at all before they were clear of the pine trees and climbing the steep approach slopes towards Covamere itself. Behind and below them the forest sprawled around the foothills and out of sight; above, the Plated Mountain revealed itself only tantalizingly as they moved alternately into gullies and up on to stony ridges.

The rock possessed an extraordinary range of colours here above the treeline. Despite the dimness of the starlight the bands of red and yellow gleamed, then gave way to blue-grey and even green rock before the black pumice finally reasserted itself and the landscape resumed its former drabness.

The stars turned about the world and they travelled cautiously upwards.

The plan was necessarily simple: they would proceed carefully until their first contact with a charmed dragon. If they encountered a large group they would retreat, hopefully without being seen, and try a new route. Their objective was to find a dragon alone, perhaps a bored sentry, whom they could pump for as much information as possible without arousing suspicion.

Being Charmed themselves, Cumber and Scoff were reasonably confident of their own safety but soon they began to generate between them the complex charm needed to divert suspicious eyes away from Fortune. His presence had to become a blank, a hole into which no dragon would even think of looking.

For his part Fortune was quite unaware that the spell was being cast. He had expected a tingling sensation perhaps, or else one of those eerie glows or crackles of magic; but there was nothing.

Presently Cumber informed him that, although not strictly invisible, he was now vague enough not to be seen by any dragon, charmed or otherwise, other than himself or Scoff. Fortune thought that Cumber was getting carried away with fancy words – if no dragon could see him then he was effectively invisible and that was that.

'Up to a point, yes,' agreed Cumber, 'but our charm works on the mind of the observer, not on your body. The word "invisible" is convenient but it's only dragons who can't see you. To other creatures you are still entirely visible, so you see, if you disturb them you may give yourself away.'

'Don't take chances,' summarized Scoff. 'Act cautious. We'll get you through.'

A fragment of rock broke loose under one of Fortune's claws and clattered away down the mountainside, kicking up dust as it fell. The tenuous nature of his invisibility became strikingly clear: he was invisible but his trail was not. He would have to take care.

Spires lifted above the next ridge; the sky towards which

they reached glowed dull yellow from the light of the city.

'Covamere!' breathed Cumber, and they scrambled to the top of the ridge. The view was limited, for a massive cliff obscured the middle ground between here and the dragon city and only over the peak of this cliff did the spires soar. Nevertheless the towers looked close. Their destination was in sight.

The ridge flattened off before them into a large plateau, a black, dusty arena which ran up to the roots of the cliff which stood square in their path. The cliff reached out over the plateau as it rose, creating a vast overhang of solid lava which erupted out of the ground in shocking defiance of its own immense mass. It was paler than the black rock from which it burst, and reached out like a dragon from the egg.

A deep crack split the bulging cliff vertically down its centre. A path led across the plateau to the base of this crack. Claws retracted, padding silently along the path behind his friends, Fortune suddenly felt very exposed.

There was no shelter in the arena, and the plateau fell away into ominous blackness on three of its four sides; the fourth side was blocked by the cliff, negotiable only by a stiff, steep flight. The place was silent and heavy.

The silence moved.

The darkness at the foot of the crack brought forth two dragons. They lumbered slowly into the scant starlight, heavy war machines hard with armour and moving with sure ease to greet the intruders.

Well, thought Fortune to himself, *I hope this cloaking charm works*.

The moon too was invisible, a blank and lightless disc against the sea of stars. The new moon.

CHAPTER 17

The Breaching of the Portal

Nineteen Charmed, corpses every one, lay in the shadow of a pair of impossibly large wings. The shadow caressed the dead dragons as the wings beat a slow, heavy time in the air.

Wraith hovered over his sacrifices, scrutinizing their sad remains, sniffing their wounds. Here he opened a belly, there he broke a skull; all the victims he examined in his thirst for enlightenment yet still it was not enough.

Another!

He would have his answer.

'Insiss!' he thundered with a voice as black as his wings.

In an instant the lieutenant was there, thin head bowed, ready to receive his command.

'Yes, my lord?'

'Another!' demanded Wraith impatiently.

'But, my lord,' began Insiss, his voice careful now that he could no longer accurately gauge his master's mood, 'they are restless. They fear . . .'

'They fear me, Insiss, remember that. As should you.'

'As you wish, my lord. Your judgement is no doubt, as ever, wise. Another I shall bring.'

Insiss ducked furiously out of Wraith's presence, moving out from beneath the vast, overhanging cowl of the Portal and into the starlight beyond.

I have many choices, he thought, his mind calculating swiftly as the future opened its myriad possibilities to his scrutiny. But he frowned. To leave the Black Dragon was surely to be hunted down and destroyed, for he knew too much of Wraith. And to stay? Much would have to change if he was to stay.

Calculating, planning, Insiss glided among the dragons ranked stolidly along the full length of the Portal approach slope. In the sky above the moon had closed its eye to the world and the night looked anything but new — it looked very, very old.

The Black Dragon remained beneath the Portal's gloriously dark roof and alighted with casual grace on the mound of corpses. He held his wings wide and free as if protecting his dead warriors from some infernal gaze. Wielding charm he created a pool of mercury in the air above him.

Looking up he contemplated his reflection in the inverted mirror of the silvery fluid's surface, his deep, dark hide, his eight spidery limbs.

You are beautiful, he smiled at his reflection. He flexed his tail lewdly at the mirror-image trapped above him and opened his wings more fully, admiring the dull light which his stored flight charm spilled into the droplets of oil which beaded their membranes. His fleshless forearms stretched extravagantly as he watched himself massage the oil into his leathery skin. He could feel Halcyon's ancient charm moving like a spice through the air around him and its scent was intoxicating: such formidable magic, such a worthy opponent!

Such a glorious triumph!

Altering the mirror's view he used it to spy on Insiss as he moved among the ranks of dragons standing to attention outside the huge cave of the Portal. Dragons parted like water as Insiss cut a path through their midst; heads were bowed and turned aside as he passed. Finally Insiss chose, picking out a single, proud individual with his iron gaze, a dragon left alone as his neighbours pulled back as though he were suddenly diseased. Under the intense, hypnotic stare of the lieutenant the luckless creature followed obediently up the slope and under the overhanging cowl to where Wraith himself waited. The rest of the crowd relaxed visibly, the tension broken for the moment.

This must be the one, thought Wraith with a stab of concern. *I cannot have a rebellion. It would not do to kill so many loyal followers.*

Dissolving the mercury mirror he turned towards the

entrance and opened his skeletal Realm forearms in welcome to his next pathfinder.

Fortune heard both Cumber and Scoff breathe a simultaneous sigh of relief. Upon seeing them the two approaching guards had abandoned any semblance of alertness and adopted expressions of limp tolerance.

'They've been on duty too long,' whispered Cumber. 'Just what we need.'

Both the sentries yawned as he raised his voice to call a polite greeting.

'Over the cliff and join the rest if you're new,' responded the larger of the two dragons as they drew close and stopped. His coarse hide would have been a brilliant turquoise had it not been dirty and ill-kempt. Together they now made a tight group of four in the centre of the plateau; it was obvious that the guards had no idea Fortune was standing quietly to one side, watching and listening. The air was cold.

'Could we rest here for a stretch?' panted Scoff, making a great show of stretching his neck and working his lungs. 'That's quite a climb.'

'Suit yourselves,' replied the other dragon, a young, silver creature with ragged claws and a slight squint. 'Training camp's just the other side of the cliff but if you want to rest suit yourselves.' He gave the impression he did not much care what they did.

'Not much training now,' mumbled Turquoise to nobody in particular.

'You've left it a bit late, to be honest,' commented his partner.

'Story of my life,' laughed Scoff, warming to his role. 'Been on duty long?'

'Don't we know it!' replied Turquoise bitterly.

Cumber held his tongue and let Scoff's banter put the two guards at their ease. He was more interested in the overhanging cliff, and in particular the extraordinary crack which ran virtually its full height. The crack was narrow for most of the way from the top but widened at its base, and the cleft it formed was too mysterious-looking to be just a cave.

Too dark to be real, he thought with a shiver. *There's charm at work here. Ancient charm.*

'Do you mind if we grab a bit of shelter?' he ventured, moving as though to step past the guards and towards the shadow of the overhang. Towards the cleft.

At once the silver guard blocked his path.

'The Master wouldn't like that,' he drawled. Cumber stopped and glanced at Scoff.

'Fair enough,' grunted Scoff as Cumber withdrew. 'Guess we'll learn his ways when we join up.'

'Likely as not.'

Ancient charm!

'He'll not escape this way then,' said Cumber, acting on a sudden hunch. Scoff frowned at him.

'Hah!' laughed Turquoise. 'Too right. Wraith's got him holed up for sure.'

So that's his name! thought Fortune, his heart racing. He could hear the exchange on the plateau clearly; the night air was crisp and sheer.

'Sooner Halcyon's dealt with the better,' said Scoff, smoothly picking up on Cumber's line of enquiry.

'Don't know about that,' replied Silver suspiciously. 'We just follow orders. Where've you two come from anyway?'

'We're from Point's Cross,' added Cumber hurriedly. 'We heard what was happening and came to join up.'

'Heard what — from who?' asked Silver, nodding to Turquoise. His partner circled behind Cumber and Scoff with slow, menacing steps. Spikes flicked out from the sentries' flanks, hissing a warning to the intruders. Silver grinned without humour and even licked his lips.

'I think you'd better answer some questions,' he said dangerously. 'We've not seen dragons quite like you before. Maybe Wraith would be interested in you personally.'

Fortune watched helplessly as the two dragons closed in on his friends. It was plain they were considerably more alert than they had first appeared, having out-bluffed Cumber and Scoff with ease and only now revealing their true colours.

Knowing that's no help, he thought desperately.

With only a few breaths in which to make up his mind he decided.

'Over here!' he shouted, racing forward.

* * *

The Portal bore a great crest of rock which formed a canopy over the high, broad cave of the entrance itself. From its scowling mouth this cave proceeded directly back into the mountain for ten tree lengths, whereupon it stopped dead in a brutal, vertical wall. Obviously artificial, this wall bore neither crack nor crevice to betray the way through to the deeper routes it guarded.

Halcyon was somewhere behind that wall.

But before he could breach the wall Wraith had to negotiate the invisible labyrinth of charm which Halcyon had set beneath the Portal's protective cowl. Nineteen dragons he had sent into that labyrinth, each aware of the route and fate of the previous one. Each had gained a little more ground than his predecessor but ultimately each had been cut down by an unknown force: charm, but of a kind even Wraith could not identify.

One more!

Surely with one more he would succeed!

'That will be all,' said Wraith to Insiss, who withdrew swiftly, his expression unreadable. Wraith ignored him – he had moved beyond such concerns now. 'Your name is . . . Lapse?' he continued.

The unfortunate dragon whom Insiss had brought into the chamber nodded dumbly. How the Master knew his name he did not dare guess.

'Come.'

By a subtle vocalizing charm Wraith's words to Lapse boomed out of the Portal to where they were heard by the rest of the army assembled in the night outside. He spoke of sacrifice and of honour and of the great victory which would be theirs, and as he spoke the dragons, including Lapse, believed. More than that – they loved.

By fire he ruled – the fire of wrath and the fire of fear – and with that fire now his words rolled out of the Portal.

'Loyal Lapse,' he concluded, 'take from me the knowledge of your comrades' tracks, so that you may be the first to breach the mighty Portal!'

A cheer echoed outside as Wraith bent his head down towards Lapse's and described in short, accurate words the details of the previous safe courses trodden by the nineteen dead dragons. They cheered, yes, but it was a cheer much quieter than those which had been raised when the first few dragons had been sent in.

Wraith hoped desperately that this twentieth pathfinder would finally solve the riddle of the Portal, but beneath that hope seethed anger that he, mighty Wraith, should be confounded by a charm set by senile Halcyon. And beneath the anger stirred the first tendrils of fear of the Maze itself, that he might never breach it.

His eyes bulging with horror at the mound of corpses, Lapse passed out from beneath Wraith's wings and into the rich darkness of the Portal. Though they could not see within, a hush fell over the waiting troops.

Lapse stepped over a line of grooves cut into the soft, porous rock floor and realized they were the marks left when the body of one of his predecessors had been dragged back from the scene of his death, presumably by a charm of Wraith's. Wraith's instructions, already spoken but now whispered again by his master as he moved, told him where to turn on the otherwise featureless floor; at times he doubled back on himself, at others he travelled straight then moved in a tight circle. All the time his inherent charm-sense gave him warning of magical triggers set invisibly in the air, but they were somehow muffled, their precise positions uncertain. No wonder even great Wraith needed path-finders. What terrible dangers were here?!

Lapse gulped and concentrated on the invisible labyrinth.

He was approaching a pool of sticky blood which had congealed before it had been able to soak into the spongy rock. Trails of gore led back towards where Wraith perched on his dead soldiers. Lapse felt a long way from anywhere.

This was the blood of the nineteenth dragon. Here the trail ended. Here his work began.

Cumber and Scoff looked at each other in horror as Fortune's cry echoed around the arena.

The silver guard flung his head round, staring straight at where Fortune stood on the other side of the plateau. A frown distorted his brow as he struggled to make out what he thought he saw there in the darkness, swaying his head

216

from side to side and squinting as if looking into the sun.

Turquoise hesitated, confused.

Scoff barrelled into Silver, head lowered, a battle-cry bursting from his mouth as he struck the guard low in the chest, knocking the wind from him and tumbling him on to his back. Silver's head struck a sharp rock outcrop and he dropped limp, his eyelids flickering briefly before he finally fell unconscious. Scoff hovered over him, suspicious – the dragon's armour was heavy, particularly around his head and neck, and he wanted to be sure he was truly out cold.

Turquoise backed away, eyes narrowed, as Cumber advanced towards him. Blue fire snaked across the guard's back as he raised a store of fire charm in his body; it writhed down his limbs and lanced out of them, solidifying into enormous, reaching claws.

Cumber crouched low, seeking an opportunity.

Turquoise pounced, and then halted abruptly in mid-air, a look of surprise splashed across his face.

Cumber, as one of the creators of the invisibility charm, could see Fortune lash out with his hind legs, clawing and battering at the charmed dragon's head.

While Turquoise was thus distracted Cumber sent a thick bolt of Realm fire into his body, stunning him instantly. His body dropped prone on top of Silver's with a dull thud.

Fortune dropped from the sky and landed neatly between his two charmed companions. They in turn looked at each other, shrugged and dissolved the cloaking charm, returning Fortune to the visible world.

'No need for that any more,' said Cumber, a wry smile on his face. 'Well done, Fortune.'

'Foolish,' grumbled Scoff, his gaze still casting over the unconscious guards. 'Clever, though.'

'I think that was a compliment, Fortune,' commented Cumber, still smiling, but as Fortune smiled back he saw the charmed dragon's face grow serious again.

'What's the matter?' he asked.

Cumber pointed past him towards the crack in the cliff. 'I don't know,' he replied. 'But I think we're about to find out.'

A crimson glow was building inside the cave – or was it

217

a tunnel? As they watched it grew in intensity and began to pulse. A shower of pebbles dislodged itself from the cliff high above and scattered around them.

The ground began to shake.

'Go on. You will be rewarded.'

The back wall of the Portal loomed close. No tunnel showed in its surface but instinct told Lapse that one had to be there, close by.

Charm seemed to buzz high to his right so Lapse turned left and took six decisive steps diagonally towards the wall.

Safe!

He paused and gently sniffed at the charm around him. It was stronger here, easier to locate, and he wove his way through a series of spirals to find himself a wing's length from the wall.

A white patch stained the floor just in front of him and the air above it positively crackled with charm. As he looked into the stain he saw a vague outline of . . . something in the rock, a flat silhouette of something not really there.

'Master?'

'Go on!'

Lapse stepped on to the pale, white stain and screamed as he was ripped from the world and sucked into another, more distant realm — perhaps the Realm, perhaps another. His mind exploded and he knew no more.

But though Lapse did not see the result of his work, Wraith did and he rejoiced. Though he snatched from Lapse's mind — as he had from the previous nineteen sacrifices — the precise details of the course he had trodden, the knowledge was redundant, for the twentieth pathfinder had broken the labyrinth.

A massive charge of crimson fire bolted back through the cave, feeding back into the countless guardian charms and destroying them in a dizzying series of implosions. Sparks rained past Wraith and out into the open air where the terrified dragons hid and prayed that it was not the Master's wrath but his triumph that they were witnessing.

The fire burst into the sky, consumed itself, and vanished with a crack of concentrated thunder.

Halcyon's blockade had been destroyed.
The Portal was open.

Fortune, Cumber and Scoff dropped to the ground as the crimson glow built and then launched a jet of fire out into the arena. The flames dispersed as quickly as they had been formed and only the earthquake remained, rocking the ground and sending a criss-cross of tiny cracks radiating out from the great cleft which already split the cliff almost in two.

'Run for the tunnel!' cried Cumber over the rumbling and as one they scrambled into the cleft as a huge slice of the rock outcrop sheared away from the rest of the cliff and tumbled to the ground.

It exploded behind them, shattering. An eerie silence followed, broken only by the rattle of the few remaining pebbles racing down from the large cavity which now disfigured the upper part of the cliff face.

A giant cairn filled the centre of the arena.

Somewhere beneath lay Silver and Turquoise; their passing was not mourned for long.

The three explorers crouched safe beneath the overhang of the tunnel entrance, gradually understanding what this place was, and what it was they had just witnessed.

Halcyon's barricade had stretched to the six lesser Portals too and so now there were seven ways opened into the Plated Mountain.

In one of the mountain's secret chambers, Halcyon waited, and watched, and wondered.

This was a dragon who had lived long and who had seen much, possibly more than any dragon deserved. But then was that not something he had brought upon himself, all those long years ago? The Maze had never permitted a successor, and he had never felt the need to die.

He was Halcyon, and he would survive to set the Turning on its course.

He rested now, as much as he could ever truly rest, wandering in his small, spare caves deep in the heart of the Plated Mountain. An unremarkable dragon he was in many ways, his papery scales brown, old and rusted. When he became still it was as if he had always been at rest in that place, immovable, rusting for aeons. He was not who a dragon might expect the Leader of the Charmed to be, but then was that title not redundant now – had not the wider world been changing for many years before that?

Had it not been turning?

Of course it had, as had always been the case, but those old, smooth changes were over now; the changes which this winter would bring would not be gentle, not at all.

The Black Dragon was on his way in through the greatest of the entrance ways. He prayed that the remaining defences would delay him long enough for the rest of the story to unfold.

He sent his mind into Mantle's chamber for a space of time, to see what dragon it was that his venerable colleague had brought to the mountain to serve his own, small part in the complexity of the Turning . . .

And he wondered too whether *any* dragon might brave the lesser entrances to enter the mountain.

The back wall of the Portal was split from top to bottom, forming an entrance wide enough to take three dragons walking abreast. Wraith approached it rejoicing, feeling with satisfaction the emptiness of the air around him. Reaching the place where Lapse had died, he scuffed at the floor, puzzled.

Lapse's dying mind had shown him a flash of white exploding from the ground as he had stepped on to this spot. Charm, of course, but with a strange flavour. Almost like . . . troll?

A trigger?

But a trigger which, when trodden upon, had demolished the entire defensive labyrinth. For what purpose would Halcyon have placed such a self-destructive oddity into his blockade?

This was too easy, Wraith decided grimly. Halcyon evidently hoped to lull his adversary into complacency, encouraging him to march straight through the broken Portal and into . . . what?

Wraith cast his charm-sense through the break in the wall. Magic stared back: he had breached the Portal only to reveal unknown layers of charm barricaded beyond. Charm still more powerful than that which he had so far faced.

And march straight into a trap? Well, not the Black Dragon. Still I shall be cautious. The mountain will be breached and Halcyon will be found, however long it may take!

But he could not suppress his rage at having been forced to reassess his strategy, to regulate his campaign not by his own timescale but by one set by Halcyon. Of one thing he could now be sure – he would not conquer the mountain tonight, nor tomorrow night; there were more defences than he had ever anticipated.

'I grow impatient, Halcyon,' he murmured with smooth anger. 'And when I do find you, you will pay dearly for this.'

He stormed out of the Portal and back into the night, bellowing summons to all his commanders. He needed all the gathered charm-sense of his best dragons to map this new magic so that it could be systematically taken apart. Dragons jumped to action as he thundered among them, barking orders and lashing at those he deemed too slow to respond. Loyal blood flowed beneath his rage and brave dragons cowered in his path.

Yet all obeyed, for their love and their fear were total.

I will take any route now, large or small. Halcyon will be conquered!

Dragons swarmed to his commands, the night seethed with glowing chains of magic as Wraith's team of charm-sensitives began to probe the mystery of Halcyon's traps and ramparts, and squads were despatched to the six lesser portals. *Any route.*

And close on three hundred were ordered into the skies above the forest around Covamere, for a different purpose.

These dragons flew with grim determination, for the orders they had been given were shocking in the extreme. The ruthlessness of this latest strategy revealed the true depth of their master's wrath.

They flew low over the trees, gathering fire in their throats.

CHAPTER 18

Separation

'Was it a fire charm?' asked Fortune, blinking away the after-image of the dazzling crimson flash.

'Of course,' Cumber replied. Then he shook his head and added, 'But there's something I don't quite understand. Scoff, do you feel it?'

Scoff nodded and said, 'Gone now. Whatever it was. Retreated.'

'What is? What's retreated?' Fortune could not hide his curiosity.

'A massive charm was guarding this entrance,' explained Cumber. 'I could sense it as soon as we came up on to this plateau.'

'I'd've said troll,' put in Scoff gruffly. 'If I didn't know better.'

'Hmm. Well, whatever it was, something's defeated it. Someone else is trying to get inside the mountain and that someone has beaten us to it.'

'Wraith,' breathed Fortune.

'Without doubt,' agreed Cumber. 'But at least he's saved us a task. He'll probably send more troops to cover this exit now that the guardian charm is breached, but at least we've got a clear run in . . .'

'If there's no more magic waiting for us inside, that is,' interrupted Fortune. 'And it's doubtful we shall have a clear run out either.' Fortune thought fast. 'Scoff, you must go back to the others – make sure they're safe. If Wraith has breached Halcyon's defences he'll probably attack straight away; it might be some time before we're able to get back out again.'

'If you get out at all,' warned Scoff.

But Fortune was adamant.

'Be that as it may, it's our task to reach Halcyon and if he's inside the mountain then inside the mountain we'll go!'

'You're mad,' Scoff replied, clearly convinced that this was rapidly becoming a pointless quest. 'But the others will need help. If there's fighting in the forest it's Charmed protection they'll need. Where will we meet again? I'll have to get the others clear.'

'Gossamer knows,' responded Fortune quietly, prompting a puzzled look from Cumber.

Scoff watched the two dragons together and was struck by their obvious closeness. *Friends with me too*, he thought proudly, feeling a little foolish at the surge of emotion which accompanied this realization. For too many years he had buried himself away at Aether's Cross, turning his back on Halcyon and on the duties he was sworn to do. For too many years he had remained aloof and friendless. But no more.

He was back, back at Covamere, back in Halcyon's domain, back with dragons he could call his friends. Halcyon needed him, of that he had no doubt, but more than that – dragons needed him. Gossamer and Brace, they needed him now.

A steady rumbling was growing on the night air.

'Listen,' said Scoff, responding first. 'Dragons. Not much time. Get in there. And good luck. Hope my eyes see you again, my friends. That I hope.'

Fortune heard the sound of dragons on the move and on the wing. An army of dragons was getting nearer.

'All speed to you, Scoff,' he said, slapping his gnarled friend on the flank.

'Look after those wings,' called Cumber.

By way of reply Scoff spread his rainbow sails and leaped into the air, flying low and fast over the edge of the plateau until he dropped out of sight on his journey back down the mountain.

Fortune watched him go and then turned to face the blackness of the tunnel. He felt . . . strange. Earlier, when he and Gossamer had been caught up in that bitter, winter wind which had come from nowhere and died more quickly

223

than seemed natural, he had felt this way too, **as though the Plated Mountain were waiting for him, speaking to him.**

Halcyon is inside, he thought resolutely.

But was there not something else in there too? **Something which moved with great power?** *The power of the stars!*

'Father!' he whispered, too quietly for **Cumber to hear.**

'Well,' said Cumber bravely, leading the **way into the** tunnel, 'it looks like it's just you and me **again, Fortune,** adventurers to the end.'

Together they entered the darkness.

'It's just the beginning, Cumber,' murmured Fortune. 'Just the beginning.'

The flash of crimson was brief and bright, and it was more than enough to wake most of the dragons sleeping in Loom's and Tillery's makeshift camp. A few breaths after that blood-red glow had dissipated the sound of its fury thumped through the trees. The Naturals roused themselves swiftly, to a dragon gazing up the mountain slopes towards distant Covamere, whence the light had come.

Gossamer woke to find her brother standing beside her, his wings spread as if to protect her from whatever danger might be descending towards them. He was trembling slightly.

It was that pose, that promise of protection, which Gossamer was to remember much later, when that long night of the new moon had passed and when she and Brace had been forced apart. There he stood, a young dragon once fat but now . . . and she found herself astonished at the transformation she saw in him. Though still solidly-built he was undeniably leaner – much leaner – and his wings had lengthened and hardened into tough and serviceable engines of flight. He stood taller and stronger and his hide, even in the scant starlight, seemed to possess a lustre of health she had not seen in him before.

Why, she thought with pleasure, *the journey has made a dragon of him!*

And as he turned to her she saw that these physical changes were accompanied by a new light in his eye, but so delighted was she that he had grown so and matured so that she did not see what inner fire it was which generated that light, nor did she see it until it was too late. For now she could only be proud.

'If only mother could see you now,' she sighed as he bent to speak to her.

'Did you see that!' Brace exclaimed excitedly, waggling his wing at the mountain. 'That was magic, no doubt about it! Something's happening up there!'

'That's as maybe, young dragon,' came the quavering voice of Tillery, 'but such things are best left unlooked-at by the likes of us. We'd best be going, and sooner than soon – sooner than now, in fact.'

Gossamer watched the crimson light dying behind the towering trees and could only worry for the safety of Fortune and Cumber and Scoff, for it seemed to her that such an explosion could only mean that some or other kind of disaster had occurred up there. She prayed that it had not swallowed up her friends and her love.

Brace, by way of contrast and for reasons Gossamer could not make out, seemed excited by the whole thing.

'What should we do, Brace?'

It was, she realized, the first time she had turned to him for guidance in this way and the moment was not lost on either of them. He was now a dragon to be trusted, a dragon to be consulted – more than a little brother, he was Brace.

But just then the sky, already dark with the night, grew darker still . . . with dragons. As the dragons descended the two youngsters huddled together, grateful that the livid red light which had broken the night had gone, for whatever fate it was they now faced was surely one best kept concealed by the dark.

Fortune had perished in the crimson explosion and here were Wraith's warriors sent to root out his remaining friends and companions.

She closed her eyes and thought of Haven, that she would some day meet her love there, although surely not in this life.

'There's something very strange going on here.'

Cumber paused, allowing his words to echo away down the sloping tunnel.

'Something very strange indeed!'

He frowned at Fortune, who stood at his side with a blank and dreamy expression.

The tunnel had admitted them readily enough. Fully aware that untold numbers of charmed dragons were already landing in the arena outside, they had marched resolutely into the blackness in the hope that there might at least be some delay before they were followed, or that the tunnels might prove confusing enough that they could lose themselves swiftly.

But they were not followed. *Not at all.*

Cumber thought he knew what was happening, but what disturbed him was that he did not know *why* it was happening. It was clear to him that some dragon – presumably Wraith – had broken the defences protecting the entrances to the mountain. Therefore he and Fortune had been able to enter.

All of which was reasonable enough, but even so it seemed unlikely that dragons such as he and Fortune would have been able simply to walk in, even after that perimeter charm had been neutralized: the tunnels within should have been soaking with charm. But they were not. Or rather, here they were not.

'What's bothering you?' murmured Fortune, clearly distracted by something beyond Cumber's awareness.

'I'll tell you what's bothering me,' responded Cumber in a state of considerable distress, 'something's letting us through, that's what's bothering me. There's magic ahead of us and there's magic behind us – Halcyon's defences or I'm no Charmed – but wherever we are, it disappears! Something's protecting us, and I don't know what!'

'Halcyon?' suggested Fortune, shaking himself from his reverie with reluctance. 'Anyway, what difference does it make now? We're here, so we might as well go on.'

Cumber exhaled noisily, an exasperated sigh, then stopped.

'Naturals!' he gasped. 'You find yourself at the centre of an inexplicable, nonsensical magical phenomenon and what do they say? They ask what difference it makes! Well, if I had my way we'd stop right here and think very carefully.'

'Cumber!' exclaimed Fortune from some way up the tunnel. 'Shut up and follow me! We've got a long way to go yet, and not much time!'

'Pah!' grumbled Cumber. 'What does he know anyway? All right, I'm coming. But be careful!'

Through the tunnels they marched, through the black, craggy depths where the only illumination was the thin, wavering light-charm which Cumber had generated and which bobbed just ahead of them, turning the rough, porous rock into an ever-changing gallery of shadows and shapes which clawed their way past until they died into the blackness behind. The air was icy and still; all was silent.

Cumber muttered to himself about the flimsiness of the bubble of safety in which they themselves were somehow contained. Fortune trudged on in front of his companion.

The tunnel offered them no changes of direction; it simply took them in and down, into the mountain and down below the ground. There were no forks and no turns. No choices. None of which bothered Fortune, for the very straightness of the route seemed to be exactly what he had always hoped for: a direct line to Halcyon himself, to the end of the quest.

But is this not just the beginning?

And the quest itself, was that not now worthless, a tasteless joke? Here they were to tell Halcyon about South Point – and of course Aether's Cross – and yet the violence had preceded them. The Black Dragon had already brought the conflict to the Plated Mountain and Covamere; their own, small story was as nothing compared to the epic scenes unfolding all around him.

Black Dragon was setting Charmed upon Charmed. *We Naturals have become irrelevant to the quest*, Fortune thought sadly. *This is a tale of charm now, for it will always be more powerful; it will always prevail.*

The cry was rapidly taken up by all the dragons in the half-dismantled camp, but it was started by Brace.

'They're Naturals!' he exclaimed as the dragons dropped swiftly into the clearing.

They were five, not at all the army they had first appeared when their large wings had first blocked out the stars, and they descended into the clearing with silent precision. There was something altogether threatening about them, Gossamer thought, something altogether . . . military.

'Who are they, do you think?' came a nervous whisper at Gossamer's flank.

Gossamer turned to see a young female dragon crouched behind her, peering tentatively around her wings at the activity. The newcomer was small and slight, with large, excited eyes.

'I don't know,' Gossamer replied with the trace of a smile. 'Who are you?'

'I'm Velvet, and I'm very pleased to meet you,' came the immediate answer, accompanied by a nervous bobbing of the head and an inquisitive craning of the neck. 'I don't like the look of them myself. What do you think?'

'I don't know,' repeated Gossamer patiently. 'Let's wait and see, shall we?'

Velvet flashed a grin at Gossamer and then frowned as she watched the five strange dragons alight on the ground before them.

There was a silence.

'Who's in charge here?' one of the intruders cried brusquely. At once Loom stepped forward and said, 'We're all of us equal, but you can address yourselves to me. What do you want with us? Speak swiftly, since we're moving out.'

No dragon listened more closely than Brace to what the stranger said.

'You are right to be moving out,' he shouted, casting his head around so that all of those dragons present would hear him. 'You must leave this place and leave it now. But think of this before you leave: there is a Charmed army descending from the mountain all across the forest. What their purpose is you may guess as well as any, but you can be sure it bodes ill for natural dragons.

'You have a choice: either go blindly and find yourselves overtaken by the Charmed and their evil magic, or come with us. We can promise you a place of safety and a chance to hit back against a common enemy.'

Brace had been gradually moving towards the newcomers as their leader spoke and only now did Gossamer realize how far apart they were. She was about to call to him when Velvet tugged at her wing.

'Do you think they're the enemy?' she hissed.

228

'Who? These dragons?' replied Gossamer, still watching her brother closely. Perhaps he had not changed as much as she had thought.

'No, silly! The Charmed, of course. I don't think they are, even if you do.'

Gossamer looked down at her with surprise, regarding her companion with sudden respect.

Loom was speaking again, interrogating the dragon about where this so-called place of safety was, and what evidence he had that the Charmed were coming.

'You will not need evidence soon, old fool!' snapped the dragon angrily. 'You will be evidence!'

'I'll come,' said Brace in a small voice then, clearing his throat, he repeated himself more loudly. 'I'll come! And I think all of you should as well. These dragons are right: it's time for us to make a stand against them before they destroy us once and for all!'

'Brace, no!' cried Gossamer, running forward. Velvet scrabbled behind her, surprised by the sudden movement but unwilling to let her new friend stray too far from her side.

'Wait for me, please,' she called. 'I haven't even asked you your name yet!'

'Gossamer!' answered Gossamer automatically, and then for the second time that night the sky burst into flame.

Fortune was finding it almost impossible to concentrate. Although his senses told him that the tunnel was proceeding ahead in the same straight line, nevertheless he found his vision blurring and his balance wavering, as though the air were thickening and the jagged floor were twisting and turning beneath his claws. Turning!

The magic groaned like a giant yawning and Fortune felt it shifting its fields into a new configuration. He imagined he could almost see the fields of magic peeling apart to admit them, and then closing again behind to seal their escape route.

Who, or what, is letting us through?

Fortune did not know, nor could he guess, but something was growing in him, a conviction that soon he would know. Or that perhaps he knew already . . .

This conviction built inside his heart, filling the hole which existed there until it took on a shape he could not see but which he knew immediately.

The shape of the hole in his heart: the shape of his father.

Ahead, through blurred eyes, he seemed to see the tunnel divided into two, a fork which offered a sudden choice in the direction they might take. The rock undulated, the two tunnels merging into one and then back to two.

The floor shook, the walls rotated, the ceiling rippled. In every direction the magic bore down upon him, hungry.

'Cumber. Which way do we . . . ?'

Turning to face Cumber, he saw that his friend was no longer there.

Cumber was, if he was honest with himself, terrified.

It's all very well for you, he thought uncharitably, watching Fortune's apparently easy progress up ahead. *You know nothing about the Maze, nor much about Halcyon, nor even much about charm. It's just all one big adventure to you, Fortune.*

Despite his fear he managed to envy his friend's innocence. Fortune would never be forced to experience the horrors of the Realm, nor the awesome responsibility it brought upon those dragons who used it. Here, deep inside the Plated Mountain, the Realm was so close Cumber could almost see it, almost smell it, almost touch it.

How could they know they were walking into anything other than a trap?

It's not a trap – Halcyon wouldn't lead us into a trap!

But what if it was not Halcyon who was doing the leading?

Again Fortune's tail was disappearing into the blackness and again Cumber increased his speed, but this time his attention had wandered so far that he did not notice a sharp ridge of rock running the width of the tunnel. He struck it painfully with both of his front legs and tumbled forward, thumping his head against the rightside wall. Light flashed inside his eyes.

He was unconscious for only a fraction of a breath, but it was enough. When he came to again, Fortune had vanished.

'Fortune!' he shouted, pitching himself forward recklessly. 'Fortune, come back! Wait for me!'

* * *

The trees on the south side of the clearing ignited in a great wave of fire which rushed through the forest, flashing away around the mountain with horrifying ferocity; it was as though the sun had risen right in front of them.

The screams of dragons caught like the trees in a burst of fire were dreadful to hear. Those who were left sprang desperately into the air, thrashing their wings against the smoke and ash which were already being pumped up into the sky to fill the night with orange clouds and coils of drifting embers. Out of the path of the flames they struggled, flying up and then away from the mountain, and they did not stop, nor even slow, until beneath them there was no more fuel to feed the storm of raging fire.

'Come on!' shouted Gossamer to Velvet over the roaring. The flames below them were white and frantic; they looked unnatural. 'Keep up with me – we can't afford to get left behind!'

'I'm trying,' panted Velvet, hauling her way through the searing air.

Ahead Gossamer could see Brace, lagging behind the main group and casting frequent backward glances to make certain his sister and her companion were all right.

'We don't have to go with them, you know,' spluttered Velvet as she battled gamely along at Gossamer's side.

'I'm not going with them,' came Gossamer's short reply. 'I'm going with Brace.'

But the fire had other ideas.

Ahead was the brow of a ridge as yet untouched by the fire. The main group had already passed over it and now Gossamer and Velvet were forced to climb above currents of air which were whipping back towards them from the other side. Relieved to get ahead of the fire – if only briefly – they glanced down to see the pines reaching up towards them from the black rock as though desperate to be rescued from the fate which awaited them.

'Hurry,' urged Gossamer, 'we mustn't let them out of our . . .'

But as they crested the ridge the fire met them again. It had already rushed around the ridge and was swarming up the opposite slope, accelerating skywards with blinding speed. Gossamer and Velvet began their descent only to be confronted by an enormous wall of white flames. It careered towards them, hot and hungry.

The two dragons screamed with a single voice and skidded their wings against the boiling air, turning abruptly back upon themselves. Back across the blazing forest flew Gossamer and Velvet, desperate now to find a space to land. Battalions of charmed dragons were sweeping low over the trees in broad, wing-like formations. In their wake the forest burned.

It was Realm fire, fast and intelligent, destroying ferociously and dying swiftly, leaving utter devastation in its place.

Gossamer and Velvet flew as low as they dared, hoping against hope that it would die swiftly enough that they might find a place where its flames were already spent before they were brought out of the sky by its power.

Fortune waited in the darkness for a while, straining to hear the click-click of claws as Cumber caught up with him at last. But he heard nothing.

His head had cleared again, but not before he had seen something, something which had called to him like a dream long-forgotten, a vision of a story he had once been told. If only he could remember . . . But the vision had faded into the mist which was its border and Fortune had returned abruptly to the real world. More alert now than he had felt for the entire journey into the mountain so far, he decided to wait for Cumber.

At length he grew impatient and started to walk back in the direction he had come. He had not gone more than ten paces before he felt the air thicken around him and he could walk no further. An invisible barrier was pressing him back and the more he struggled against it the more rigid it became. For a few more breaths he tried to force a way through but eventually fell away and sat on the rocky floor, panting from the exertion.

He tried once more and gave up even sooner.

'Cumber!' he called, but there was no reply.

He was alone.

It dawned on him that he could still see, even though Cumber and his light charm had disappeared. He realized that there was a faint glow in the depths of the tunnels, far,

far, ahead, a pale blue light which flickered and wavered as though it came from some dying flame. He hurried down one of the tunnels in pursuit of its source.

This tunnel, unlike its predecessor, was wild. It dipped, it turned, it narrowed and writhed and widened and twisted, yet always the light was flickering ahead, teasing him and leading him on through the mountain. Time had stopped now for Fortune: all that mattered was the rock and the light, and whatever lay ahead at the end of his quest.

Halcyon! he thought excitedly as the tunnel widened unexpectedly into a broad cavern. Was this his audience chamber? But no, the tunnel forged on again at the far side of the cave, the blue light flashing invitingly just around the next corner.

His thoughts ran sharp and clear now as he ran through the dimly-lit tunnels, and it occurred to him that he could no longer sense the magic around him in the way he had earlier.

I must have passed through whatever defensive zone there was and reached the centre of the mountain!

A small pile of boulders blocked the way but Fortune forced a way through it keenly. Directly before him the tunnel shrank to a narrow vertical slot, beyond which the light was blinding.

It was hot here, hot and bright. Heat baked his skin. Flames roared before his watering eyes. The air stank of burning wood.

'No!' he howled.

He was on a sloping ledge overhanging the forest. Flames thundered skywards beyond the ledge. He swirled around to face the tunnel which had just spat him back out on to the side of the mountain. But there was no tunnel there, just a blank wall of rock.

Above him, the stars seemed very far away. He was outside.

But I haven't finished yet! What about the quest? What about Halcyon?!

Out of the corner of his eye he saw a brown shadow against the white of the flames. Another dragon, some distance away on the far side of the ledge.

A rumble made the cliff shake. Looking up he saw the

233

sky obliterated by a mass of flame and debris as a section of the cliff laden with burning vegetation broke free and grew massive in his vision. He felt the heat of its approach blistering the skin around his eyes and mouth as he dropped into a crouch and prepared himself for the end.

The other dragon moved.

Cumber had little time to reflect on his separation from Fortune before he felt himself snatched by sudden magic.

His body tingled as he was hauled into the Realm. Trapped beast-spirits howled and clawed at him as he swept past them, lancing magic towards his vague and hurtling form. The trip was virtually instantaneous, but no less disturbing for that.

Then, suddenly, he was standing wide-eyed in a large, spherical cavity which could have been a black facsimile of Ordinal's cave at South Point. Before him was hunched an old dragon, small and slight. He was black.

The Black Dragon!

But, of course, it was not. Scales not glossy but more like burned bark clung to the dragon's body as if in fear of sliding off. Here was not the terrible, ebony beauty of the Master but the shadow of great, great age. Humour and wisdom, not rage and ambition, vied for control of the sparkle in his eyes; behind them Cumber thought he detected a massive sadness.

As Cumber looked closer he saw that his scales hugged a skin dark yet translucent. Veins and muscles and – Cumber shivered – even bones seemed to be visible beneath that skin.

Blue light rose from a disc-shaped charm embedded in the floor, throwing deep shadows into an expression Cumber took to be a smile of welcome. As if he had read his thoughts the dragon nodded his head and said, 'Welcome, Cumber.' He moved across the polished floor with an easy grace which reminded Cumber of Fortune's economical gait. 'I am Mantle. Now, where should I begin?'

Fate, or whatever chain of coincidence was working that night, compelled Brace to look back at the very instant the fireball exploded over the ridge: Gossamer and Velvet were specks set against the distant pall of smoke, then a mountain of flame erupted into their path with appalling ferocity. And Gossamer was *gone*.

Unable to speak, Brace sliced his wings into the torrent of hot air behind him and turned his whole body around to face this latest devastation. The burning wind pushed him away and he drifted in the blazing air, eyes streaming, looking . . . despairing.

Then he was joined by another, who swooped from high above and matched Brace's wingbeats beside him. It was the leader of the group of dragons who had urged them to fight the Charmed.

'My sister!' sobbed Brace.

'It is a terrible thing to see your family burn,' responded the dragon, his voice hard. Yet he spoke as though he knew – really knew.

Brace looked at the other dragon, who said, 'You could do something. Come with us.'

'Revenge?' asked Brace.

'If you like.'

Before they rolled as one and sped away from the burning forest, the newcomer asked, 'Do you have any other companions?'

Brace thought hard. 'No,' he replied. 'No dragon else, just me and my sister. Just me, now. My name is Brace.'

'All right. Keep up, we've a long way to go. My name is Wood.'

CHAPTER 19

The Old Dragons

'But what about Fortune?' insisted Cumber, standing his ground despite Mantle's best efforts to draw him closer to the blue light which was set in the floor in the centre of the cave. Like Ordinal's cave, this was a troll burial chamber, and the ancient bones stared down at them in patient silence.

'Oh, very well,' grumbled the old dragon. He scratched irritably at his flank with one tattered wing and lowered one horny eyebrow. 'Your friend, Fortune, is safe enough. Or at least he has left the tunnels safely enough — what happens to him thereafter is out of my control, I'm afraid.'

'So we were being controlled?' asked Cumber, pursuing the point relentlessly. Much as he had warmed to this wizened creature he felt determined to root out all the answers he could. After all, had they not travelled half the world to reach this place, and were they not entitled to some sort of explanation? 'But what about Halcyon? What's all this got to do with you? Who are you?'

Mantle sighed heavily.

'Dear me,' he exclaimed. 'Are you the best Ordinal could come up with?'

Cumber blinked. He opened his mouth, then closed it with a snap. He blinked again.

'I hope you're less foolish than you look,' said Mantle, scrutinizing Cumber's face from a distance which the youngster found uncomfortably close.

Cumber blinked again, then managed to say in a small, damp voice, 'You knew Ordinal?'

Mantle raised his head and tutted, swinging his weathered horns from side to side.

'Well of course I did, young Cumber,' he intoned impatiently, 'and a fine dragon she was too. Never met her, of course, but we shared the same sense of humour.' He turned away and bustled across the cave.

Ordinal? And this . . . Mantle? Sense of humour?

Cumber stepped gingerly around the disc of blue light and followed his host. Mantle was busying himself with some kind of structure set partly into the wall. To the side of the strange device a great troll's bone lay partly-buried in the rock, its surface rich grey and pitted with marks. In the blue light it looked curiously alive, as though it might suddenly start to move.

'You never met her?' Cumber prompted. 'You knew her and yet you never met her?'

Crazy though the idea was he had no doubt that it was true, for this Mantle seemed as fond of the enigmatic response as had his old teacher.

'Of course,' the old dragon replied, spinning around briskly, 'there were ten of us then. Still, times change.'

Cumber lowered his head and forced himself to suppress his growing temper. When he raised it again, it seemed to him that the ghost of a smile had crept across Mantle's face.

'Could you please,' he began wearily, 'just tell me what is going on?'

'Nothing would give me greater pleasure,' beamed Mantle. 'But first I want to show you something.'

Halcyon sent his thoughts out through the mountain towards Covamere. Almost immediately he felt the first of the five layers of defensive charm he had set between his innermost stronghold and the Portal. Wraith, as he had predicted, had broken through the Portal with ease and now only these five inner layers remained, formidable every one, dangerous every one, but none of them invincible, not to a dragon like Wraith. That he would destroy them all and reach Halcyon – and, of course, the Maze – there was no doubt; what mattered now was how long it took him.

That's all the defences ever were – a play for time.

There was one other factor which might slow Wraith, and that was the possibility that he would expect the remainder of Halcyon's army to be waiting for him inside the mountain and therefore be cautious. This was Halcyon's final and most dangerous gambit.

For only he and Mantle were left.

Only he and Mantle knew how weak his support had really become. There was the Hardship, of course, that core of loyalty which Wraith had somehow managed to subdue . . .

The Maze had something to do with that. Treacherous, to the last!

But Halcyon's sight stretched rather further than that of Wraith, and he could see things entirely hidden to the Black Dragon. Things which, once seen, could not be unseen.

And then, he thought finally, *there is the Sleeper. What that will do should it ever awake is beyond my power to foresee – or control.*

Isolated, old, Halcyon pushed his mind out beyond the outer layer of charm which had so far protected him from the forces of the Black Dragon and inspected the devastation which his adversary had dealt upon the Plated Mountain.

The hideous Realm fire had burned with impossible heat and unnatural speed, incinerating and sterilizing the ring of forest by the time the first strands of sunrise began to filter into the cloud-filled sky. When the sun rose, Halcyon spied upon Wraith and felt with a shudder Wraith's cold satisfaction at the dry, black desert of the mountain slopes, covered now with ash and smouldering charcoal. Not for Halcyon the sanctuary of a concealed escape route through some hidden part of the forest, not for Halcyon the chance of retreat. A few small stretches of woodland remained, those specifically ordered by Wraith to be left untouched, but for the most part the forest was gone, cleansed with brutal efficiency.

Halcyon could feel Wraith's certainty of victory, which was sharpened by anger. The Black Dragon turned back into the Portal and consulted the commander of the charm-sensitives who were hard at work mapping the first layer of magic Halcyon had constructed behind the hole in the wall. Most of the investigators agreed that there were at least four layers, but certainly no more than six.

'One day each, at least,' sighed the commander, already exhausted. It was demanding work, and potentially lethal.

'One day each,' agreed Wraith, taking the dragon at his word. 'No more.'

He was angry that it should take so long to break Halcyon's defences. But underneath Wraith was confident that Halcyon had nowhere to go. He felt invincible. And he was angry for another reason, Halcyon learned, without understanding its import: Insiss had disappeared, leaving him to deal directly with his lesser commanders.

Then the anger turned to something more sinister and Halcyon sensed that Wraith found a new pleasure in working more closely with his dragons rather than through the mediation of that slippery creature. His dragons were working hard for him, harder than they had ever worked before.

'It's moving!' exclaimed Cumber after he had observed the bone for a space of time. He could hear nothing, but he could definitely see the movement, almost imperceptible but undeniably there.

'It's moving,' agreed Mantle, squinting at the bone. 'Like the rest of them. Like many things these days.'

'But what's making it happen?'

'Ah,' replied Mantle. 'Now there's the question. Care to guess?'

'Well,' began Cumber, eager to appear something more than simply a foolish young dragon who knew nothing about the world, 'it's a troll's bone, that much we know. It's old, and it's moving of its own accord back into the rock. Um . . .'

'Well done. You have just stated the obvious. But you asked why.'

'All right then. Why?'

'I don't know,' beamed Mantle with infuriating glee. But before Cumber could retort the old dragon lowered his brow and pulled his young visitor close. 'But listen to me now, young Cumber, for I don't mean to be flippant with you. It's true that I can't tell you why this phenomenon is happening, but what I can do is give you a wide view. Now listen. Did Ordinal ever tell you that the world was turning?'

'Well, yes, but . . .'

'But you never understood what she meant? All right,

then I'll tell you – I'll tell you as much as I know, for it may be that you'll discover truths that even I've not yet come across.

'The world is turning, Cumber. Take these bones, for instance. They have lain here long years, dead and still, but now they have started to move. They are slipping deeper into the rock, burying themselves beyond reach so that they might never be found again. But there is more, for as they move they are also growing older; their past is changing. It is turning.'

'I don't understand.'

'These bones,' continued Mantle with growing excitement, 'are changing from trolls' bones into something else altogether, into the bones of creatures our kind, our world has never known. But which the new world will have known. The trolls were old – thousands of years old – but these creatures will be older still – they will be millions of years old. Can you imagine that?'

Cumber shook his head dumbly, trying to imagine what creatures might ever have existed which were older and stranger than trolls, but in his mind the dawn of revelation was gradually casting up its first rays.

The world is turning, he thought with wonder.

'You see,' Mantle went on, 'the trolls were charmed. In old times, when our world was new-born, all creatures were charmed, and this state held true until comparatively recent times. A few generations ago the natural creatures started to appear and those Charmed who knew the signs saw that the world had started to turn, to turn towards a new course, to turn towards the future, away from charm.'

'So the charm is dying?' blurted Cumber, unable to contain himself. 'That's why magic is harder than it used to be, and why the trolls died out, and why charmed dragons are going mad and . . .'

'It's hard to see the whys of everything,' cautioned Mantle, staring hard into the blue light which lay in the middle of floor. 'But many things change when the world turns, and many things die.'

'I see,' said Cumber. 'I think I actually see!'

'No, you don't!' growled Mantle, his voice suddenly angry. Cumber took a step backwards, shocked at this unexpected change of mood. 'You don't see at all! But you will, I'll make sure of that!'

Cumber found himself backing towards the recessed disc of light. He stopped just short of it, glancing nervously back over his shoulder into the blue-white glow. Mantle loomed over him, leering in the harsh light.

Then the old dragon relaxed again.

'Oh,' he sighed, 'perhaps it's all very simple, in the end. Look: every so often the world turns, like you or I might turn in our sleep – perhaps the world is asleep, although I have no idea what might happen should it ever wake up.' He chuckled, as though the idea amused him, then continued. 'When it turns, everything changes. The last Turning saw the birth of charm and the next Turning – this Turning – will see . . .'

'. . . its death?' quavered Cumber.

'Perhaps. It doesn't necessarily happen like that, but . . . perhaps. Probably. But the important thing for you and I to understand is that there is always – always – a way for disaster to be averted. It just has to be found.'

'There's a way to save the magic?'

'Save the magic?' exclaimed Mantle as though the idea were ludicrous. 'Save the magic . . . young Cumber, if the magic were all that needed to be saved then we might consider ourselves fortunate. The world starts to turn of its own accord, by some cosmic reflex we cannot know, but it cannot complete the action on its own. Only by positive intervention can it be made to turn true.

'And the world must turn true, or else it will be destroyed.'

Halcyon pulled his senses free from Mantle's cell where he had been observing Cumber's enlightenment, such as it was. Something in Wraith had changed, and the change was noteworthy.

Wraith had flown to the small belt of forest he had allowed to remain at the bottom edge of Covamere, the forest where once the zirafae had roamed, and by the time he reached it he had all but erased Insiss from his thoughts. He was buoyed to see the machinery of his army working around him, his goal was in sight now, the end of his quest comfortably within the grasp of his claws. And it was his.

241

Alone. It was then something happened. The mood suddenly changed.

The Black Dragon was afraid!

This was new, and not entirely unwelcome. But it made Wraith even more unpredictable. It was from the ghosts amongst the trees, or rather from the past which they represented, that his fear came.

'Too much history,' Wraith announced to the dawn sky. 'Too many dragons.'

He was afraid of the past, but Halcyon could not see how that meshed with the rest of the weave.

Lost dragon, he thought, not without contempt. *The Maze had you by the throat, Wraith, and it took a Natural to drag you free. Only you, and I, and Mantle remember that day now; only we remember the lost dragon.*

What from that past could possibly return to threaten the Black Dragon now? This close to the Turning anything was possible.

Then there was Mantle and this newcomer sent by Ordinal. The young dragon was coming to terms with the revelations which were being opened before him. That was good; he was strong. Ordinal had chosen well.

But why did she send the Natural? Have we done right in rejecting him?

Halcyon wondered briefly if he should not have taken more interest in Mantle's role in all of this. He had been content enough with the division of responsibility at the time – indeed his own chosen task of fortification and confrontation was by far the more demanding role – but now . . . should he not have vetted these two visitors more closely?

But no. There was only so much any one dragon could do, and even Halcyon was only one dragon. Mantle it was who had chosen to admit Cumber and send his companion, the Natural, back into the fire. These were hard times, demanding hard decisions, and for all he knew Mantle's decision had been the right one.

Time would tell.

'Before I tell you what I need you to do,' said Mantle gravely, 'I want to show you this.'

242

'An illuminated floor?' replied Cumber wryly. 'It's very
. . . nice.'

'Don't jest! What sort of a job did Ordinal do on you then,
young Cumber, if she didn't teach you to show respect in
the presence of your elders?'

'Oh, all right, but tell me what you want from me. I need
to find Fortune; I've got to see if he's all right.'

'Who? Oh, your friend. Yes, well, there'll be time enough
for all that I'm sure, but first . . .'

Even as Mantle moved Cumber felt the Realm pressing
against the back of his skull, as though it had leaped from
a great distance and was now panting there, its jaws wide
and ready. He slammed his mind shut, suddenly conscious
of the tiny leaks of charm which he emitted constantly from
his own reservoirs of magic. The Realm chattered and
smoked with invisible hunger.

Mantle reached over to the contraption with which he
had been fiddling earlier and pressed his right wingtip
against it. It was a squared-off fold in the rock wall, plain
and dull but obviously humming with charm, for tiny bolts
of lightning were stabbing their way from its skin like quills.
Some of them struck Mantle, and where they did so his
charcoal scales glowed orange.

Looking back into the blue light, Cumber saw that it was
opening.

Like a great eye it opened, peeling its fire back into the
floor to reveal a flickering chasm of immeasurable depth.
The light twisted somehow as it withdrew, draping itself over
the upper reaches of the pit to send claws of blue fire down
into the void. Cumber gasped and gripped the edge tightly,
vertigo threatening to tug him down into the darkness.

Behind his mind, the Realm moaned and tried to push
him in.

Cumber tried to look away and found he could not. The
chasm, striped with bands of blue light which receded into
sullen shadow, hypnotized him, called to him, pulled at him
as the Realm pushed. He was falling, falling . . .

'Steady, Cumber!' laughed Mantle, grasping the young
dragon's haunches and hauling him away from the drop.
'Let's keep a respectable distance, shall we?'

Cumber could hear the light as it thundered into the

chasm. He could feel the pain in his head as the Realm tried
to tear its way through him to reach whatever it was that
lay below.

But you know what lies below, don't you, Cumber? he thought
desperately.

'Is that . . . ?' The words were like fire in his throat.

'. . . what you think it is?' Mantle concluded for him. 'Yes.
What you are observing is the only way into the greatest
challenge any dragon can ever face. This is the entrance to
the Maze of Covamere.'

Cumber dragged his eyes away from the brilliant blue
light to stare Mantle in the face. The movement was agony.

'Then you . . .' he whispered.

'I am Mantle. I am the Keeper of the Maze.'

He turned again, extended his wing and the hole in the
floor slammed shut before Cumber could blink. There was
no sound, but Cumber felt his ears thump as both the Maze
and the Realm retreated instantly to their own, strange resting places.

He dropped to the floor, shaking very badly.

'Don't worry,' whispered Mantle, folding a wing over him.
'You don't need to go in there. But there is something you
can do for me. I must tell you now and I must tell you
quickly, for it is time for you to go.'

Halcyon could judge little from Cumber's reaction to the
Maze. Most dragons reacted like that at first; it was only
successive encounters which proved their mettle – or their
lack of it.

But then Mantle had been right about one thing – no
dragon would need to enter the Maze ever again – except
one.

Now that Mantle was rapidly drawing his meeting to a
close, Halcyon withdrew from his chamber for the final time.
Cumber would be returned to the outside now using charm
borrowed from the Old Earth Dwellers, having been charged
with his task now, a relatively simple one but no less important for that. And so another strand of the weave would be
set in its place.

But could any of them ever see the whole pattern? Halcyon suspected not.

Only the Sleeper might see that far, should it ever awaken. But then if it does so, all that Mantle and Ordinal and I have planned may come to nought.

Halcyon bent his head, massively, incurably tired. Soon, he hoped, there would be an end to it all. Very soon.

He looked up at the black ceiling and swiftly entered the escape route which the Dwellers had prepared for him and which Wraith would never find.

This way is too subtle for his eyes, he thought with satisfaction as he glided through the rock and into new spaces formed from gentle, living charm.

Charm not of fire but of the earth. Well, it makes a change for Halcyon!

Up moved Halcyon — not fleeing, since before the dawn had fully broken he would be back in his prison, this time with no hope of escape — up through the mountain. Soon Mantle would join him and together with the Dwellers they would seek the answers which had so far eluded them.

Time was short, and perhaps the stones would bring them the insight they so desperately needed.

CHAPTER 20

Summit

Earth charm differs from fire charm in many ways. It is weaker, certainly, but in its way it is kinder. Where fire charm confronts, earth charm complements; where fire charm stimulates, earth charm soothes. The magic of the fire can all too easily bring death, but the magic of the earth is always about life.

This both Halcyon and Mantle knew, and their hope was that somehow the magic of the earth could be brought to bear upon the Turning, so that the new course of the world might be one not of death but of life.

This they hoped, but the hope was a slim one, and one in which neither of them had much conviction.

Weak magic. Earth charm is so fragile that even the cycle of time affects its power. Longest and shortest days stretch and compress its influence, and the times when it is at its most potent are the magic hours of dawn and dusk, when light and dark are distracted by their opposites and room is left between into which the sheerest, gentlest spells may be slipped.

Weak magic; fragile charm.

But *beautiful*.

The promise of dawn caressed the summit of the Plated Mountain.

A rugged but largely regular cone for most of its prodigious height, the mountain levelled off at its peak to form not a wide crater, as the other mountains had had before they became the Injured Mountains, but a flattened plain.

From here the view was unparalleled. To the north, the black foothills blended into pale desert and the distant, dis-

246

tant green of the Heartland. To the south the blackness continued further, the wasteland of the Injured Mountains laid open in all their terrible beauty. To the east lay the inner seas and the pale jags of the Ice Peaks, while to the west, beyond formidable cliffs, was the sea.

All of these things an observer might see, might taste, might inhale, from the top of the mountain; all these things held their splendours like gems woven into the fabric of the land.

But now, at the end of this long night, the mountain was different. The world was there, far away and fair, but in the dullness of the threatening dawn it looked cold and dead. Dying fires sparkled hopelessly in the ashes of the forest. Smoke wreaths trailed in endless loops. The silence was like the edge of death. The mountain itself looked colder still.

The summit was bare and white, the black rock concealed beneath the ever-present ice which clad it here at this great altitude. The air was thin and subtle; the sky was cold.

In the dark sky there gathered clouds, obliterating the remaining stars and racing the sun towards the day. And yet, there was a light. Not the dawn, not yet, but a magical light which chased in circles around the summit, a sequence of pulses which shone briefly, weakly just beneath the ice and which then melted into the rock below. The lights flashed, then disappeared, but the circle they had defined remained, for where each point of light had glowed there rose a small stone, no more than a pebble, each a different colour and each generating its own tiny reflections to form a mosaic of crimsons and ochres and cobalts fleeing across the ice like a shattered rainbow.

Soundlessly the stone circle raised itself from the ice, and when it had risen the dragons rose within it.

This was a journey Mantle rarely made, but it was one which always humbled him, for those who made it possible for him did so with little real power but enormous skill. The earth charm which they generated was weak, but it was wielded so accurately that its weakness did not matter. By comparison, his own use of fire charm — or even of earth charm itself, for that matter — was so crude that he felt

ashamed of what he could only perceive of as his own bru-
tality.

But it was not that he was brutal; it was just that they
were so gentle.

As he emerged into the cold, thin air at the top of the
mountain, Mantle reflected on his encounter with Cumber.
He had communicated his needs to the youngster well
enough, and he felt confident that the tasks would be carried
out according to his instructions. Cumber had been terrified
by the Maze, but then that was only to be expected.

So what is the problem?

Try as he might he could not isolate the feeling of unease
which had crept over him since he had sent Cumber back
outside. He regretted having sent the Natural back without
meeting him first, but then sending two dragons had never
been part of the plan – what had possessed Ordinal to do it
he could not imagine – and besides, the tasks which needed
to be done were tasks achievable only by charmed dragons,
namely himself and Halcyon and, in Ordinal's absence,
Cumber.

And Wraith, of course. We cannot forget his part in all of this.

Mantle, like Halcyon, remembered Wraith. The day two
dragons had emerged from the Maze had been a memorable
day indeed, for he had not long been appointed by Halcyon
as Keeper of the Maze, and as such was still regarded as a
novice. His handling of the situation – the careful quarantine
he had imposed upon the Natural and the instant dismissal
of the young Wraith – had brought him much praise and
respect, and had perhaps ultimately assured him his place
on the Secret Council.

Ten of them there had been on that Council, dragons
of no special merit other than great age. Their wisdom as
individuals varied but that simply added spice to their congress, and the collective decisions they made were generally
good ones. Their leader, naturally, had been Halcyon, and
Mantle had enjoyed greatly the melding of minds he had
shared with him, with Ordinal, and with the others. Foreth
and Reciter and Archan . . .

But over the years they had died. At least, he assumed
they had died; they had faded from contact. Other dragons
had occasionally joined the meeting of minds but now they

248

too were gone, now Ordinal, dear Ordinal was gone, and only he and Halcyon remained.

Were he less modest he might have admitted to himself that it was he who had sustained Halcyon over recent years, giving him the strength he needed to raise the great weights he had never thought it would be his own destiny to raise.

And now he had brought Halcyon here, slipping them both under Wraith's lightning gaze with the help of the Dwellers, their bodies flowing like enchanted water up through curious spaces in the mountain to emerge here at the summit, here inside the occasional ring of stones, the ring which was focused into reality only when the powers needed to sustain it could truly be justified.

Only when councils needed to be called.

Or when worlds needed to turn.

Two charmed dragons were lifted through the ice and deposited softly upon its skin, where they stood to await the arrival of their hosts, the Old Earth Dwellers, the Makers of the Ring, the Gentle Ones.

The two dragons said nothing to each other as they waited but they stood close, partly to share each other's warmth in the bitterness of the mountain air. However, any dragon watching from afar might have seen a deeper connection, for of the two there was one who leaned and one who stood foursquare.

Mantle it was who stood strong in the cold, supporting most of Halcyon's weight as he had supported his spirit over the long, desolate years of decline. Too old they were now, both of them, but Mantle had managed to retain something of his old fire. Halcyon was still powerful — frighteningly so, Mantle sometimes considered — but he was tired. The magic was there but its fire was gone.

But he is controlling so much magic, even now, Mantle reminded himself. *Even now he is refining the defences, misleading Wraith, protecting the Maze.*

But for how long could he keep it up?

The ice sheet vibrated and Mantle felt Halcyon shift his weight away so as to support himself again. Glancing sideways he saw something like a sparkle in the ancient Leader's watery eye.

249

Above them the sky was filling with great sheets of cloud but here on the summit all was still. Nothing disturbed the silence until . . . until the ice trembled again and a splinter of light raced from the centre of the circle to one of the perimeter stones.

The stone absorbed the faint glow and began slowly to grow, and as the light raced on around the circle so its fellow stones grew, lifting silently up towards the massing clouds until they towered over the dragons. Like watching sentinels the slender stones crowded into the ring of ice, thickening, watching . . .

The ice at the centre of the circle parted, and Mantle held his breath as the faeries emerged.

Like captured snow their bodies crystallized before him. Ethereal beings, the faeries existed normally as spirits, no more substantial than the air itself. But very occasionally, at their own hundred-year council or at other extraordinary times they made themselves real, briefly assembling physical bodies which housed and represented their spiritual selves.

This was such an extraordinary time.

Many years had passed since Mantle had last seen the faeries, and he had forgotten how beautiful they were. He gasped, drawing in the frigid air with sudden surprise as he looked upon the Old Earth Dwellers.

Thirteen they were, almost identical, tall and slim with intricate features and long, expressive limbs. The earth charm from which they had formed these bodies glowed within them and held them close to yet clear of the ice, so that they floated. Large eyes gazed sadly from thin, pointed faces and gossamer wings which were not wings but spectacular reservoirs of earth charm surged from their backs like sculpted and dew-soaked cobwebs.

As they floated towards the dragons the ice lifted tiny crystals towards their dancing forms, as though the land had released them only reluctantly and wanted them back, so much did it love them.

Mantle knew how much effort it had taken the faeries to bring not just him and Halcyon here, but themselves too, and he felt humble in their presence.

But can they help?

He had to admit that he thought not. But he had to try.

'Greetings to you,' he said softly, fearful that even the sound of his voice might blow these fragile beings apart.

'You are most welcome here, Mantle,' replied the lead faery, her voice a fragrant whisper. She clasped her slender hands against her breast and tilted her head to one side. A charming smile illuminated her sad face. 'And you too, Halcyon.'

'He is not strong,' said Mantle, indicating his companion with a nod. 'I will try to speak for us both, if I may.'

'We understand,' said the faery. 'Halcyon spends much power even as we speak, this much I can sense. The black one is powerful, and even Halcyon's fire is enough only to slow him. Nothing can stop him, it seems.'

'It seems,' agreed Mantle.

Halcyon closed his eyes, content to let them speak, for even here he could feel Wraith's dragons probing at the mountain defences, slowly beginning to unravel the magic he had woven into the rocks and the tunnels. As they searched so he strengthened, unwinding charm here, rebuilding it there, constantly upgrading, constantly confusing. For how much longer he could maintain his vigil he was not certain, nor to what ultimate purpose; he knew only that he must.

'The Black Dragon must be slowed,' he whispered before he dropped into a shallow slumber. 'The Maze must be protected at least until the moon is full again. After that . . . no creature can say.'

The faery bent her head as her companions assembled into a perfect semi-circle behind her. Mantle noted that their bodies were more transparent than hers, and that their eyes were tight shut. They would not participate in the discussion, he knew, for they were here only to support their leader. Their magic would combine to give her the energy she needed to communicate on this earthly plane, and no doubt they would contribute to her thoughts with their own too, supporting her in spirit as well as in charm and body.

'We have little time before dawn,' began the faery, 'but then there is perhaps little to be said.'

'Perhaps,' agreed Mantle. 'Can you help us?'

The faery sighed. Her breath condensed before her and it

was with undisguised joy that she watched the vapour roll away into the night.

'Such beauty in the physical world,' she exclaimed, her voice like sunlight in the darkness. Then she caught Mantle's eye and half-raised her hand to her face. 'Such a thing for a Dweller to say,' she added cautiously, as though he had witnessed something a dragon should not have seen.

'Changes?' asked Mantle gently.

'Changes,' nodded the faery. 'Not only into the world of dragons is this new nature intruding.'

Her expression proud and infinitely sad, she lifted her chin and opened her arms wide, exposing her whole body to Mantle's gaze. Her own distress was reflected in his dragon eyes for he saw the new shapes which were growing beneath her skin, the hard bone which was pressing out against the pale flesh, the rude skull which was beginning to distort the fluid contours of her head. The natural creature which was building itself inside her ethereal form.

'Each time we make ourselves real it becomes a little stronger,' she mourned, sketching her hand down her body. 'These new bodies weigh heavy on our spirits; we cannot for much longer maintain our charm. There are new faeries in the world now, Mantle, natural faeries, and they are not our friends.'

'I only hope you do not fight them as we fight our cousins,' replied Mantle, dismayed but not surprised by this news. But the faery shook her head.

'They will fear us, I think,' she said softly. 'And envy us. And we? We will fade, in time. All things fade, in time.'

'Will you become natural yourself?' asked Mantle as kindly as he could manage. The new skeleton was apparent and gaudy beneath the faery's subtle skin – beneath all the faeries' skins – and yet she seemed not to accept it. She shook her head.

'I shall not be corporeal again,' she said. 'Nor these, my brethren. Mantle, you are witness to the last council of our clan. Ethereal we shall remain for ever more, for to take on bodies again will be to take on these bodies, and all the nature and mortality which they bring with them. As spirits we may not be immortal but we are at least free. And we have our charm, at least for a time.'

'For a time,' agreed Mantle. He took a deep breath and went on. 'But we are here tonight for a purpose, and since you have spoken of charm I feel I must speak of it myself. I ask as fire to earth, as crude to fine, as bringer of death to bringer of life. The world is turning. As wielders of fire, dragons are working to help the world turn true, whatever the outcome, for the alternative is too terrible to contemplate. Is there anything you can do to aid us in this task? Is there anything we might have overlooked?'

A shaft of pale light opened across the underside of the looming clouds, turning the blue-black to brown and then to gold. Deep in the ice the dawn light reflected back into the eyes of the faery.

'Please,' he urged.

The faery closed her luminous eyes and considered Mantle's words for a long moment, then she opened them again and said, 'Our friends across the world have done much which you may consider foolish, but even the smallest act might be of help when histories are balanced as delicately as they are tonight. Our friends have made circles, and the circles will help when the Turning comes. Do not underestimate the power of the earth, Mantle, nor the power of the stones. You have already sent another to work with the stones of the mountain – that is good. But do not dismiss this new force, this nature, for all things will have their parts to play before the moon is full again. All things.

'But as for help, you already know we have none to give. It is the turn of the dragons now, Mantle, for our time is long past, as will yours be some day. Take your turn well; it is how you will be remembered, if any are left to remember you.'

Already the sunlight was washing through the ice and brightening the sky. The faeries seemed thin and broken, as though they were dissolving.

'We must return,' whispered the faery. 'Come with us now, or you will be missed.'

Mantle walked obediently back into the circle with the retreating faeries, ushering the drowsy Halcyon along with him. Only the faeries' charm had carried them free of their prison and only that charm could return them now without Wraith detecting their movement.

As he felt the gentle magic pulling him away from the dazzling sky and the bitter air, he looked up to see the clouds peel open. Silvery, acidic, sharp as the winter they heralded, snowflakes cascaded out of the sky and soon covered the shrinking, vanishing stones. The faeries and the dragons merged back into the frozen ground and the new snow cast a blankness over the place of their retreat, while across the mountain the final fires died, and the ashes turned white, and all creatures stopped and looked to the skies, for while the year told that the summer had barely ended the skies told a different tale, a tale which had begun in some distant, frozen land called the past and which would end none knew where.

Too soon the winter had come to the world and no creature, charmed or natural, could say whether spring would ever be seen again.

PART 4
WINTER

CHAPTER 21

Awakenings

Once it had had a name.

Once it had had many things: the companionship of its deathless brethren, the citadel they had carved for themselves then abandoned ... Once, but no more. Now, it simply slept.

Old memories – the oldest – submerged themselves in its dreams. Worlds – this one and others – were spawned from primal light, and it watched their births with a fascination which could not last.

Eternity is a long time to have lived, and many worlds live and die in that immeasurable time. Fascination gives way to boredom, and eventually despair. The despair of the deathless, that they must see everything before they themselves can die. If they can ever die.

The Sleeper, one of the Deathless, had lived forever, and would live forever, and when this knowledge had finally numbed its every nerve, clogged its every thought, it had chosen the only course of action left open to it, the same course of action long ago chosen by each of its five brethren as they had realized earlier: that eternity erodes. And that the only way to deal with it is to turn away.

And yet even in its sleep it could not escape the curse of its deathless state, for eternity intruded even into its dreams. Worlds lived and died, worlds congealed and crumbled. Worlds turned.

In its dreams it felt its spirit fill and refill its body. Many bodies it had used, yet always a new one was ready at the point of death, ready for the weary, aching soul to be transferred into its new and vital flesh. If such a being existed who was responsible for this damnation, this resurrection

257

without end, the Sleeper could not guess, though it had spent long millennia searching for such a god. It had a plan for any supreme being it might come across in the course of its unending life, and the plan had very little to do with a quick death.

But, through the individual life spans of its successive bodies – each identical to the previous in its lack of sex, its powerful charm, its sheer resilience – it had travelled far across many worlds, and in all that time it had found no god to blame, nor to punish.

It dreamed those travels now, and all the failures which had loomed at their conclusions in dreaming it lived out those failures again . . . as it slept in a shallow reservoir of charm beneath the mountain. The Sleeper had finally buried itself beneath the nightmare of its existence and lifted its barriers against the world. Aeons had passed, and the reservoir had deepened, strengthened as charm had gripped the world more fully and shaped its course through the stars.

The magic had grown and with it, at its core, the Maze had grown too. Undisturbed by this, the Sleeper had dreamed on, but recently the charm had begun to do more than merely swell – it had begun to move.

Sluggish at first, then increasing to breathtaking speed as the dragons had manipulated and distorted it. Even with the Maze as its anchor, the magic had been drawn clear of the mountain deeps and, most recently, put to work building barriers of its own, setting rivers of charm in the solid rock, constructing defences . . .

Around the Sleeper the charm now flowed like lightning, and the lightning had a taste – the taste of dragon, and of one dragon in particular: Halcyon.

Halcyon flitted occasionally through its dreams, for he was one of the few dragons to have lived long enough for the Sleeper to take notice of him, however fleetingly. But his magic alone, even though it now rushed past the Sleeper's inert body like a waterfall trapped in the narrowest gorge, was not enough to wake it.

That would take something special.

Something dangerous.

Halcyon had done what no dragon had ever dared. In funnelling his magic around the place where only he knew the Sleeper lay, he had bravely, foolishly gone one stage further.

He had focused the charm into the Sleeper.

Like a lens, the sleeping immortal was amplifying Halcyon's magic beyond all reason, splashing it out into the mountain in wild and fabulous configurations. This ancient charm Halcyon then trapped again and set to work within his defensive structures, layering his own creations with the old and powerful magic which Wraith and his front line could sense, but not identify.

They had never before encountered it, so how could they possibly have known what it was?

The risks of such an experiment Halcyon could not calculate, but he knew that they were great. His one hope was always, always, that the Sleeper would never wake.

What would happen if it did, he could not imagine.

Halcyon's magic flowed, and piece by piece it was dismantled by Wraith's team of charm-sensitive dragons.

Hidden in the torrent, the Sleeper dreamed.

Until . . .

Deep inside the Plated Mountain, deep within the inner rocks, silver and featureless eyes were exposed as lids which had been closed for aeons moved silently open. Surrounded by magic, bound in by the dragon charm which had been woven around it in some pitiful attempt to guard the mountain against attack, it opened its eyes.

Deep underground, at the threshold of the Maze, the basilisk awoke.

Dull fire burned down Fortune's left side as a moving shadow cast darkness over his closed eyes. Bright light flickered sporadically, hurting him.

He opened his eyes.

A dragon hovered over him: male, huge, a silhouette against a blinding white sky. A Natural. Fortune found that he was relieved.

'Feeling better?' the dragon asked in a deep, slow voice as he wound his wings against sky. 'Stay here — I'll get you some water.'

He swooped out of Fortune's vision but swiftly returned with a huge, waxy leaf held bunched in his jaws.

259

'Gently now,' he rumbled, carefully releasing his load of water into Fortune's mouth. 'Only leaf for far around, I reckon. Drink slowly.'

Fortune drank, the water as cold in his throat as the light in his eyes. The other dragon squatted on the ledge at his side. He was huge, with bright eyes half-hidden between gnarled brows; his hide was dark, but as Fortune watched it slowly began to turn white. Then, when his eyes had adjusted to the brightness, he realized that it was snowing. Snowing hard.

'My name's Tallow,' said the dragon carefully, as if the statement required some thought. 'I'm glad you've recovered. You'll be well enough now.'

He spoke with enormous certainty, as if an idea once spoken became truth, and Fortune liked him instantly.

'Where am I?' he blurted. 'How long have I . . . ?'

But Tallow hushed him with another mouthful of icy water.

'I'll answer your questions presently. Just relax and let your body come round. What's your name?'

'Cumber!' cried Fortune suddenly, his mind switching suddenly to a new train of thought.

Tallow frowned and pondered for a moment.

'That's an odd name for a natural dragon,' he suggested, glancing suspiciously at the blank cliff face behind them.

'What? No, I'm sorry, my name's Fortune. My friend's name is Cumber. Have you seen him?'

'I saw only you,' came the steady reply. Again a glance at the cliff.

'Oh.'

Fortune appraised Tallow in the silence which followed. He was a huge dragon by any standards, fully twice Fortune's size yet well-proportioned and lean. Bright, intelligent eyes filled his broad face and his wings, a deep, nutty brown like the rest of his body, looked powerful and well-groomed. Fortune observed him as closely as he could, for it seemed that he would soon disappear beneath the skin of snow which was gradually forming across his body.

Formidable but friendly, he thought, welcoming his presence.

Gingerly he raised his head, wincing at the sudden pain which lanced down his flank. Snow crumbled from his back and fell at his side.

'Don't move for a while,' warned Tallow amiably. 'A day's rest should see you fit enough to fly.'

Fortune gingerly moved the muscles in his chest and wings and felt a tightness about his shoulders.

'You'll be right enough,' Tallow assured him. 'You'll have a scar down your left flank and your left wing's lost some flight surface. You're probably not as pretty as you were, but you'll do.' He smiled, an expression which Fortune imagined might be a rare visitor to that earnest, honest face. He felt honoured that Tallow had blessed him with it.

He also felt very tired, and very, very sad.

'I saw you come out of the mountain,' Tallow blurted suddenly, then looked down, embarrassed. 'It's all right,' he went on hurriedly, 'it's just . . . I'd keep it to yourself if I were you. A dragon might get the wrong idea.'

'You mean a natural dragon might get the wrong idea?' replied Fortune with a smile.

'Something like that,' mumbled Tallow, looking away in embarrassment. 'It's up to you, of course, but most Naturals have no love for the Charmed, and you don't want to be telling them you came out of their mountain.' Tallow spoke quickly, then shrugged and slowed up again, concluding, 'Me, I don't fret one way or the other.'

Fortune sighed, torn between growing respect for this great rock of a dragon and a numb, emotional exhaustion which seemed to be creeping through his every pore. It was cold, very cold.

'They're just dragons, Tallow,' he said.

'It's not me you have to convince, Fortune,' said Tallow.

'Who says I have to convince any dragon?'

'Well, you know best.'

'I didn't even know it was winter,' said Fortune forlornly after a silence. 'Do you think I could have some more water?'

The big dragon spread his wings, shaking the snow from them with an easy flicking motion, then loped obligingly off the ledge, soaring away into the storm of white flakes. Despite his size he was graceful in flight, making even the

261

short journey down to the tiny pool he had found seem effortless.

Fortune lay back, exhausted. Beside him was piled the great mass of tree and shrub which had fallen blazing upon him as he had emerged from the cliff – from the tunnel which was no longer there. The foliage was now merely a heap of ash and charcoal, largely hidden now beneath a drift of snow, but he shuddered at the thought of what might have happened had not Tallow come to his rescue.

Did he block its fall or simply drag me out from underneath it?

But it didn't really matter. Tallow had saved his life, and right now he was exactly the sort of dragon Fortune needed around, strong and resourceful. *Because all my strength has gone!*

The tears came hot and sudden as he gave in to the shock at all he had lost, all he had worked for. They trailed down his face, melting the crystals of ice which had gathered around his mouth and cheeks.

He was alone, his quest had failed, and for all he knew his friends were dead.

The devastated forest below reminded him of the razing of South Point, except this was surely a thousand times worse. He could not imagine how many Naturals must have died in the flames, nor could he conceive what evil plan of Wraith's could have demanded such a purge.

But he didn't kill at Aether's Cross. Maybe his purpose here was different too.

But unlike Tallow, whose easy-going attitude towards the Charmed was surely untypical, the other Naturals who escaped would be baying for blood, hungry for revenge, and what dragon could blame them?

Even here the war would continue.

'But that doesn't make it right,' Fortune muttered under his breath. 'The fighting has to stop sometime.'

And he was surprised to find that already his tears were drying, for despite the terrible ache he felt within, the colossal grief that he had lost his companions and failed in his quest, he began to wonder if there were not other things to be done, other quests to be undertaken. To discover the fates of his friends was of primary importance, but he would need help.

'You say I'll be fit to fly tonight?' demanded Fortune when the big dragon returned bearing fresh water.

Tallow nodded slowly as he alighted, narrowing his eyes with curiosity. 'Where will the natural dragons go now that the forest is destroyed?' Fortune asked.

Tallow's brow rolled down into a maze of creases, but Fortune gained the impression that he was pondering not so much the answer itself as whether or not to say.

'So be it,' replied the big dragon at length, his voice strangely tight. 'I'll take you to where they have gone. But first we must get off this ledge,' he pronounced. 'This snow will kill us if we remain. There's a cave immediately below us, near where I found the water. That'll protect us until tonight. It's only a short glide for you; you should manage it well enough.'

'What are we waiting for?' replied Fortune, gingerly extending his wings and grimacing at the stiffness he felt at their roots. 'Lead the way, Tallow.'

'It's what I do best,' said the big dragon with a broad smile.

The snow filled the day. In the cave the two Naturals were safe enough from Charmed patrols, but Tallow ventured out periodically to observe the elaborate patterns which Wraith's dragons made in the sky. Drifts piled up at the entrance to their hideaway, but the dragons would be gone before there was any threat of their being blocked in. Even out of the wind the temperature was low, and Fortune, who should have been resting, found himself compelled frequently to pace up and down the length of the cave in order to keep himself warm.

'They're filling the sky,' commented Tallow as he returned from another sighting trip. 'It'll be hard to slip through the patrols. Night's the only way. If we're lucky the snow will keep up.'

'If we're lucky?' exclaimed Fortune.

'Yes,' responded Tallow, his face straight. 'With a name like yours, how can we be anything else.'

The day passed slowly. Fortune told Tallow a little of his quest, but although he trusted the big dragon he found himself reluctant to reveal too much of his tale. He felt safe enough here in the cave but something seemed to be prowling behind him, whispering at his back or biting at his tail and fleeing before he could turn. Something in the mountain.

It was an uncomfortable sensation, yet despite its curious and disturbing presence he felt reluctant to leave the mountain behind. But it did make him reticent in his conversations with Tallow, as though that unseen presence might catch his words and use them somehow against him.

Fortunately Tallow did not seem to notice, or if he did then he did not mind. Though slow of speech, he proved himself an able storyteller as Fortune quizzed him on his own background, and what life was like for the natural dragons who lived – had lived – here in the forests of the Plated Mountain.

'It was an adventure,' was Tallow's summation. 'A dragon's life was one big journey with no start and no finish – other than the obvious ones, of course.'

'You would just travel round and round the mountain?' Fortune asked, disbelieving.

Tallow nodded. Though Fortune did not know it, he was not usually so talkative, let alone so eloquent. But he had reached a turning in his life, like so many dragons that night. All he had left were memories. He needed to find the words to share the memories before they faded the smallest amount, but it was not easy. 'A new camp every season. Move on, and by the time you come round the land is fresh again. It's a big forest –' he hesitated, but did not stumble '– I mean, it was. And a good life. When there were four of us . . .' This time his hesitation was long and the bleakness in his eyes was deep. 'There's just two of us now. Just Volley and me.'

'What happened?' asked Fortune softly.

For years, for as long as they could both remember, he and Volley had been one half of a foursome, a group of young male dragons who had revelled in the freedom their nomadic existence offered, their lives one long adventure. But three had always looked up to one. To Weft. Weft it was who had the ideas; the adventure was always really *Weft's*. He was not really a leader, it was just that things happened when Weft was around.

'He was a fine dragon,' sighed Tallow with a melancholy smile. 'I miss him.'

Weft's enthusiasm had known no bounds. He was a dragon who would fly in a storm for the thrill of it, accept any dare no matter how dangerous. Together with the youngest member of the group, Piper, they had seen many parts of the forest, but Weft was always eager to see more, and eventually he had been swept away by a bold idea. They would explore one of the forbidden belts.

'Forbidden belts?' interrupted Fortune, for although he could guess where the story was leading he felt gripped by it. Had he not been tempted to explore forbidden realms back home in South Point? Had not his own curiosity taken him underground into the caverns of the Charmed, and finally brought him here, on his own great adventure? Already he felt he knew this Weft, and he liked him.

'Parts of the forest which the Charmed have marked off,' explained Tallow. 'No dragon knows why – they're just forbidden. But there were always stories, you know, the sort that you tell youngsters at night when you want to scare them.'

'I know the sort you mean,' smiled Fortune. 'I've heard a few in my time.'

'Hmm,' replied Tallow, breaking his thoughts for a few breaths so as to appraise his young companion. 'I believe you might tell a few too, Fortune.'

He went on with his tale.

At the boundary points of the forbidden belts the Charmed had carved red claw-marks into the trees.

Tallow had not wanted Weft to go in there, but Weft had grinned and said, 'Don't worry, Tallow my friend. We'll be in and out in a couple of blinks. Now, who's coming?'

Volley had shuffled over to where Tallow stood resolute but young Piper – Pipsqueak! – had allowed himself to be led past the red slashes and into the forbidden belt. Piper had looked nervously back at the others.

At first all seemed well. Piper had begun to smile and wave at his friends and Tallow and Volley waved back reluctantly, urging them to get out while they still had the chance.

Then Weft had said, 'I think we should go back now, Piper.'

His words had been clearly audible to Tallow and Volley, although they were spoken in barely a whisper. They were the last words he spoke.

'It was all so sudden,' murmured Tallow, his deep voice shaking a little at the memory. 'They were walking out again – they were actually walking back out – when ... when the ground just opened up, like a mouth, and there was this ... light. It shot upwards like a geyser – I saw one once, on the other side of the mountain – and took the flesh off their bones. Their skeletons dropped into the hole and it snapped shut again. Just like that, so quick ...'

He sighed, a long, breaking sound which saddened Fortune despite the wan smile the big dragon offered him.

'That was ten years ago,' Tallow added, 'but you don't forget, do you?'

Life went on for Tallow and Volley but the adventure had come to an end. The years passed and the memory of their friends' deaths crushed their spirits.

Until the day the forest burned.

Already things had been changing here on the mountain. Dragons once content with their endless circuits of the forest now spoke of other places, of breaking free; still more dragons spoke of how they should stand up to the Charmed. After all, was this not their land too? And some, inevitably, spoke of war.

The latter Tallow and Volley had ignored, for they did not really believe that war could ever happen. But the talk of exodus, of freedom from the mountain which for years had held them prisoner without them even realizing it ... now there was an adventure even Weft had never dreamed of.

To leave their homeland and journey across the world!

But could they do it without Weft? The urge to travel was strong in both of them but equally strong was the urge to follow. Neither one of them was a leader, and the years of doubt following the deaths of Weft and Piper had sapped their confidence. So, like their fellow dragons, they spoke of escape, and did nothing about it ...

But then, barely five days before Wraith's Charmed razed the forest, natural dragons actually began to leave. Careful enquiries revealed their destination – an ancient and deserted troll fortress to the north of the mountain, a place free of the forest yet close to Covamere. Dragons were gathering there, it was said, natural dragons both from the mountain and from other parts of the world.

Tallow and Volley believed that this could mean only one thing – that conflict was possible, that these dragons were preparing for war on the Charmed. But after considerable discussion they decided they would follow on regardless, in the hope that this might be the first beat of the wing on the greater flight which they both hoped some day to take: the journey around the whole world. The Fortress would be a convenient way-station from which they would soon strike out.

Soon. Not tomorrow, but perhaps the day after that . . .

By then both dragons knew that it was Tallow who would make the final decision on when they should leave, but the decision kept being postponed. Either the weather was not right – which was unheard-of for Tallow, a dragon who could fly anywhere in any conditions – or there were things more immediate to be done.

They had been on the verge of leaving twice, and the third time was the night of the new moon, the night when Wraith broke through the Portal and the forest burned . . .

'Perhaps the decision is made for us now,' Volley had suggested, struggling to hold back his tears.

Tallow had remained strangely silent, as though he were listening to an inner voice. In truth he heard nothing, but something – the mountain? – tugged.

Before Volley could react he had leapt into the air and flown off towards the fire . . . 'I flew straight to this spot,' said Tallow as though he were challenging Fortune to deny it. 'I don't know why – it's not a place I know well. But when I got here, I saw . . .'

'Me?' asked Fortune.

'You.' The big dragon sighed, his breath a billowing cloud of vapour in the confines of the cave. 'You were coming out of the mountain. There was no time to think – I just bundled you out of the way of those falling trees. Then the tunnel you came out of . . . it wasn't there any more.'

'You saved my life,' said Fortune gravely, touching his companion lightly on the wing. 'But you said you felt . . . tugged here,' he went on. He was curious, for the sensation

Tallow had described seemed familiar. 'What do you feel now?'

Tallow rewarded his question with a slow smile, brilliant as sunrise.

'Like I've been asleep for far too long,' he replied. 'And I've just woken up.'

Outside the cave the evening gloom had turned the falling snow to a deep blue mosaic. The two dragons could see little activity in the sky but both knew that Wraith's dragons were still up there, patrolling and surveying the land they had exposed with their strange charmed senses. Visibility for their own natural eyes was appalling; they could see only three or four tree-lengths into the darkness, and it was getting worse.

'It's time for us to go,' announced Tallow suddenly, lifting his great body on to his wing-arms with one fluid movement. 'If you feel fit enough, that is.'

'I feel fit enough,' acknowledged Fortune, 'but look at the weather! We'll never get anywhere in this. And the Charmed . . .'

'A little extra cover is just what we need,' said Tallow with the barest of smiles. 'As for the patrols: they follow a pattern — a complex one, but a pattern all the same.'

'How can you . . . ?' began Fortune, exasperated. But Tallow scooped him along with one massive wing and pushed him gently out into the snow. Spreading his wings reluctantly and shivering at the impact of the cold air which seemed to be radiating off the drifts piled high against the cliff, Fortune looked out into the blank wall of dusk.

'Well,' he sighed, 'if you're sure you know where you're going.'

'Fortune,' replied Tallow opening his enormous wings grandly. 'There aren't many things I'm good at, but there's one thing I'm great at.'

'And what's that?' chuckled Fortune, an unexpected wave of confidence warming him just enough to fire his muscles into action.

'Flying!'

The basilisk possessed many levels of awareness. Only its outermost barriers dropped when Halcyon's flood of magic became powerful enough to make marks against its peripheral senses. Its inner core remained unmoved by such trivialities, leaving the sentries to deal with the problem as they saw fit.

These senses: like none a natural creature could ever comprehend, each with its own intelligence, each living like a parasite on the skin of the greater being – the basilisk itself. If the basilisk thrived, the senses thrived; if it died, they died. Yet their duality was such that they *were* the basilisk in as many ways as they were not, and so they shared too its yearning for oblivion, its ultimate death-wish.

Awakened, hungry for information, the senses sucked at the magic which roared past them, extrapolating from it an image of the world they had not experienced for millennia . . . *Charm . . . Dragon charm . . . No troll . . . Little fire . . . and the world is turning!*

So, the basilisk had been disturbed at a crucial moment in the life of this world. But it had already seen many Turnings; there was nothing special about this one, nothing special . . .

The senses, having dredged information from across the entire world in the time it would take most natural creatures to blink once, were about to close their own parasitic eyes and lower the basilisk back into the totality of sleep in which it had previously been immersed, when something made them pause.

These dragons . . .

The dragons had been in the world for only the briefest of times when the basilisk had gone to sleep, and it had paid them little attention. Perhaps, in some small way, they were brethren, for they shared the charm of fire and perhaps, had history unravelled in a different way, they might have found a way to share that power together. But history, for its own reasons, had chosen to keep their two species apart, and now the basilisk drifted towards wakefulness to find them lords of the world.

Creatures of influence.

A tornado whirled through the basilisk's sleeping mind, a wind which carried dragon voices and dragon scents and dragon thoughts and dragon hearts. The basilisk drank dragon for the merest fraction of an instant, and in that minute slice of time it understood the news which would soon cause it to awaken fully, to stretch its time-locked limbs and move once more out into the world.

What it realized was this: this Turning was different. This time it was the turn of the dragons. And this time there was a very real possibility that the world would not turn true.

That the world would die.

And if the world died, then maybe the basilisk would too.

Interested now, floating in the borderlands of sleep, the basilisk directed its senses deeper into the mountain in which its body was locked.

CHAPTER 22

Ring of Stone

To sleep in the open that night was surely madness, yet that was just what Gossamer and Velvet were eventually compelled to do. As they flew back towards the mountain they saw the fires, having burned with ferocious and magical speed, already beginning to gutter. Exhausted, the fates of their companions uncertain after the fireball had separated them, they gradually swooped lower and lower over the sporadic flames until at last they could fly no more. They touched down in a field of ash, the fire a blazing wall now some distance away and retreating into the night. If they were seen by Wraith's dragons then they were ignored — two natural females were perhaps not considered to be a threat by the Black Dragon — but even if they had been challenged they would have had neither the strength nor the desire to resist; they simply curled up where they lay and fell fast asleep.

The new day brought a sliver of dawn light, but it was quickly consumed by the icy, grey clouds which over-whelmed the mountain and unleashed winter upon the land. In the end it was the cold which awoke the two young dragons, not the meagre, colourless light which was strug-gling through the clouds from far above. They woke sud-denly, both of them lurching up as one and shrugging off the thin layer of snow which had already turned their bodies into some abstract part of the landscape. Had they slept on they would perhaps have become imprisoned there, lulled into deeper and deeper sleep by the sinuous frost, their bodies revealed only when the thaw finally came. If it ever did come.

Each of them read these thoughts in her companion's eyes and they huddled close, sharing their warmth in the storm. The snow continued to fall, as indeed it would all day, and already their bodies were white again.

'We can't stay here,' announced Gossamer, tilting her head down protectively and squinting into the wind. Flakes of snow busied themselves around her face, coating her lips and tongue as she spoke.

'I don't know anywhere that's safe any more,' replied Velvet disconsolately. 'I don't even know where those dragons were taking us.'

'Can you tell where we are?'

Velvet looked around with pained, jerky motions, spitting out the snow as it forced its way between her lips.

'Don't know,' she shrugged. 'Not far from where we started, I should think. Covamere's over there to the south. We're a long way from shelter now the forest is . . .'

Her voice trailed away as she realized what she was saying. Again she turned her head into the wind but now her mouth fell open and stayed open, despite the driving snow which pressed its way in.

'What have they done?' she wailed. 'The forest is all I've ever known. Where am I to go now? What am I to do?'

But of course Gossamer had no answers, and so she could only hug Velvet close and let her cry as the enormity of what had happened to her homeland struck its blows against her young heart. All this dragon had known had been destroyed in a single night and Gossamer struggled in vain to find words with which to console her.

'Velvet,' she said presently, 'welcome to the clan.'

'Th-the clan?' Velvet managed to say, confused enough for her flow of tears to pause.

'We've all lost so much that we've got nothing behind us now,' went on Gossamer, trying to convince herself that her words meant at least something, 'so do you know what we do?'

'No,' snivelled Velvet.

'We don't look behind — we look forward!'

The triumph in Gossamer's voice was false and unconvincing — at least that was how it seemed to her. Yet at her words Velvet brightened visibly and actually smiled.

'You know,' she sniffed, 'you're right, Gossamer. We're young, and we're alive. Trees will grow again, and we're still alive! Let's look forward together, Gossamer, you and I!'

And there was something in Velvet's bright, young voice (for although Gossamer was at most two years older, she still thought of Velvet as a very young dragon) which made Gossamer wonder if there had not been power in her words after all. Despite the blizzard, despite her own despair, she found that Velvet's resilient innocence was drawing her back from the brink too, back into a world where a dragon could shape her future even as it unfurled. A world where winter might soon turn to spring.

'Come on,' she said, giving Velvet a playful tap. 'Let's find ourselves some shelter before we're snowed in.'

But as she prepared to move off Velvet grabbed her, her eyes shining.

'Hold on!' she exclaimed. 'Look where we are! Look where we landed!'

Gossamer stopped and looked around. All she could see was white. The wind had strengthened, whipping the snow into madness.

'I can't . . .' she began.

'Look down, look down!'

Gossamer looked down, and she saw.

'Stones!' exclaimed Velvet, trying to keep herself warm by hopping up and down on the spot.

Gossamer bent to examine the humps of snow which were spread around them in a broad circle. Blowing the fine flakes away from one of them she did indeed reveal a small stone lying on the ground.

'This is the stone circle we were in when Loom and Tillery found us,' she said slowly. 'I'm sure of it, even with the trees gone. The lie of the land is the same. I've been here before.'

'Do you think this means something, Gossamer?' cried Velvet, growing more excited with each breath she took. The snow flurried around her, joining her dance.

'I don't know . . .'

Gossamer hurried around the circle, brushing snow away from odd stones until she had uncovered twenty or more. Although the snow quickly recoated them it seemed to her that it did not settle as quickly here as it did elsewhere; within and immediately around the ring of stones the fall was lighter.

Odd, but for some reason she was not surprised.

She crouched down, pressing her muzzle against the ground and trying to work out what it was that seemed so strange about this place. She could feel magic at work, of that she was certain, like the magic of the sprites she had so liked to watch back at Aether's Cross. *Back home*, she thought with a stab of pain.

She rose again, and as she rose the ground within the circle appeared to drop slightly, as though some invisible giant had trodden upon the ground. The snow creaked as it was crushed, its surface flattening visibly while the two young dragons watched in amazement.

Then something rose from the centre.

The snow cracked as the emerging form was pressed up from below. Sudden gold flashed behind the storm of white flakes and a creature unfolded itself from the cocoon of charm which had protected it on its journey here from deep inside the mountain.

From the middle of the ring of stones, into the blizzard, beneath the gaze of Gossamer and Velvet, borne on the subtle charm of the faeries, rose Cumber.

He gasped as the freezing air invaded his lungs, then flapped his small wings with absurd frenzy as though by shaking them hard enough he might prevent the snow from landing on them again. Blinking and sneezing, coughing clouds of vapour into the wind, he stumbled towards the perimeter of the circle and then stopped short.

'Who are you?' he exclaimed, catching sight of Velvet.

For her part, the young Natural goggled at this staggering golden beast which was evidently a charmed dragon yet who seemed so . . . unwieldy.

'Cumber!' shouted Gossamer from behind him.

He turned, and was bowled off his four feet by Gossamer, who had flown across from the opposite side of the ring. They ploughed through the snow together and came to a halt right in front of Velvet, who looked down on them with a broad grin.

'I'm Velvet,' she proclaimed happily as Gossamer and

Cumber clambered to their feet. 'And you're the very first charmed dragon I've met. You do look a little peculiar, I suppose, but if you're a friend of Gossamer then you're a friend of mine!'

'Well, thank you, er . . .' spluttered Cumber, too taken aback by her brashness to be offended.

'Velvet!' she repeated, rolling her eyes. 'Really, Gossamer, are all your friends so forgetful?'

'Don't mind her,' laughed Gossamer, but beneath her laugh Cumber heard the tension. Their gazes locked and their smiles vanished. 'Where's Fortune?' she demanded.

'We were separated,' replied Cumber, looking back into the ring of stones. 'I haven't seen him since we went into the mountain.'

'Into the mountain . . .' breathed Velvet in awe.

'But it was only supposed to be a scouting trip!' exclaimed Gossamer. 'You promised, you both promised!'

Cumber frowned.

'Didn't Scoff explain?' he asked.

'I haven't seen Scoff since he left with you.'

A long and telling silence followed, during which Velvet, for once, kept diplomatically quiet.

'We had no choice,' muttered Cumber. 'We had to go in: Wraith's dragons were right on our tails.'

Gossamer shuddered and let out her breath very, very slowly.

'It's all right, Cumber,' she said at last. 'I understand – I understood when you left, I think, it's just . . . I didn't want to believe it.'

'You're sure you didn't see Scoff?' pressed Cumber.

'Of course.'

Another long silence, during which Gossamer began to cry silent tears.

'Fortune is safe, Gossamer,' said Cumber suddenly, jostling her flank with his wing.

'How can you know that?' she sniffed. Velvet pressed against her other flank, warming and reassuring her with wordless nothings.

'Mantle told me,' answered Cumber with pride.

Gossamer fixed him with a look which burned through the tears.

'Who's Mantle?' she demanded. Then she sighed. 'All right, Cumber. Tell me everything that happened, from the beginning.'

'Can't we get under cover first?' whined Velvet, for the snow was falling even faster and heavier now.

'No,' snapped Gossamer. Then she added more gently, 'Cumber's story first, dear, then shelter. Cumber?'

The cavern had swallowed them effortlessly, its mouth even wider and even higher than it had appeared from a distance. In a breath they had passed from the blizzard and into comfortable shadow, and if Brace remembered any one moment of his arrival at the Fortress it was when he glanced back over his shoulder, shortly after passing through that gaping maw.

The mouth of the cavern had extended to the limits of his vision to both sides, spreading wide and high. The world outside was framed in rock: a storm of white, the only feature visible through the snow the vertical slash of the Dead-fall tower. It had looked like nothing so much as a staring white eye, its pupil a hard, alien line of stone. Brace had looked quickly away, but he felt the glare of that eye burning into him long, long after.

Inside the Fortress, dragons awaited them.

Wood's cry, 'The Fortress!', had coincided with the first glimmer of dawn. The light rolled up into the sky with a speed matched only by the speed of the snow clouds which pursued it. The heat of the fires left far behind them, the band of dragons had flown on through air like fragmented ice, sharp and cold.

To each side the hills receded in an identical, featureless march, but in front the Fortress rose with uncompromising solidity. It broke from the surrounding foothills like a wave as big as a mountain captured in the act of breaking. From a ragged forward edge the wave rolled away and over until its back was hidden, while beneath it was a long, low cavern, dark and mysterious. It was towards this cavern that the dragons had flown.

Even then the feature of the landscape which had captured Brace's attention was the great pinnacle of light grey rock, standing in front of the wave of rock, free of the black landscape and in startling contrast. Even the equalizing whiteness of the snow could not disguise its alien qualities.

As high as the crest itself, this intruder was slender and slightly curved, like a dragon's claw, but the real wonder was what it held at its flattened tip.

On top of the claw, balanced impossibly against the wind and the pull of the land, was an enormous boulder. Banded with colours beneath its exquisite cap of snow and too large by any standard for the tower which supported it, the boulder waited there, poised, its massive bulk filled with the threat of imminent collapse, its rough sides rich with strips of deep green and hard blue and fiery red, as though it had been sliced from many mountains and reassembled here for some unknowable purpose.

Brace flinched as they passed beneath the defiant shadow of the Deadfall tower. In its lee they were free of the blizzard, if only briefly, but as he gazed at the curiously smooth sides of the pinnacle he found himself eager to distance himself from it again. The tower gleamed like bone in the grey light beneath the shadow of the boulder which filled the sky above them.

Wood must have brought them here by this route for a purpose, Brace decided, for no dragon in his right mind would fly so close to this monster by choice. Whether he intended them to be impressed or terrified Brace did not know; he was both.

The snow returned, borne on a gale which blasted them off course and threatened to suck them up towards the giant boulder. Wood lead them on steadfastly, his indomitable strokes forging a way through the storm towards the approaching shelter of the wave crest. Brace followed with growing enthusiasm, for now that they were leaving the tower and its terrible load behind he found himself excited by the prospect of what might await him in this mysterious place which was not so much a cavern as a whole land enclosed beneath a roof of stone.

For the first time since his ordeal at Aether's Cross his thoughts ran clear, and although the loss of his sister burned like a beacon in his mind, it was with hope and vigour that he flew with his new comrades into the shadow of the

Fortress roof which lunged from the winter land like a stone ocean crashing against the sky.

Alone in the storm, the pinnacle stood resolute, while inside the Fortress, dragon eyes grew accustomed to the dark and drank in the wonders which awaited them there.

Wood, with whom Brace felt he had established at least the beginnings of a rapport, disappeared almost immediately, leaving them under the jurisdiction of a burly dragon whose name he never learned. After a slow and tedious flight to the far end of the cavern, they were marshalled into a wide corridor of rock at the end of which a team of dragons took them aside individually and questioned them at length about their histories and allegiances. Brace lied fluently about his companions, conveniently omitting all mention of Fortune and especially of Cumber and Scoff, but he did not hide his hatred of the Charmed; in fact he revelled in it, exaggerating and even inventing stories of the purge of Aether's Cross. Determined to be noticed here in this stronghold of the Naturals, he pitched his voice loud, hoping to be overheard by the dragons who milled around this recruiting centre. Hoping to be remembered.

Whether it worked or not he could not tell, for in the end he was simply cleared for entry – as indeed were all the dragons of his intake. Some suspicious part of him doubted the validity of the clearing procedure, wondering if these dragons would not have taken any Natural who turned up at their claws, but that part he suppressed, preferring instead to believe that he had passed some test of his resolve and initiative.

The light in here was cool and muted, filtered as it was by the cascade of snow outside, and the effect on the interior of the Fortress was to wash the pale stone with even paler bands of illumination. Grey where the mountains outside were black, the Fortress was as much an intruder in this land as the Deadfall tower which guarded its entrance.

The floor ascended towards the rear of the cavern in a series of wide, smooth terraces which curved up to either side like ribs. These met the back wall at a sharp point from which the ceiling exploded out in a great, soaring vault, its surface prickling with growths and hanging strands of rock. Simple, awesome, the Fortress swelled around the dragons like a gigantic egg, its promise of protection reassuring, its permanence undeniable, its purpose being shaped even now by the army of natural dragons which filled its spaces.

All of the new recruits were assigned to a training camp situated right at the back of this far corner of the Fortress, and as he flew there along with his comrades Brace drank in the sights. What an army!

The noise was deafening. Everywhere Brace looked the terraces were swarming with dragons; he had never seen so many of his kin. There were surely thousands of Naturals here! Over the next few days he would hear many stories about what had led them here. Many of them were refugees from the devastated forest but just as many were travellers from across the world – in flight from fire or in pursuit of the rumour of a Natural army.

But the name on all their lips, now they were here, was a name Wood had spoken once to Brace before they had parted. Brace heard it many times again that day, often whispered in wonder. This dragon it was who had journeyed from far in the north to lead natural dragons to victory and freedom; this dragon it was who had already defeated the Charmed once, and who could defeat them again. This dragon and those who followed him would be the ones to inherit the new world, the world without the Charmed. This dragon would conquer; this dragon would bring an end to charm. This Shatter.

Brace listened to the legend as it grew around him and found himself thrilled by Shatter's alleged exploits, found himself hungry for the same action Shatter was said to have seen – indeed, to have initiated. Here was a dragon to adore!

But then one of his colleagues, in answering a simple question, set his mind wondering if there was not more to Shatter's story than first appeared to be the case. In answer to Brace's question about where exactly Shatter and his followers had come from, a particularly well-informed dragon had replied without hesitation, 'Some little island called Torr. South Point, they say – that was the name of the place where he conquered the Charmed. It'll go down in history too, mark my words.'

South Point!

For the first time, Brace was grateful that he had been so

cautious about mentioning Fortune and Cumber. If they had shared their home with this Shatter and his cronies, then . . . then what? But something about this revelation bothered him, though he could not decide what. Perhaps this special knowledge meant nothing, but then again . . .

So Shatter shares his birthplace with my lost companions. Knowledge like this could make a dragon valuable – could make me valuable.

Brace pondered this for the rest of the day as his new commanders began to drill him and his fellow dragons in the art of warfare, and even as he collapsed into a makeshift nest, exhausted from forced flights and marches, still he wondered what he might make of this secret, if there were indeed anything to be made of it at all.

Fortune and Cumber, he mused as sleep lapped against him like a rising tide. *I wonder if they ever even met this Shatter, or what they would do if they met him now. Perhaps I shall never know.*

Outside the Fortress, the white day had turned to a sullen blue dusk. Still the snow fell.

'Look!' cried Velvet. Frozen, exasperated, fascinated by Cumber's story yet irritated by its erratic narrative, she had finally had enough. 'Are we going to get out of here or what? I don't know about you two but my wings are just about frozen to my sides and if we don't get moving right now we'll never move again.'

'Well,' replied Cumber with a frown, 'I suppose I had just about got to the end. After Mantle said it was time for me to go he just sort of closed his eyes, and the floor melted away and the faery charm brought me here and, and, well, here I am.'

'Excellent,' pronounced Velvet, 'now come on – I've thought of somewhere we can go for shelter until this storm dies down.'

She began to stamp off into the blizzard, rattling her wings free of snow and ice and sniffing loudly.

'I shouldn't be surprised if we've all caught some terrible chill now,' she called back over her shoulder.

'Oh, all right then,' called Cumber. 'Gossamer, are you . . . ?'

But still Gossamer hesitated, staring into the ring of stones, which was now all but unrecognizable beneath the drifts of snow.

'Come on,' repeated Cumber. 'What's wrong?'

'You haven't finished, Cumber,' she replied, her voice distant as though she was emerging from a dream. 'What else is there?'

'What do you mean?' Cumber replied. In the distance, shrouded by the billowing snow, Velvet clapped her wings impatiently.

'What are you waiting for!' she shouted.

'What else did Mantle tell you?' pressed Gossamer.

'What?' Cumber was confused. He felt cold and tired. The earth magic had left him drained, not to mention the trip into the mountain in the first place, and losing Fortune, and the encounter with Mantle . . . 'I'm sorry, Gossamer,' he grumbled, 'but I am rather weary, you see, and I don't really see what . . .'

'Oh, come on, Cumber,' groaned Gossamer.

'Yes,' echoed Velvet. 'Come on, this way!'

'What?' he responded yet again. By now he was ready to curl up on the spot and the weather be damned.

Gossamer closed her eyes and said, slowly and patiently, 'You don't mean to tell me Mantle brought you all the way here just to tell you that the world is turning – whatever that's supposed to mean.'

'But I told you what it means.'

'Cumber – what did he want from you? What did he ask you to do?'

Cumber wobbled his head uncertainly, began to say, 'I don't underst—' then grinned broadly as he finally remembered. 'Of course!' he cried triumphantly. 'I knew there was something I'd forgotten!'

He bounced forward in glee and ran a little dance in the snow. Velvet, still fidgeting in the distance, giggled but Gossamer merely graced him with a caustic smile.

'Cumber?' she growled.

'Hmm? Yes?'

'What did he ask you to do?'

At this Cumber leaped into the centre of the ring of stones and swept his short tail around in a tight circle, scattering snow into the air where it joined the rest of the flurry. Cracking sparks between his teeth, he exhaled a great draught of hot air – not fire but simple heat – around the perimeter of the ring, melting the snow which had covered the stones. Velvet watched agog; Gossamer looked on with growing excitement.

'We can do something, can't we?' she exclaimed.

'Oh yes,' answered Cumber with a smile.

'Something to help Fortune?'

At this the smile faltered, but Cumber bravely rebuilt it and said, 'That's not what it's meant for but . . . well, I think perhaps . . . yes, I think we might just help him. Don't ask me how, but we might.'

'That's all I need. Now – show me what we have to do.'

Cumber stood as high as he was able on his short legs and puffed out his chest. Surveying the ring of stones with a proud and regal air, he glanced at his Natural companions and proclaimed, 'We break the circles, dragons, that's what we do!'

And with that he turned the heat of his breath to a lance of fire and blasted the stones out into the blizzard with one dramatic sweep.

Where the ring of stones had been only a crude circle of steaming slush remained.

Cumber felt it, and Gossamer felt it too: where the circle had gone so had its charm, as though the faeries who had made it had never existed at all.

'All of them?' whispered Gossamer.

'Every circle in the forest and on the mountain must be destroyed,' confirmed Cumber.

'But . . . how many are there? And where are they all?'

At this Cumber faltered.

'Er, well, you see . . .' he stuttered, his confidence evaporating swiftly.

'I know,' announced Velvet, trotting up through the snow. 'Now come on, before we turn to snow ourselves!'

'You know where all the rings of stone are?' demanded Cumber.

'Of course. This is my home, you know. Now come on!'

And this time they came.

Behind them the snow fell hard into the ring where once

the stones had held their power, erasing that place of charm from the world so that if the thaw ever did come, no creature would know what power had once been stored there.

As they flew low through the cold, Gossamer kept an image of Fortune warm in her heart, hoping desperately that these acts of destruction which they were commanded to perform might somehow bring him back to her again.

How that could possibly be, she could not imagine, for powerful though her intuition had become here on this mountain of charm, still it was not enough to answer the question which some unknown beast had planted into her heart.

How can I save Fortune from the fire?

CHAPTER 23

The First Layer

That night — the first night after the Portal was breached, the night when under cover of the blizzard Fortune and Tallow made their first flight towards the Fortress, when Brace slept exhausted after an intensive afternoon of military training, when Cumber, Gossamer and Velvet slept in the lee of the two great rocks known locally as the Twins . . . when dragons both natural and charmed turned in on themselves, turning away from the snow, away from the unwelcome breath of winter and contemplated their own dreaming hearts — that night, Wraith's dragons broke through the first layer of Halcyon's defensive magic.

There was no glory in the event, no splendour. No fire lit the stormy night sky, nor did any charm lance through the air nor thunder disturb the silent snow.

But dragons died all the same.

Wraith knew of this first success the instant it happened, for the soundless, invisible concussion echoed through the Realm where it was detected by his ever-present arms. Bones flexed at the end of those skeletal limbs, unseen in this world, folded the ripples of magic as they skated past on their way to some unknown destination; bones which touched and sensed and scented, and learned.

Wraith withdrew this new information and turned it over in his mind.

The sensation was the same as that which he had experienced the previous night, when the Portal had finally collapsed its charm and admitted him into the mountain.

Part-way into the mountain, he thought bitterly.

Ancient. Not troll. But though he tugged at the smell, though he tried to peel through its many layers and see to its centre, still he could not identify the source of the charm which was holding all Halcyon's defence network together.

Nor had he any chance of doing so, for Wraith had never before encountered the scent of basilisk.

His introspection was disturbed by a dragon's voice. Around him the snow fell heavily through the trees of his protected woodland; he could almost imagine the zirafae picking at the icy needles, almost hear their soft hooting . . .

'My lord,' began the intruder. It was not Insiss but one of Wraith's lesser commanders; Insiss had not been seen since his disappearance the previous day. But Wraith was not concerned.

I have relied on others too much, he had decided. *Especially Insiss. What use to me is power if I do not use it directly?*

'You have broken the first layer,' he responded, his voice deep and authoritative. It was a statement, not a question, and its weight was not lost on the commander, who bent his head humbly.

'My lord sees much,' he said.

'Well, your report, please.'

The dragon coughed nervously and glanced back up towards the mountain. Nothing was visible beyond the nearest trees but Wraith gained the impression that this dragon was afraid.

'My lord,' he stammered. 'We have indeed discharged the first of the five barriers, but at a terrible cost. It seemed at first that nothing had happened, but then . . . my lord, dragons have died, many dragons!'

'Speak slowly, dragon,' commanded Wraith. 'Tell me what you saw.'

'Yes, my lord.' The commander took a deep breath. 'We had been working well. The front ranks stood back when they agreed the time had come to make the final connections – I myself was in the third rank, at the rear. Ten dragons we assigned to the ten triggers we had uncovered, and they set them off in the sequence we had calculated to be correct.'

'And?'

'And it worked, my lord. The barrier just crumbled – we all felt it revealing the next layer of charm beyond, just as we had predicted.'

'But?'

He glanced behind him, as though he feared that some beast might have pursued him here. 'But there is something else in there, my lord, something which is channelling the magic. The broken charm did not dissipate, nor even explode: it vanished. It was sucked away, my lord, into some vacuum we could not detect, and then spat back out . . . but with such venom! We saw nothing; we heard nothing; even our charm-sense felt very little. But when we looked again half our number was gone.'

'Gone?'

'Dead, my lord. Dismembered.'

Wraith stood motionless in the tumbling snow, hearing the commander's words and tasting again the charm he had sensed in the Realm. So! Was there another adversary than Halcyon for the Black Dragon? But what was it?

'So be it,' he rumbled. 'The dragons who died will be replaced. The second layer will be broken by tomorrow night. This changes nothing — do you understand me, dragon?'

'But, my lord . . .'

'Listen to me!' Wraith's voice thundered in the night. 'I shall defeat Halcyon. I shall prevail. Do you doubt it?'

'N-no, my lord.'

And indeed the cowering commander, like all his fellow dragons, had no doubt that Wraith was in some way chosen, that the Black Dragon was supreme. Invincible, many said.

'Believe it, dragon! And as you believe it, consider this: would you rather prove your allegiance to the Black Dragon, or be punished by him when he finally takes his place at the heart of the Maze of Covamere? That punishment you cannot conceive, dragon. Do not test it.'

'My lord, we are already at work,' stuttered the poor commander, bowing hurriedly out of his lord's presence and braving again the unknown power of the mountain where perhaps there was still a beast awaiting him.

But then, he wondered, could there be any worse beast than the beast he had just left among the trees?

Wraith did not watch him leave, for he was confident that his orders would be carried out to his satisfaction. Despite the cold the blood pumped hot through his veins, filled with charm and fire. He felt triumphant, for the departure of Insiss had reminded him of his true power here.

And as the snow drifted against his mighty form, he found himself doing something he rarely did: speculating. Always a dragon of action, Wraith's relationship with the future had always been a pragmatic one. He planned, and then he implemented those plans. Speculation was irrelevant, for his plans always succeeded.

A distant, inner voice would occasionally chide, *Once you failed, lost dragon.* The night before in this ghostly place he had heard that voice and he had shuddered, for once unable to face his thoughts . . . *will a Natural come for you next time?*

But now he found himself enjoying this novelty of speculation, for it seemed that Halcyon had managed to prepare some tricks for him. Far from scaring him, the discovery thrilled him, for what did it prove if not that Halcyon was scared of him? The old dragon, terrified that at last a dragon had come who would depose him, had resorted to tricks and gimmicks in an attempt to repel the dragon who would surely succeed him.

For many years Wraith had planned his final confrontation with Halcyon, and for years it had seemed so simple: they would meet, and Halcyon would either bow or die.

But now it seemed the old dragon retained some spirit.

And perhaps a helper, Wraith thought, remembering the strange-tasting charm.

Perhaps the old dragon would put up a fight.

Wraith decided, in the snow and the dark, that nothing would please him more.

287

CHAPTER 24

Flying Lesson

A dragon balanced on a wedge of cool air flattened between the darkening clouds and the blue dusk of the ground. The snow fell around him, but its touch was soft now, its flakes spare and calm. A breath of air stirred his wings and through their forced motion he detected its intentions. As the gust came he rose with it, flying free, supremely aware of the junction between his body and the sky, new apprentice to the mastery of flight.

For the whole day Fortune had been in the air, and what a day!

Only Tallow's towering confidence had given Fortune the courage to strike out from the Plated Mountain into the jaws of the blizzard the night before. His wings had grown heavy and white with snow and he had panicked.

'Tallow! My wings – the snow! We have to stop!'

But Tallow had forged on.

'Many untruths are spoken about the cold!' he had answered. 'Shake your wings periodically – they will ice up less slowly each time. Flying warms them. They will not freeze.'

They had not frozen. In front, Tallow had beat his wings on and on, up and down, their great, steady strokes mesmerizing Fortune and hauling him on through the wind when he thought he could go no further. Life had become a closed circle of wingbeats repeating themselves endlessly in this eternal cloud of snow. For a breath or two Fortune was convinced that they had long ago become trapped inside a whirlwind and were simply flying round and round over the same spot again and again and again . . .

But the miracle was that the two dragons had at last left the blizzard behind, and as the sky lightened, although it snowed still, the wind had dropped away and the air relaxed about them. The ground had returned, a pale and featureless blur some incalculable distance below, and with it the faint horizon, a reminder of the distant world which surrounded them still and into which they had finally been returned. With the sky bright grey and the falling snow a gentle cascade, the two dragons had at last, as dawn revealed them, alighted in the shelter of a long crevice where they had intended to spend the daylight hours in hiding from Wraith's patrols.

Instead, except for the two occasions they had returned to the shelter of the crevice − for though the Charmed patrols had been far away, Tallow had thought it prudent − the day had been spent gloriously in the air!

When they arrived at the crevice that morning, Tallow announced, his breath billowing around him, 'That went very well. We're where we should be, at least.'

At this Fortune nearly choked.

'What?!' he exclaimed. 'Where is here, then? We could be anywhere after a night like that. I can't even tell what side of the mountain we're on, let alone which way we need to go now.'

'But you are not a local, Fortune,' replied Tallow with a small grin.

'Well, forgive me,' said Fortune, bowing low. 'Which blob of snow do we head for then, oh local dragon? This one, or perhaps that one?'

Fortune's sarcasm was thoroughly good-natured. Still, despite his concern, he could feel no anger against Tallow. The big dragon was simply too . . . honest. Even though he doubted that any dragon would have been able to find his way accurately through such a storm, he trusted that Tallow would be able to read the surroundings well enough to set them back on course and bring them eventually to their destination.

'We fly this way,' decided Tallow instantly, pointing his wing in what looked like to Fortune some unspecified direction. All he could see was that it was away from the mountain and therefore, presumably, the same general direction in which they had flown all night.

'So we were going the right way then?' Fortune said incredulously. 'I don't believe it. Even if we were it would have to have been pure chance.'

'No chance,' responded Tallow gravely. 'Only skill.'

'All right,' laughed Fortune. 'Come on, really which way?'

'Really this way, Fortune,' repeated Tallow without a trace of humour in his voice. 'I do not joke about such things. Such things make me the dragon I am.'

Fortune held his gaze for a breath or two and then burst out laughing. The laughter erupted from him like some beast that had been imprisoned for far too long and with its release he felt some great cleansing process sweep through his body; he felt the tug of the mountain fade; he felt a calmness descend which embraced the loss of Gossamer and his friends; he felt his past — including his dead father and the mother for whom he still searched — lock around him with comforting wings; he felt complete again.

The quest had failed, but there were other quests.

He looked at Tallow, at his puzzled frown, and burst with laughter again.

'I'm sorry, Tallow. It's not you, my friend, it's not you. Well, perhaps it is. It's just that you look so earnest. Here we are in the middle of nowhere and you're just so confident.'

Tallow rewarded him with a broad smile, but a little of his former frown still remained.

'You do not believe me, Fortune,' he said slowly, tilting his head to one side.

'It's not that I don't . . .' began Fortune, only to be interrupted by his companion.

'No, you are right to doubt. It is a long time since I have had to prove myself, but I am happy to do it to you, Fortune. You of all dragons, I think, need this proof.'

'I do?'

'Fly to that ridge,' continued Tallow with a mischievous grin, indicating a low line of snow in the middle-distance. Just as Fortune was about to open his mouth he added, 'Don't ask why, just do it. And count your wingbeats.'

Fortune obliged, flapping his way across to the waiting ridge, alighting, and returning at more or less the same pace. When he landed back with Tallow he announced the tally.

'Sixty-eight strokes there, seventy-nine strokes back.'

'Agreed. Now watch me.' Tallow opened his wings with a flourish. Once more Fortune remarked on this dragon's sheer size: he and his massive wings were like the mountain itself. 'Count wingbeats.'

Saying no more, he beat his way upwards with three powerful strokes and then set off towards the ridge. As instructed, Fortune watched him closely, counting the steady rhythm of his flight. Even before Tallow reached the turning point he noted the regularity of those wingbeats and the unchanging angle his wings made against the clouds. A few breaths later Tallow landed, by now a small dragon-shape in the bare, white landscape. He called back to Fortune,

'How many?'

'Forty-seven strokes!' cried Fortune.

'Agreed! Now count again!'

So saying, Tallow struck out on the return stage, finally dropping lightly on to the snow at Fortune's side.

'How many?' he repeated.

'The same,' replied Fortune, impressed. 'Forty-seven. The rhythm, the power of each wingbeat – it's exactly the same.'

'That is the first part of good navigation,' said Tallow, 'and the first lesson of good flying. A dragon whose rhythm is good knows exactly how far he has travelled each time he beats his wings. Counting beats gives you distances, Fortune, lets you know where you are.'

'But what about direction? What about wind?' Fortune was gripped. For him flight had always been an arbitrary muscular activity, a reflex action without grace or form. He had learned it in a hurry the night South Point had burned and he had never considered it to be anything more than a useful means of transporting himself about the world.

But Tallow had refined it to an exquisite degree! Fortune looked again at the big dragon's muscles: they were not only large but well-formed, shaped by constant and considered practice. His wings: large again but so obviously efficient. Here was a dragon truly tuned for flight!

Even as Tallow started to answer his questions further ones leaped into his head.

'Direction is more subtle,' the big dragon replied. 'Wind

291

is a factor, of course, but many things can help a dragon through the sky: the stars, the pull of the ground, simple landmarks and the lines which run between them.'

'But when you can't even see, like last night?'

'Then a dragon relies entirely on his body. It can be done, Fortune. I have proved it before and can do so again.'

But Fortune no longer doubted.

'What about when you fly high and the air gets thin? What about when you get tired – doesn't your wingbeat get erratic? And changing height? And what about . . . ?'

'Fortune!' exclaimed Tallow. 'I set out to prove something to you, not to teach you my life's work.'

Fortune stopped speaking abruptly. Though he no longer felt its pull he could sense the mountain looming behind him, and though he knew not its location he could feel the Fortress waiting somewhere ahead. The former he had abandoned for now, and the latter would reveal itself only too soon.

There is only today, then, he decided.

'Teach me, Tallow!' he blurted. 'Teach me all you know!'

The big dragon narrowed his eyes and pondered this for so long that Fortune thought he was about to burst.

'Took me a lifetime,' he answered slowly. 'And I'm still learning, even now.'

'The basics, then!'

'We should get to the Fortress tonight,' warned Tallow. 'No dragon is safe at large now. And something is happening tonight I think you will want to see.'

Fortune looked around at the grey sky, still brightening as the new day finally gripped the world.

'Then let's get started,' he beamed.

And thus the day had been spent above the landscape of winter. All was white, reformed and unrecognizable. The sky beckoned, its dome an infinite chamber, a vast emptiness on which a dragon might lose his past and his future and become a being only of the present, alone in flight.

Alone in the empty sky, Fortune mused. *That's what dragons are. We are the only creatures who fly.*

His thoughts scattered as Tallow dived close by, the sud-

292

den wake disrupting his own easy glide. A broad smile lit up the big dragon's face. He swooped back and forth above Fortune, casting a critical eye over his pupil's attempts to regain his composure.

'Never trust an airstream!' he announced, then took several deep breaths. 'The winter is beautiful from up here!'

And Fortune had to agree. Below them the world was clean, the snow coating it with its own inert magic. The blue-grey light which filtered through the clouds cast a pale aura across the landscape, making it glow from within.

At the limits of their vision, in the opposite direction to the Plated Mountain, was the flaw on the horizon which Tallow insisted was the Fortress, although how he could tell at this distance Fortune did not know.

'We should go there now,' urged Tallow, following the line of his friend's gaze.

'Shortly,' promised Fortune. 'I could stay up here forever.'

Throughout the extended flying lesson neither dragon had alighted other than on those two occasions when they had landed to avoid the patrols. Having lain low for a space of time, taking the opportunity to snatch refreshment in the form of fruit which grew in the lee of the crevice and ice-water, they had returned promptly to the air, making the most of the dull light and the wintry sky. That day they had simply flown, sharing the wind and learning together.

Fortune proved himself a keen and able student, willing to admit his own mistakes and work hard to correct them. While it would be many years before he could even begin to understand the subtlety of Tallow's navigational skills, he still managed to learn the rudiments of wing control and the regulation of his rather erratic flight rhythm.

But what he enjoyed most – and what seemed most important to him – were the speed and the aerobatics. The flying.

Tallow began with Fortune's body, explaining anatomy and aerodynamics. He explained how most of a dragon's bones were hollow, how the retracting blades of cartilage at the leading edges of his wings, when deployed, would greatly reduce his stalling speed, allowing slow and complex manoeuvres; these were particularly useful when landing on precarious ledges. He explained how Fortune's deep breastbone was really a keel on to which were anchored his most powerful flight muscles.

'How do you know all this?' Fortune marvelled, for although this information seemed familiar, like a scent remembered from infancy, Tallow articulated it so precisely and simply that he was swept away with the sheer elegance of it.

'Flight is symmetry,' Tallow explained. 'I have had to learn this through experience. You're lucky – you've got me!'

So Fortune flew, and in flying he felt utterly alive.

'I suppose flight was my response to forest life.' As Tallow spoke Fortune noted how much more animated he was up here than on the ground. His voice was still slow and thoughtful, but flying appeared to bring out an expressive tone he had not really heard the big dragon use before. 'Most forest dragons are tied to the ground, introverted. Their wings grow short; they shamble. But my element was always the sky. Can you imagine, Fortune, life without flight? The sky was not meant to be empty.'

He spoke again of his friends, of Volley and of course poor Piper. And Weft.

'If Volley were here he would sing!' he laughed. 'If Weft were here . . .'

'But he isn't,' said Fortune gently.

'No,' agreed Tallow. 'But you are, Fortune. You are.'

The day turned around them and the world turned beneath them as they flew. In the afternoon light they swooped and soared, and as dusk approached they glided and spun, until at last the lesson drew to a close. Reluctant though both of them were to end such a perfect day, time pressed against them again.

'You've taught me well, Tallow. Thank you,' said Fortune, bobbing close to his friend on a rising shaft of air.

'You wanted to learn,' Tallow agreed.

'Yes.'

But there's more to it than that, isn't there?

'In fact,' continued Tallow, 'a dragon might say you needed to learn.'

'You may be right, Tallow.'

He did not tell his friend about the peculiar sensation which had been growing inside him ever since they left the mountain.

It pulled at him, this sensation; it was like a claw raked into his heart and it tugged at him. It was weaker now than when they had first taken to the air but still it tugged, trying to drag him back towards the mountain.

Back towards . . .

It was not a pleasant feeling, nor was it painful, but it was . . . insistent. Fortune felt able to resist it now but could he continue to do so forever? He thought not. He thought that soon, not today, nor perhaps tomorrow . . . soon he would yield to that pressure to return, to follow the direction of that relentless pull until he reached its source.

And then?

He could not say, but some inner part of him yearned for that time to come, for it knew into which piece of his heart that strange claw had been hooked.

Ahead was the Fortress, the prospect of which pulled at his mind; behind was the mountain, which dragged at his heart.

For now, he beat down his heart and journeyed on.

They talked a great deal as they flew on towards the Fortress. Fortune was astonished to find that he was not tired from the day's exertions.

'That's because you flew well,' explained Tallow. 'A dragon uses less energy when he flies well.'

'You haven't told me much about this place. How many dragons are there?'

Tallow pondered this for a few breaths, during which time Fortune found his attention more and more drawn towards this dragon stronghold which clung to the horizon ahead. It had by now taken the appearance of a great hump of rock slashed down its centre by a single vertical line, wider at the top than at the base.

It looks like an eye, he thought with a shiver, remembering a dream he had not thought of for some time.

'I would guess,' replied Tallow slowly, 'that there are two thousand there. No more than three.'

'Three thousand?!' exclaimed Fortune, his wings faltering.

'Three thousand dragons? I had no idea there were so many in the world!'

'It's quite an army,' agreed Tallow. 'The Charmed will be challenged, that much is certain.'

'Three thousand,' echoed Fortune. 'Tell me about them. What sort of dragons are they?'

'Many from the forest; even more since the fire, I should think. As many still from elsewhere, especially from the north.'

The north!

Tallow went on.

'Dragons have been living at the Fortress for many years, but only recently have they become united. The Fortress is a big place, you see, one in which up until recently there were many separate communities. And many Naturals still fear it, for it was once a place of the trolls. But it is a safe place, a stronghold, and most important, it is a place the Charmed never go.'

'Why not?'

Tallow shrugged, the gesture sending ripples down his wings. Fortune noted that he adjusted his rhythm automatically to deal with the tiny motion.

'I cannot say. You know the Charmed better than I.'

'Then what has made the natural dragons band together? Why now?'

Again the shrug.

'There has been much disturbance at Covamere in recent times,' the big dragon sighed. 'Lights, sounds. Dragons say the Charmed are growing restless; some say that they are making an army against Naturals. They feel vulnerable in the forest, so close to Covamere, but they feel angry too, for the forest belongs to them as much as to the Charmed. Forest dragons have been fleeing to the Fortress for several moons now.

'And then came the dragons from the north.'

'What dragons?'

Suddenly the air temperature seemed to drop. Darkness was almost upon them now, the sky a purple canopy of cloud. Fortune felt a curious doubling of time, as though he knew what Tallow's words were going to be even before he opened his mouth.

'The one they call Shatter,' revealed Tallow.

The name fell casually from the big dragon's tongue yet it crashed into Fortune's ears like a landslide.

Shatter!

The dragon from the north!

CHAPTER 25

The Rally

White was all the land now beneath the untimely winter.
Even the mighty crags and turns of the Plated Mountain lay
hidden under overwhelming snow, with only the bleakest
of them standing proud and black above the frost. Grey
cloud shrouded its summit and shadowed its root, while in
every direction its flattened neighbours sprawled into the
pale distance.

White was the land and, as far as any dragon could guess,
so was the whole world.

Charmed dragons flew a complex lattice in the sullen sky.
Their purpose: to spy upon and prevent any followers of
Halcyon from escaping the mountain by secret means. With
the forest destroyed this should have been easy, but the
coming of the snow had blurred even the most perceptive
of the senses these patrolling Charmed were employing. The
snow tricked the eye and dampened even the subtle prob-
ings of charm, and so it was possible for careful dragons to
evade the network, to slip between the claws of the patrols
and trace their own paths across the mountain.

Cumber looked out over the field of snow, taking time to
enjoy the cast of the rising sun. Since coming to the mountain he had been surprised to find himself beginning to take
pleasure in such things.

He sighed, remembering friends and teachers and contemplating his task at hand, to break the circles the faeries had
so carefully made. The low light rolled over the drifts like a
wave on the shore, leaving behind it a fine pattern of orange
crest and blue trough and only gradually reaching up to the
cleft in which the three dragons rested. Velvet had led them
to a tiny cave there, an uncomfortable but welcome shelter.

The coming day would be the second since Cumber had emerged from the faery ring. The work had gone exceptionally well the first day, Velvet tirelessly tracking the rings despite the disorientating snow. Once located, they proved easy enough to neutralize – only a single stone needed to be displaced for the earth charm contained therein to be dispersed.

Why Mantle had sent him on this curious errand was still a subject for speculation. Already each of the three had his or her own, secret ideas on the matter.

A dark arrow loitering in the sky.

'Dragon!' he hissed.

He hurried back to Gossamer and Velvet in the cave and they all watched fearfully as the charmed dragon swooped low over the terrain they had crossed the previous evening in order to reach their sanctuary, arching its neck as it scanned the drifts for any suspicious marks. What had drawn it here they could not guess, for the cave was surely invisible from the air, but here it was, and here they were . . .

'It's coming back for another look,' whispered Velvet, huddling close against Cumber as the patrolling dragon glided slowly by again, this time in the opposite direction. They all squinted into the early light, desperate to see if they had left any marks in the snow that might betray them.

Then the dragon landed.

She hopped clumsily through the snow towards the steep cliff in which the cave lay concealed. Her scales were white, her wings long and slender; had she not been wearing such a stern and unapproachable expression Cumber might have considered her beautiful.

'We could overpower her, the three of us,' suggested Velvet suddenly. Cumber jumped, for her mouth was right next to his ear. He could feel her body heat against him and was surprised to find the sensation somewhat enjoyable. For her part Velvet was delighted at least that he did not shy away. Cumber fascinated her, for in him she saw confounded all the old stories she had been told of the monstrous evil which charmed dragons wrought upon the world and upon their cousins, the Naturals. But Cumber was neither monstrous nor evil; he was good and he was . . . funny.

'Don't be foolish,' he was whispering. 'She'd soon be missed, and besides, she's stronger than she looks.'

Indeed, the nearer she came the more formidable she appeared. Those slender wings were barbed and strengthened with glistening rods of charm, living webs which made the almost transparent membranes glow with stored energy. Her eyes glinted like cold, hard jewels.

Cumber looked around the cave but saw only what he already knew — there was no other way out.

I could always escape through the Realm, he thought with a shudder. *But I would have to leave my friends behind.*

The dragon was almost close enough to smell.

'Solice!'

The voice boomed out of the sky. The three trapped dragons squinted up into the bright patch of cloud behind which the rising sun was obscured and saw there a second Charmed, beating its wings hard against the wintry sky.

'Solice!' this newcomer repeated. 'What are you playing at all the way out here? We should have finished this quarter already!'

The female — Solice — stared resolutely into the darkness of the cave, her eyes narrowed and unreadable.

'I thought I saw something,' she murmured in a low voice which carried with uncanny strength across the ice and into the cave.

'Oh, you're always seeing something,' grumbled her partner impatiently. 'Come on, I need a break. We haven't eaten all night!'

Solice stood there for a breath or two, then shook her head.

'Oh, very well,' she sighed. Silently, hardly daring to believe their good fortune, the three hideaways sighed too.

With a flourish Solice opened her wings. Flashes of light chased across their membranes and without moving them further she rose majestically off the ground. Gossamer and Velvet watched open-mouthed.

'She's just showing off,' muttered Cumber. 'What a waste of magic!'

'Can you do that?' asked Velvet eagerly as the two charmed dragons flew away into the tumbling snow.

'Of course, or at least, I could if I wanted to,' acknowledged Cumber briskly, 'but there are far more useful things a dragon can use charm on if you ask me, far more useful things.'

'Like what?' Velvet pressed.

'Well,' replied Cumber, looking pensively at the tracks Solice had left in the snow, 'there's this for a start. Follow me.'

He led them outside. Still the snow was falling, but more gently now, and despite the recent danger the mountain seemed marginally more welcoming than it had the previous day. His friends followed, Velvet with an eager spring to her step, Gossamer with the slightest of smiles at the behaviour of this young dragon around Cumber.

'Stand here,' Cumber directed, pointing to arbitrary spots in the snow. 'I should have done this yesterday, but I didn't think of it and anyway it's only today that I've begun to realize how much power there really is around here. The snow disguises it but it's there all the same, in the ground, under the ground, even in the air – it's there.'

'Excuse me,' piped Velvet, a little bashful now that Cumber had taken charge. 'What's there?'

'Charm,' replied Cumber.

'Magic,' elaborated Gossamer.

'Oh, that,' said Velvet.

'This whole mountain is filled with it, you see,' went on Cumber, his voice rising as he became more animated, 'and that means that the sort of charm which is now so difficult to perform back in the Heartland – and is even harder on Torr and beyond – here it's so much more effective. Why, I could make magic here I would never have dreamed of back at South Point. I'm only just beginning to see what possibilities there are here, you see, because to do such things . . .'

'Cumber,' interrupted Gossamer patiently, 'what are you going to do?'

'Ah, I thought you'd come to that. Well, if you don't object, I'd like to do this.'

So saying, Cumber closed his eyes and hunched his back. Around his claws the snow crackled and melted away, and between his scales there flared sudden fire, darting through the gold like thousands of tiny tongues. Through gold they sprang . . . but they retreated into white.

301

Cumber had changed colour.

'Gosh!' exclaimed Velvet after a suitable pause. 'That's incredible!'

'Well, Cumber,' smiled Gossamer, walking around him as though inspecting his work. 'Do you want to do me first or Velvet?'

'What?' Velvet cried.

'Oh, I hope you don't think I was going to . . .' stuttered Cumber, suddenly embarrassed, 'I mean, I was going to ask first if I could . . . you see, it would be for the best — camouflage and everything — although I'll quite understand if you don't want to . . .'

'Cumber!' laughed Gossamer.

'Yes?'

'Just get on with it!'

'Oh, er, very well. Velvet?'

Velvet, for once, could find no words so she simply nodded her head. Gossamer, seeing that she was trembling a little, went over to her and supported her with a motherly wing.

'Don't worry, my dear,' she said. 'If you don't like the way you look, I'm sure Cumber will be more than happy to change you back again. You never know,' she whispered, 'he might prefer you in white!'

Before Velvet could respond to this a warm tingle spread itself through her body, starting from the tip of her snout and speeding back to the end of her tail. She shut her eyes instinctively and blurted,

'Tell me when it's over!'

'It already is,' replied Cumber at once. 'The white dragons — that's us. Maybe we can give the Black Dragon something to think about, what do you think, Gossamer?'

Gossamer looked down at her new scales. They shone in the pale light, sheer and beautiful. Beside her Velvet shone too, her own scales gleaming with a radiance beyond mere whiteness. She shivered, a trace of fear invading her heart, yet was at the same time thrilled by this unexpected transformation.

If a dragon can change colour then what other changes might be made in the world? she thought suddenly. *What warm futures might we carve from the cold snow?*

Velvet surprised Gossamer yet again by saying, 'I like my new coat, Cumber. Thank you! I want to stay like this forever! Now come on, you two — there's work to be done.'

With genial groans and light hearts, Cumber and Gossamer joined Velvet in the air and together the three white dragons set off towards the next ring of stones.

A day which had begun with fear took on a new and optimistic air. As they laboured, working from one ring to the next around the mountain, the initial gleam of their new hides wore off, leaving a dull yet more effective whiteness in its place.

'That's the left-over charm falling away,' explained Cumber. 'The colour will stay forever — or until it's changed again — but the magic always fades, sooner or later.'

That night they slept long and deep in a shallow cave which Velvet discovered high among the eastern foothills.

'Stay close now,' warned Tallow as they flew in close formation through the jaws of the Fortress. 'And leave the talking to me.'

'I understand, Tallow,' responded Fortune. 'I would no more put your life at risk than I would any of my good friends.'

At his remark Tallow allowed himself a smile.

'Don't forget,' he said, needing to labour the point for Fortune's sake, 'dragons here know little of the Charmed. Most despise them. The Black Dragon's name is not known, nor are any of the secrets you carry with you. Be discreet, Fortune, or you will put us both in danger.'

From the flutter of the snow outside they swept into the massive bubble of air which was held captive beneath the soaring wave of rock. Tallow had been right: there were dragons here — thousands of them!

They filled the terraces and slopes of the Fortress floor, clustered together in a huge, straggling audience which spread itself in a rough half-circle centred about a stony outcrop near the back of the colossal chamber. The heat from their bodies rose into the colder night air, and with his new sensitivity Fortune felt himself adjusting his wings automatically to the changing density of this subtle rising

303

draught. With the warmth there rose a great blur of conversation — the murmur of the crowd, the voice of the army.

'So many dragons,' he whispered in awe. 'Can they all despise the Charmed so much?'

'That you will find out soon enough,' muttered Tallow. 'But first we must find Volley.'

Fortune did not even question the big dragon as he led them lower and lower, skimming across the crowd in a tightening spiral with wings spread wide and flat. If any dragon could find another in such a gathering it was Tallow.

They circled, scrutinizing the ranks of dragons below. As Tallow searched, Fortune found himself captivated by the raised knuckle of stone towards which all the watching dragons were directing their gaze.

'He's not at his usual spot,' grumbled Tallow. As he spoke Fortune saw in the corner of his eye a pair of burly sentries lift themselves briskly into the air to their left. They stroked their way across to the circling dragons and called them to a halt. The four of them hovered together, Fortune and Tallow staying close while the sentries took station on either flank lest one or other of them should try to make a break.

'And what are you two playing at?' the first sentry drawled. He was big and bony and had an easy, casual air which was more kindly than threatening. His companion, by contrast, was sharper-looking, with an acidic, greenish hide.

'Yes,' agreed the sharp one. 'You should be on the ground. It's an insult to Shatter, that's what it is, trying to steal the attention like this. I've a good mind to report you both.'

'All right, Mulch,' drawled the other. 'That's enough. You,' he went on, 'you're . . . Tallow, aren't you?'

'I am,' Tallow rumbled.

'Hmm. I don't know your friend. Is he new?'

'I was new yesterday, sir,' piped Fortune with exaggerated enthusiasm. 'Tallow was just showing me around and I'm afraid I've made him a bit late. We were just looking for somewhere to land. I'm terribly sorry — it's all my fault. I'm just so keen to hear the speech, you see, and it's made me quite giddy!'

Fortune could have kicked himself. The gauche manner

he had adopted sounded so phoney to him that he was sure the other dragons would see through it immediately. He was supposed to let Tallow do the talking. But it seemed to work nonetheless. Mulch appeared satisfied that here were loyal followers of Shatter, and his big companion seemed to know Tallow well enough to trust any dragon in his company.

'See any other dragons out there?' Mulch leered, still probing. He darted in towards Fortune with a sudden thrust of his wings. 'Perhaps you had reason to be flying outside on such a cold night, eh, Tallow? Perhaps your loyalties don't stretch as far as you might have us believe?'

Fortune's puzzled glance at Tallow was genuine enough but Mulch picked up on it at once.

'And don't pretend you don't know what I mean, you little runt!' he snapped. Evidently he was an irritable dragon and intended to exert his authority on these two latecomers one way or another.

'Come on, Mulch,' yawned his colleague. 'Give it a rest, why don't you? They're up to no harm.'

'But they could still be traitors,' whispered Mulch angrily.

'Tallow's no fool,' came the lazy reply. 'And this young-ster's no Flight dragon, anyone can see that. Now let them land and let's get back to our places. You don't want to be caught up here when Shatter starts his speech.'

Looking nervously down at the crowd, Mulch reluctantly rejoined his colleague, although not without first casting a venomous look at Fortune and Tallow.

'Go on then,' he hissed. 'And don't let us catch you like this again. Shatter might tolerate dragons like you but that's no reason we should!'

'What was all that about?' whispered Fortune as the two sentries glided back down to earth.

His words were almost drowned by a sudden gasp from the crowd. It began at the front, nearest the stone knuckle, and rushed back through the throng like a wave, jerking the dragons into alertness. Something was about to happen.

'This is not the time or place,' cried Tallow over the sud-den clamour. 'Follow me down and I'll explain later. Ah, there's Volley!'

* * *

Although none of the natural dragons gathered that night in the Fortress — nor indeed any dragons on the Plated Mountain other than those few Charmed who were direct witnesses to the event — were aware of it, at more or less the same moment Fortune and Tallow joined the crowd waiting to hear Shatter speak, Wraith's pathfinders penetrated the second of Halcyon's walls of charm.

This breaching was almost identical to that of the previous night — silent and dark — except this time, to the great relief of the Charmed who released the final levers of magic, there was no loss of life. When it came to it, the wall, a tall and undulating mirror of charm which flexed in and out of the rock like a huge, flattened serpent, simply melted into the floor like snow in spring.

With Wraith visibly excited by this latest triumph, and with their own odds of survival significantly improved, it was with renewed enthusiasm that the elite squadron of charm-sensitives bent to their task of unfolding the third layer.

This third was as invisible as had been the first, and sent back precious few clues as to what triggers might have been set into its mysterious surface. All that faced the line of investigators was a smooth wall of stone crazed with fine etchings.

With a collective sigh, and a set of grim glances exchanged, the pathfinders went back to work.

Again, they had a single day in which to solve the riddle, with two more walls yet to come, and each hoped secretly that in three days' time he or she would at least be still alive.

Tallow shouldered his way through the pressing crowd to a large, tan-coloured dragon who awaited them with obvious delight. Fortune guessed at once that this was Volley, for although he was not as big as his friend, nor as dark in colour, he carried himself in exactly the same way; to see them together was to see two dragons who had spent a near lifetime together, and who were as relaxed in each other's company as it was possible to be.

'Tallow!' exclaimed Volley warmly, slapping his flank. 'Don't you fly off on me like that again! I was beginning to worry about you, old fellow!'

His voice was a rich and marvellous baritone, and Fortune remembered Tallow remarking that he liked to sing. He hoped he would hear that voice put to good use one day.

'Well,' replied Tallow, his own voice slow and deep, 'I couldn't let a bit of fire and ice get in my way, now could I?'

Volley grinned, the expression sitting more comfortably on his broad face than it did on Tallow's. Fortune decided that this dragon was one who set out to enjoy life's physical pleasures and not dwell too much on any matter which demanded too much thought.

'And who might this young dragon be?' he enquired, bending down to Fortune's level. Although Fortune was almost full-grown he felt dwarfed in the company of these two dragons. But safe too, he decided, for he warmed to Volley almost as quickly as he had to Tallow.

'This is Fortune,' said Tallow with uncharacteristic haste. 'I think he might keep us here for a while longer yet.'

Volley raised one eyebrow at his friend, leaving Fortune to wonder quite what information had just been exchanged. He was about to ask a few questions of his own when the buzz ran through the crowd again. This time however it was cut short as almost every dragon present suddenly sucked in his or her breath.

A dragon had appeared on the knuckle of rock.

The light was poor, and every dragon strained to see, but only when the silence was total did he finally speak.

'Welcome,' said the dragon. 'I am Shatter, and I welcome you all to my fortress.'

Wood was not surprised to find himself largely unmoved by the speech.

I've heard it all before, he thought listlessly as Shatter boomed on about glory and revenge and victory and justice. Wood felt restless here behind the platform, remote from the crowd to whom Shatter was making his address and strangely unexcited by the prospect of finally going to war against the Charmed.

But was this not what he wanted? Was this not the moment he had made inevitable as soon as he had made his choice on the forbidden ledge in the Great Chamber at

South Point, as soon as he had dived into the midst of the fighting, making for Ordinal, screaming to his father? Was this not the future into which he had at that instant flown? His mind told him it was, but his heart . . . ?

His heart did not know, for it was still bound up with his father. Poor, burned Barker, who was now nearly blind and who could not fly without terrible pain, and yet who had crossed the world rather than abandon Shatter, and who still maintained his place among Shatter's small number of advisers. Loyal to the last, Barker adored his leader. And Wood adored his father, he admitted that at last, and that was the real reason Wood was here.

After their uneventful passage through the Low Mountains via Aether's Cross, the journey here to the Fortress had been arduous. Shatter had set a cruel pace, urging his small band on at great speed, flying by both night and day and stopping only for the shortest of breaks. Had it not been for Barker's stubbornness, his determination to follow his master across the world, Wood would have abandoned the party after the first day, but stay he did, if only for his father's sake.

They arrived among the Injured Mountains one full day after Mantle's messenger earthquake had finally closed the ravine of Aether's Cross and set Fortune and his companions on their own journey south. Shatter, his red eyes constantly roving, flew through the landscape as though he owned it, until the Fortress loomed on the horizon. They made straight for it.

Shatter's reaction to the place was odd, for while the others in the group were awe-struck by the sheer scale of the place, and in particular by the astonishing, gravity-defying spectacle which stood outside the entrance, Shatter himself seemed to regard it as nothing more than what he had expected.

Barker went so far as to ask Shatter why this was so and Shatter replied, his voice curt and disinterested, 'It has existed for a long time inside me, dragon. There is no surprise for me here! The rock outside is the ''Deadfall''.'

They found dragons already living inside, and more gathering there daily, and it was only a matter of time before Shatter did again what he had done at South Point and appointed himself rouser of rebels, condemner of the Charmed. Leader.

This he did over the ensuing days, the gathering Naturals eagerly listening to his speeches, eagerly spreading word that here, at last, was a dragon who had seen real action against the Charmed and who could lead them to final victory. Small rallies became active flights into the forest, some of which Wood participated in if only to keep his mind off the awful prospect of a lifetime under Shatter's rule. He even began to wonder if the Charmed needed to be battled with after all.

But then, during the last such expedition in which he managed to recruit most of the dragons of Loom and Tillery's clan, he saw them burn the forest.

And in the flames he saw his home burn too. In the ashes he saw his father's twisted body.

The Charmed had to be punished!

The rage came to him again now, a reflex he could not suppress initiated not by Shatter's words but by his own inner thoughts. He was powerless to shake off the anger so he supposed that it represented his true beliefs, and if ever he doubted its right to exist he had only to look at his father's broken body, to remind himself of the dreadful harm a charmed dragon was capable of dealing upon an innocent Natural. The harm that Ordinal had dealt upon Barker.

But he attacked her!

But that thought and those like it he banished before they could truly form. Easier to believe that his father must be avenged, that Shatter must be supported, that Ordinal had been the one to attack first, that Fortune had been wrong all the time . . .

Fortune, if only you were here now. Then I could show you what a terrible mistake you made, how you chose the wrong path. Shatter will succeed, the Charmed will be destroyed and you will have chosen the wrong side.

That he had chosen correctly he did not doubt, for this he believed: whether right or wrong, Shatter would succeed. Looking around him now at this vast army he could not believe that even the charmed dragons of Covamere could defy an army of nearly three thousand! Despite their wiles, despite their spells, they would be defeated. In the last great battle of the dragons, only the Natural would survive.

He wandered around to the side of the knuckle of stone and looked out across the crowd. Here, hidden in the shadow cast by the faint snow-light outside, he could observe the army without himself being seen. He felt safe here, cocooned and anonymous among thousands of his own kind. His own family broken and torn, he had adopted this as a surrogate. Here were wings big enough for him to hide beneath; here was a sympathetic flank in which he could bury his face and forget all that he had seen.

Here, for a while, was escape.

Faces stared back from the throng, gazing up past Wood towards the top of the rock where Shatter paced, hurling his words back at them like projectiles. He could see the awe on their faces, the respect, and the love. He knew that look – it was the look his father reserved for Shatter.

If only he could look at me that way, he thought with a shiver. *If only I could know that he is proud of me.*

'Standard fare,' commented Volley drily as Shatter spoke on into the night. 'Although he's getting on to tactics now. He'll make his move very soon, I reckon. Still, we'd have more fun listening in on the Flight if you ask me.'

Fortune nudged Tallow's shoulder.

'Come on,' he whispered, 'you can't keep avoiding the subject all night. What's this "Flight" I keep hearing mentioned?'

The big dragon's eyes met Volley's for an instant. The two dragons seemed to breathe as one briefly, and Volley frowned slightly, then they both looked down at Fortune.

'Very well,' began Tallow gravely, 'we'll tell you.'

'It's very simple,' put in Volley. 'Don't drag it out.'

'I won't,' replied Tallow patiently. 'But I think we should be interested in Fortune's thoughts on the matter.'

'Oh, really, Tallow,' protested Volley genially. 'Don't you think you're building this up to be . . .'

But Tallow interrupted him.

'Weft would have been interested,' he said slowly.

Volley shut his mouth with a snap and adopted the quizzical expression again.

'Go on,' he murmured, regarding Fortune with renewed interest.

Once more Fortune felt disconcerted that information had passed him by without his fully understanding what was going on.

And yet, maybe I'm beginning to see a pattern . . . he thought.

'Not all dragons here agree with Shatter's ideas,' explained Tallow, 'especially when it comes to fighting the Charmed — or fighting at all, for that matter. The problem is what to do about it. So far they haven't decided *anything* . . . except to call themselves the Flight.'

'Rebels!' exclaimed Fortune. 'So tell me, Tallow, Volley — are you dragons of the Flight?'

'Us?' exclaimed Volley. 'You must be joking! We're out of here altogether after tonight, or didn't he tell you?'

'Tallow?'

'That was our plan,' agreed Tallow. 'But I'm interested to hear what you've got to say, Fortune, in the light of what I've just told you.'

Again that shared look between the two friends. This time Fortune got the impression that Tallow was holding Volley back from saying more, and all at once he felt like the subject in some bizarre test.

'I think,' he replied slowly, 'that I would like to meet these dragons of the Flight myself. Would you care to join me?'

Now the look which Tallow flashed at his friend was one of triumph. Volley simply shrugged non-committally, but Fortune could see from the big dragon's manner that the response had been to his liking.

'Can we go now?' he asked, but Tallow shook his head.

'It would not do to walk out on Shatter while he speaks. That would be too conspicuous, even for three dragons who plan to join with the Flight.'

'Who said anything about joining them?' put in Volley.

'Tomorrow night,' suggested Tallow, hushing his friend with one flap of his enormous wing. 'Besides, you might care to listen to Shatter a little longer.'

'I think I've heard enough,' murmured Fortune as Shatter, his eyes blazing red enough to be seen even from here, halfway back in the crowd, spoke louder yet.

* * *

It was not really Shatter's words which mattered that night, nor even his voice. In the end it was simply his presence and his timing which proved the inspiration to the dragons he had gathered together and who were already trained and ready for action.

This, as all those dragons there that night knew, was surely the last age of charm. This night, and those which followed, would be the markers for the beginning of the rule of the Natural in the new world which awaited them all. The Charmed were all but finished, and Shatter had simply brought together the right dragons in the right place at the right time.

These facts notwithstanding, his voice boomed out across the chamber as though propelled by magic, and his words were a barrage of rhetoric which made hot the blood in the veins of the listening dragons. Half the night he spoke, and by the time he stepped down his voice was rough and broken.

What made this speech particularly inspiring, apart from the perfection of its timing, was that Shatter went on, after thrilling his audience with a general call to battle, to define his campaign in considerable detail, revealing the extensive knowledge his scouts had gained of the mountain territory and even of Covamere itself. That Covamere was their ultimate target he left no doubt, nor did any dragon doubt that Shatter had the ability to lead them to victory within its walls.

So it was that dragons retired that night both roused and challenged, for now each squadron had been given a specific assignment in the greater campaign, and even within those squadrons each dragon had a specific part to play. More than inspired, these dragons felt needed, needed by the war, needed by Shatter.

Shatter had manipulated his army by the most effective means: he had flattered them.

Which for a dragon roaming the borderlands of insanity, and who believed that no other dragon than himself was even real, was an astonishing feat.

As the crowd broke up, Tallow and Volley invited Fortune to share the limited comfort of their scrape near the eastern end of the entrance. Fortune gladly agreed, and it was as they were strolling casually back towards that part of the cavern — there had been enough flying that day even for Tallow — that the night presented to him its final surprise.

The dragon stood a little way ahead, poised on a low, curved ridge of grey rock and staring back towards the platform from which Shatter had delivered his speech. In the scant light he appeared nondescript, and Fortune would have paid him no attention — but at last *something* about the dragon registered with Fortune. He stopped short and whirled around, grabbing the stranger by the wing and pulling him not without some force from the ridge on which he was standing.

'Hey . . . !' the dragon exclaimed, and was about to tackle Fortune bodily when their eyes met and they finally recognized each other.

CHAPTER 26

Dragons in the Snow

Higher and higher up and around the mountain they went.

There were more alerts to begin with, for it seemed that the patrols had been stepped up, and more than once they were forced to freeze in the open, flattening themselves against the snow and trusting their new camouflage to protect them against the keen eyes of the Charmed. In this way, although the rings proved relatively easy to find, and even easier to demolish, their work was demanding because they had ever a wary eye upon the sky. As evening approached, the dragons collapsed together in the shelter of a deep cleft of rock largely free of ice and snow, panting hard in the thin air and looking out with satisfaction across the lower slopes which they had, in implementing their mysterious strategy, somehow cleansed.

Here, despite their success that day, the mood was melancholy, and at first they said little to each other. Then, as shared warmth slowly relaxed their bodies, Gossamer said suddenly,

'I'm going up the slope a little way. I'll be back soon. I just need to be alone for a while.'

And before either of her companions could protest she was gone. Cumber started up after her but Velvet pulled him back.

'Leave her for a bit,' she said.

'But she shouldn't be . . .'

'She'll be all right. She's missing her Fortune, that's what her trouble is, any dragon can see that.'

Cumber sighed.

'I didn't see it,' he said presently.

'Never mind,' Velvet consoled him. She shuffled closer to

him, pressing her slim body against his bony haunch.

'It must be marvellous to be so in love with a dragon,' mused Cumber. 'I never really thought about it much until I came here, to the mountain, I mean, but you see, this place is the place I always dreamed of coming to when I was small, and so to actually be here is like being in a dream. Only it's real.'

'So do you believe dreams can come true?'

'Well, I suppose this one has, but then it's so different to what I actually expected that it's not like it's my dream at all — it's as though I've fallen into another dragon's dream altogether, if you see what I mean.'

'Not really,' murmured Velvet, nuzzling him affectionately.

'You see,' went on Cumber, warming to his subject, 'there is just so much here for a young charmed dragon like me — there's the charm itself of course, enough for a lifetime, but there's the history too, and the quest and all its strange twists and turns — and this task of ours here on the mountain. Now there's a puzzle!'

'Mmm.' Velvet had snuggled as close to Cumber as it was possible for two dragons to get. His scales were warm and resilient, and if she had thought him impressive as a golden dragon, now that he was white she felt quite swept away in his presence. She listened as he talked on about charm, only half-understanding yet wholly thrilled that she, Velvet of the forest, should be sharing so much with this dragon of magic.

But he's not just that, she thought cosily. *He's Cumber. And maybe I love him!*

The thought was a shocking one, for it drove against everything she had been taught. A Natural and a Charmed? Nonsense! Even were they not monsters such a thing could never be; it was simply not in the way of things. A dragon should stick to her own kind and leave well enough alone of things she did not understand.

But Velvet, despite her occasionally timid air, was nothing if not an independent dragon, and all she knew at this instant was that her closeness to Cumber was good and warm and special. She was comfortable against him, comfortable enough to close her eyes and let his voice and his heartbeat lull her towards sleep. And comfortable enough to dream of the possibility of love, yes, even between charmed and natural dragon.

Cumber's voice interrupted her drifting thoughts.

'I said, how many more are there, do you think?' he repeated, and from the exasperated tone in his voice it was apparent that he had been asking the question for some time.

'Oh, oh, I'm sorry,' yawned Velvet, reluctant to leave her dreams but anxious to please this dragon in particular. 'How many more what?'

'Rings, of course, my dear. Stone rings. How many more?'

Dear! He called me dear!

'Oh, well, let me think. There was a rhyme once, if only I could remember it . . .'

She frowned and tapped her claws as though counting. Deep memories from infancy slowly rose to the surface and at last she remembered. Reciting in a low chant, as she had learned it many years before, she spoke the old verse:

'Seven guard the trees
In the greatest of rings.
Five on the towers
Of the dragon kings.
Three close by
Where the high water sings.
And one without end
Which the fire will send
When the mountain stings.'

Cumber looked at Velvet as though he had only just realized that she were there; in a way, he had. He felt the proximity of her body to his and for the first time appreciated the way her curves made smooth and abstract shapes against the snow. She was so close to him that she had ceased to be a dragon – she was simply Velvet.

'That is fascinating!' he exclaimed excitedly, the verse she had spoken whirling through his mind with sufficient velocity to sweep away any notion he might have been developing simply to lie there with this young female and enjoy this strange new intimacy. 'But what does it mean, I wonder? "The greatest of rings"! What's that, I wonder.'

Velvet allowed herself a hidden smile, for while she felt increasingly frustrated by Cumber's inability to relax for more than a few breaths, she acknowledged that it was exactly this trait which made him so appealing. As he fidgeted next to her, she leaned back a little on one wing and said, 'That's the forest, of course.'

'The forest!' echoed Cumber, puzzled for a moment. Then it dawned on him. 'Oh, I see. Yes, of course. We've already found those – seven stone rings concealed inside the greater ring of the forest, except the forest is gone now. Still, I suppose that made them easier to find. Now, let's see . . .'

Velvet groaned in exasperation as Cumber sprang to his feet and marched up and down the length of the cleft, muttering to himself.

'Five rings . . . what was the next bit, Velvet?'

'"Five on the towers of the dragon kings",' tutted Velvet, resigning herself at last to this exercise. 'We found those today. "The towers of the dragon kings" is just a fancy name for those weird rocks that were nearby.'

Cumber nodded with growing enthusiasm. They had indeed found and dismantled five rings of stone today, all clustered within a short flight of each other and overlooked by a crown of rocky spires which burst clear of the snow, like the claws of a monster locked into stasis at the instant of its birth from the mountain.

Who knows, Cumber had thought with a tingle of dread, *perhaps trolls were once that big!*

'So that leaves the three near the water and the one . . . where was it?'

'The rhyme doesn't say,' admitted Velvet. 'But you're right: we've already broken twelve rings and there are only four left. And I've got a good idea where we might find the "high water" the rhyme speaks of.'

'You have? Where! You must tell me.' Cumber flashed a glance out across the darkening mountainside. 'Is it far?'

'Far enough not to go there today,' laughed Velvet. 'Oh, Cumber! Can't you just come and sit with me for a while?'

'Hmm? Yes, in a while. I just need to think first. Your rhyme made me think of something but it's gone again. Stay there – I won't be long.'

And out into the low afternoon light he hurried, leaving Velvet wistful and alone in the shelter of the cleft of rock. Presently Gossamer returned and huddled up close to her young companion.

'Did you tell him?' she asked.

Velvet looked up at Gossamer. She could see the marks of tears dried on to her white cheeks.

'Tell him what?' she replied, resting her head on Gossamer's flank.

'That you love him.'

Velvet did not reply, but as they pressed their bodies close together and stared out at the sky, watching the cloud turn first blue, then red, then finally a rich purple, she wondered why, if her feelings were so obvious to Gossamer, she could not make sense of them herself, much less express them to Cumber.

Perhaps he, like Gossamer, would see them too, and so she would not have to explain.

The sun went down, and they slept.

'Fortune!'

'Brace!'

Fortune looked down at Brace's wing, which he held tight in his claws. Seemingly mesmerized for a breath or two, he at last came to his senses and shook free his grip, taking a step back as he did so.

Brace glared at him, but for now Fortune did not read his sullen expression, so overjoyed was he by such a chance encounter.

Yet, when later he looked back on their exchange, he saw that even then, at the beginning, the anger had been welling inside him.

'Brace!' he repeated. 'Thank . . . you're all right! I never thought I'd see you again.' He glanced around, as though expecting to see his other companions appear from the night, and went on, 'The others – are they all right? Where's Gossamer? And Scoff – did he . . . ?'

'There's just me, Fortune! All right? Only me!'

Brace's voice cut briskly through Fortune's, and had he been listening more closely Fortune might have realized quite what a cry from the heart that admission was. But suspicion was already getting the better of him and he heard hostility creeping into his words.

'What do you mean?' he barked. 'Where's Gossamer? I told you to take care of her, Brace – you could do that much, surely?'

He knew his words were cruel and he felt ashamed, but he could not help himself. His anger at finding Brace alone without his sister – nor any other of his friends – came swift and clean, and for the moment it seemed easier to hurl it at Brace than to face up to the truth.

'We were parted in the fire,' retorted Brace, obviously unimpressed with Fortune's wrath. 'I did all I could, Fortune. Where were you?'

The words stung, and Fortune felt momentarily sorry for what he had said. But then he thought again of his dear, sweet Gossamer and his heart swelled with fear and rage. Looking at Brace, he saw the shape of her face mirrored in that of her brother, saw a reflection in his eyes of the light in hers; saw the promise of her. But it was a promise Brace could not keep.

'You don't know what it is to love another!' he snapped, and then his anger flooded out in a torrent of words which later, as he looked back in shame, he could not even remember. Even as he ranted at Brace his heart heard what he was saying and pleaded that they not be spoken, but some terrible engine inside was spewing it out, out of control. 'You're responsible if anything's happened to her, Brace!' he raged. 'Your protection is worth nothing; you're worth nothing, Brace, do you hear me?! Nothing!'

He paused, his eyes red and misted, panting. At a discreet distance Tallow and Volley were watching and mumbling to each other in an undertone.

They must be wondering who they've taken up with here, thought Fortune, and the thought was like a fresh wind through his head. Briefly he saw Brace as he really was – a young, proud, frightened dragon who was surely the last of his line, lost in a land of which he had little understanding and searching for a way to rebuild the life he had seen collapse about him. He closed his eyes and lowered his head, unable to meet the gaze of his one-time companion.

But then, just as he was seeking for the words he needed

to begin his apology, another horror entered his thoughts. He looked up again, but instead of trying to rescue the situation he demanded,

'You're the only one? What about Cumber? What about Scoff? Scoff at least came straight back to you. What happened to him?'

'We never saw him,' Brace snapped back, clearly fed up with Fortune's barrage. 'Both your charmed friends could be dead as far as I'm concerned, Fortune, and so could you! I don't care. Now just leave me alone!'

Scoff!

Cumber's whereabouts Fortune could not even begin to guess, and to hear this news about Scoff piled worry upon worry.

Where are you, my rainbow-winged friend?

But that question could no more be answered than could any of the questions and so, as Brace forced his way past and disappeared into the gloom of the cavern, Fortune was left with his two new friends and a heart filled with the painful spaces left by his old friends — and his love, Gossamer.

Try though he did, he could not believe they were dead. Not Cumber, not Scoff. Not Gossamer, please not Gossamer. They were simply . . . gone.

And so, it seemed, was Brace.

Rejoining Tallow and Volley he began a halting and awkward apology for his behaviour, but the other two waved him silent, reassuring him that he had no need to explain. Fortune was grateful for their understanding and discretion, but the shame did not leave him, for even if they could forgive him he could not forgive himself. Worst of all was the unwelcome notion that Gossamer, wherever she was, might somehow have sensed his anger, somehow heard his words, for in attacking Brace had he not also been attacking her?

Then too he felt at last the full effects of his day in the air. He had flown long and hard, and had stood alert for half the night listening to the rhetoric of Shatter. The temperature in the cavern was dropping gradually lower and it seemed to him that the weight of the entire world had dropped with casual ease on to his shoulders.

Feeling lost and alone, stranded on a pathway of doubts and regrets, Fortune plodded on behind his companions wishing that sleep would claim him now. But even when they did reach the scrape, and when Tallow and Volley had curled themselves around and settled quickly into a gentle rhythm of snores and grunts, still sleep eluded him and he was left alone with his thoughts.

The weight pressed down on him with ferocious power, and by the time his eyes began finally to droop and his mind to wander he had grown confused, so that it did not seem to be the weight of the world at all, but rather the weight of a huge boulder poised on top of a great tower of grey rock. Around it swarmed dragons, and they all looked to him for the answer.

But he had no answer for them, only a rage without direction, a rage which flowed through his veins like a source of power waiting to be tapped.

It was a simple need that had driven Gossamer away from her friends for a short time and up the mountain: the need for a view.

Not that the view from the sheltered cleft was not impressive enough — vast, rolling humps of snow were stacked below them, their intricate folds tumbling away into the deeps where they melted into the drifts and ridges of the lower slopes — but she needed something more, something different, something she could not quite define . . .

Something to help me think of Fortune!

She clambered slowly up the steep incline, unable to see much higher due to a large, overhanging crag of rock. Behind her, the sky was dimming rapidly towards night. Above the crag a sliver of white light flared against the brightening stars — a night dragon, falling through the heavens on some unimaginable quest of its own.

The caution of the day put aside, Gossamer spread her wings and flew boldly up over the crag to perch on its peak, digging her claws into the ice to secure her hold upon the slippery surface.

She surveyed the land. Was this the view she had sought?

With the mountain to her back she looked out due east into the twilight. She could see nothing different in that

321

direction to what she had already seen from the cleft, nor had she expected to. Behind her the mountain obscured all landscape but for its own indomitable wall, so instead she scanned the terrain to her right.

Fields of snow; rocky bulges thrusting forth; the dim horizon nearly invisible now as night hunched over the mountain. Nothing remarkable.

To her left, then – due north.

The same: the close, snow-covered mountain and the distant world beyond.

Except . . .

Except it seemed to Gossamer that she did see something different. No, not see but sense.

Tipping her head forward and half-closing her eyes, she blinked into the flickering snow and tried to make out what it was she thought she saw.

A network of faint lines laid over the landscape? Or rather under the landscape? They shimmered at the periphery of her vision, clearest at the corner of her eye and practically invisible wherever she looked most intently. How real they were she could not judge, but there was something there . . .

As she observed them she began to discern a pattern. She saw that the lines were arranged in concentric rings radiating out from the mountain, their broad arcs receding into the distance as far as she could see – or rather sense. What she was sensing had to be some kind of charm, for she had sometimes detected similar lines in the form of auras about the bodies of the water sprites whom she had so loved to watch back in Aether's Cross. Those tiny filigrees of magic had shone with pale colours and cloaked the darting sprites with radiant cloaks, but these lines, though similar, were in another way altogether different.

They are bigger, she thought, laughing out loud at her own understatement. The laugh broke the spell under which she had fallen, and as she widened her eyes again the lines began to fade. But before they did so entirely she saw one last feature of the pattern which she had so far missed: within the concentric rings there were anomalies, strange shadows cast on the net like bruises on the skin of a fruit. She counted ten before the lines vanished altogether, spaced in a regular circle perhaps a day or two's flying time out from the mountain.

Things – something – spaced around the mountain like the stones in the rings we are working so hard to destroy . . .

The puzzle was too great. Darkness was near, and her head was beginning to ache, and so she hopped back over the edge of the crag to return to her friends.

I haven't even done what I thought I had come out to do – think of Fortune.

The realization and the remembrance of him brought with them not the pain she might have expected, but a sudden and overwhelming tranquillity, for it seemed to her that this evening, now, he was with her. Involuntarily she looked towards the north again, not realizing that the point in the darkness towards which she gazed was the very place her love resided; without even knowing that she was doing it, she looked straight at the Fortress, and in doing so she knew with devastating truth that Fortune was alive.

The revelation blasted through her like a hot wind and then fiery tears sprang forth, blazing down her cheeks and falling into the snow, which melted beneath them. North she looked, without understanding why, yet in that prospect she knew that everything that mattered to her was out there for her to reclaim: the magic, the fear . . . and Fortune.

And although she could not see her love, nor again the magical network which had been so briefly revealed to her, she knew that the power of both were at her disposal, and that sometime soon she would be called upon to use it.

Fortune waited, and the land waited, and Gossamer could only look on and weep, knowing that the final task would take all her strength and probably more, and many more lives than their own two would depend upon her understanding a mission even Cumber could not explain.

North she looked, and long she wept, but in the end she was not sad, for as she returned to the sheltering cleft of rock she sensed that time was at last closing in upon them all, and that it would be during the next few days that the true course of the world would be set.

Would it turn true, or would winter consume it forever?

'Why am I being shown these things?' she whispered to herself as she turned the corner to rejoin Velvet. 'For surely, in the end, it is Cumber who will see this task through. Surely, in the end, it is about charm that the world will turn.'

But even as she spoke these words she looked again towards the hidden north.

Tonight I have been primed, she thought with wonder. *But for what?*

That she could not say but she could guess from what direction the answer might come, and when.

'From the north,' she murmured. 'Soon.'

Cumber too looked to the north, but he enjoyed none of Gossamer's revelatory excitement. Instead he saw ... nothing.

'I'm in the wrong place,' he said grimly as he gazed out into the new night. 'I don't know where I should be, but I'm in the wrong place.'

Four rings were left to be dealt with, and Cumber felt confident they would be dismantled tomorrow. But then what? And would it really take three of them to do the job?

'But Mantle told me,' he protested, uncomfortable with the direction his thoughts were leading him. 'I have to see it through, or else ...'

Or else what?

He sighed heavily and thought about Velvet. A strange young dragon, that one, but ... intriguing. If only there was time to get know her a little better.

The sky was showing clear patches for the first time in days and Cumber looked up to see stars shining in the breaks. It seemed to him that the light they gave was falling everywhere but here, that the whole world was illuminated by starlight except for this particular spot on this particular mountain.

I'm in the wrong place!

'All right,' he argued. 'Where do you think you ought to be instead, Cumber, hmm? Tell me that!'

I don't know. Just . . . not here.

Above, a night dragon streaked across the sky with all the surety of a dragon certain of its path and of the events it must influence.

Uncertain, restless, Cumber paced uneasily back to where

his friends already lay asleep and rejoined them, squeezing himself into their warmth and eventually drifting into restless dreams about lost dragons and forgotten quests.

Outside, the snow stopped.

Brace dwelt long on his terrible encounter with Fortune, but in the end he found that he had cause to thank Fortune for at least one of the cruel things he had said.

'You're worth nothing,' Fortune had said, words which had struck at the heart of the frustration Brace had felt since arriving here at the Fortress.

Shatter's words had inspired him, of course; no dragon had listened to the oration more intently than Brace. But still, more than anything, he felt unimportant, still he needed to prove himself. Until he could remedy this he felt that no other dragon would be able to recognize his true worth.

And then Fortune had actually called him worthless!

That barbed statement had finally made up Brace's mind. He would show them. He would show them all!

And so, instead of sleeping that night, Brace made himself a plan. He would prove himself. He would find his challenge. And then, when at last he flew triumphant, dragons like Shatter and Fortune would be forced to look at him and say,

'There goes Brace — a dragon of worth!'

And perhaps Gossamer too, wherever she was, would look at him and say proudly,

'There goes Brace. He's my brother, you know.'

Dreaming of love, Brace crept past the sleeping forms which surrounded him and launched himself out into the snow-filled sky where flew the dragons of the Flight.

CHAPTER 27

The Time Between

There was no stranger time in all that unexpected winter than the two days which followed. That night, when Cumber, Velvet and Gossamer slept together on the mountain, as yet unaware that they were soon to part, many dragons crossed into a weird territory, a reality through which they seemed to move at odd angles, a world which seemed somehow tilted away from true. No dragon, in looking back on that unearthly time, could define what was wrong, only that something was wrong.

That night, when Brace set out on his most perilous adventure yet and Wood wept to hear the pain of his father's dreams, when Fortune slept the uneasy sleep of one who knows a storm is building greater than any that has broken before. That night, when Wraith punched through to the penultimate layer of defence, so near now to the very core of the Plated Mountain and the Maze of Covamere. That night, a night so full of events both great and small, when the snow finally stopped as though it knew that the world had reached some mighty pause in its endless turning. The days which followed were clear too, and after that the fog came and not even time, much less snow, mattered much on the mountain any more.

Nor indeed anywhere in the world.

It was the time of the Turning, and so the meaning of time had started to change out of all recognition.

The first of those two dreamy days passed swiftly enough for the three white dragons labouring on the Plated Mountain. Rejuvenated by the sight of a clear sky, they positively leaped up the steep slopes, following Velvet's directions towards the place she suspected to be the 'high water' of which the rhyme spoke: a broad tarn high on the southern reaches of the mountain. By noon they had reached it and under the midday sun they located the first of the rings of stone, a tiny circle of no more than twenty pebbles located on a little island near the centre of the open water. This they successfully broke up and by sundown the remaining two rings had also been dismantled.

Which left only one.

There were fish in the tarn, which Cumber caught deftly by means of a charm he did not even try to explain to his companions. Velvet watched in adoration as he roasted the fish over an open fire and gasped in delight at the rich flavour created by the smoky flames.

'It would be worth getting caught for this!' she exclaimed, tucking into a third portion with obvious relish. 'Oh, Cumber, you're so clever!'

'They're pulling in the patrols,' responded Cumber distantly. 'Wraith is getting ready for the final assault. We won't be spotted now.'

Gossamer eyed him suspiciously.

'What's wrong, Cumber?' she asked. 'I thought you'd be curious about this last ring? Surely time's running short now?'

'It is, Gossamer. Very short.'

Cumber would be drawn no further on the subject of the last of the rings and only later, after sunset, did Gossamer manage to coax him into a proper conversation. Velvet lay peacefully asleep some distance away as they crouched near the remaining embers of the fire. The dying flames turned their white hides golden, causing Cumber to glance wistfully down at the scales on his flanks.

'Getting bored with being white?' chuckled Gossamer. Despite her humour, she recognized there was something infinitely sad in Cumber's expression. She thought she knew what it was.

'I can't see it through,' he blurted, staring mournfully into the fire. 'I know I'm failing Mantle but . . . I can't do it, Gossamer. I shouldn't be here at all – I should be . . .'

'Yes?'

Cumber exhaled slowly.

'I don't know,' he intoned. 'Not here.'

'Where then?' pressed Gossamer gently. 'With Fortune? With Mantle? With Wraith?'

'Don't joke about it — I'm serious.'

'So am I, Cumber.' Gossamer pulled herself closer to her Charmed companion. 'Look, Cumber, you're trying to tell me that you need to leave, to let the two of us complete the task that Mantle originally set for you. Then do it, Cumber. The task will get done. No dragon knows the mountain better than Velvet, and I . . .'

Here she faltered and Cumber, for once, picked up on the hesitation.

'Yes, Gossamer? You what?'

She smiled at him, and it was at that moment that he knew that he would leave them, and that it would be all right to do so. He did not understand it, and he still felt guilty about — as he saw it — letting down Mantle, but somehow he knew that it had to be so.

'You said you shouldn't be here. Well, as strongly as you feel you shouldn't, I feel that I should.' She glanced to the north, a gesture which was becoming as automatic as blinking or breathing. 'I'm waiting for something, Cumber, and I need to be here when it comes.'

'Me too,' Cumber echoed. 'But I need to be . . . somewhere else.'

For a time that seemed to be enough, but neither dragon professed to feeling tired so they simply sat there together for a while, watching the fire die away and the stars track slowly through the black sky. It had been an odd day, a day of triumph in their work yet one also of impatience, of irritability, as though each of them were waiting for something none of them could explain. Now, in the comfort of the night, some of those tensions were gradually ebbing, and there was growing, at least between Gossamer and Cumber, a feeling of decisions made and destinies planned.

Then, deep in the mountain beneath them, the thunder started.

The ground trembled, powdery snow dancing beneath their claws, and the air resonated with the echoes of the underground storm. With a yelp Velvet awoke and scam-

328

pered over to her friends, clutching them against her in her terror.

'What is it?' she cried, looking around with fear.

As she spoke, the rumbling died away.

Gossamer and Cumber exchanged a glance.

'Wraith,' they said in unison.

The next morning they parted, and Velvet surprised Cumber by crashing up against him again when he thought that all the goodbyes had been said. Wrapping her wings completely around him she clamoured, 'Oh, please take care of yourself, dear Cumber! I couldn't go on if I thought something was going to happen to you! All of yesterday I knew you were planning something but I didn't dare ask what, or even think about it. Please come back to me soon, please, promise you will!'

With difficulty and not a little embarrassment Cumber extricated himself from her grip and backed gently away, fending her off with his own short wings.

'Of course, my dear, of course I'll take care – and of course you must too, you see, I mean . . . well, just make sure you look after each other, and whatever you do, find that last ring and break it up like we did the others. You promise that and I'll promise to be careful.'

'We promise!' blurted Velvet through her tears. Snuffling, she drew one wing across her face and then suddenly pushed him away. 'Go on!' she cried. 'Let's get this over with, at least. Come back to me soon!'

'I hope we'll all be together again soon!' called Cumber over his shoulder as he trudged uncertainly off into the snow.

'Goodbye, Cumber,' whispered Gossamer, who had already said her farewell and could only stand and watch yet another of her companions disappear into the landscape.

Together they stood, watching until Cumber could be seen no more, then they turned to face each other.

'Any ideas?' said Gossamer with a half-smile.

Velvet frowned, wiping away her tears, then bounded right up to her and exclaimed, 'I just know we'll see him again, and your Fortune, of course! Ideas? Oh, yes, I've got plenty, but I'm not really sure about any of them, although there's only really one direction we can go from here, isn't there?'

'And where's that?' laughed Gossamer. Velvet's instant change of mood had infected her with a new lightness of spirit and even the sudden departure of Cumber seemed part of some greater scheme which would soon reach its resolution.

'Up!'

For Fortune, those days of waiting before the fog came were days of pressure. Around him Shatter's forces were completing their training and preparing for battle, their tension and readiness reflected by a similar tension inside his own heart. What its ultimate cause was he did not know, but it was there all the same, brooding like a waiting storm, like a beast ready to pounce. Perhaps it was simply the threat of the coming war, but beyond even that were other pressures, such as the possibility, however remote, that if Shatter was here then other dragons, dragons whom he loved, might be here too. This above all else pushed down upon him, but so great was his fear of not finding them that he did not even try to do so.

Soon, he thought, and, *Perhaps they will find me. Yet there seems to be no time!*

And then there was the revelation of the Flight.

Fortune had spent the day after Shatter's rally in contemplation of the tremendous activity going on all around him. Having arrived at the Fortress so late in the proceedings, and having the formidable Tallow and Volley as his guardians, he was not bothered by any of the squadron commanders, all of whom had far better things to do than chase up odd dragons who may or may not have been loitering away from their duties. He received a few odd looks, and Tallow fielded a few unwelcome questions, but otherwise he was allowed to wander with his companions more or less where he pleased, and this he did.

'There's so much to take in!' he gasped at one point as a battalion of five hundred Naturals hovered in perfect formation above one of the terraces towards the middle of the Fortress, the draught from their wings a veritable gale.

'Shatter's here at the right time,' replied Volley. 'These

dragons are itching for a fight – have been for years. There'll be songs about these times, you mark my words.'

'And you'll be there to sing them, I suppose?' laughed Fortune.

Tallow smiled without humour. Such a display of military force was impressive, as he had already admitted, but he did not have to like it. He watched Fortune closely as he bantered with Volley, and soon realized that the young dragon's laughter was entirely artificial, and that something far more sinister was lurking beneath. He recalled the venom Fortune had spat at Brace the previous night and briefly doubted his own judgement in choosing to follow this stranger who had flown out of the mountain and into his life.

But then Fortune caught his eye, and the glance they exchanged was full of understanding.

My laughter may be false, he seemed to say, his eyes boring into Tallow's own, *but I am not! Bear with me, Tallow.*

Casting his doubt aside, Tallow followed his friends for the rest of the day as they gradually toured the great vault of the Fortress, assessing the army's strengths (many) and its weaknesses (few), gleaning from other dragons details of some of the strategies which were planned for the imminent attack on Covamere, absorbing, learning, preparing.

But preparing for what? wondered Tallow.

A little of Fortune's tension eased when night came, for instead of killing time in the confines of the Fortress, he was able to fly out into the darkness and learn about dragons for whom he felt far more affinity than those who paraded within. As he followed Tallow and Volley out from the over-hanging wave of rock and into cold air blissfully free of snow for the first time in days, he felt a thrill of anticipation. His wings felt strong and new, and with Tallow's training helping him through the air he felt able to take on any dragons Shatter – or Wraith for that matter – might have cared to throw at him.

The meeting place of the Flight was well-known to many of the dragons who occupied the Fortress. Sometimes Shatter posted guards to ensure that no hostile action came of their meetings, but tonight, with all the activity inside the stronghold, the sky was almost empty.

'They're usually to be found down here,' called Volley softly as they glided low over the Fortress roof. The great wave of stone rolled past beneath their wings, grey and hard in the faint starlight. Ahead, Fortune could just make out a cluster of shapes hovering in the darkness which could only have been the dragons of the Flight.

Sudden light carved the surface of the surging rock beneath them into a maze of cracks and splinters of rock, each with its own brilliant leading edge and black, streaking shadow. They gasped at the rage of light and turned into the glare to seek out its source.

As they looked the light died, but they all saw the place from which it had come: a spot low on the western slopes of the Plated Mountain.

Covamere! thought Volley and Tallow.

Wraith! thought Fortune.

Then the rumbling came, a tremor which rattled the air around their wings and reverberated in the structure of the rock beneath them, a sound which went on for many long breaths and only slowly faded into the cool silence of the night.

Some part of the rumbling pulled at him even as it died in his ears, an echo of the force which had tried to prevent his coming here at all but which he had resisted. The pull of the mountain. It was like a reversal of the pressure which was building on him here, a vacuum which threatened – or did it promise? – to drag him back to its source.

Should I have resisted it before? he wondered. *Should I be here at all?*

He looked ahead to the dragons who awaited their arrival and put his doubts to the side and opened his heart and mind to the here and the now, for he was anxious to learn just what dragons these were who openly defied their mad master.

'Greetings,' cried a loud, female voice from some indeterminate place within the group. 'We've been waiting for you.'

The Flight, as Fortune learned that night, comprised some forty dragons, over half of whom were females. They gathered here most nights for fellowship and mutual support, for many of them were assigned to the most active of Shatter's squads and by the end of each day were desperate to release the anger they felt about what was happening here.

'Why don't you just fly off?' suggested Volley, ever the practical dragon. 'If you hate it that much just up and go — that's what we were planning to do,' he added, eyeing Tallow meaningfully.

'Ah,' sighed the dragon who had first spoken to them, a middle-aged female whose name was Werth. Although she was not the leader — for the Flight had no leader, nor even internal hierarchy of any kind — she seemed to speak for the group as a whole. 'We join here at night because we care, and it is because we care that we cannot leave. If we stay we might make a difference; if we go we will have achieved nothing.'

'Very noble,' acknowledged Volley. 'Damn foolish, though, if you ask me.'

'We didn't,' replied Werth good-naturedly. 'What do your friends say?'

'Admirable,' agreed Tallow after a pause. 'But in practice you are achieving nothing.'

'We share our dissatisfaction,' called another dragon from the main group.

'Ideas spread,' said another. 'Our numbers are growing, you know.'

'But too slowly,' said Tallow grimly. 'Shatter will attack before many more days are out. Then dragons will begin to die.'

There was general agreement with this last statement, then Werth piped up again, this time directing her words at Fortune.

'You haven't said much, young dragon. What do you think of all this?'

Fortune pondered this then replied, 'You said you'd been waiting for us. What did you mean?'

Another stirring in the crowd, then Werth answered.

'Well,' she said hesitantly. 'It started like this: when we came here tonight no dragon wanted to say much at first. Then, when we did get talking we all agreed that it had been a strange sort of day.'

'That's right,' put in yet another dragon. 'Very strange!'

'Thank you, Kale,' muttered Werth. 'If I could continue? Where was I? Yes – a strange day. Anyway, when we went through our usual roll-call it appeared that we were three dragons short on last night . . .'

'Sleet, Whittle and Dredge!' prompted Kale again. 'And good riddance!'

'Exactly,' said Werth. 'Well, wherever they've gone, they've gone. But it seemed to the rest of us that since our numbers have done nothing but grow since we started meeting here, there were bound to be some other dragons along sooner or later to make up for the loss. And now here you are!'

Werth beamed at the newcomers, while behind her the rest of the Flight, all beating their wings against the night air with a steady communal rhythm, offered varying degrees of welcome and suspicion.

But mostly welcome, noted Fortune with surprise.

'How do you know who we are?' he asked. 'We could have been sent by Shatter. Shouldn't you be more cautious?'

'Oh, nonsense!' exclaimed Werth. 'Tallow and Volley we know a least a little about – they've no love for Shatter, I'm sure of that.'

Tallow and Volley grunted non-committally at this, although both seemed pleased that their reputation had preceded them thus. Werth smiled at them, but it was Fortune whom she examined most closely with her keen gaze.

'But you,' she continued. 'Hmm, you're a little different, aren't you?'

'And then there's the light,' came a voice from behind her. 'Don't forget the light!'

'I was coming to that,' tutted Werth. 'You see,' she explained, approaching Fortune more closely now, 'there was that light, you see – when you came over the ridge just now. And the rumbling. It happened . . . it was just when you appeared . . .'

For the first time Werth seemed at a loss for words and she looked behind her for support, but before any dragon could offer it Fortune said slowly, 'That was charm. Magic. From the Plated Mountain.'

A hush descended upon all the dragons of the Flight.

Tallow and Volley held their breath, watching the proceedings intently.

'Wraith is trying to penetrate the mountain,' explained Fortune, the words seeming to crash from his mouth. Suddenly all the pressure which had backed up inside him came flooding out, and on its crest rode the words he now spoke. 'Great changes are coming to the world, changes of which we could all be a part. Even Shatter and his dragons are a part of it. Even me. And perhaps even you.'

After a long silence in which only the steady rush of air beneath dragon wings could be heard, Werth let out a long, whistling sigh.

'Well!' she announced. 'It looks like you're the one we were waiting for all right. Tell me, young dragon, what's your name?'

'Fortune.'

'Well, I suppose that will have to do.'

Much was spoken that night and much was learned. Fortune related most of his story to the dragons of the Flight and all who listened did so intently, including Tallow and Volley, neither of whom had heard the whole tale before.

'So you see,' concluded Fortune, 'it was only by the two of us – Cumber and me, Charmed and Natural – coming to Halcyon that there seemed any way of preventing the conflict from sweeping through the world like the fire swept through the forest.'

'Only it didn't work!' called a voice – Fortune thought it was Kale.

'No,' he admitted, 'it didn't. Something led me out of the mountain before I was able to reach Halcyon. I've lost my companions and I've failed in my quest. I don't really know what I can do, but . . . but . . .'

'But what, Fortune?' asked Tallow kindly, his gentle rumble a sudden comfort to this young Natural who found himself floundering in the middle of a situation he was now desperately trying to bring under control.

Control! he thought. *That is just what I've been lacking up to now!*

'But,' he continued, breathing deep and looking out over his audience, 'I will say this: the Charmed are not evil. I know you feel this in your hearts. It is only fear and prejudice that have caused this divide – and the faults are present on both sides. There is good and bad in each race; after all, what is Shatter if not a monster?'

And what is my good friend Cumber if not the best of dragons?

'Listen to me, dragons of the Flight, as you have never listened before. Between them, Shatter and Wraith have brought the dragon world to a critical place in its history, a turning point if you like. Behind us, Wraith is fighting to destroy all that the Charmed have ever built – for all I know he wants to level the mountain as he has already levelled the forest. His ultimate ambition I cannot guess, but why should he stop there?

'And Shatter – he in his turn is fighting to destroy Wraith and all that he and his charmed dragons stand for. I have seen just such madness destroy entire dragon communities; you yourselves have all seen the power of the Charmed destroy the great forest of the Plated Mountain; we know the might of Shatter's army.

'So I ask you, what will come of this if not the complete destruction of the entire dragon world? And, given the terrible power of fire charm, and the dreadful ambitions of dragons like Wraith and Shatter, of the whole world itself?'

'You speak knowledgeably of this magic,' came a wary voice from the crowd. 'And you seem to know many things – until you came no Natural even knew the name of the Black Dragon, yet you speak it as though you had met him.'

'I have not met him,' replied Fortune at once, 'nor do I ever wish to, but yes, I do know something of charm. And if every Natural here knew what I know, then we would be some way to making a real difference in the world.'

This last remark brought a chorus of approval which quite overwhelmed Fortune. Without realizing it he had spoken half the night away, conducting his own rally in the cold night air above the Fortress. Tallow and Volley, he noticed, had gradually moved their position around from one of opposition to one of containment within the larger group of the Flight, while he himself had adopted a high and solitary post looking down on his audience.

What is happening? he wondered. *Can it be that I am here to lead these dragons?*

'What must we do, Fortune?' demanded Werth with a smile from the front rank. 'Tell us and we will listen. The words you speak are good words; now all we need are actions to go with them.'

Actions?

Fortune considered this for some time before responding. The speech he had so far made had not, it seemed to him, come entirely from his own mouth and now he felt devoid of the inspiration which had kept his words flowing. The initial thrill of holding so many dragons in his spell was losing its grip upon him and he felt suddenly very young and very small and very embarrassed.

He thought in panic, *What can I possibly do for them, here of all places and against such overwhelming odds?*

To Fortune's relief, Tallow spotted his mounting distress and slipped smoothly through the air to his side, where he spun elegantly around to face the Flight.

'If I may make a suggestion?' he boomed.

'Of . . . of course,' replied Fortune gratefully.

'We have debated long tonight,' said Tallow slowly and carefully, 'and I feel that it is too soon for such important decisions to be taken.'

Thank you, Tallow!

'Yes,' agreed Fortune, taking up his friend's lead. 'I suggest we all use tomorrow as day of observation and, where possible, further recruitment. We should meet here again tomorrow night and only then decide what is to be done. But . . .' and here he paused and frowned, '. . . but tomorrow night we must decide. Time is running too short now, too fast to delay any further. Tomorrow night . . . will be the start of it all.'

To a general hubbub of agreement and anticipation, the Flight gradually broke up then, each dragon flying off across the roof to his or her own place of rest. As she said her goodbyes, Werth said to Tallow, 'Look after him well, this youngster. There's more to him than meets the eye.'

'I will,' Tallow rumbled in reply. 'Be sure of it.'

Fortune watched the dragons disperse until only he, Tallow and Volley remained. Far in the east, dawn was promising a new day and he yawned wide. He felt drained, but worse than that he felt dissatisfied. Although excited by the events of the night, and by the prospect of new allies and new challenges, at the same time he felt empty.

There are too many holes in my heart, he thought sadly. *Once it was only my father that I missed; now there are so many dragons. When will I ever be healed?*

As though hearing his thoughts, Tallow nudged him and murmured, 'This night is a great one in your life, Fortune, though you may not think so now. Ride on the coming storm, do not fight it, and perhaps it will soon bring you to the place you really want to be.'

As they flew back to the shelter of the Fortress, Fortune noted the long shadow cast by the Deadfall tower in the low rays of the rising sun. It lay across the distant snowfields like a felled, flattened giant, or perhaps a magical claw pointing westwards . . . where?

The place I really want to be. But where is that?

They flew beneath the tower's shadow and the day began.

In the eternal night of the mountain deeps, the basilisk stirred in its sleep, a sleep which ebbed away from it now like a tide of worlds from a shore of stars. Light and sound mixed with its greater senses as tiny dragons pecked at the mesh of which its own, brutal magic was an integral part. Colour invaded its dreams – black and red and gold – and with the colour came shapes.

Dragon shapes, small and fragile, scurrying through time in their desperate, mortal race.

The mountain, as deep as it was high.

A claw, and a boulder, and a broken ring set into white snow.

Many things. Some of them now of interest.

On the threshold of awareness, the basilisk began to growl.

CHAPTER 28

Deadfall and Light

Fortune pondered the fact that he was risking death by waiting here, but found little fear in the threat. Here, of all
places, he was beginning to feel right.

I am meshing with the workings of the world, he thought
dreamily, then laughed out loud.

'You fool, Fortune,' he chuckled. Above him a night
dragon soared, swiftly followed by a group of others. Their
threads of fire started high in the north and streaked south-
wards behind the Plated Mountain, which loomed sharp
and high in the middle distance.

Only starlight illuminated the mountain, for the glow of
the night dragons was weak by comparison and there was
no moon. This last observation sent a chill through Fortune,
for the moon should have been visible on such a fine, clear
night, if only as a thin, waxing crescent. It would be many
days before it would approach fullness again but still it
should have been there.

It was not.

Time is not just short – it's wrong!

As he waited for the Flight to come, Fortune examined
the land between the forbidden place where he was perched
and the mountain. The distant foothills flattened gradually
as they descended the mountain slopes towards the broken
plain of the Injured Ones. Although covered in snow, this
plain clearly demonstrated its subtle sculpturing: it looked
like a great, frozen pool of water into which the mountain
had long ago been dropped. Waves rippled out from the
centre, radiating towards the peripheral hills ... and
towards the Fortress.

From here, Fortune could see that the Fortress rested at

the low crest of one of those ripples; indeed, this minor mountain was itself like a great wave of stone upon the frozen pond. Looking out around that crest was like looking around a line which some mighty dragon had scribed in a colossal arc which circled the entire mountain.

A ring of stone . . .

And then there was the Deadfall.

He did not know what had drawn him here tonight. He had needed to be alone, but why here of all places?

Here, at the topmost point of the huge boulder which was poised on top of the Deadfall tower. If Shatter's dragons found him here, in the place Shatter himself considered most holy, he would almost certainly be killed.

And yet there was no fear.

The giant rock squatted beneath him, perched impossibly on the slender spire of grey stone which erupted from the snow in front of the Fortress mouth. The slightest breath of wind would surely send it tumbling to the ground, and yet the layers of dirt and vegetation which were packed around the junction between the two proved that it had rested there for many, many years.

In defiance of the pull of the ground, it rested.

Though the mountain pulled at him, and though new duty called him forth, Fortune rested too, while above him the night dragons began to play.

Werth had come to him early that morning, glancing around suspiciously and muttering that she could not stay long, and that they should not be seen together.

'I came to tell you something,' she announced in hushed tones. 'Something I didn't want to say last night, not with the others around.'

Exhausted by the strange pressures of the previous day and the effort of speaking so long to the Flight, Fortune had slept deeply, and now he felt considerably more refreshed than he had anticipated. The new day was cold and clean, and as yet the Fortress had not woken; the air beneath the overhanging roof was quiet. Looking up at that roof he saw wonder in the encrusted icicles which had formed there over the past days, the frozen remains of the breath of three thousand dragons.

'What is it, Werth?' he yawned, moving away from the corner where Tallow and Volley still slept peacefully.

Werth fretted, tapping her wingtips together. Fortune noted that her eyes were kind and motherly. At length she sighed.

'Well, no doubt I could be doing you wrong by telling you this, and then again maybe it's something you already know,' she began hesitantly.

'Just tell me,' smiled Fortune.

'All right. There's other dragons of South Point here apart from Shatter.'

If Fortune had not felt alert before then he certainly did so now. His eyes widened and his breathing accelerated. The cold air bit at his throat and chest but he paid it no heed.

'Go on,' he murmured.

'There's Shatter, of course, but you said last night that you knew him only by reputation, and that I believe. There are a few others – one of them an adviser to Shatter, though a sorrier specimen of a dragon you could scarcely wish to find anywhere. He's badly burned, you see, by a charmed dragon, they say.'

'Barker!' blurted Fortune, unable to stop himself.

'Then you do know him.'

'He is not a bad dragon,' said Fortune sadly, 'but I think Shatter has seduced him into thinking his way is right. Yes, I know him – I was there when he was burned. His son was my friend.'

Werth took a deep breath.

'There is far more to you than even I had guessed, Fortune. There when he was burned, eh? Well, my next piece of news will mean as much to you if not more: this Barker is tended by a young, fit dragon. It is said that he is his son.'

'Wood?' asked Fortune faintly.

'Yes. What will you do? Both seem loyal to Shatter, and both would surely betray the Flight as soon as take a breath. You understand I must say this to you, Fortune; I must do what is right, but I must also protect the dragons for whom I care.'

Fortune pulled himself back from the distant thoughts which were gradually claiming him.

341

'Of course I understand, Werth,' he sighed, 'and I would do nothing to compromise the Flight, believe me. Thank you for telling me this, but as for what I shall do . . . I just don't know.'

As she turned to go, Werth placed a motherly wing upon Fortune's own.

'The other dragons who came here from South Point were just a couple of common rogues,' she added. 'I'm sure they were not known to you. Nor loved by you.'

'No, I suppose not.'

'Until tonight.'

'Goodbye, Werth. And thank you.'

So Werth made her way off into the waking Fortress, leaving Fortune full of news and indecision. He had found Wood . . . and surely lost his mother forever. And if Wood were here, should he try to find him? It would not be too hard to locate a dragon close to Shatter, even among three thousand.

But do I want to?

For the rest of the day Fortune pondered this question as he roamed with Tallow and Volley among the excited dragons of Shatter's army. Wherever they looked dragons were flying, dragons were clashing in mock-conflict, dragons were deep in discussion, scratching maps on the dusty floor or arguing tactics and strategies. Never had Fortune seen dragons so motivated.

And yet he could not summon the courage to face Wood. Not here, and not now.

What would we say to each other? he thought dismally. *If we were not already growing apart at South Point then surely we have grown apart now.*

And then there was the Flight. Wood would know Fortune's allegiances the instant he saw him, and that alone might be enough to bring Shatter's full wrath to bear upon the innocent dragons of the Flight. Though he trusted Wood not to betray him personally, the chance was too great that Barker, or perhaps Shatter himself, would somehow hear of their meeting and prise the information from him. No, the risk was too great.

The decision tore at him, for it felt like cowardice, yet he

342

knew it was right both for his own safety and for that of his new friends.

If only we could have been reunited somewhere else, far away from the world where only we would matter.

But, of course, such things could never be.

It was midday before Fortune reached his decision, and shortly afterwards he took his leave of Tallow and Volley. His excuse was that he wanted to explore parts of the Fortress he had not yet seen and that he could cover more ground alone. His friends did not believe this for a moment, but let him go all the same, recognizing his need to be on his own.

'There's more to him than meets the eye,' said Volley as they watched him depart.

'Still want to fly away, Volley? Still want to see the world? We could go, if you wanted.'

Volley considered this for a moment, then said,

'Well, Tallow, my old friend, it seems to me that there's quite a lot of world around here at the moment. Maybe we should stick around, just for a bit longer, what do you say?'

'I think that's just what Weft would have done.'

Fortune came close to going back on his decision to avoid Wood. Late in the afternoon, when he had already begun to think about flying out into the sky to await the other dragons of the Flight, he found himself in the rear section of the Fortress, where the roof curved low towards the ground, the rib-like structures which supported it standing proud as the low sunlight caught their contours. Here Shatter had his headquarters, a tight and ordered system of caves and constructed walls in which he held his councils and took his decisions. Guard dragons paced and soared, covering both ground and air; this was not a place for a dragon without business to be caught.

Yet here he loitered all the same, flying a few low passes over the headquarters in the hope of . . . of what he could not really say, for even had he seen Wood down there he surely would not have stopped to greet him, nor even called down from the air.

After three such flights he retreated, for one of the sentries seemed to be growing suspicious and began to follow him.

343

He turned his back on Shatter and flew swiftly out towards the sunset, not looking back.

And now here he sat, as he had sat all evening, on top of Shatter's forbidden Deadfall. Night had fallen, the night dragons flew and soon the Flight would come.

Soon.

But not just yet.

Despite the fears and hopes which danced in his heart, he found himself captivated by that which had sat with him all through his vigil. That which shared with him the silence of the night and the stark beauty of the snow.

That which, like him, was waiting.

The Plated Mountain.

It pulled at him, a terrible engine of force which sucked at the roots of his soul as though wishing to tear them loose from the world to which they clung . . . and yet which whispered to him with the gentleness of a warm autumn breeze rich with the scent of fallen leaves. Its presence with him here was more than simply its presence on the horizon — it was *here*. It was as close to him as his own body and yet still it tried to pull him nearer.

High in the darkness, night dragons flew fast, showering and splintering so that the sky became ablaze with their light.

And still the mountain pulled.

Beneath his claws, the boulder trembled.

'Fortune!' the voice floated through the cold air, a hoarse whisper. Tallow coasted up to where he sat clinging to the rock and hovered at his side. 'What are you doing here?' he hissed urgently. 'For the sky's sake get clear. If you're found here . . . !'

'No,' replied Fortune. 'You get clear. Gather the Flight at a safe distance and . . . and watch. Just watch.'

'What are you talking . . . ?'

But then Fortune turned on him, and if Tallow did not complete his words then it was no wonder, for a sudden light fell upon him, a powerful, glorious, terrifying light which seemed to have as its source so many things, the mountain, the boulder, the very snow on the ground . . . and Fortune's eyes.

'It's all right, Tallow,' said Fortune, his voice strangely

344

normal despite the fiery glow which had surrounded his body. 'I'm still here. I'm not sure what's happening, but I think it'll be all right.'

Speechless, Tallow back-tracked through the air and called to him the rest of the Flight, who had been waiting just above the mouth of the Fortress.

'To me!' he boomed. 'And go no closer!'

The light came from the mountain. It had become a dark wedge bisected by a horizontal slit of light across its base. As the dragons watched in awe, the light began to pulse, sending shock waves of energy through the ground powerful enough to lift the snow and shake the air. The light narrowed, then focused, its target clear: the Deadfall.

On top of the boulder, Fortune opened his wings and soared into the air.

With one, final pulse, the light exploded from the mountain and struck the Deadfall boulder at its very centre. Terrifying energies seemed to fill Fortune's body, sending the fire coursing out from between his scales, and this strange inner light joined that of the stars and the night dragons in their dance.

A dragon of light flew through the sky.

Fragments of the fire illuminated the boulder beneath him, overpowering the dying light from the mountain and fleeing beneath its icy skin like worms into soil until the rock glowed from within. The stars dimmed as a greater light exploded from the dragon-dwarfing boulder, firing the ice into angry jets of steam which arched out into the air where they condensed anew to form a fog of tiny crystals suspended all around the frightened dragons of the Flight.

Through the fog swept Fortune.

Vapour spiralled from his wingtips as he skimmed the surface of the Deadfall and accelerated upwards until he was powering into a sheer climb which left behind the rock, the Flight, the Fortress and, it seemed, the whole world. Impulses not his own worked his wings as the wintry land receded.

Cold air burned his lungs as he played the sky and his head grew light as the air thinned around him. High as the Plated Mountain itself he paused, held on air taut and fragile as a spider's web. Below him the world revolved, starlit and magical.

Lights danced inside his eyes as he laboured in the tenuous air. The cold penetrated his whole body like winter falling on the land. Frost crackled across his scales with every beat of his ice-heavy wings.

His mind expanded.

Far, far below him the Deadfall rock glowed with a light he could recognize as neither real nor unreal, natural or charmed. Nevertheless, it glowed. Though he did not know it, it was the glow of the Maze.

Far, far in front of him, on the slope of the Plated Mountain where Covamere was built, a second glow blossomed, bleeding red into the distant snow like a maze of translucent veins. A bitter wind seemed to howl upwards from the Deadfall, pass through Fortune and then, as though redirected by his body, continue across towards the mountain. The wind struck far-off Covamere and returned, doubled in strength, to strike Fortune afresh.

He swivelled on the two opposing winds.

Equally distant but suddenly there in Fortune's heightened awareness was another point of light, this time high up near the mountain's summit, and from that point a shaft of light launched itself up into the night sky like a glorious blade of golden grass, sending its own piercing wind back across the snow, back across the land and into the maelstrom which was building around the fragile, flying dragon.

Fortune wrestled the gale into submission and rode it with both the skills Tallow had taught him and with a greater skill, the source of which he did not dare imagine.

The fourth light birthed before him.

He saw it reflected in a cascade of ice crystals breaking from one of his horns, a bright blue flame burning deep inside the mountain. As he turned to face it, it too sent a storm into his path, a wind hot with the stench of death. This wind too Fortune marshalled into submission until he felt the winds bucking beneath him, slaves to his new mastery of the sky.

They're alive, he thought, looking to the various lights in turn.

'They're all still alive!' he cried exultantly.

346

He felt as though air drawn from the farthest edges of the world was gathering beneath his wings and that as he hovered there he might beat it in any direction he chose; he could direct the winds and they would drag the world on to any course he desired.

He breathed in the storm and felt his heart pound its energy through his body. As he had when Tallow had taught him the glory of flight he felt alive, but this time he felt the presence of the world too, and it was alive with him.

'They're alive!' he cried again, his song torn into a symphony of joy.

The winds gathered beneath him in one final, momentous gust and he expanded his throbbing wings until it seemed his chest would be ripped open. Scales warped and slid over each other as his back bunched itself tight with the pressure and then, with one immense thrust, he directed all the winds, all his new joy, all the light and all the air he had gathered from across the land and sea . . . down!

The ball of energy spilled out across the snow, but not before its core had struck the Deadfall. The dragons of the Flight, reduced to the size of dust motes by the sheer scale of the colossal explosion, fled the scene to cower under the protective overhang of the Fortress. From so high Fortune began to see a pattern in the rock, a new shape to the land . . .

The Deadfall shuddered and the land moved.

Crusts of ice splintered and mixed with shattering rock as the Deadfall tower bent in massive judders at two points along its length.

Abruptly the winds stopped and the magical lights – both the eerie glow surrounding Fortune and its more distant echoes over the mountain – were extinguished. Only the still, faint starlight remained; no night dragons flew now.

Fortune gasped as he hovered in air now calm and clear after the storm, watching pieces of the land fold themselves into new and awesome patterns.

The huge spire of rock on which the Deadfall was trembling and rocking twisted violently about its joints. Four new towers burst from beneath the snow to take their places at its side. They drew together, closing up to support the shuddering boulder.

Together the cluster of five spires was easily twice the size of Shatter's entire fortress.

The base of the cluster shook, sloughing off its coat of snow and ice, then it too bent like the Deadfall tower and with a subtle, animal motion tipped the mighty boulder itself off its perch of centuries to fall tumbling into the narrow valley below.

The very mountain shook.

The snow exploded as the Deadfall rumbled through it, white clouds billowing into the freezing air only to fall anew, coating the watching land far and wide. On and on it rolled, cutting a vast swathe through the whiteness until at last it reached the next crest where the slope turned against it. After a brief climb it slowed, stopped, then turned back upon itself, rolling back along the path it had just cut until it finally came to rest at the foot of the valley in a shimmering cloud of snow and pulverized rock which only gradually began to settle around it.

Like thunder the noise of its passage reverberated around the mountain for what seemed like eternity, and even when the echoes had died Fortune heard them yet in the sky about him.

The silence which followed was massive.

The stars had tracked across the sky some distance since Fortune had first emerged from the Fortress that night, and now the young Natural flew higher to confirm what their meagre light told him.

From this height the shape of the land was laid out in stunning relief.

Around the Plated Mountain lay a troll. Its form was quite distinct, but so huge that only from this extreme elevation was it possible to make it out. Fortune saw that the low hills which surrounded the mountain were not hills at all but the troll's wasted body.

Like the earth giant, he thought, *it is both land and troll*.

Its head was lost or buried from sight, but the curve of its back was clearly visible in the hills, the ranges of ridges and valleys betrayed its flattened ribs and the moving cluster of spires from which the Deadfall had tumbled was clearly an outstretched hand. Fortune could not guess at what the true, living shape of the troll had once been, but what he could see made him feel small and utterly insignificant in the face of such vast and ancient power.

The troll was dying, or dead already, but with its last effort it had tipped the boulder it had held aloft for so many years so that it fell and joined its fellows on the ground.

For this was the other pattern Fortune now saw: a ring of regularly spaced, giant boulders which now, with the addition of the Deadfall, encircled the mountain entirely.

Like the earth giant he and Cumber had watched that night so long ago, this creature of legend had once laboured to create a circle of stones, tiring at the end of its momentous task so that the ring had remained unmade until tonight.

Until Fortune had intervened – or something had intervened through him.

The events of the night were growing hazy in his memory. The troll's dead fingers were there below him, motionless now, evidence as undeniable as the great scar in the snow leading to the fallen boulder, but the idea seemed suddenly impossible – a natural dragon pushing a dying troll, a charmed troll, to complete some unfathomable task? Nonsense! He had simply been in the way.

And yet . . .

Debris fell back to the ground, clouds settled and Fortune turned to drop once more down to earth. Then he stopped, cupping the air, as starlight glinted off another body in the sky with him.

Another dragon was labouring through the high, thin air, close enough now for Fortune to hear its breathing as a series of hoarse, frightened grunts. Its shape was natural, its body stocky.

'Wood?' murmured Fortune as he struggled to make out the dragon's features. Then he recognized it.

'Brace!'

As he called out Brace looked up, agony contorting his face. Then the young Natural seemed just to give up: he folded his wings and tumbled towards the ground, out of control.

Fortune tucked his own wings close and whipped himself into a crashing dive which took him below Brace's plummeting form. They collided, the impact winding them both but jolting Brace back to sensibility so that he opened his wings again. Together they glided down to land in the snow-field inside the five towers of rock which had once been the fingers of a troll.

Fortune held Brace close, wrapping his wings tight around the youngster's frozen, trembling form.

'I'm sorry,' wept Brace. 'I'm so sorry. Help me, Fortune. Forgive me.'

Fortune hushed him.

'It's all right, Brace,' he said. 'It's all right. I'm sorry too. I should never have said the things I said. I'm sorry.'

The towers stood guard around them as they warmed each other in the cold, the miracle of their second, sudden reunion banishing the winter from their hearts, and soon Brace stopped shivering and looked up.

'Anything you want, Fortune, I'll do for you,' he said. 'I want to join the Flight. I want to join you. I'll never let you down again.'

Fortune heard the conviction in his words and, for an instant, saw the light of Gossamer's love in her brother's eyes. Tears stained his own cheeks and crystallized in the cold.

'Everything's all right, Brace,' he said. 'They're all all right. Now, why don't you tell me what's happened?'

CHAPTER 29

The Eve of the Battle

Shatter woke suddenly, his eyes filled with fire.

A cold, brilliant light had brought temporary day to his Fortress. It flickered and flashed, a weird lightning renewing itself with constant energy, and a terrible rumbling shook the bones in Shatter's tensed body.

There was a taste of magic in the air.

Forcing his way roughly between the two guards who stood, stupid and astonished, at the entrance to his quarters, Shatter rushed on to the platform beyond and looked out across the Fortress.

His quarters were in many ways a reconstruction of the secluded caves in which he had grown up, a dark network of chambers and tunnels excavated from the softer rock which made up what was in fact, did Shatter but know it, part of the prone body of a dead troll. From here he could see virtually the entire complex laid out below, and also maintain a commanding view of the valley and mountain beyond the Fortress mouth.

Though he now ruled an army of three thousand dragons, Shatter was still the coward he had always been, and lest he be trapped there, he had personally overseen the cutting of an escape tunnel, clear through the body of the troll to the low foothills behind the Fortress. So that their work was guaranteed to be forever secret, after the completion of the tunnel he had slain the four dragons who had excavated it.

He could kill well enough, he did not need to prove himself in battle. If the four excavators had unwittingly helped him bury them alive in a second tunnel — by obeying Shatter's order to dig it! — they were fools, tools. As his parents had been. Used and destroyed.

He remembered little of the past now. The journey here from South Point was a vagueness of wing and breath, and his coming to power over these many dragons of the mountain had been so inevitable it was unworthy of memory, a distraction. Shatter had moved into a dark world of the now and the near-future. A world dominated by his Deadfall.

This mighty rock was the rock he would drop on to the heads of any dragons who saw fit to defy him. For this was his warped and hopeless strategy: that his army would draw the Charmed out of the mountain and back to the Fortress, where Shatter would be waiting, ready to unleash the power of the Deadfall upon their unsuspecting souls.

He reached the platform in time to witness the awesome event taking place in the valley outside. The Deadfall boulder, displaced by some force he could not conceive, was falling. It thundered through the snow surrounded by an unnatural blue aura — a magical aura — shaking the ground and crazing the air with its momentous passage.

Charm had reached into his Fortress and plucked his Deadfall from its perch. Some dragon had betrayed him — the fallen boulder was a sign — and that dragon would know Shatter's wrath before the night was ended.

He watched as it slowed . . . and stopped. Cold rage filled his empty heart.

He was betrayed!

The two guards backed nervously away as Shatter began to mutter to himself. Unwise dragons called him mad but the guards, being wise, retreated and kept their silence, awaiting their master's command.

'Betrayed,' growled Shatter hoarsely. 'No dragon to be trusted. Charm reaches even here. Seduced. Betrayed! But I won't fall; I'm no rock. This is my war, my land. I won't fall!'

The guards flinched as he turned on them.

'Fetch my lieutenants,' he rumbled, red eyes blank, unfocused. 'The war is upon us. This is the signal!'

The departing sentries occupied only a brief part of his attention as he was left alone on the platform.

As he had always been, he was alone.

For Shatter the world around him had always been a mere extension of the world inside his own mind; outside, as inside, the only true being was he, the only true dragon himself. Only he existed.

Now that his power had grown he had managed to shape this outside world into an image of his own making — he had found this Fortress, recruited this army; this world he had moulded to be truly his own, unreal though it certainly was.

Yet the more time went on the more real this world seemed to become, and so for the battle he longed to wage against this intruding reality he had come to rely almost totally on his ultimate weapon: the Deadfall.

A rock to fall upon them, to crush them out of the reality into which they had, unwelcome, started to insinuate themselves. Charmed, Natural, all would be crushed in the end, but then that was right, for from the beginning it was only Shatter himself who had ever really existed.

But now he saw that he had been seduced.

The Deadfall itself had been his betrayal. The primary defence of his Fortress, now stinking of charm, had revealed itself as the traitor it was, shaking his world both outside and in, taunting him with its unruly motion, its flagrant denial of his command.

The world he had created had ceased to obey him and so now it had become an irritation, a distraction. An itch.

And the time had come for Shatter to scratch.

He glared deep into his one, true, interior world and considered.

Charm had overturned the Deadfall, therefore the Charmed would die.

For the Charmed to have known of the Deadfall a Natural must have betrayed its existence.

Therefore the Naturals would die.

The land itself, Shatter's new world, had shifted under the collapse of the Deadfall.

He would destroy the land.

Only Shatter, the one, true dragon, would remain.

After a lifetime on the brink of insanity Shatter stepped finally into the pit.

Unaware that they were being observed, Fortune coaxed Brace's story from him.

'I thought I was being clever,' the youngster began, trembling. 'I happened on them by chance – I was going to infiltrate the Flight and betray them to Shatter. But I ended up following those three. It was just after we'd argued, you and me, and I wanted to prove myself.'

'Oh, Brace,' sighed Fortune, full of regret. 'Who did you see? Tell me from the beginning.'

'Three renegades from the Flight. Sleet and Whittle and . . . I forget the other one's name. They were talking just outside the Fortress mouth, saying how they were going to betray Shatter to the Charmed. I thought at first I'd just report them, but when I saw they were actually about to set off, I thought maybe I could tag along. I suppose I had some idea about talking them out of it or even fighting them down. Either way,' Brace added in a small voice, 'I thought it was my chance to be a hero.'

He breathed in heavy, juddering breaths. Vapour solidified in tiny pellets before his frightened face.

'That Sleet, he's a *bad* dragon, Fortune. Was, I should say. At first I thought he was just a typical Flight dragon, you know, just trying to stir up trouble for Shatter, but soon I realized it was any kind of trouble he was out to stir up. He sees no single enemy – every dragon is his enemy. He's just . . . bad. *Was* bad.

'We ran into trouble almost straight away. The Charmed are everywhere on the mountain now; I think if we hadn't betrayed Shatter they'd have found the Fortress soon enough. Anyway, two of them pounced on us when we were barely halfway to Covamere and they killed Whittle and the other one. Just like that! Only Sleet and I got away . . .'

Brace was shaking now but Fortune urged him on. The story had to be told.

'I don't know how we escaped,' he continued, his eyes wide and unfocused. 'We found ourselves beside a camp, the one the Charmed had come from. There were still trees there.'

Here he paused, clearly unwilling to go on, great shudders raking his body.

'This camp,' prompted Fortune, hardening his heart with difficulty in the face of Brace's obvious distress.

'This isn't going to be easy for you to hear, Fortune,' said Brace, his voice a plea.

Fortune's blood was ice water as he listened to Brace tell him of the Charmed prison camp.

'It was a clearing in this patch of forest they'd left untouched. Obviously so they could keep the prison there. They had cages of fire, like globes hanging in the air. They were covered in flickering blue flames and there were dragons trapped in every one. Charmed dragons, Fortune — their own kind.

'A few had been mutilated. Sleet couldn't look but I did. Some had no legs, some just had great scars on their bodies, or their eyes put out. I recognized something, you see, lying in a corner, just forgotten in a corner.'

Another shuddering breath. Ice crystals fragmenting the air.

'What did you see, Brace? Tell me!'

'Wings,' blurted Brace with a sudden gasp. 'A pair of dragon's wings.'

Now Fortune too shivered. For a dragon to lose his wings was like . . . like nothing he could conceive. A wingless dragon was a cripple, an outcast, worse than dead. A dragon would sooner lose its eyes, its tail . . . anything but that.

'A charmed dragon might grow them back,' he ventured cautiously.

'Perhaps,' replied Brace without conviction.

'But what was it you recognized?' urged Fortune, although he already knew.

'They were red and blue and gold and every colour you could imagine. Like a rainbow. They were Scoff's wings, Fortune. They were Scoff's wings!'

Brace spilled this out, his chest heaving, his face a mask of horror as he saw again the terrible scene, but Fortune could feel only numb. The strange ecstasy he had experienced in the path of the winds fled like a sudden ebb tide and was replaced by . . . emptiness.

Scoff!

Dear, brave Scoff, who had once saved them all by slaying Brutace, and who had further risked his life to help bring them to Covamere. Crippled by his own kind.

'Was he . . . ?'

355

'He was alive,' said Brace, hitching his breath in great gulps. 'In a cage, like the others. I couldn't even get close. There were hundreds of cages, Fortune. Hundreds. And it was then that I finally realized.'

'Realized what?'

'That they're just the same as us.'

And Fortune at last understood Brace's remarkable transformation from sullen adolescent to rational adult.

'I started crying,' confessed Brace. 'I couldn't help myself. It came over me so suddenly I couldn't take it in. I realized how unbearable I'd been, how cruel . . . how evil.'

'No, Brace,' replied Fortune, 'not evil. Just unsure.'

'Well, I was ashamed and I cried. I'm sorry, Fortune; I was so wrong, and now Gossamer's gone and I didn't take care of her and, and . . .'

Fortune let Brace weep long and hard again, holding him close and rocking him in the snow, a nugget of warmth held close in the troll's dead embrace.

Somewhere, at the periphery of the circle of towers, their hidden observer waited.

'You must tell me the rest, Brace,' said Fortune at length. 'Tell me what happened to Sleet and how you got back here.'

'Well,' Brace began, sniffling and brushing at the icy tears crusted on his face, 'I don't know how long I crouched there feeling sorry for myself but when I looked back into the camp I could see Sleet down there, surrounded by four Charmed. They looked, you know, like Brutace – big, savage.'

Fortune nodded. He remembered Brutace only too well.

'Sleet's voice only just carried up to where I was but I heard him telling them about Shatter and where the Fortress is. Then, when he'd finished, he just stood there as if he expected them to thank him.'

'What did they do?'

'They cut him in half.'

Fortune found it hard to mourn for Sleet but he shuddered nonetheless.

'I just fled then,' Brace concluded. 'All the way back I was convinced I was being followed. Every breath I waited for the fire to knock me out of the sky, but I made it. I made it . . .'

He was visibly more relaxed now, much of the horror of what he had seen purged in the telling of his story, and Fortune saw a new confidence in his eyes, sensing for the first time a surety of purpose, of his role in the greater story in which they were all of them inextricably caught up.

He pondered momentarily on a memory, chewing it like a forgotten fragment of food: the inner light which had felled the Deadfall.

That was the greater story.

The memory of light flared across his inner eye and he heard again the waking troll, its subsequent death, the thunder of the rolling Deadfall; saw the dragons of the Flight scatter like seeds on the wind.

The Flight! Tallow!

He looked anxiously around, a sudden, cold gale freezing the easy flow of memory, seeking out his friends, and found himself looking straight into the eyes of their silent observer.

The spy uncoiled his stout, muscular frame from behind the troll's outermost finger and stalked into the lee of its palm, every step a quiet threat.

'Wood?' breathed Fortune. Though he knew the shell of his friend, he did not recognize the spirit which drove it.

'Give me the traitor,' said Wood reasonably.

Seeing the emptiness in Wood's eyes, Fortune tensed his muscles for the attack he knew must surely come, but at the same time felt his heart break; what story was it that could turn them to this point on its unimaginable circumference?

'I do not want to fight you, Wood,' he said. 'But, I beg you, do not cross me. Not here, not now.'

'It's not you I want,' Wood replied, his approach through the snow slow and relentless. 'Just give me the traitor.'

Brace stood, shaking, next to Fortune, and was about to speak when his companion silenced him.

'Go behind that rock,' ordered Fortune briskly. When Brace protested he added, 'You are a dragon of the Flight now, Brace, and as such you will obey me! Go!'

The unexpected authority in Fortune's voice caused Wood to falter momentarily. Brace retreated with some reluctance, watching with wide eyes and pounding heart as Fortune and Wood faced each other in the cradle of the troll's hand.

'If you have a quarrel with Brace,' continued Fortune in the same, commanding tone, 'then you argue with me.' But then he relented. 'Wood, it's me! How much fury can you have for me?'

A cruel smile appeared on Wood's face.

'Can this be the dear, sweet Fortune I remember of old . . . ?' he began, then stopped as he realized that in front of him was not the Fortune he had known at South Point but a dragon changed.

Wood faltered.

Everything about this dragon was Fortune, but more. Once-brown scales now glowed with a deep, rich, coppery lustre; young muscles were now firm beneath belly-skin and flank; fine, delicate features had become handsome. Beautiful.

And an inner light filled his eyes with radiance.

Wood recalled an old vision of Fortune – so long ago it seemed now: the young dragon caught in a beam of late sunlight in South Point's old sector, his face radiant, the future captured in his smile. Beautiful.

'You shouldn't have flown over Shatter's quarters like that,' he grunted. 'I saw you clear enough, and it was quite a shock, I can tell you. I thought you were dead. Drowned.'

'Then it was you I saw in Ordinal's cave!' exclaimed Fortune, taking a step towards his old friend.

'Just give me the traitor,' sighed Wood, his anger all but gone now. 'He must be brought before Shatter, so he can explain how he has betrayed us all.'

'Brace stays with me,' replied Fortune.

Wood felt uncertain again as Fortune stared back at him with surety, with confidence, with power.

'He comes with me,' he responded, grimacing as old conflicts swelled in his heart. He did with them as he always had done – he pressed them down to the self within himself.

He set his wings wide in the snow, a fighting stance.

Brace watched agog as the two dragons circled each other, low, dark shapes on a field of starlit snow, a cluster of stone towers piercing the ground in an arc around them, blue shadows slicing across the mountain behind. The wind sloughed snow from the surrounding drifts and cast a layer of white powder across the arena.

Wood sprang.

Anticipating the move, emitting an agonized cry as he accepted that he must fight his oldest friend, Fortune slipped neatly to his left, kicking snow into Wood's face as he leaped across his shadow. Wood struck a bank of packed ice and floundered, struggling to regain his balance.

It was with a murderous expression then that Wood turned to face Fortune.

'You're behind all of this,' he growled. 'If you hadn't led us into those caverns none of this would have happened!'

Fortune shook his head, ferociously searching his mind for the words he knew must exist which might turn Wood back to his side, back to his heart. But Wood sprang again, and this time Fortune failed to react so quickly. His opponent powered straight into his outstretched wing, crushing it painfully against the base of one of the troll's fingers. Small bones snapped. They grappled together, falling as one into the snow.

'You and your Charmed friends!' growled Wood. 'Why don't you ever learn?'

Wood battled as though possessed, and it soon dawned on Fortune that he must truly fight for his life. His neck choked tight by Wood's coiled tail, he thrashed in the snow, each breath like fire.

The world was growing misty when Wood's face flashed across his vision, teeth bared.

He lunged desperately, clamping his own mouth hard across the back of Wood's neck. Tough scales resisted his bite but his adversary grunted in pain. Claws scrabbling, Fortune raked at Wood's belly with his legs and gradually prised himself free of his tail.

Wings spread, he leaped straight up into the air, striking out with his legs as he did so and drawing a deep cut across Wood's face where the scales were soft as they blended into the skin under his throat. Hovering in the cold wind he watched as his opponent clambered free of the snow and spread his own wings wide, ready for the leap he never made.

Fortune watched, puzzled, as Wood's upturned face registered first shock, then anger and finally fear.

The wind shivered to his right and suddenly Tallow was beside him.

Volley swooped in from the left, and then the air positively boiled and all the dragons of the Flight were there, fifty or more of them, crowding the tiny slice of sky held between the troll's outstretched fingers.

At the sight of them all, Wood's courage finally failed him and he backed away, his pace increasing as his fear and sullen anger grew.

And then Fortune offered him what he thought was a final chance, but to Wood was the final insult.

'Join us, Wood,' he said. 'Please. We'll accept you, if you'll accept us.'

But Wood could only curse an incoherent reply as the shadows claimed him. He vanished from the arena, his shame great, his thoughts a storm.

In that storm the winds blew first one way then the other as he was buffeted by new and forgotten loyalties. But though anger denied him any decisions, one idea alone cut through the storm and decided his next course of action.

Shatter will know of this. He will know of it all.

'Did he hear us talking, do you think?' called up Brace, his voice thin and broken in the growing wind. Snow flurries moved like ghosts, paling his body against the white ground.

'Every word,' called Fortune in reply then, addressing the rest of the Flight, cried, 'Shatter is betrayed. But worse, Wood will tell Shatter of the betrayal and of our part in it, through the actions of Sleet. The time is here at last, my friends; this is truly the eve of the battle.

'Our intention was to use tonight to plan, but there is no time now. Perhaps it is better that way. Each of you must do what you feel is right; only you can turn the tide. Go now and speak the truth of the Flight, and perhaps when the battle is done there will be some of us who survive.

'Do not ask me to tell you what you must do. We have never discussed action, nor shall we now. Do as your hearts tell you. Recruit. Convince. Do not fight.

'Speak the truth.'

Fortune's words both roused and chilled his tiny group of volunteers so that, with the brisk speech made, they flew off carrying hope and fear in more or less equal measure. They were the seed, the seed of doubt Fortune hoped to see planted in Shatter's ranks, the seed of truth.

Into the darkness he cast them, and he could only pray that the harvest would be good.

Only Tallow and Volley stayed. Initially wary of Brace, they swiftly warmed to him as Fortune related his story in shortened form.

'If you trust him then so do we,' was Tallow's grave response, and yet again Fortune was shaken by the big dragon's capacity for loyalty.

This one is a good dragon, he thought. *Let him live through this.*

'We'll wait a while so that Brace can rest,' he said. 'Then we must get out of here before Shatter comes.'

'We could go after Wood,' suggested Tallow. 'Shatter doesn't need to find out.'

'No!' said Fortune sharply. He looked at the trail of destruction left by the Deadfall. 'Shatter knows already that he is betrayed. His mind works differently to ours; believe me, he knows. Time is short, in any case.'

'Where are we going?' asked Brace.

Fortune gazed keenly into the distance, but did not reply.

A madness different to that of Shatter sped through the icy corridors of the Fortress that night. Wood, angry and humiliated, rushed for support to the very dragon he despised yet whose sheer power could not be denied.

Only his father's unshakeable loyalty to their insane commander had kept Wood with Shatter's army of dragons for this length of time. He hated Shatter, and many times had pleaded with Barker to flee with him. But his frail, scarred father would say, 'I know he seems cruel sometimes but he fights for the truth, so that Naturals may live by their own rules, not those of the Charmed. These are his scars I bear, not my own. I'll never leave him.' And so they stayed.

But Wood knew, as he rushed through the fortress towards Shatter's quarters, that he and Shatter were not so different, for they both hated the Charmed, and it was this thought which hurried him forward in his blind anger, the thought that he would bring down the might of Shatter on the betrayers, on the Flight, on Brace and Fortune and all those dragons who believed in the Charmed way. Could they not see how wrong they were? Were they not ashamed?

Could it not be I who am wrong?

The thought pierced his anger with sudden pain. He had not betrayed Fortune when he had seen him take up his post on the Deadfall, but his friend's outrageous confidence in flying up there had angered him.

And after that the anger had simply grown out of all proportion. He had watched dumbfounded as events had exploded around Fortune — the falling boulder, the strange story of Brace . . . *How can it all be happening to Fortune? I was the one who chose right, not him.*

As he drew near to Shatters quarters he was stopped by an aggressive young sentry who barred his way with out-stretched claws.

'Can't go up there,' the massive dragon intoned. 'Big meeting. No interruptions.'

Wood nearly tried to force his way past, but the sharpness of the other dragon's claws and the easy set of his powerful limbs warned him off. With a deep breath he said, 'But I must go up there! I have important news for Shatter!'

But the sentry was resolute.

'No interruptions,' he repeated bluntly. 'No exceptions.'

Frustrated, Wood stamped the snow and stretched his neck in an attempt to see up the sloping channel which led to the platform above. Faint voices shivered down the ramp and he strained to catch the words.

'With respect,' one voice was saying, 'I see no evidence that our position here has been compromised.'

'Believe it!' came a rumble which was unmistakably Shatter's. 'I am betrayed.'

Wood cursed.

'I must go up there,' he protested. 'Shatter must hear me!'

'No exceptions,' growled the guard, his back muscles stiffening, his claws slipping again from their sheaths.

Shatter grew more and more impatient as the argument on the platform went on. At last he bellowed, 'We attack! I decree it, and so will it be!'

'You are wrong, Shatter.'

The new voice was one which Wood recognized at once. It was that of his father, Barker!

He held himself utterly still, his every muscle straining without motion towards the sound of his father's voice as though the tension might bring him closer.

'If we attack, we will all die,' continued Barker calmly. 'We are well defended here — that's why we are here. You have given us all of this, Shatter. Why would you take it away?'

Breaths were held. All dragons knew Barker — poor, burned Barker — to be Shatter's most loyal follower. Was he truly disagreeing with his master?

'We attack!' repeated Shatter, as though he had not heard Barker's words.

'Forgive me, but I cannot agree!' retorted Wood's father with reckless anger. 'Shatter, I have followed you across the world because I believe in your crusade. We must wipe out the vile Charmed for what they have done to our kind. I myself lost my own dear Eleken to a storm brought on by their treacherous magic . . .'

A loud, scraping noise masked Barker's words momentarily but Wood was only partly aware of it. *He believes the Charmed killed my mother*, he thought desperately. *That's not right — it was a storm, just a storm.*

And here his hatred for the Charmed wavered. An image of Fortune flew into his head and he banished it.

But all the same, his father was wrong.

'. . . to attack now would be folly,' Barker was saying, gabbling now, his words tumbling over one another. 'You would see us all die, Charmed and Natural alike. The battle would be death to all dragons, to all . . .'

Again his voice was cut off but this time Wood heard a more terrifying sound — a sharp, slicing hiss, a short gasp, a heavy thump.

Silence.

Beside him the sentry looked up the ramp uneasily.

Wood seized the opportunity, springing past the distracted guard and racing up the walled channel, claws showering splinters of frost into the air. A terrible anticipation crawled under his scales.

363

White ice flashed past his eyes as he surged up on to the platform. As the ground levelled out it turned pink. Then red.

An arc of twenty dragons, fear shadowing their features.

His father's body, prone in a lake of freezing blood.

Shatter, his claws buried deep in the dead dragon's neck, his eyes red and soulless.

Red death. For Wood, the end of all hope.

'Father!' he howled, hurling himself at Shatter with the reckless fury of a dragon to whom life no longer matters.

A nearby dragon rushed forward loyally to prevent the attack but Wood lashed out viciously with his sharp tail, catching the other high on the head and shattering bone. The dragon fell unconscious, one eye filling with blood. The others held back, more cautious.

His blood still hot from the fight with Fortune, Wood turned to face his father's killer.

Shatter struck out with bloodied claws and knocked Wood to the ground. Winded, the young dragon found himself face to face with his dead father.

Death had already filmed Barker's sightless eyes; blood hung solidified in his gaping mouth. Wood felt nothing.

He whirled round to face Shatter.

A series of stunning blows forced him back to the edge of the platform. The other dragons, reluctant to intervene, shuffled back to give the combatants room. Shatter paused, eyeing his opponent.

'Traitor!' he shouted suddenly.

'No,' mumbled Wood, his jaw aching, several teeth loosened. His mind felt dull — did he care about dying or not? He was not sure. Despite his uncertainty some deeper part of himself surfaced and pleaded for life. 'Not me — the Flight. You were right, you are betrayed, but not me, not . . .'

'You!' howled Shatter, beating the air with his wings. 'You are my betrayer! Like your father. Traitors both of you!'

'No!' Wood looked around the circle of dragons but found no support. His senses began to sharpen again as they dropped their gaze to the ice, relief daring to show on their faces as they realized that Shatter had selected the dragon he would blame.

364

Everywhere was cold.

He looked desperately back at Shatter himself, into those frozen, red eyes . . . and saw that Shatter had gone!

His body remained to be sure, and to a degree his mind. But some greater part of him had retreated forever into that interior darkness which served as his reality.

Wood saw that he was more dangerous than ever, yet a strange calmness filled his veins.

'My father was right,' he warned, speaking now to the dragons in the semicircle around him. He backed away until his claws clutched at the very edge of the platform. 'He will kill you all. He's gone beyond his promises now. He won't rest until you're all dead.'

Shatter began to laugh.

Wood poised himself on the lip of the platform, wings raised.

'You killed my father, Shatter. For that you will pay.' Then he added, 'As for you others . . . perhaps there may be a chance – if you can find it.'

Shatter's commanders watched, puzzled, as Wood turned and flew off through the Fortress.

He flew high, hugging the underside of the great rock canopy so as to lose himself in the matrix of crevices there.

The mad dragon's laughter followed him out into the night, filling the passages and corridors, the caves and tunnels, the paths and corners, into every pore of the Fortress, casting its shadow of insanity and fear across the hearts of three thousand natural dragons for whom, up until now, Shatter had been the single, warm light in a world turned dark and cold.

Many dragons moved through the Fortress, gathering about the platform, eager to hear their master, eager to trust him, eager for reassurance. Most realized that this was the eve of the battle.

In between the waves of laughter, behind the thrall of Shatter, moved the dragons of the Flight, and in their movement they hoped to avert a war.

CHAPTER 30

Illumination

Where the light had come from which finally toppled the Deadfall from its age-long perch no dragon would ever know for certain, nor would that knowledge ever be revealed to any mortal creature.

But one creature knew, its very immortality part of the fabric of the ancient world from which that magical light had come.

It stirred now, this creature of old, this basilisk, memories spurting through its wakening veins. Trollbirth, the shaping of the land, the oceans condensing from a living fog. That world ending and another in its place. Cycles. The rise of giants, the rise of mountains and the powdering of both to sand. The coming of dragons.

The fall of charm.

Alone in the maelstrom of Halcyon's magic, it sensed the gathering of the forces of time about the mountain, it perceived the way events were beginning to lock together. It knew the futility of the efforts these pitiful dragons were making to direct the course of the turning world, for it had seen every Turning since the beginning which had never been. Such was the nightmare of infinity.

And yet . . . this time, this Turning, it knew it would awaken, for something else had begun to interfere. The basilisk was aware of the strangeness of Halcyon's defences, and also of the Black Dragon's approach to their destruction. Other dragons might have concentrated their power into creating single, impregnable strongholds, or else beating down their enemies with relentless and single-minded campaigns. Not so these dragons. Halcyon had built his fortress in layers daunting yet ultimately assailable; the Black

Dragon seemed content to play Halcyon's game and take the defences piece by piece instead of risking all in a single onslaught.

It occurred to the basilisk then, as it appraised the dragons' behaviour against the greater forces which were gathering, that their own feeble confrontations might for this reason coincide with the one it had now begun to plan. Strange, and probably of no consequence. But . . . interesting.

As for the basilisk, this nameless relic with no love for the future and only hatred for the past, only one thing beckoned loud enough to draw it from its eternal slumber, only one thing did it now love enough to stir itself: the prospect of death.

If, like it, the Maze of Covamere was waking to participate in this final end of all that had gone before, perhaps there was a way in which they might together expose some flaw in the structure of eternity. That the Maze was waking again it had no doubt, for it had felt its power unleashed this very night, in the form of a bolt of hot, blue light sent north to – of all places – a natural dragon stronghold formed from the remains of a dying troll. Yes, that light it had observed, and the collapse of the Deadfall too, and the subsequent formation of the final, greatest ring of stones.

All brought about by the Maze of Covamere. Yet through a dragon!

The urge to wake fully was now overwhelming, and at last the basilisk began to move its physical body. Weak despite its strength, stiff despite its suppleness, it poured charm into its core and flushed away the fatigue of aeons. Careful not to disturb the flow of Halcyon's magic around it, it stretched and turned and scented and . . . was curious.

For he first time in an age of ages it was curious!

The feeling revitalized it more than any charm could have done and it settled again, quite alert now yet content to wait for the day of confrontation, when the mountain would at last be breached, and it would face the Maze and the dragons . . . it would find out just what part the dragons were destined to play in this oldest of games.

The blue light which Fortune had seen last of all had been, though he could not know it, the light of the Maze. But two other fires had joined in that weird dialogue, fires of far more concern to dragon than to any beast of mountain deep or time immortal. And two dragons had answered the call of the light, and in doing so both had found their own illumination.

The first of these dragons was Wraith, for at the instant he had turned his terrible, noble head to the north and seen the explosion of light on the horizon which told him that charm was at work on the edge of his territory, his tiring warriors had broken through the penultimate layer of magic set by Halcyon against him.

They were working deep in the rock now, far below the level of the Portal and beyond the reach of even the brightest sunlight, let alone the dim starlight by which they now laboured. They were dragons exhausted, dragons disillusioned, dragons beginning to doubt their leader and mourn their fate. Though they knew the end was in sight, they were also terrified, for all were aware that progress so far — though fearful — had been much easier than any dragon had dared to hope; what did Halcyon have in store for them at the end?

The third layer had collapsed without drama the previous night, and now it looked as though the fourth would be overcome at any moment. Indeed, so confident was Wraith that this was so that he had stationed himself at the head of the excavation, just inside the Portal, to oversee the final stages of the operation. His presence there, though intended to inspire, served only to threaten and cow his operatives labouring in the darkness, but there he stayed, formidable and resolute. If he sensed dissension he paid it no heed; still he led, and still he would prevail.

Dragons came to him that night with pleas for mercy, and especially for a relaxing of the relentless time scale he had set upon his workers, for although fewer dragons had died than had been expected, still the toll was high and the work arduous.

'Progress is adequate!' Wraith would boom. 'Some would say easy. Do not tempt me to raise my expectations of you.'

And dragons quaked. Could any dragon ever confront this black monster and live? No, they said, tomorrow night the mountain will fall and Halcyon with it. The Black Dragon will take on the Maze itself and then we shall know once and for all whether or not he is truly destined to be our leader.

And many dragons prayed that he was not, and that having entered the Maze, he would not return.

So it was with no greater emotion than relief that the dragons on the front line took apart the last fragments of the fourth layer of charm to find no hidden traps, no terrible destructive magic awaiting them. No dragon died that night, and all silently rejoiced. And silently feared for what tomorrow would bring.

One event alone marked the breaking of the charm, one which no dragon, not even Wraith, fully understood but which all interpreted in one way or another. As the last pieces of charm dissolved away a cloud of red vapour gathered about the cracked, black wall which was revealed. As the vapour swirled and compressed, the dragons backed away nervously, afraid at what might be about to spring at them from the mist.

But there came only light, a brilliant, red light which shattered over them and fled for the surface; those dragons who spoke afterwards of it said that it was like being bathed in blood. Upwards it streaked until it broke into the Portal itself, where many dragons witnessed what happened next.

The light struck Wraith head-on. He opened his wings at once, absorbing its power in an instant, yet many of those who watched the scene more closely believed that it had taken him utterly by surprise. Though his hard features remained unmoved, there was something about his movement, his poise, which spoke of nothing but shock.

Swiftly, jerkily, as though his body were under the control of some force unknown, he swivelled his neck until he faced north. Then he opened his great mouth wide to expose his dreadful fangs and spat the light out towards the horizon, where it flashed through the night and snow to join a distant, white flare which had just appeared in the distance.

On and out boiled the light, seemingly sucked from Wraith by whatever magic it was which drew it north. On its journey it was joined by a second light, a golden glow from high on the mountain, and a third, blue flash from

. . . but no dragon could say where that had originated, only that it seemed to be *down*.

The lights met and grew, and on that distant spot there was another mighty flash . . . and then all was gone. The night was dark again.

There Wraith remained, his mouth still gaping, seemingly lost in some remote place. Only slowly did his awareness return, but with it returned a little of the awe in which he had previously been held by his dragons. It was with renewed respect that they watched him pace majestically down the dark slope and into the mountain to inspect the night's work, for although no dragon could say what event it was they had witnessed, all agreed that Wraith had been at its centre.

Thus was the Black Dragon's position of power assured for a few more days at least. After that, perhaps, little would matter but what the Maze itself would bring forth.

All that day Gossamer and Velvet had climbed, aimlessly circling the mountain as the air became cold and raw around them. Breathing became a battle with the elements and it seemed sometimes that they were not moving higher, but that the mountain was shrinking beneath them. On they laboured, and in all that time they saw no sign of dragon nor indeed of any living creature, much less anything resembling a ring of stones.

'What did your rhyme say?' panted Gossamer as they called an impromptu halt. ' "One without end"? Well, this journey certainly seems to be one without end.'

They collapsed together against a bank of hard ice. At this altitude the snow and ice were a permanent part of the scenery, and together they made the going difficult in the extreme. They flew intermittently, but in air this thin that too was exhausting work so they were reduced to switching between the two. They had travelled a great distance, despite the hardships, but still they seemed no nearer to their goal.

'We can't go on today,' wailed Velvet, huddling close to Gossamer. 'Oh, I wish I was more help to you, Gossamer, I really do.'

'It's all right, it's not your fault. We'll rest here tonight –

it's as good a place as any, and maybe tomorrow we'll hit upon the answer.'

Obviously needing no more encouragement than that, Velvet snuggled closer and within a few short breaths was fast asleep.

Some time later, when the sun had gone down, Gossamer eased herself free of her young companion and took a few steps out across the ice to look down the mountain slopes. She was worried about Velvet, for despite her buoyant nature she was weaker physically than Gossamer – and she was also pining for Cumber.

We must find it tomorrow, she prayed. *But we need help, and who can help us here?*

She gazed down over the snow and rock, wondering where Cumber was amid that great wilderness. She gazed west, towards Covamere, which she knew to be there, hidden behind the curve of the mountain, waiting.

Is that where you've gone, Cumber? Where you always thought the end of your quest would be?

And then she looked north and thought of Fortune as she had only two nights before, before Cumber had left them.

'Fortune. Where is our haven now?'

Later still, when she had slept a while near the warmth of Velvet's body, she awoke to see lines of light in the sky above. Lying back on the ice she watched the night dragons carve their shapes upon the heavens and again she thought of . . .

'Fortune!'

This time his name was like a call to action, a stab of excitement in the night. Leaping up, she rushed out to the spot where she had earlier looked out over the land and strained her eyes to see in the dim starlight. The mountain felt poised beneath her claws, coiled as though ready to leap; the air smelt of charm.

Then came the light.

She received it in rapture. It invaded her every pore and she spread her wings wide in welcome; it broke over her body like a wave, crashing into her senses and tracing its way down through her veins and out into the millions of crevices in the icy ground beneath her claws. Absorbed by the mountain.

The darkness returned, but only briefly, for the light exploded again beneath her, entering her body, filling her with light, with radiance, with Fortune!

Golden now, searing and ecstatic, it flew from her into the north, joining now with other light, one red, one blue, to meet again that white fire in the distance.

To join Fortune.

Drained now, rejoicing, laughing and crying tears which themselves glowed with internal flames, she rushed back to where Velvet sat rubbing her eyes, mouth agape at what she had just seen.

'What was that?' she asked dumbfounded.

'Fortune!' exclaimed Gossamer, her voice like the light itself in her throat, his name like the fire in the sky.

'Fortune?' responded Velvet. 'Your Fortune?'

'The same! And you know what? I know where to go now!'

Velvet shook her head and shivered. This was too much — interrupted sleep, bitter cold, and now a mad companion.

'You do?' she said doubtfully.

'You said it yourself when we set out earlier.'

'I did?'

'Yes! We have to go up. But not like we've been doing so far, just gradually working our way. We've got to go up! All the way to the top!'

Velvet sighed and managed the briefest of smiles.

'Can I get at least a little more sleep first?'

PART 5

THE MAZE OF COVAMERE

CHAPTER 31

The Prison

The snow had ceased, but the weather still had new games to play with the many dragons who moved within it. Fog rolled silently in towards the Plated Mountain from the sea and surged about its base, brooding and motionless. Eyes were blinded by cloud so thick as to obscure even a dragon's own snout; ears normally sharp were dulled by its damp folds.

In moved the fog, settling and slowing as time itself seemed to be settling and slowing. The full grip of winter was now upon the world for the air, though moist, was cold and deadly. Above the fog perhaps the sun and stars and lost moon moved as they should, but to the dragons lost within the gloom it seemed that those constant companions had ceased to exist.

The Plated Mountain was a place outside time.

Four dragons approached the mountain through the tumbling fog. If dawn had come they did not know it, for their world had contracted to a grey blur. Brace groaned as the fog grew thicker.

'Worried, little one?' laughed Volley good-naturedly. 'Don't be – you couldn't pick a better set of dragons to be lost with.'

Tallow's strong, measured wingbeats led them on through the thickening fog. Dragon shapes diminished to dragon shadows and soon vanished altogether, so that only their voices kept them together.

'I'd sing but I fear that would drive us apart!' joked Volley, although a quaver in his voice betrayed a certain tension.

'On the contrary,' came Fortune's voice. He sounded

somewhat relieved. 'Tallow's wings may gauge our course but we'll lose each other if we don't do something. Sing out, Volley! I've been promised your voice for far too long – now I'd like to hear it!'

After a brief, half-hearted protest, Volley began to sing an old, mountain song, deep and haunting. Its melody lingered in the cold air like a trail of smoke, weaving into the mists its mournful tale of betrayal and lost love. On they flew, quite invisible to each other now, but following Volley's song, and when pathfinder Tallow heard the words grow faint in his ears he would call out gently, bringing the minstrel back on course.

Thus together did the four friends proceed slowly – painfully slowly – towards the mountain. Fortune was convinced that Covamere was his ultimate destination . . . but something nagged at him, a new task gnawing at the back of his mind and one which urged that it be done fast . . .

'Brace!' he called suddenly. 'Where exactly did you see Scoff?'

By some unspoken command the party halted, hovering in space as Brace struggled to remember the location of the Charmed prison camp. Tallow and Volley tried to help with suggestions based on their vast knowledge of the forest. But Brace could not recall enough about the place, and Fortune reluctantly concluded that they would never be able to find it.

'Why would you go to this Charmed prison?' inquired Tallow doubtfully.

'Scoff must be freed,' replied Fortune simply.

'Fortune,' said Tallow in his deep, steady voice, the sense and reason he emanated moving in almost visible waves through the fog, 'we would never come away alive. Those Charmed monsters are . . .'

'Are dragons!' barked Fortune. 'You don't know charm, Tallow. It's not the evil you think.'

'I saw it slaughter Weft and Piper!' retorted Tallow. 'If that's not evil I don't know . . . !' But his anger dissipated as soon as it had flared and he concluded, quietly now, 'I'm sorry, Fortune. We are the Flight now – I should have known better.'

'No, Tallow, I'm to blame,' responded Fortune at once.

'Tallow, all of you, there is evil in charm just as there is evil in nature, and you are right to fear it. We should, we must all be afraid.

'Brace and I owe Scoff a great debt of gratitude,' he began with a heavy sigh.

'You owe us no explanation,' interrupted Volley. 'We trust you.'

'That's exactly why you deserve one,' Fortune replied. 'Scoff saved our lives — Brace's and mine. Without his intervention Brutace would have killed Cumber, and then us, Gossamer . . . all of us. Our mission would have been over when it had barely begun.

'But more than that, think about this prison camp; think about us. We are the Flight, the crack in Shatter's scale. Well, Scoff and his companions may be the crack in Wraith's! If I know Scoff at all he will have argued for unity just as we do — he may even be their leader.

'We must try to free them. They will die in the coming battle if we don't, trapped as they are. They are the Flight too. They are Charmed, but they are our friends and allies. And our kin. They are dragons!'

A stab of wind pierced the fog as Fortune concluded his speech and for a breath or two he could make out his friends, just visible in the dank greyness in front of him. He looked from one to the other, dragons of dark cloud in a heavy sky, and was struck by the dreadful conviction that one of them was soon to die.

That is up to me, he thought deliberately. *It need not happen that way.*

Then, as the mist thickened once more, Brace's voice rang out, strong and resolute.

'We approached the camp from the west,' he said, concentrating hard. 'There was a high spur of rock to the right. I remember now — it looked like a pine cone, all ridged. We crossed a stream, no, two streams, both running from west to east. The camp was in a dip just beyond the second stream.'

Tallow and Volley renewed their questioning as Fortune listened on, then conferred for a moment.

'Bottom end of Whare Vale,' said Volley confidently at last.

'No doubt about it,' agreed Tallow.

'How far?' Fortune asked.

'About two hundred wingspans,' replied Tallow grimly. Then he took a deep breath. 'Straight down.'

'You mean . . . we're there?' blurted Brace.

'Quite a coincidence,' agreed Tallow.

With the fog clinging to them closer than ever they flew into a tight group, holding the damp air and sharing their trepidation. What force had moved them to come here when their destination had at first been Covamere?

Scoff's world was a net of blue fire.

Sparks writhed as he shifted his position uncomfortably in the spherical cage of charm which kept him trapped here alongside the rest of the traitor dragons of Wraith's army.

Why doesn't he kill us? he thought, the question rattling through his head as it had so often of late.

He had thought the same of the natural dragons of Aether's Cross. Why had Wraith taken so much trouble to create a gaol for the Naturals? Why had he not killed them? Was conquest not his goal?

Questions, only questions, with no hope of answers.

The stumps of his once-proud wings itched terribly. The pain had passed now; although he had largely managed to suppress it with an anaesthetic charm, the moment of amputation had been agonizing.

They had held him down, the guards, and drawn fire from the Realm with which they had severed his wings. Even now they lay within his vision, dull and brittle, poking out of the snow like fallen leaves.

His capture had come scant breaths after he had left Fortune and Cumber at the cliff. He had never reached Gossamer. A squad of warrior dragons had hustled him off to Covamere where he had been questioned by none other dragon than Insiss, and here it was that he had found himself with a choice.

'You are a stranger here,' Insiss had drawled, 'and you were found leaving the site of an . . . unusual incident.'

Wraith's slippery lieutenant was of course referring to the landslide which had killed the two guard dragons outside the minor portal through which Fortune and Cumber had entered the mountain. Scoff's suspicious presence there had been enough to ensure his arrest but now he saw that there was a chance for him to secure his freedom here in Covamere simply by concocting some tale, pledging his allegiance to Wraith and melting into the huge army he saw massing all around him.

Simple enough to convince this dragon, he guessed, for although Insiss was clearly intelligent, sly even, Scoff guessed rightly that there were nevertheless ways of mis-leading him.

Flatter him, he thought. *Make yourself look a fool and he'll let you go.*

This may well have been so, and to his later shame Scoff did indeed consider such action, if only briefly. But then he thought of his companions and how they had trusted him – how Fortune had trusted him to keep Gossamer safe. He remembered the long journey across the Heartland during which he had seen Cumber fly the storm of Realmshock and emerge older and wiser on the other side of the clouds. He thought of his companions . . . no, his friends.

And he thought of Halcyon.

He had lived here for a time in Covamere many years before when he had been a young and naive dragon. Then it was that he had joined the great, global ranks of Halcyon's envoys and had been trained and assigned to his first – and last – posting: Aether's Cross. He had joined, he realized now, at the beginning of the end of Halcyon's regime and so all he had known of the once-great system had been its slow decay. Thus had he grown bored and disillusioned and self-centred and in Aether's Cross he had stayed.

Now here he was again in Covamere, back in Halcyon's land – and yet under the power of the Black Dragon!

'Dragon!' he announced, standing up square to scrawny Insiss and half-opening his glorious wings. 'Dragon! You are speaking to one of the appointed representatives of Halcyon, Leader of Dragons and Ruler of Covamere. Ambassador Scoff I am, and from Halcyon alone will I take my com-mands, not some usurper. Your authority I do not accept; you have no power here. My service belongs to Halcyon and Halcyon alone, that is my pledge. You may do with me what you will, but I should warn you that there is only one true Leader.'

'Indeed,' replied Insiss icily, a thin smile drawn across his face. 'There is, as you state, only one true Leader. That is, of course, our lord Wraith, the Black Dragon, Master of Covamere and soon to be the Taker of the Maze. Your loyalty to the venerable Halcyon is noted and you will be dealt with accordingly. Guards!'

Without further ceremony he summoned four hefty guard dragons who led Scoff away, their orders unspoken but evidently understood. Scoff did not struggle. As he passed Insiss he said, 'Think carefully, dragon, which side you wish to be on. The Black Dragon will fail. Where will that leave you?'

Five days ago that had been. Upon arriving at the camp Scoff had estimated the number of prisoners to be around three hundred, possibly more; the numbers were still growing.

Why doesn't he kill us?

Whispered conversations between the prisoners had strengthened the bond between them all, and quickly he had learned their name: Wraith's Hardship. Scoff, as one of the more widely-travelled of the dragon captives, was in constant demand for his stories, of which everyone's favourite was the Battle of Aether's Cross, where he had beheaded Brutace in the smoky aftermath of his friends' flight through the tunnels. In his tales he spoke with affection of his friends, Charmed and Natural alike, and his fellow prisoners listened with silent admiration for this dragon who had lived, at least in part, the dream they all shared. The dream of Charmed and Natural flying side by side, dragon kin in a world without conflict. The impossible dream.

Daylight showed briefly that morning before the thickest fog Scoff had ever seen billowed in through the surrounding trees. The air tasted damp, still retaining the bitter scent of charcoal which rose from the burned forest beyond this isolated patch of woodland.

The fog approached, sealing the gap between ground and sky . . . and then it lifted, rising above the dragons as though sliding over a bubble of air protecting them from its cloak. Spare tendrils crept occasionally into the camp but otherwise the air immediately around them remained perfectly clear.

Isolated thus on every side by a sheer white wall, and capped by a ceiling of solid cloud, the prison cages sparkled like gems in a seam of crystal, cut off from the rest of the mountain, a solitary world where, suddenly, anything might happen.

Glancing around, Scoff saw the restless stirrings of many of his fellow prisoners; likewise the guards paced nervously, unsettled by this strange phenomenon.

The tension gradually built. Scoff turned his mind to consideration of the charm — for charm it had to be — which was holding that fog in check, away from the camp.

Ancient charm it had to be, like the charm of the cages.

Tentative probing of the blue strings of fire from which his cage was constructed had convinced Scoff that the magic was not dragon-made. It tasted old, too old for him to be able to identify its source, but of one thing he was certain: the cages had existed — if not here then elsewhere, underground perhaps — for a very long time, perhaps for longer even than dragons had been in the world at all.

He suspected that their original purpose would remain forever a mystery, but their efficiency as prison cells was impressive. Like a valve, each cage's outer membrane would admit any living creature passing through it from outside to inside — but refuse exit thereafter. Inert matter such as food or waste could pass freely in either direction but an imprisoned dragon attempting to leave the cell would be rewarded only by a flash of light, agonizing pain . . . and a blocking force as solid as a wall of rock.

Once inside, a dragon was trapped forever.

In this way the prison camp was unique, for charmed creatures are notoriously difficult to hold captive. Indeed, Scoff's first instinct had been to open an escape route into the Realm by which he might flee to another part of the forest.

But the Realm had not been there!

Inside the cells charm had no power. Charmed dragons were merely dragons, stripped of their magic and their pride. And their liberty.

Whare Vale was a prison indeed.

Scoff had had plenty of time to consider these strange fire cages. Wraith had commandeered the complex as his gaol for outcasts, and though Scoff could not imagine why the cages had been created in the first place, he thought he knew at least what had created them. He remembered the stories of the Maze's 'experiments' in the forest!

Perhaps a battle had been fought here aeons before; perhaps the Maze had once broken the surface here; perhaps this complex was part of its very structure.

This last idea Scoff suspected to be closest to the truth, and his conviction grew when the fog had been so dramatically . . . *repelled* by the cages.

The guards, eight warrior dragons, huddled together near the entrance to the vale, their scales shimmering in the eerie blue light cast by hundreds of cages flickering with sparks as prisoners strained at their cells. These sparks illuminated the belly of the fog like lightning, turning it blue, a shroud of smooth colour. And then, salvation!

Scoff saw them first – four dragons descending from the ceiling of cloud with the cold precision of expert flyers. He saw the surprise on their faces, surprise which might at first have been that of dragons who have explored eternity to find a single, lonely world at its heart, but was, Scoff realized, only shock at emerging from the fog into unexpectedly clear air.

Naturals they all were, balanced on massive, muscled wings, and he found no surprise in the fact that at their head was Fortune. Brace he recognized too, although the youngster looked leaner and harder than he remembered. The others he did not know but was at once impressed by their size and grace, especially the larger of them who flew close to Fortune and beat the air as though he owned the sky itself.

Salvation? Four Naturals to help . . . us?

The guards had seen nothing, but the other prisoners began to look in their direction, hopefully. A few of the captive dragons groaned with disappointment. What could four Naturals do against fire charm? The guards looked round, alerted. Two of them took to the air to force the Naturals down.

As Scoff watched, his heart thudding, Fortune barked a command at the other three, who all vanished at once into the fog. Simultaneously the air above the cages thickened with charm, although he could not determine which dragon was wielding it.

Fortune held his station as the two warriors flew confidently towards him, staring them out with an arrogance meant to enrage them. Just before the guards reached him, the big Natural plummeted from the cloud above and struck with unerring aim at their heads. Scoff was astonished to see that the Natural's eyes were tightly closed. Both guards received a crippling blow to the base of the neck and dropped from the sky in a tangle of wings and limbs which ended in a single, shattering impact as they crashed together into the remains of a thicket wrecked by fire. One twitched and turned, his underbelly pierced by spears of volcanic rock and broken tree trunk. Blood pooled around them both, black in the cold, blue light.

The other six guards froze, then, to a dragon, turned their gazes up to where Fortune and his companion hovered above them. Of the other two Naturals there was no sign.

CHAPTER 32

Ancient Charm

'You're a marvel, Tallow,' Fortune said with conviction.

Only then did Tallow open his eyes.

'There's something else here besides me,' muttered the big dragon. 'I'm not this good. And it was not my intention to kill them.'

'I know,' responded Fortune, 'but whatever it is we cannot rely on it. It has motives of its own.' Fortune studied the guards clustered on the ground perhaps four trees below them. 'I think you're about to get your first taste of fire charm, Tallow.'

For the moment the guards seemed panicked, indecisive, but they would surely jump to action soon enough and what then? With the advantage of surprise lost what could four Naturals do against six Charmed?

But there were hundreds of potential allies here! What if they could be freed?

'Brace! Volley!' he bellowed. 'Go to Scoff!'

Every dragon in the camp heard his cry. His gamble was that the guards would not know the names of individual prisoners, and indeed they did not react, perhaps assuming that he had sent his friends to sanctuary elsewhere.

Fortune's cry did however rouse the guards from their stupor and now, with their backs turned on the caged dragons and their attention focused entirely on Fortune and Tallow, they crept forward as a single unit, their bodies beginning to generate and store charm in crackling patterns of light and shadow.

Behind them, behind the cages, Brace and Volley dropped silently out of the fog and on to the ground. They moved swiftly among the captives, whispering, questioning, seeking.

Fortune was about to suggest to Tallow that they gain some time by retreating back into the cloud when one of the dragons arched its neck and spat a long tongue of flame up into the sky. The two Naturals avoided it with ease, but before Tallow could remark on its poor aim they saw that its purpose was something more subtle than mere attack.

The flame shot past them but when it met the fog bank it splashed across it like water on to rock, spreading over its underside to form a glowing, white-hot net which expanded, swelled until it clad the entire perimeter of the camp. Hot, pulsing, alive, it burned skin and charred scale when either of the Naturals approached within a wingspan of it. Now they were prisoners too.

Fortune noted however that the advancing guards were now five. The sixth – evidently the one who was operating the net of fire – had stopped and was hunched into a ball, his back curled over to present only armour and spike to the sky.

Good. Five against four, thought Fortune grimly.

Then the net began to contract.

Fortune glanced back up to see the fire descending towards his back. Tallow regarded the phenomenon with more curiosity than fear as, with this skin of flame drawing them ever lower, they slowly descended towards the waiting gang.

Despite Tallow's calm, strong presence, Fortune began to despair.

We cannot die now, not here, not like this!

But in they were pulled, and though they flew completely around the ever-contracting web they found not a gap, not a chink through which they might escape into the open sky.

'That way! That way!' urged a caged dragon, sending Brace and Volley scrambling down a short run of cages to where . . . 'Scoff!' cried Brace, running up to the last cage in the line.

He stopped short, tears welling, for the charmed dragon was thin and tired, and without his beautiful rainbow wings he looked quite the saddest and most dejected dragon Brace could have imagined. And yet on seeing the two Naturals he beamed, a massive smile which banished Brace's tears before they could reach his eyes.

Five warriors leered up at Fortune and Tallow, no longer angry — just amused. The web had stopped shrinking at a single tree's height; to the sides it extended to just beyond the cages but no further. Silence reigned, broken occasionally by the crackle of charm.

Tallow's features were set rigid, his muscles were tense; he was ready to fight. But Fortune, after his brief attack of panic, felt calm again. He felt as though he could see things, sense things he had no right to be aware of.

The waiting guards, for instance — they seemed insubstantial, bony relics with fog for flesh.

The ground was pale and watery and beneath it, far beneath it . . . a scheme.

A scheme of lines, crossing, dividing, spreading, erupting into a pattern more complex than a mountainful of spider's webs, vibrating with life and solid, real, somehow more real than the rest of the world combined. It tasted of nature, it tasted of charm. It tasted of change.

It was the Maze.

He saw it, or its shadow, though he did not know what it was. And even though he knew it not, something about it was devastatingly familiar, as though he had been here before. Dazzling in its mystery, the Maze showed a fragment of itself to Fortune and he guessed that here was the power which had worked through him to take the Deadfall from its tower. Here was the power.

Before Fortune could even contemplate what he might do, Brace exploded from the cages of fire. He took the guards completely by surprise as he skimmed over their heads and swooped up to where Fortune and Tallow hovered.

A moment frozen in time.

'For Gossamer,' Brace said. 'Charm is yours.'

So saying he turned on a wing and dived towards the guards, crying out in a deep, sure voice,

'Charm is *ours*!'

Four of the warriors scattered but the fifth, more level-headed than the rest, leaped up and wrestled Brace from the sky. They fell to the ground, and the charmed dragon seized Brace about the neck and spread his jaws wide for the kill. To make a show of his power in front of these presumptuous Naturals, he paused. Raising his muzzle to the sky he gaped wide, belching fire high in a clean gout of yellow light. As he roared his jaws abruptly doubled in length and spears of bone sliced out through his cheeks, sharpening as they grew into deadly blades.

His tongue transformed into a flame, a white lance in the yellow pyre his mouth had become; his teeth lengthened, thickened, grew deep serrations; his lips curled away out of sight.

All skull, all fang, this charmed monster bent its neck to turn its fire on Brace.

But it had given Tallow all the time he needed. At once awed and revolted by the warrior's boastful display of magic, Tallow bolted from Fortune's side and clamped his own jaws hard into the belly of the extrovert who, quite engrossed in his own performance, did not even see his attacker coming; his chest and underbelly shredded, the charmed dragon died instantly.

But his charm did not. Realm fire exploded in all directions, throwing Tallow off to one side where he fell unconscious to the ground. Brace too was blown clear of the explosion and staggered further backwards, dazed and weak.

The fire boiled from the empty space where the dragon had once stood, sending feelers out to weave strange patterns in the air. Fortune watched, curious, as the flames twitched and jumped, and then bulged as though countless distorted creatures were inside them trying to get out. The fire turned red, then green, then brilliant blue, the glow spreading across the clearing until, just as the terrible Realm spirits began to slice their claws through into this world, one of the dead guard's companions sprang forward and fired a charge of pure white light into its midst.

Thunder closed the breach between this world and the Realm, and Fortune saw the pathway between the two.

An instant without time.

Looking up, Fortune saw the stars, visible despite the fog. Looking down, he saw the Maze despite the solid ground

387

which separated them. Reaching out, he opened a gateway into the Realm.

Something was behind him, giving him the strength of charm his natural body lacked. Nevertheless the gateway was his own.

The Realm backed away from him, as though it feared his presence. Indescribable beasts slithered through his mind as he floated through theirs. Outside the real world, the Realm admitted but did not welcome this intruder, this charmless alien.

The Realm was dark yet into it Fortune brought light. Everywhere it shrank from his touch, his look even, as he drifted through, searching for, searching for . . . *There* was the source of the light which was his to use. He left the Realm and found himself . . . elsewhere.

A numbing glow filled the distance and by some sense he could not comprehend Fortune knew that this searing point of light occupied the gap between the Realm and the real world. Both worlds, both realms, were in its thrall; it hung suspended between them like a drop of dew at the heart of the web.

The web was the Maze.

It spread in every direction that was real and many that were not. The light, the world, the Realm, all were dewdrops on the web of the Maze, the fabric on which everything rested. It opened its pores to Fortune, beckoning, inviting, pulsing with life, throbbing with death.

Its labyrinthine form transcended time and space. It breathed like a living thing, although it was much more than that. It was old long before time had begun to move.

Fortune coasted through the void, although he knew he was not really here, he vanished into insignificance, aware of the immensity of creation around him, aware of the sudden proximity of the searing light, aware of his own fragile, natural spirit in this ocean of charm.

When he turned in a direction he could not define, the light vanished.

Fortune was back in the real world, back at the prison camp, although now a brilliant white light illuminated the entire valley. He looked in vain for its source until he realized that he was the light.

Looking down he saw charmed dragons in cages, blue spheres of fire turned dark and spectral by the brilliance of his own light. He stroked the air and the cages turned white in a dazzling instant, then folded slowly, reluctantly, into the enveloping ground. The earth hissed and buckled as the magic subsided. Four hundred charmed dragons dropped to the ground and looked up at their saviour – their natural saviour – with puzzled wonder.

Where the cages had been was now a criss-cross of scars, as though the land had been wounded there – but long ago.

A huge tiredness came over Fortune then, invading his body as he had invaded the Realm. *Was I there?* he wondered vaguely as his body tumbled gently into a shallow drift of snow.

Dragons crowded around him, charmed ones all, peering down with concern at this strange creature which appeared a Natural yet had wielded magic to banish the ancient charm none could comprehend. Their faces swelled in his vision, thrusting forward with sympathy and surprise, strangers he had travelled half the world to meet yet for whom he could find no words. His blood crashed in his head and blackness hovered at the corner of his eye.

'Fortune!' cried a familiar voice. The crowd opened as a dragon shouldered his way to the front. 'Fortune!'

The dragon's face filled Fortune's narrowing vision as welcome darkness, neither world nor Realm, closed in around him. The contracting net of charm vanished at last as the guard responsible was overpowered along with his four remaining companions and the fog, held at bay for so long by forces as old as the mountain itself, descended along with blackness. The last thing he saw before he fainted was a particular face bearing an expression torn between joy and concern.

'Scoff,' he said weakly.

Fortune dreamed. No charm now, just a dream full of reality, solid. Natural.

Dragons over the sea. The air fresh and salt, the wind

389

invigorating. Waves reaching up for daring wings, clouds racing for the sun. Brightness, clarity.

A chain of islands in a wide circle, a reef at the centre. Lush, green-fronded trees and white sand. Ocean the colour of turquoise.

Voices in the flawless air, voices he knew, his mother's and Gossamer's, even Wood's, their words passing him like fugitives, rushing, 'The world is turning,' they whispered together. 'It begins here,' the voices chanted, 'It ends here.' Countless voices of dragons he did not know yet who even now flew with him. The voices of the Flight, and of the Hardship. With the rhythm of the chanting was a throbbing which Fortune knew to be the wingbeats of the Black Dragon.

The words twisted away, interchanging, fluid in the sun-filled sky, and Fortune was left quite alone. He was upside down and the light was not the sun but came from where his feet seemed to stand. The realization turned him the right way up, and brought terror to his comprehending eye. He saw a labyrinth both strange and familiar whose ending was shrouded in mist. With an immense effort he stretched a claw across the chasm to touch the mysterious wall of the pathway he was on, lost and alone, surrounded by dark turns and grasping shadows. With a jolt Fortune's eyes found other eyes and their gazes locked. The eyes were jet black like his own and he knew his father Welkin, for that frozen instant, that endless age, stood beside him. He felt the world shedding its skin. In the distant fog something moved with the power of the stars.

He saw the stars above him and felt immense joy. But there were wingbeats invading the silence . . .

He awoke to find that he had been unconscious for only a few breaths. Scoff still leaned over him, only now he had been joined by Fortune's Natural friends — Tallow, Volley and Brace. They crowded in, their expressions of worry so earnest that Fortune instantly found the whole situation funny and started to giggle. Nonplussed at first, his friends quickly began to smile, and then to laugh, until at last even the confused throng of Charmed in the background were joining in. Through the snow and the fog the laughter rang, healing wounds and lifting spirits, and it was many long moments before it started finally to die away again. Fortune by then had decided that the dream must be sealed away in his mind for another time. What had happened in the real world was strange enough.

But he smiled at Tallow and said, 'You're a great dragon, Tallow, and such fine teeth!'

The big dragon boomed with a broad grin, 'But it was not just me, Fortune, as you well know.'

'No,' agreed Fortune at once. 'Volley, you did well too. And you, Brace . . .'

At mention of his name the young dragon stepped forward to embrace Fortune, as though eager to confirm that they were indeed both still alive.

'You are a hero,' concluded Fortune as they parted again. 'Your bravery saved us all.'

'And you saved us!' exclaimed Scoff, unable to contain himself any longer. 'Makes us equal!'

Fortune's heart expanded as Scoff leaned over to pat his head in a rather fatherly way. How he had missed this dragon! Then he caught sight of the rough scars on his back, only just beginning to heal over, and cold horror sent his joy into sudden retreat.

'Oh, that!' said Scoff grimly in response to Fortune's glance. 'Well, flight's possible without wings. For a while at least. They'll grow back.'

He tried valiantly to sound philosophical about it. Yet of all things Scoff did not sound bitter, and Fortune suddenly felt as though he had gained a flash of insight into what Scoff once had been like.

'It's good to see you again, Scoff,' he choked.

'Likewise.' Scoff reached out to help his friend. Fortune staggered upright with some difficulty, his eyes glazing again as he tottered in the snow. 'Charm taken it out of you, eh?' Scoff continued, his eyes beginning to twinkle a little now. 'Not for your sort, that business. What were you playing at?'

Fortune managed a smile.

'Subtle as ever, Scoff,' he answered. 'To tell you the truth, I'm not really sure what happened. I remember seeing . . . a light. And there was some kind of web, like a maze of lines hidden beneath the mountain.'

His friends were hushed as he battled to remember, and the tension among the charmed dragons who were gathered close around this small group was stretched tight.

'Maze?' prompted Scoff.

'Yes ... or something. I don't really know, Scoff, but whatever it was it saw fit to work its magic through me. It's not the first time. Strange, but the main thing is you're all free. That's all that matters for the time being.'

There was a buzz of conversation throughout the dragons of the Hardship now as Fortune shrugged away these momentous events.

'Thinks the Maze is working through him!' exclaimed Scoff. 'Always thought you were odd, Fortune. Now I know it!'

'Then what I saw – it does exist?' asked Fortune excitedly.

'The Maze of Covamere,' Scoff announced solemnly. 'It exists.'

Fortune let out a deep breath.

'Are you all right, Fortune?' put in Tallow with some concern for, although he did not really understand what was going on, he was well aware that his friend had been through a great ordeal. But Fortune, despite his obvious fatigue, flashed him a disarming grin and laughed,

'I'm all right, Tallow. Most of me is ready to drop but inside ... inside I'm ready now. We're near to the real quest now, I can feel it, near to the heart of it all.'

'Well then,' pronounced Scoff. 'What's the plan?'

'Plan?' came Fortune's reply. 'What makes you think we need a plan?'

They talked. Some of the charmed dragons set fires in the snow using unburned timber from the surrounding trees, the flames bringing welcome warmth and keeping the fog at bay at least to a degree. One of the first things Fortune learned was the name of this group of charmed dragons.

'Wraith's Hardship,' he smiled. 'I like that! And you are all loyal to Halcyon?'

'We are his dragons,' replied Scoff, clearly the spokes-dragon for the whole assemblage of Charmed. 'Ambassadors, like me. Warriors, like Spar here. Or servants and officers. But Halcyon's, all of us.'

'It was to speak to Halcyon that I first came here,' mused Fortune. 'I wonder if I ever shall; I think perhaps the real reason for us all being here is something altogether different. The Maze, Scoff, tell me about it.'

'There is much to say,' began Scoff. 'The Charmed fear it. The Maze is . . . many things.'

'Too much to tell now?' suggested Fortune. Scoff nodded, grimacing with pain again. 'All right,' Fortune agreed, 'for now. But — Wraith is afraid of this Maze?'

'Most dragons are.'

'Hmm.' Fortune had no desire to push Scoff on a subject which seemed to distress both him and his Charmed companions, and anyway, even if he did not understand their reticence he had himself at least tasted something of what this strange Maze was about. The rest would come later — if it mattered — of that he was sure. He needed to know about this Hardship, about Wraith's army. Spar, a lean, scarred warrior, spoke at length about the various factions, and about their numbers.

'Then the fifteen hundred Charmed still with Wraith in Covamere represent his long-term supporters?' Fortune asked finally.

Spar nodded and replied, 'But don't think that necessarily makes them loyal. Many of their number are as disillusioned as we are with the Black Dragon and his ways — the difference is that they know him better, and so fear him more. That will make them weaker than their numbers suggest.'

Tallow cleared his throat, the rumble of his breath effectively silencing the debating dragons and drawing all attention to him. Even in the company of these brave Charmed he stood tall and confident, his great wings twitching impatiently; evidently he was hungry for more action.

'What of Shatter?' he said in slow, measured tones. 'This army which the Black Dragon commands: it numbers scarcely one half of the one which masses even now in the Fortress to the north. An army of Naturals,' he added for the benefit of those Charmed to whom this was news.

'Not many Charmed left in the world,' commented Scoff with uncharacteristic sadness.

'Plenty at Covamere, though,' said Fortune, smiling grimly at Tallow. 'Don't be fooled by numbers, Tallow. The

Charmed of South Point were outnumbered tenfold and look what happened there.'

'Didn't have Wraith's Hardship at South Point,' Scoff reminded him.

Tallow coughed again. Fortune smiled to himself as he saw the new light in his big friend's eye. He had rediscovered the adventure at last; he was doing something Weft would have been proud of.

'Shatter's attack is imminent,' Tallow said. 'The Flight is working even now to undermine his authority but it is already too late to prevent the coming battle. We can hope only to lessen its impact.'

'A river cannot be stopped, but it may be diverted,' murmured Fortune in a voice so low that only Brace, who stood close at his side, heard. He looked with concern at Fortune and whispered, 'I don't understand what we can do here, but I know one thing — there's dragons on the mountain more important to me than any army.'

Scoff interrupted their exchange with an impatient cry.

'Plans!' he shouted. 'Time moves fast, though the fog hides it.'

'No, Scoff. No plans.'

Fortune's quiet voice cut through the drifting fog, reaching out to every dragon ear. He sensed that the point of decision had been reached, that debate was of no further use. Here before him was Wraith's Hardship, and yet it seemed to him that he saw only the dragons of the Flight, to whom he had already denied his leadership. He saw hope and resolve and trust etched into every face and knew that he must reject them all.

'No plans,' he repeated heavily. 'No leaders. We must all decide individually, or none must decide at all. Tallow is right: the battle is coming. You had already defined your greater role long before I came to the mountain: to subvert Wraith. Very well, go and do it. I have done all I can for you; you must let me complete my quest.' He paused, then added, 'Winter has come to the world. Let your task be to bring the winter to an end. I cannot tell you the way; you must find it for yourselves.'

Fortune's brief speech ended, the debate broke up. Dragons puzzled, dragons argued, until soon dragons began to cluster into smaller groups. Before long these groups had become squads and dragons were exchanging farewells and lifting into the fog on unknown missions into the darkness. Unspoken though most of the decisions were, all were headed for a common destination: Covamere.

'They're good dragons,' came Scoff's voice at Fortune's side as he watched the charmed dragons slowly disperse into the gloom. The fires they had set were dying now and the fog was rolling in again. All seemed damp and barren, a lost world with no current of time to bring it life.

'Wraith's Hardship,' smiled Fortune. 'It's a good name. They don't need me to lead them, nor any dragon for that matter; they know what they must do.'

He thought of the weird clarity of vision which had come to him when he had broken the cages in the clearing – and now he could see so little. Such a contrast, like the difference between life and death, the world and the Realm.

Nature and charm.

Out of the fog came Tallow, Volley and Brace. With Scoff and Fortune, their little band, the last left in the deserted clearing, numbered five. The Hardship had finally gone, the vanquished guards had long since fled and now they were alone here.

'Will Shatter's army find Covamere in this weather?' asked Fortune of Tallow as the big dragon lumbered up to him.

'He will find it,' responded Tallow. 'Nothing will stop him now.'

Brace was hopping impatiently at the edge of the group.

'What are we to do?' he kept asking, opening his wings and flapping them enthusiastically. 'Are we going to Cova-mere too?'

'Not quite,' replied Fortune enigmatically. 'Not just yet, at any rate.'

'Plans, Fortune?' quipped Scoff with a broad grin. 'Not like you.'

'No, Scoff. Not plans. Destinations!'

Presently the clearing was utterly empty. The last five dragons had set off on their own course through the fog and now only a dark grey shroud occupied Whare Vale, chill and icy. No dragons here now, only winter, as there was winter everywhere on the Plated Mountain, and possibly everywhere in the world.

CHAPTER 33

The Attack

Of all the inexplicable events of the fateful time of the Turning, one of the most strange was the way Shatter was able to lead his army through the overwhelming blankness of the fog.

While for charmed dragons the fog was merely an inconvenience, a haze which sixth and seventh senses might penetrate with relative ease, for the Natural army it came as a devastating blow. Dragons primed for attack, dragons ready to give their lives for Shatter, dragons ready to wipe magic from the world, all despaired when the fog rolled in. Dragons stood at the mouth of the Fortress, looked out into the grey nothingness and howled their frustration; some even wept. Surely now the attack was impossible, surely now they would have to wait.

But they were so ready! And to add to their urgency, Shatter had proclaimed that they were betrayed, that the Charmed knew of their stronghold and their purpose. In addition, he had maintained that, with the Deadfall downed, their defensive capabilities were greatly weakened and so attack was the only option.

This last declaration was greeted with some confusion, for few dragons had believed that the Deadfall had been anything other than a curious feature of the landscape. Nevertheless, all knew of the superstitious importance their leader had placed on it and so now, with it fallen, it was apparent that there was nothing to keep them here. All was clear: the time was now. But the fog!

The day moved on and there was no word from Shatter. Dragons grew dejected and it was now that others began to speak to them, solitary dragons who whispered rumour of

Shatter's madness (which was suspected by most already) and, more strangely, news of the charmed dragons who awaited them in Covamere.

They too were dragons, said the whispers. They too followed a leader who had over-stretched his wings. They even spoke of the name of that leader, the name of the Black Dragon himself: Wraith!

The whispers spread, and if twenty dragons rejected them then at least one listened, and thought, and perhaps spoke back to the dragon who had brought the rumour, curious to hear more of these charmed dragons who were so hated and yet so remote.

In this way the Flight dragons began their work within the very ranks of Shatter's army, all of them hoping that the fog would bring enough time for their task to be completed and for the minds and hearts of dragons to be set on a new and more peaceful course. Such idealism may have been naive, but they all knew that the seeds of doubt had to be planted if ever the world of dragons were to be changed for the better; from the tiniest of beginnings great events might be brought about.

As Shatter might have agreed, the smallest of pebbles may start the greatest of landslides. But in the end it was Shatter himself who decided on the setting of such a pebble in motion. Before the day had reached noon – if any passage of time were discernible within the cloak of fog – he called a council of war, a brief affair in which his chief commanders were given one simple instruction.

'Follow me,' Shatter grated, his red eyes burning through the dense mist. 'We attack.'

And he would hear no protest from any dragon. His commanders, the memory of Barker's death still fresh in their minds and themselves anxious to keep their impatient troops happy, agreed and retreated with further instructions to gather every available dragon at the mouth of the Fortress. The strategy was simple: they would fly through the fog to Covamere and attack the Charmed on their own territory. Shatter would lead the way.

The news burned through the army like a forest fire and it was all the commanders could do to prevent a stampede for the cavern entrance. In what seemed the blink of an eye the mightiest Natural army ever assembled – a force just short of three thousand hungry, angry dragons, was poised on the huge rock ledge. Ahead was an empty abyss into which they would fly in the wake of the dragon who had brought them strength and purpose. For although his temper had shortened beyond measure, and although his eye now glittered with a cold, distant light, still he was their leader. He was the dragon who had at last stood up to the Charmed and made a difference.

To the head of the army he flew, and where he flew dragons gazed up open-mouthed, for his red eyes seemed to pierce the fog like beacons. And so they launched themselves after him, wave upon wave of dragons, squadron after squadron soaring off into the dismal fog, each wave hanging on the tail of the one before, commanders calling through the gloom to maintain formations, wings thumping against the sky like a multitude of heartbeats, breaths clouding, voices cheering yet at the next moment calling for silence and secrecy. Out they flew and south, these natural dragons, and leading them on was the dragon who had never before led from the front, the dragon coward who had always pushed from behind then retreated to safety.

His senses wildly distorted now, his mind roaming far beyond the confines of sanity, Shatter had retained the ability to rule, to command, but beneath the façade was a pit of black madness the depths of which no dragon would ever know. Perhaps in that pit he had found some inkling of magic, an extra colour in his red eyes which enabled him to pick his way through the all-enveloping fog, or perhaps it was simple luck which carried him on towards Covamere that day.

Once there, he would turn the world into the pit in which he now found himself, and he would be free again. Shatter alone.

Cumber flew fast and low, dodging in and out of the maze of snow-laden tree stumps which curled around the mountain and led inevitably to Covamere. He sprayed charm ahead of himself, drinking in the reflections which told him where the hidden world was beyond the obscuring fog. He tried to judge the time but could not; all he knew was that time was short. He suspected that it might already have stopped altogether.

Heat to his left indicated an outlying sentry post; he was nearing Covamere. A high ridge shielded him from probing charm as he swept past, a silent wind in the broken forest of grey.

After parting from Gossamer and Velvet he had wandered on the mountain for a time, concentrating on avoiding the Charmed patrols, although they had been all but abandoned now. Then, in the night, he had seen the light in the north, and the three answering lights from the mountain: red from Covamere, gold from near the summit and blue from . . . within. From the Maze. He knew it. He had been there. At that instant he had seen clearly what it was he had to do.

'Guides!' he had exclaimed into the night. 'Gossamer needs Velvet, and Fortune needs me!'

It was so simple as to be devastating. The quest was not over at all! He and Fortune still had to enter the mountain, although he no longer knew why. He suspected now that their final goal was not Halcyon at all but something quite different.

Mantle will know, he thought with certainty. *I can find his cave again and it's there that I must lead Fortune now. Now that the time is right.*

The decision made, the means of achieving his goal was less easy to formulate, for not only did he suspect that all entrances to the mountain were now heavily guarded but he had not the slightest idea where Fortune was nor even, if he was honest with himself, if he was alive at all, whatever Gossamer might have protested to the contrary.

'No matter,' he muttered to himself as the new day approached. 'I must try.'

And so, in the end, that second decision was easy too, for if he was to guide Fortune then it had to be by a way he had already travelled.

'Back to the tunnel,' he said, surprised that the answer was so obvious. 'We went in that way before, and so we shall again.'

If he could get back to that lesser portal where he and Fortune had gained access to the mountain tunnels before, then perhaps everything else would fall into place.

No sooner did he set off down the mountain than the fog billowed up around him. He slowed, the constant use of charm-sense tiring him more than he had anticipated. He blinked into the fog, the magic he was using weakening suddenly. Frightened, as though he might at any breath be blinded, he touched down on a snow-covered rock outcrop.

His course had brought him down towards Covamere in a broad spiral so that now, only a brief flight short of the central spires he knew must be looming in the distance, he was on the borders of the enormous settlement. Focusing his mind despite his exhaustion, he projected charm into the fog and pulled images from the land where no images existed.

The forest belt was a trail of debris below, Covamere an intricate construction of rock and timber sprawling snow-swept in the dank air. Dragons heaved in its narrow passage-ways; noise filtered in dull waves up the mountainside.

The rest enabled Cumber to quell his sudden panic. 'The tunnel first,' he muttered to himself. 'Then I'll worry about Fortune.'

As he waited, looking into the revealing charm, some-thing rumbled deep in the ground beneath him. A heavy swelling of charm surged . . . and receded, and as it did so Cumber's head cleared again. *The Maze is shifting!*

He swiftly calculated. In order to reach the plateau where the tunnel entrance was located he would have to descend through or at least close to Covamere. He could go round, but time pressed so heavily upon him now that the thought of unnecessary delay filled him with terror. Still . . . there seemed to be a lot of confused activity down in Covamere; perhaps he could sneak through unnoticed. He gave himself no choice.

He flew casually down to a group of three small towers, wooden turrets white with frost, a back entrance at the high eastern perimeter of the settlement. Huge fires pressed back the fog, allowing the sentries to view the terrain with a little more ease. The guards seemed distracted and admitted him without a word although even as he passed into the broad yard beyond a group of ten warrior dragons lumbered up to the gate and took up posts there.

'Naturals!' he heard one of them grumble.

He sighed with silent relief — these dragons evidently had more on their minds than checking every charmed dragon who wandered in and out of the settlement.

Dragons bustled all around and Cumber did his best to match their busy mood as he travelled through the vast complex. Fires blazed at every corner, keeping the air relatively clear. All the dragons he saw were obviously intent on some task or other, and most of them, he noted with growing concern, were very heavily armoured. Virtually every dragon he saw was a warrior. Spikes and claws were long and dangerous, and most bore the sheen of recent force-growth. Here was an encampment put recently on to war readiness.

He moved cautiously around a large arena, catching occasional glimpses of the activity there through the radial passages leading up the shallow slope on which it was built. The local flow of dragons led inexorably into the wide, open space and by now Cumber was having to push against the pressure of bodies trying to force him up the wide channels. The ground was smooth and black, solid lava worn flat by the passage of countless dragons over the years. In contrast, the walls and tunnel structures loomed high and rough, some natural thrusts of once-molten rock, others deliberate constructions, all sharp and possessed of a certain primitive elegance.

This place is old, thought Cumber, but his thoughts scattered as a crush of bodies gathered him up and propelled him sideways towards a gaping passage. Just when he thought the pressure was too great and he was sure to be dragged into the arena it suddenly lessened, then dropped to a mere trickle. A few solitary dragons scurried anxiously past him and then he was alone in the corridor.

Acutely aware that he should take this opportunity to cross the settlement and escape down the mountain to the plateau, he hesitated, curious to know what would happen. As he did so the rumbling of voices dropped to a whisper, then a hush, and the crowd of dragons he could see through the radial passage all turned their heads skywards.

Cumber looked up and for the first time saw Wraith.

A monster had invaded the sky. Black against brooding cloud Wraith clenched massive wings on the air and

402

descended majestically into the arena. His head, long and sharp, turned and swept with a gaze intense as Realm fire. Skeletal limbs twitched and jerked, their ends disappearing into invisibility, their spiny contours flashing with charm. Cumber shrank warily into the shadows, afraid that the Black Dragon might see him hiding in the corners of his kingdom.

Wings flexing with sinuous grace, Wraith dropped like a great, airborne spider out of Cumber's view, disappearing behind the high, spiked wall which protected the crowd. Excitement swelled, a buzz of anticipation. Cumber waited, gripped.

The air began to thunder all around.

At first Cumber thought that Wraith was building a spell, but then he realized that the charm was coming from underground, from somewhere deep inside the mountain. He backed away, puzzled, for the magic tasted at once old and powerful, yet restrained, and he recognized in a part of it the rumble he had heard in the ground earlier. Charm was moving beneath Covamere, old charm, but it was not ready to show itself. Waiting, it warned.

The Maze!

In the crowd dragons murmured, puzzled like Cumber. Of Wraith there was no further sign. The rumbling slowly ceased . . . but something remained. Something was wrong. Something Wraith had not planned. Cumber began to flee, presentiments of danger firing him into action. The rumble of charm had stopped; what was building now was a rumble of nature. The rumble of dragons!

He skidded round a corner which took him away from the arena and spread his wings, intending to complete his escape in the air. But the air was no longer above him.

The air had become a vast mat of natural dragons crossing Covamere, the fog above merely a series of grey chinks in the patchwork of their wings. The corridor he was trapped in resounded with their battle cries and the draught of their passage whipped the snow in angry flurries. The Naturals were attacking Covamere!

Darting into a side alley Cumber found welcome shelter in a network of tunnels carved through the rock. Even so this was not a place in which to be cornered. He wove through the icy channels, charmed senses leading him down in the direction of the plateau. Outside, fire charm began to blast as the battle was joined.

Where the Natural army had come from Cumber could not guess, knowing as he did nothing of Shatter or the Fortress. But the attack itself did not surprise him; after all it was merely proof of Ordinal's prediction that dragon would fight dragon until none were left on the face of the world. Dragon destroying dragon and a world without magic! The idea bit deep into his heart and he emerged from the tunnels in fury. His anger undoubtedly saved his life.

Eight or nine Naturals blocked his path as he lunged into the swirling mist; they turned on him as soon as they registered his presence.

Furious with the world, with all dragons who fought, with his own need to fight his own kind to survive – for Cumber counted all dragons, charmed or natural, as his own kind – he sprang into their midst and ripped a crude opening into the Realm.

What emerged was neither fire nor monster but form.

Realm wind sucked snow from the surrounding passage, a wide thoroughfare studded with side tunnels, building it into a shell of ice which contracted about him like a second skin. Thick in section as a pine trunk, it was hard as rock yet flexible as a dragon's tail.

Encased in this strange armour, Cumber battered his way through the bemused dragons, neither harming them nor allowing them to harm him. They struck and bit at the weird, glassy creation which swept past them, but their blows raised only chips of ice swiftly healed, and the armour's slippery curves afforded no purchase for their claws.

Held in this mobile cocoon Cumber spent his anger on the huge energies he needed to maintain the integrity of the protective charm and vanished down the maze of corridors beyond the tunnel exit from which he had burst, leaving the Naturals confused, amazed and quite unhurt. As soon as he was out of sight he dissolved the web of energy which had held the ice against his body and returned it to the Realm.

Hot and trembling with the exertion, he hurried on through the settlement, close now to the lower perimeter, anxious to leave the battle behind.

CHAPTER 34

Time

Like a boulder in a stream, like the forgotten basilisk waiting in its river of charm, the Plated Mountain sat motionless while time itself flowed around it in a never-ending torrent.

The current of time had flowed long across the world, meeting many obstacles in the course of its meanderings, all of which had sooner or later been broken free from their roots or else worn away to dust, to nothing. But the mountain was different. Wrapped up in the fabric of the Turning, it was more solid. Time flowed up to it, broke, and passed on round unable to exert even a fraction of its massive power upon this mighty obstacle. The normal passage of time ceased and in its place came the fog; in the place of normality came limbo.

For the dragons on the Plated Mountain time moved either erratically or else not at all, and the outside world was no longer of any concern, if it even existed.

The heart of the Turning was drawing near.

Weaker than he dared to consider, Halcyon stood at the threshold of his secret chamber and stared at the wall. Around him was the black rock of the mountain, smoothed by magic, soaring into a dizzying spiral of sculptured lava whose heights were lost in the haze of countless floating light charms. This place was an old conceit. Halcyon ignored its glory now, lost instead in contemplation of the dragons who moved a mere scale's width beyond the flimsy stone which protected him still. Sheer though the stone was, however, its strength had been elevated to something near infinite by the colossal river of charm he had directed through it, a river which formed an almost impenetrable barrier. Almost.

Beyond the barrier the dragons worked and probed and Halcyon felt the changes they made in the flow of the magical river. Very soon they would be through. He sighed, and the brittle sound fled up into the spiralling roof where it was lost in the haze of light. *Soon enough*, he thought despondently. *Time is everything*.

He knew that on the mountain outside the battle had already begun and that time was drawing its many strands together to bear upon this great blockage in its inexorable path. The world was turning, it wanted to turn with something close to desperation and yet . . . And yet the time had to be right.

Halcyon thought of Mantle and of Wraith and of the countless small dragons who even now were playing their part in the turning, but above all he thought of time. *Wraith must break through at exactly the right moment. He cannot enter the Maze too soon.* Time, and timing. That was all that was left for Halcyon now, for he knew already what the future held for himself and, to his surprise, he found himself quite without fear. In fact, he felt only relief that soon it would all be over, one way or another.

His thoughts widened briefly to contemplate other dragons he had known, the whole world of dragons he had once held in his influence. Had those times been good? He thought so – that was how he remembered them. The great dragons with whom he had communed across the continents – Ordinal and Archan and all those noble, worthy dragons – were but memories to him now, and even those were fading. He could not even recall clearly how his empire had formed, nor for what purpose it had been maintained.

Its formation was simple enough, he reminded himself. *I survived the Maze. Dragons follow heroes and such I was – for a time*.

Inertia it was, he supposed, that had sustained his power over the centuries, that and the fact that no dragon had emerged either strong or wise enough to take on the Maze as he had. Not that it was really power that he had wielded, for his reign had been one of peace and enlightenment, one in which he had taken pains to avoid confrontation.

Communication had been the key, he decided, a world network of like-minded charmed dragons, individual leaders in constant touch with Covamere, ambassadors mediating and keeping the peace, all problems — wherever possible — resolved without bloodshed.

There had been mistakes, of course, too many for Halcyon's liking. Still no dragon appeared to challenge the Maze with any hope of success and so Halcyon prolonged his life, feeding himself with charm until his age became irrelevant, even to him; he simply was.

At last time had caught up with Halcyon, and as it raced towards him like a hungry predator he turned to embrace it with his wings held wide. Now, at last, he was ready.

After an arduous climb interspersed with short flights through the thin, cold air, they reached the mountain peak. A rugged place this, white and wild, a flattened cone of ice broken in places by jags of black rock and scatterings of rubble. A roughly circular plain, open on all sides to the horizon over a low rock wall, an arena on top of the world.

Exhausted, they rested for a while in the shadow of a short spire of lava, contemplating the ring of stones which dominated the plain. Small these stones were, unremarkable in many ways yet clearly imbued with great power. Gossamer could feel it even from here, earth charm, the charm of the sprites and the mountain, of the giants and the faeries. In its presence she felt humbled, for she was reminded of both the strength and the beauty of this quality which was slowly leaking from the world.

What sort of place will this be when all the charm has gone? she wondered with dreadful foreboding. *Can anything ever take its place?*

What could the future possibly hold for a world without magic?

So it was with humility and regret that she took the few short steps up to the nearest of the pebbles of which the summit ring was made, and with sadness that she lowered her snout and nudged it out of line. A tiny movement, but one of terrible importance and tremendous influence, for as that one, small stone settled into the ice Gossamer felt the magic flee the circle and evaporate into the wintry air.

Gone!

Velvet wisely kept her distance, sensing her companion's distress. She smiled as Gossamer paced heavily up past her again and wandered up to the highest point of the low ridge which ran most of the way around the plain of ice, but she could not long contain herself and soon hurried up to where she was standing.

'Well?' she cried breathlessly.

'It's done,' sighed Gossamer.

'Then we can go? We've finished our work here?'

'I don't know, Velvet. Let's stay here a little longer, just to see.'

And so they stayed, and the fog came and with it the night, and it seemed that they had nowhere to go. Above them were only the stars, too far away ever to be reached, while below them the land had been obliterated.

'No moon,' whispered Gossamer presently.

The two dragons gazed down on the fog. Night spread beyond the mountain but somehow did not seem to touch it; it was as though the night stopped short of its slopes, afraid to breach some invisible barrier, afraid . . .

Grey and dim in the starlight, the fog moved with slow, heaving waves, occasional ripples disturbing its surface and sending wisps of vapour in long, reaching claws which turned over and over before gradually descending again into the back of the beast which had spawned them. Showing nothing, hiding all, the fog surrounded the lower half of the mountain in a massive blanket from which the upper slopes thrust like an island from a calm, grey sea.

And although the battle was already raging, there was no sign of dragon either above or within its folds.

'It looks so peaceful,' whispered Gossamer, looking down into the bank of cloud.

'It looks cold and damp to me,' commented Velvet with a shudder. 'You don't want to go down there, do you?'

Gossamer shook her head.

'We'll stay here for a while longer,' she replied. 'At least until that fog's cleared. Then we might stand a chance of finding the others again.'

'Oh yes!' exclaimed Velvet. 'I'm looking forward to that

more than anything! Do you think Cumber will be all right? Oh,' she added, 'and Fortune of course.'

Gossamer shivered too then, and shrugged. She did not reply at first, for although she shared Velvet's yearning to leave these cold slopes and rejoin their companions, their loves, indeed simply the warmth of other dragons, she felt that their task here had been too easy, that their work here was not yet done . . .

All the circles are broken, she thought restlessly. *Why? I know not, but it is done, even the ring at the summit, even that.* So why did she not feel content?

No light from the outside world reached into Halcyon's chamber yet he knew when the sky began to change. The light charms which spiralled up into the glare wavered and bobbed as the heavens lurched above.

Halcyon scented through the river of charm; the dragons beyond had gone, their task incomplete, no doubt summoned to join the battle.

Now he will come, he thought grimly. And with relief. While above, the stars moved.

'Look!' exclaimed Velvet, waggling her wings frantically in the air. 'Look, Gossamer! The sky's moving!'

Open-mouthed they both stared up at the stars, they alone witnesses to the spectacle. Sure enough, the sky was moving. The Eye, the single, brilliant star about which all the others turned, remained as immobile as it had across the aeons but its countless neighbours were all undergoing a strange transformation. A wave seemed to ripple through the blackness of space, distorting the stars in front of which it passed and leaving them dimmed and repositioned in its wake. From north to south it swept, gathering the stars in its relentless passage until familiar patterns were broken; with the power of the stars it travelled, and the stars themselves it moved as it went.

What remained when it had gone was a sky changed, a sky alien to the two dragons who gazed up into its secret depths. They trembled, afraid, and then the blackness split in two.

The moon, absent for so many days, returned from the

409

timeless limbo which had claimed it, bursting through into the real world with an explosive burst of light which sent tiny sparks racing through the field of ice covering the flat mountain peak. What power had taken it from time's influence no dragon would ever know, nor from whence it had returned, but both Gossamer and Velvet had tracked the days they had spent on the mountain and knew that it should have shown a mere crescent, waxing perhaps but still a mere sliver compared to its full glory.

But the moon returned full, a bright, blue-white orb ringed with crystals of white which danced in the air and created a glowing, shimmering halo. It seemed expanded, a mighty observer beyond the influence of the world and caring neither for it nor for the tiny creatures who crawled across its surface. Cold and dispassionate it watched these two dragons, casting its icy rays across the summit, across the stones . . .

The moonbeams flickered, caressing the ice. Muffled sounds started underground. Gossamer and Velvet watched the light pouring down from above and followed its line with their gaze until they too looked upon the ring of stones.

Noise again, a faint crackling. The ice shook.

The moonlight bleached the arena.

Then, one by one, the stones began to grow. As they had before Mantle and Halcyon they grew, except this time they did not stop until they dwarfed the two frightened dragons who stared in awe at the astonishing events taking place before them. Up they lurched like tattered giants, shaking off ice in great tumbling flakes, rocking from side to side as they reached towards the reborn moon, full and bright, which was drawing them skywards, and only gradually did they slow and eventually stop, settling a fraction back into the cracked ice with reluctant groans, their black, ragged shapes stretched and twisted as though some inner spirit in each was still trying to reach for the stars.

Dumbfounded, Gossamer and Velvet looked from moon to stone then back to moon again, and even if they did not understand what power had brought about this strange happening, a single exchanged glance confirmed that they both knew for certain that their task here on the summit of the Plated Mountain was not over. Not at all. In fact, it had only just begun.

The wall was thin, scale-thin, that much Wraith could sense. Yet the charm which shored it up was charm of such devastating power that even he was daunted by it. He tapped at it delicately with his bony Realm-arms but it did not yield. Solid as eternity, fluid as time it flowed in every direction through this fragile rock barrier, now the only thing separating him from Halcyon and the inner chambers of the Plated Mountain. And the Maze.

Reports had reached him shortly before warning of the imminent attack of the army of Naturals. The sentries from Whare Vale, who had been too dismissive of Sleet's original story to consider it worth warning Covamere, had returned in terror after fleeing the breakout at the prison. Shatter's army, they claimed, had launched a surprise offensive against the prison and they had been forced to retreat against overwhelming odds. Even now, they said, the army was behind them. Covamere must be prepared, they said, and Shatter defeated.

Their lies Wraith had spotted, but he did not doubt the truth of their claim that this army of natural dragons was indeed on its way towards Covamere. Having listened to their frantic tale he at once called an assembly in one of the principal arenas of Covamere, an assembly by which he planned to rouse his army to readiness for war and simultaneously prepare the way for his own triumphant entry into the mountain and the Maze.

And here it was that the Black Dragon made his first error of judgement.

Although he believed that there was indeed an army of three thousand natural dragons bent on the destruction of Covamere, he did not believe that mere Naturals would be able to find their way here through the fog. No, they would wait until visibility had improved before they attacked, thus giving him time to plan his own defences and inspire his own warriors with speeches. So it was with leisurely grace that he descended into the arena on a cushion of charm. He drank in the moment, savouring the sight of the upturned faces, many of whom still adored him, all of whom still feared him. Dragons – his dragons, ready for his command. A command he never gave.

For no sooner had he landed than the Naturals attacked! Wave after wave of these crude, muscular dragons flooded into the arena, breaking out of the fog in an endless flow of body and wing and claw. Many hundreds of Charmed died in that first attack, the Naturals' advantages of surprise and massive numbers far outweighing the superior fighting power of their charmed adversaries. Retaliation began soon but not soon enough for Wraith's liking, for already too many Charmed lay dead or dying, the crush of the crowd only exacerbating the terrible situation into which he had led his army; with the Naturals crashing on to their heads from above, the charmed dragons found themselves not in an arena but in a trap, unable to rally quickly enough to fend off the first, dreadful assault.

But rally they did at last, and Wraith's confidence was restored as he saw *his* dragons lifting into the grey air. Light began to slice through the fog, boiling the vapour and cutting through flesh. Now it was the Naturals who were trapped, penned in by the sheer weight of their own number, unable to turn quickly enough to avoid the lances of fire charm now being launched into their midst. Blood and bone began to rain down from the mist, scattering over the broken bodies which already lay piled in the arena, and soon the sky was alive with flame.

First blood to the Naturals, but second and third to the Charmed. Wraith did not wait around to see the rest.

'Fight, my dragons!' he roared, his voice resounding through sky and soil, through world and Realm. All dragons heard his words, for they echoed like no thunder that had ever been heard before. 'Fight and you shall prevail!'

As he bellowed, the fog twisted, opening a shaft of clear air directly upwards until the sky was briefly visible through the long, narrow gap. Dark at first, the sky suddenly flared blue. Then the fog closed in again and Wraith took his cue.

'The moon returns to us and it is full!' he rumbled. 'The time of prophecy is here! Fight for your lives and for your leader, for when I return to you the Maze of Covamere will be mine. Charm will prevail, dragons!'

With those words he slashed his way brutally into the

Realm and disappeared from the view of those few dragons left alive in the arena, while above and beyond the place he had left empty the battle raged and dragons began to die in ever-increasing numbers. Magic filled the bank of fog with lightning, fire pulsing in the gloom like a hidden heartbeat.

Dragon fought dragon at the turning of the world, and Wraith fled underground towards his own fate. The battle left behind he travelled swiftly down through the passage which his pathfinders had already opened for him. Finding them loitering uncertainly at the final barrier he dismissed them at once, assigning them to various battalions which even they knew they had no hope of finding in the mêlée. It was some measure of their fear of the Black Dragon that they fled his presence, choosing instead the battle outside.

And now here he stood, waiting in the dark, feeling the charm which Halcyon had laid before him, scenting at the challenge, savouring already the glory which would soon be his.

Before him, a smooth, black wall, solid lava polished and made perfect by the flow of magic across its surface. The tunnel which it blocked was narrow but very high, more a slot than a passage. Wraith looked up into the blackness which concealed the ceiling and sent his sight out into the Realm.

Tiny monsters wriggled beneath his gaze in this other world, but he was their master. Multi-legged, many-brained, they struggled in his embrace until finally they succumbed to his influence. Bloodless and cold they lay limp in the clutches of his strange, distorted claws as he drew them through into this world.

He crushed them until white juices flowed from their diamond bodies. Flinging the juice high against the wall he watched intently as the droplets shattered on the rock. As they fragmented they met the cascading charm and boiled to vapour instantly, but in the pattern of steam they left Wraith saw things he had not detected before: shapes, weaves . . . Weaknesses!

Eyes fixed, wings opened, he elevated himself two trees high until he hovered close to a light spot on the wall. Here he sprayed a little more of the pale juice and noted with satisfaction the way it shuddered before vaporizing. Closing his yellow eyes and extending his skeletal forearms deep into the Realm, Wraith thrust talons of magic into the space behind the wall and then pulled them back towards him, puncturing the barrier of charm from the opposite side and thus sending the unleashed energies spraying out into the chamber beyond.

At once he felt an answering thrust from another dragon – Halcyon! – as this released torrent was diverted harmlessly into some waiting void far off in the Realm. With a tremendous groan and a flicker of deep orange flame the river of charm embedded itself into that other world, leaving only the rock itself between the Black Dragon and his prey.

Lowering his head, Wraith broke open the wall with one, gentle tap then, with his jaws gaping, he bit into the remaining fragments of rock, tearing them apart and spitting them out into the glowing, spiralling cave which awaited him. He surged forwards and grasped the lip of the hole he had made in the wall.

There below him, looking up with old, tired eyes, was the hunched form of Halcyon, brown and feeble, surely no match for the great conqueror who had finally emerged to confront him. Wraith's eyes flashed, and his mouth opened again with hungry expectation.

Then he paused, for two things occurred which he did not expect.

The first of these was a sudden flurry of movement behind and directly below him. Glancing down he saw a flash of white as another dragon forced its way through the bottom part of the wall of rock. He saw Halcyon register surprise as this newcomer burst through immediately in front of him and floated before his tired gaze, bobbing a scale's width above the ground, his scrawny neck turning a thin, bleached face up towards where Wraith himself was perched. It was Insiss.

Wraith hissed, and as he did so the second revelation came to him, for as he drew breath a weird aftertaste invaded his mouth. The remains of the charm from which Halcyon's barrier had been constructed still sparked fitfully around the gap he had forced in the wall and it was these that he could taste. The flavour was odd, the same as that which had

414

danced at the limits of his senses ever since he had started this invasion of the mountain. Old. Powerful. Awake. Not dragon.

He looked beyond the spot where Halcyon and Insiss stood together, staring up at him. The chamber stretched away into the distance, high here but lowering as it turned towards the deeper tunnels which led, Wraith knew only too well, to the centre of the mountain and the entrance to the Maze. From those depths he sensed massive powers building but for the moment his attention was captivated by something rather nearer.

Directly opposite where he crouched, near the bottom of the illuminated spiral chimney, was a crack in the wall. Light wriggled there, chasing up and down, back and forth. Light and movement. As Wraith watched the crack widened into a hole and the light grew in intensity. Something moved within, something with blank silver eyes and a long, sinuous tail. Something ancient and reptilian, whose breath was like a shadow and whose gaze could kill. Something which had slept and which was now awake.

Moving slowly into the light of its own making, out-staring the Black Dragon, this interloper into its own, time-less world, ignoring all else, moved the basilisk.

CHAPTER 35

Confrontation

If the mountain was a point of time frozen amid the turning of the world then Halcyon's chamber was at the heart of the ice of which it was made. Here beneath the high spiral roof all was still, the chill air held tight between the pressure of the winter without and the charm of the Maze within. A held breath in the throat of a motionless beast.

Of all the creatures present in the chamber that night — if night it was and not simple darkness — Insiss was the one most out of his depth. To some degree they all were uncertain, Halcyon, Wraith, even the nameless basilisk, for nothing now could be clear, nothing predicted. But for Insiss the situation was doubly strange for suddenly he found himself present in circumstances wholly out of his control. A dragon who thrived on manipulation, who over the years had influenced even the Black Dragon into taking decisions he might not otherwise have made, he floundered, unsure of what he should do or say. It was his very uncertainty which prompted him to speak, and so it was with these words that Insiss began the first of the great confrontations of the Turning.

'My lord!' he cried, aiming his words carefully so that it was not clear whether he was speaking to Wraith or to Halcyon. 'I am here to do your bidding, whatever it may be. My counsel is yours; ask and I shall serve.'

His words raced up the twisting ceiling and were lost without echo, as though the rock had sucked them away in contempt, recognizing their lack of worth in these eminent surroundings. Insiss inhaled sharply, glancing first to Wraith, then to Halcyon, then to the still form of the basilisk, poised high in the wall above. Both Wraith and

Halcyon ignored him; for the moment they only had eyes for each other. Insiss retreated slightly, overwhelmed by the intensity of their gazes. He waited and watched, curious and afraid, for he sensed that the future was being made even as he observed. *And I will be a part of it!* he resolved.

The lazy air seemed to stir a little as Halcyon raised his bony head higher and tipped it a little to one side so that he looked obliquely at his adversary. This small motion appeared to unnerve Wraith, for he drew his wings up in a gesture which seemed almost nervous and glared down in disgust at this withered, brown dragon who dared to offer him opposition.

'Who do you think you are, dragon?' he boomed, his voice like fire. 'Do you believe you can withstand me? Do you believe this time is anything but mine, or that any will prevail but the Black Dragon?'

Halcyon said nothing, but dared to smile.

'Are you afraid to reply, dragon?' roared Wraith, enraged now. 'You dare to *mock* me?' Then he pulled back his anger and presented a thin smile of his own. 'Or perhaps you wish to challenge me as I challenge you,' he continued. 'Is that it, dragon? Do you truly believe that a creature as feeble as you can defy the might of the Black Dragon?'

Wraith took a deep breath and spread his terrible claws high into the space below the tortured ceiling. Flame darted between them, chasing along their bones and up the hard tendons of his neck to emerge through his mouth in a broad jet of orange fire.

'Then I accept your challenge, Halcyon!' he thundered through the hiss of the fire. 'Choose your moment well, for it will be your last!'

The fire died and his words, like those of Insiss, were absorbed into the rock. The basilisk watched implacably from the opposite wall, its silver eyes blank and unreadable, its body pale and indistinct, its breath a lethal cloud about its blunt and ancient face.

Halcyon continued to smile.

Insiss flicked a glance at Halcyon but reserved most of his attention for his master. Surely Wraith would prevail as he had long promised, and so vital to Insiss now was the opportunity to repair the damage he had already inflicted on their fragile relationship.

Since their final argument Insiss had crept his way through the deepest of the tunnels of Covamere, stealing food and information where he could and planning his course of action. He had long known that this confrontation would be the turning point for Wraith and so had long decided that he would be present himself. But whose side should he take? Who, in the end, would live? Halcyon or Wraith? One would die.

And this new creature, which he could only guess to be a basilisk, this creature which he looked upon with awe and horror, what of that? Would it spare any of them, victor or no? Did it even care?

'Lost dragon.'

The words filtered through the cold air like smoke, drifting up to where Wraith was poised high on the rock wall. As he heard them he boiled in anger, his yellow eyes widening in rage while Halcyon looked peacefully up.

'Lost dragon,' repeated Halcyon. 'Yes,' he went on, 'I know you, dragon. I knew you when your colour was not black, before you took on all the weight you call charm but which is only shame. I knew you when you came to this chamber once before and passed beyond these tunnels and into the heart of the mountain. And I saw you when you emerged again, when the Maze spat you back out. When you were lost, and when you were saved. Yes, I know you, Black Dragon. I know your past, and perhaps a little of your future. How much do you know of me?'

His voice was pitched low but his words were hard and strong. Wraith spat back his reply.

'I know you are old, Halcyon,' he responded, speaking his adversary's name for the first time. 'I know your time is past and I know that my time is here. I can see all of your future, Halcyon, for it is short. It starts and ends here; your only choice is the manner of your downfall.'

Halcyon tilted his neck a little further and rubbed at his shoulder with an outstretched claw. 'Would you not rather come down here, lost dragon?' he suggested, wincing slightly. 'We could talk more easily.'

Wraith laughed. 'Tired? In pain? No, I will stay here a

little longer, for it is you who are lost. I know my place here; it is a pity you do not.'

'Pain?!' exclaimed Halcyon abruptly, his voice expanding with terrifying power so that ice crackled on the walls and Insiss cowered. 'What do you know of pain, lost dragon? Do you think to be leader is to know anything but pain? When a dragon dies I die too; when pain is felt it is felt by me. All dragons come to me and all dragons are me. Even now I feel the war which you have brought to my lands, even now the pain is mine. Is this what you want, lost dragon, all this pain?!'

So saying, Halcyon whipped back his tattered wings and reared up on his legs, exposing his breast to Wraith, and it seemed to the Black Dragon that the battle was brought before him, for his vision was filled with blood and his ears with screams and his nostrils with the scent of death. Fang cracked and scale shattered, wing folded and claw sliced, and all this happened within the spread of Halcyon's wings. The chamber was bathed in a deathly red light, a light which emanated from Halcyon's breast, from his heart it seemed, and Wraith saw that the words he had spoken were true: to be leader was to share the pain of one's subjects one hundred times over. He shuddered, horrified by this awful display yet at the same time inspired by it. *For is the counterpoint of pain not the glory?* he thought. *Shall I as leader not know the ecstasy as well as the agony?*

He too spread his wings, unfurling their great, black sails until they seemed to fill the whole roof space. The red light pounded against them and was sucked away by them, pulled into Wraith's own body even as it left Halcyon's, shedding droplets of magic on to the floor, the wall and even the upturned face of Insiss as Wraith took on the very pain with which Halcyon was trying to scare him.

Insiss looked on amazed at this bizarre congress, at Halcyon pouring out the horror of the carnage they all knew to be occurring above ground, and at Wraith drinking it in as though it were the purest of spring waters, revelling in the nightmare in which he was bathed. He sidled closer to Halcyon, aware of the anger he would cause Wraith but his mind at last made up. Against his instincts he chose his patron before the outcome of the contest was clear. He took the risk, for after all, was life not simply a huge and lethal game in which only those who dared to risk all could truly be said to have won?

Through the red glare Wraith saw the subtle movement which brought Insiss silently to Halcyon's side and knew that he had been betrayed. The realization brought him cold pleasure for he had good reason to dispose of Insiss too. As Halcyon slowly relaxed, folding his wings away again and sagging back as though exhausted by the staggering performance he had just put on, Wraith pulled in the last of the sensations he had unleashed, although he kept his wings wide open still.

'Insiss!' he called with soft menace. 'I see you now, and I see that your choice is made. Very well, I accept your decision.' Here he paused. 'Now accept mine.'

It was done with horrible swiftness.

As Insiss cowered against Halcyon's grizzled flank, the Black Dragon wrenched a chunk of lava from the wall at his side and hurled it down towards his former lieutenant. This projectile Insiss ducked with ease, but as it struck the floor at his side it exploded into a million tiny fragments, each of which leaped up from the ground towards his face. Halcyon watched impassively as the minute flakes moved with astonishing speed to cluster around their quarry's head before embedding themselves in it from every direction. Insiss jerked once and his head fell to the floor with the crash of stone upon stone. His body, its neck tattered and exposed, was left to slump to the floor.

'Enough!' cried Wraith before the deadly swarm could go to work on the rest of his corpse, and with a flourish he banished the charm into the Realm from which it had come. The noisy writhing of the head ceased. The air all about it was stained and somehow violated. Thus did Insiss make his choice, and thus did he die.

'And now?' prompted Halcyon.

'What is your choice, dragon?' replied Wraith at once. 'Is it to be pain, or something worse?'

He dropped silently from his perch and alighted in front of Halcyon, close enough to touch him though for the moment he held back. Again the basilisk blinked, and although it was not possible to track the line of its sight, perhaps it leaned out over the precipice to which it clung, better to observe the events unfolding in the chamber below. Reflected in its featureless eyes were the twin forms of Wraith and Halcyon, facing each other in this ancient chamber while beyond them the Maze busied itself with concerns elsewhere.

As they stood poised, each waiting for the other to make a move, both became aware that the temperature in the chamber was rising. Winter had come too soon, defying time itself in its premature arrival, but something now was challenging it.

On top of everything, this dragon. No sooner had the stones undergone their strange transformation than he appeared, crawling painfully over the lip of the far ridge and slumping down at the edge of the stone circle. Gossamer and Velvet looked on uncertainly as the dragon – obviously a Natural and obviously badly wounded – struggled into the shadow of one of the highest stones and collapsed there. Now he was quite motionless, possibly dead, and still they looked on, unsure of what they should do.

'Who is it?' whispered Velvet fearfully.

'I don't know,' replied Gossamer. 'But we must find out.'

The circular plain of the summit stretched away before them, the ice and snow which covered it dull despite the moonlight, disturbed by the giant stones standing black and tortured together. All seemed dead, yet despite this sensation Gossamer was convinced that there was still charm here, whatever she had felt earlier.

Charm, thought Gossamer suddenly. *Whatever my work here may be, I cannot do it without charm.*

Blue shadows shivered off the stranger as he shifted his weight. So he was still alive! A deep groan issued forth, cut short by a sharp intake of breath, then silence fell again. A deeper shadow was spreading now, moving across the ground where the other shadows were still, a black pool reaching like water out from where the injured dragon lay. Like water, or . . .

'Blood!' hissed Gossamer, starting forward impetuously. Whoever this dragon was he was hurt, and he needed help.

If it were Fortune I would help him!

421

'But it might be . . .' began Velvet.

'We must help him!' responded Gossamer, shaking off Velvet's clutch with a roughness she instantly regretted. 'Stay here,' she added, more gently this time. 'I'll be careful'

She spread earth-red wings in the high, cold air and glided rapidly across to the opposite side of the ring of stones, coming to ground a wingspan short of the hunched figure of the stranger. As she crossed the centre of the circle – a slightly raised hump of ice – the ground seemed to hum slightly, as though acknowledging her presence. She felt heat there.

Charm! But not for me, not yet.

The dragon was indeed a Natural, a strong, young male with a dull brown coat and a slightly paler underbelly. Dark eyes glowered at her from the shadow of the stone against which he lay at an awkward angle. He moved again, then grunted, and at last Gossamer saw his misfortune. His left wing was all but destroyed. It stuck forward crazily from his flank, blood caking the entire span of the delicate membrane, its edges torn and raw. Halfway along its length the supporting bones were broken clean in two, white splinters piercing the skin and glinting with horrific cleanness in the moonlight.

Crippled, obviously in dreadful pain, the dragon reached his good wing out towards Gossamer and whispered,

'Leave now. He'll kill you. Get away while you can.'

'You're hurt,' Gossamer replied, leaning forward towards him, but he shrank back, wincing as he did so.

'Get away!' he cried. 'There's no defeating him. He'll follow you and he'll kill you!'

'Who?' she demanded impatiently. 'Who did this to you?'

'It's too late,' came the dragon's reply, his voice suddenly tired. 'Go.'

Then his eyes widened.

Air brushed against Gossamer's neck as she moved still closer to the crippled dragon. Snow crunched behind her.

She whirled around to see . . . Velvet landing heavily in the snow behind her. Her heart thumped in relief.

'I felt like I was being watched,' Velvet blurted. 'What's happening? Who is he? Gossamer, I'm scared!'

'Listen to me,' said the stranger, urgently cutting through

Velvet's babble. 'He's still around here somewhere. I came up here to . . . to think, to get away, but he followed me. He found me. He did this to me.' He half-lifted the remains of his wing with a grimace. 'Just go. He's mad. He won't spare you.'

'Who?!' cried Gossamer in frustration.

The stranger blinked back at her, surprised.

'Shatter, of course,' he replied. 'He's here!'

If he had been expecting a response then he was disappointed. The two females stared blankly back at him; obviously the name meant nothing to them. He began to laugh.

'I wish Fortune were here,' he chuckled. 'He'd find it funny. And that friend of his . . .'

'Fortune?!' exploded Gossamer, utterly confused by this dragon's ability to make no sense whatsoever.

And then, as her shock subsided a little, she found herself looking more closely at his features for, although she knew she had never met this dragon before, nevertheless there was something familiar about him. Something in his voice, his accent, the look in his eye. Something from Fortune's stories? Something in common . . .

Then she had it.

'You're Wood,' she said softly.

Now it was his turn to be surprised. His jaw dropped open and he lurched back, his pain temporarily forgotten.

'Who . . . who are you?' he challenged, his voice fearful.

'It is Wood, isn't it?' pressed Gossamer, reaching out to touch his face.

Wood nodded dumbly, then looked hard at her. A weak smile reached up into his face and he managed another chuckle.

'Well, well,' he coughed, spitting flecks of blood on to the snow. 'So you love him, then.'

Gossamer looked away bashfully, at once horrified at Wood's injuries and delighted by the instant rapport they seemed to share. If only they could have met earlier. She looked back to find him scrutinizing her face closely.

'Do you have a brother?' he asked suddenly.

She nodded.

'His name is Brace,' she replied in wonder.

'He's alive, or at least he was when I last saw him, although that was several days ago.'

Tears of relief filled Gossamer's eyes and for a few breaths Velvet had to hold her up.

'And Fortune too,' added Wood, although now his own eyes were downcast and full of tears of their own, and he would not speak further of his old friend save to reassure Gossamer that he too lived.

'Oh, my dear,' said Gossamer presently, looking again upon Wood's terribly wounded wing, 'you're so hurt. We must help you.'

'It's too late for that,' came Wood's response.

Around them his blood was staining the ice, but it did not freeze. Instead the ice began to run with it, trickling across the ground and creating pools of water in the lower depressions. Heat was rising from underground, even to the summit of the mountain.

'It's too late for me,' whispered Wood.

The basilisk was surprised to find itself actually interested in the confrontation between these two charmed dragons. Although the heat of great magic was escalating in the labyrinth of inner tunnels beyond this one chamber, although in those deep places the Maze itself was casting off its interest in time, the basilisk found itself captivated by this scene and, for the moment, unwilling to move.

And above all it was captivated by Wraith. This one, this dragon seemed more real than any other it had encountered in its long life. This great, black dragon was more solid than a dragon had any right to be. He loomed in the cave, he dwarfed Halcyon, he impressed the basilisk with his sheer presence. His very existence sparked memories in the basilisk which had lain dormant for aeons, memories which flowed freely again but too fast to be properly perceived.

But although it could not remember clearly, the basilisk found that it was able to do something else most efficiently.

It found itself able to fear.

Their eyes – Wraith's hard and yellow, Halcyon's brown and watery – were locked together, their thoughts untrackable. For what might have been years, or merely a few breaths, they stood there motionless, lifeless almost, each waiting for the other to take the initiative.

As the basilisk watched, struggling to keep its broad and timeless perception focused on this one, tiny scene, it saw that there was in fact motion. The two dragons were moving with agonizing slowness across the floor of the chamber, Wraith advancing and Halcyon retreating. Slowly, so slowly, Halcyon's tail brushed against the rear wall and coiled itself around, drawing itself up until his haunches and eventually his back legs were pressed up against the rough black rock. Only now did Wraith halt, his breathing shallow, his head held high and steady.

A pause, then a hiss of air. 'Yield,' murmured Wraith.

Halcyon said nothing, although he looked down at the headless body of Insiss sprawled before the hole in the wall through which he had entered the cave. Then he shook his head and lowered his gaze to the floor.

'Yield!' repeated Wraith, louder now. 'Or die.'

Again Halcyon shook his head.

'Refuse and you will die!' cried Wraith, his voice cracking now. Although his body was still, there was clearly great turmoil within. Halcyon looked up.

'I do not refuse,' he said softly. 'So do not pretend you offer me a choice.'

Confused, growing more angry with every breath he took, Wraith reared back on to his hind legs and raised his quivering Realm claws above Halcyon's head, which was offered up to him now as if in sacrifice.

'Yield!' he roared, lightning cracking between his claws.

'But remember this at the end, lost dragon: you must give it up if you are ever to prevail. On that fact everything will turn. Remember it, if you call yourself dragon!'

Enraged and quite bewildered by what he considered to be the ravings of a senile dragon, Wraith's patience found its end here and he swung his claws down towards Halcyon. But instead of slicing into his body they embraced him, lifting him clear of the ground, and held him close to Wraith's breast as the Black Dragon whirled around to face the watching basilisk. Then they vanished.

There was silence in the chamber then, if only briefly. The basilisk tracked their progress through the Realm with casual ease and flicked its silver eyes to the right to locate their re-entry point into this world.

With a crash they appeared, Halcyon still hugged tight against the Black Dragon's heaving chest. Except now there was no flesh within his skin.

Wraith filled his lungs and issued forth a roar which was surely heard by the dragons who fought above ground. The sound surpassed any definition of word or even voice: it was the sound of triumph and terror, of power and magic and of a lost dragon who thought he had found himself again. On it went, and as it gradually died Wraith opened his claws and let Halcyon's empty skin drop to the ground. Scales scattered and lay like dull autumn leaves on the black lava.

Halcyon was gone. Now the basilisk moved.

The drama here was over and in the end, as so often before, it had been disappointing. Dragon had killed dragon and the victor had deluded himself that such action had increased his own power. Even now the Black Dragon's head turned towards the entrance to the tunnel which would take him on and down towards the Maze and what he undoubtedly saw as his final glory.

No matter, the basilisk would get there first.

But as it coiled past Wraith, it heard the dragon's voice again and was compelled by some ancient memory to stop and turn. Some memory and . . . fear?

'What are you?'

The basilisk had no intention of speaking, if indeed it could remember how, so long had it been since it had been called upon to use such a crude means of communication. It exhaled its deadly breath and blinked its lethal eyes, surprised that this dragon showed no fear of his own.

For his part Wraith looked upon this strange creature with fascination. Exhilarated, his blood pounding through his massive heart with such force as he had never known before, he felt able to take on anything, to defeat any dragon who might defy him. And now . . . this.

It was small, this creature, no bigger than a small bear cub, yet unmistakably reptilian. Creamy scales covered a narrow, twisted body and it had only two visible limbs, long articulate forearms with sensitive fingers and many joints.

The rear half of its body narrowed into a muscular tail with which it propelled itself. Its head was broad and bony, its mouth partly obscured by the cloud of vapour which seemed to hang permanently around it. Its eyes . . .

Wraith could not look at them, for in them death lurked.

Yet it fears me! he exalted, dizzy with the power he wielded now that Halcyon was no more. *I can be its master if I so desire! And I shall be!*

Of course he was wrong, for it was not Wraith that the basilisk feared but the evil which Wraith could force upon them both.

As he paced towards the lurking creature Wraith was at last able to put a name to it, and this he spoke.

'Basilisk!' he hissed. 'Where are your kin, basilisk? Or are you the last of the six? Yes, you are, I sense it. Well, basilisk, does legend not tell of the union which dragon and basilisk might enjoy? Perhaps Halcyon did not dare such a thing, but I do!'

By now he was towering over the diminutive creature, his wings spread and his yellow eyes blazing. The basilisk appeared hypnotized by his words, although in fact it was trapped by them. Wraith had indeed recalled what had so far eluded it: the fact that dragon might join with basilisk to form a greater entity, a symbiotic monster with such powers as had never been unleashed upon the world. What those powers might be neither Wraith nor the basilisk knew for no such union had ever before been made, but what trapped them both now was the inevitability of that union once the circumstances for its enactment were right.

Clearly they were right now.

The realization of what was about to happen evidently unsettled the basilisk for Wraith saw it lash its tail in a vain effort to escape the inescapable. For forces greater than they were drawing these two creatures together now, and in the flow they both floundered as though caught in a whirlpool. Closer they approached until their bodies touched, yielded, merged . . .

At the point where dragon scale met basilisk flesh the very air bubbled. Living meat was briefly exposed, then new skin snapped around it as the two creatures slowly began to fuse into one. Now both struggled to escape as the enormity of what was happening dawned on them, but it was already too late. Whatever ancient curse it was that had predicted this congress held more strength than even these two mighty beasts and now they had no choice but to succumb to its influence.

Wraith howled with pain as the basilisk's thrashing body was absorbed into his own. Either because he was the larger of the two, or because it was decreed, it was his form which survived the transformation and that of the basilisk which was sucked within. Soon only the basilisk's lashing tail remained, protruding from Wraith's flank like an angry snake, and indeed there it remained.

No witness was there to this incredible joining of bodies, for both Halcyon and Insiss were dead. Perhaps the Maze knew of it as it stirred, or perhaps not, for now the Turning was so near that the world was made slippery by the passing of time and the decay of charm.

A new entity combining such strength and such magic had never before been seen. Were its true abilities ever to be demonstrated, even such events as the turning of the world might fade into insignificance for what could it do if not turn back time, or build its own charm without need of earth or Realm? Would it not rule all forever? Could it not turn the world in any direction it chose?

If the Maze did indeed observe this transformation here in the defiled glory of Halcyon's chamber then it did not betray its thoughts any more than the dragon-basilisk betrayed its motives.

For now, surely, motives were all. If it was Wraith's desire which drove the beast on then it would undoubtedly head straight for the Maze and ultimate triumph; if the basilisk's . . . then maybe it would seek its own self-destruction and thus end at a stroke the potential nightmare of its own creation. Or the potential glory, depending on the point of view.

Its pace slow and heavy, the unearthly creature which seemed dragon but which was so much more passed away into the darkness of the deep tunnels beneath the Plated Mountain. Somewhere ahead the Maze waited, alert now and hungry.

The heat grew.

CHAPTER 36

Closing In

Some way behind Shatter's vengeful army flew a small group of dragons, some natural, some charmed. They made their way around the mountain as though the dense fog were but a wisp of cloud, as well they might for at their head they had Tallow, navigator supreme.

Again Volley's song held them together as they sped through the darkness which was not truly night, except now it was no mournful mountain tune but a song of resolve and anticipation. Its chorus soared with them in the sky and filled them all with hope.

'We're drawing near,' called Tallow. 'Perhaps you should keep it down, Volley.'

'No,' cried Fortune at once. 'Let him sing. The time is past for skulking and hiding. We fly now, Flight and Hardship, and let no dragon doubt our purpose!'

So on they flew and on Volley sang. The terrain raced past unseen beneath them as they kept up a punishing pace despite the gloom.

'We're nearly at the cliff!' shouted Tallow over the noise of the rushing air. Snow exploded beneath their wings as they swooped low over a hidden ridge and out into clearer air.

Here the fog billowed. It was thinner in the lee of the cliff and now they could see why: great fires were blazing in Covamere, only a short flight to the west, and the heat from the flames was driving back the mists. As they watched they saw lightning arc up from the ground and pierce the filthy sky.

Below them the landscape swam and then, as the tendrils of mist parted further, locked into forms recognizable to

Fortune and Scoff. This place Tallow knew by virtue of his own travels around the mountain, but for Fortune and Scoff it was a place of ill omen, the place where they had been separated from each other and which had led Fortune from Cumber.

Nothing had changed here: the ragged, grey cliff still reached out over the plateau in a huge overhang, the great, vertical crack bisecting its face and concealing the entrance of the lesser portal. In the centre of the plateau itself was a snow-covered mound of rocks, the cairn which had formed there after the collapse of the upper cliff wall.

I suppose those poor, crushed dragons are still under there, thought Fortune with a shiver, the place filling him with a dread he had not anticipated. In the distance the sounds of the battle rolled in on a cold wind which disturbed the billowing fog even more. The cliff loomed large and threatening.

Then, between the sheets of cloud which boiled above their heads, there came a glimpse of darkness beyond. Tiny points of light pierced the veil and with them came a rich, blue glow.

'The moon!' exclaimed Brace.

Sure enough, the full moon hung high over their heads, and though they saw it only fleetingly through the churning fog, the sight of it took their breath away. Huge, bright, surreal and unexpected after it had vanished from the sky so many days before, it had returned, impossibly full, unbearably bright and ringed with a halo of white crystal which stared blankly down at them from the unattainable heavens. Ominous it was, and thrilling, and all five of the flying dragons halted in the air and gazed up at it in rapture, hardly daring to believe it was there, not wanting to consider what events – terrible or wonderful – its return might herald.

For Tallow and Volley, plain-thinking dragons of sky and forest, to see it again was simply good, for it surely marked a strengthening of the natural order. For Brace and Scoff, both of whom had witnessed horrors at closer quarters, its presence now was more frightening, more mysterious. And Fortune, in seeing the moon, saw something different again. He saw an impartial eye which looked down upon the land, an eye which looked down on them just as it looked down

430

on Wraith, on Shatter, on Gossamer . . . An eye with no sense of good or evil, right or wrong, nature or charm, but one which simply observed.

It is down to us, he thought bleakly.

The thought filled him with terror, and at that instant he wanted to do nothing else but turn around and flee. He dropped suddenly from the cloudy air, landing on the snow with a thud and whirling round to stare at the entrance to the portal. There, in the tunnel, he saw Wraith!

The great, spidery dragon-monster scrabbled towards him, limbs thrashing, wings slicing the air, fangs bared beneath wild, yellow eyes . . . and then the apparition was gone. He staggered back as snow flurried around him. Concern grew on the faces of his descending friends as he glanced up at them, panic-stricken.

'I can't . . .' he mumbled haltingly, stumbling on the slippery ground.

'You can!'

The cry came from the top of the cairn of fallen rocks. Dragon necks turned to face that way. Fortune looked up at the figure stood there, set against the flickering moon with an artful sense of timing and composition. A dragon. A charmed dragon. 'CUMBER!'

Fortune bounded up the slope with a sudden, glorious rush of energy, leaving big Tallow reeling in his wake and squinting quizzically past him at this strange, scrawny visitor.

White scales flickered as Cumber spread his wings wide to embrace his friend but even that welcome was not enough.

Fortune bowled him clean head over haunches in his joy and they tumbled together, snow exploding in all directions, down the other side of the mound and out of sight of their comrades. There they fussed and pummelled like infants until at last, their initial excitement at least somewhat abated, they strode together over the rock pile to an even greater reunion where Cumber wept for Scoff's wings and Brace for the first time embraced the young Charmed as a true friend.

The darkness which had been welling in Fortune's breast burst in an agony of joy at his friend's safe return, leaving exhaustion but also adding new light and hope for, as they had begun the story so too would they end it — friends together.

'And Gossamer?' he had asked in his first frenzy.

'She's all right,' Cumber had replied. 'She's near. You'll be with her again soon.'

Light and hope. And an end to the winter in sight. *Perhaps*, a voice warned, which was neither that of Gossamer nor his mother.

'Your wings!' he exclaimed, staring at Cumber. 'Your scales!'

'Do you like it? I had my doubts as to its effectiveness, of course, but then I always say that if you don't try a thing out then you'll never know if it will succeed, although having said that . . .'

'You'd blend in if you didn't talk so much!' quipped Brace and they all laughed together again.

As they caught their breath in the shadow of the cliff, a titanic explosion sent a fireball high into the sky over Covamere. They all turned their heads towards it.

'Dragons are dying,' rumbled Tallow. 'There is work to be done.'

'Tallow's right,' agreed Scoff, his face suddenly serious. 'We part again, Fortune?'

Fortune looked around at the faces staring in at him and noticed, not for the first time, that he seemed to be at the centre of the group. He nodded.

'I'm afraid so,' he said. 'Cumber? We have been this way before. Do you care to try it again?'

'Well, Fortune!' came the eager reply. 'I'd like to see a dragon try and stop me!'

Cumber's response raised a chuckle among the dragons but it was weak and short-lived. It was clear now that they would indeed part again and the division was quickly agreed: Fortune and Cumber would journey again into the mountain in search of Halcyon, while Tallow, Volley and Scoff would continue on to Covamere in an attempt to join with the rest of the Flight and the Hardship . . . and somehow try to put an end to the fighting.

'Brace?' prompted Fortune, for he alone stood apart from the group. 'What do you wish to do? You can decide — any of us would be proud to have you at our side.'

432

Brace hung his head, embarrassed.

'Well,' he said at length. 'It has taken me a long time to find my place in all of this. When I saw poor Scoff here in that awful prison, it was then that my mind was made up. The conflict must end, and there's only one place where that can be made to happen – in the heart of the conflict itself. I will go with Scoff.'

'Well said, young dragon,' murmured Scoff with approval.

'Good luck, then,' said Fortune, staring hard at Brace and seeing with pleasure that the youngster was more than capable of holding his gaze.

'Good luck to you, Fortune.'

With that they parted, Fortune and Cumber standing close together as their comrades lifted into the bleak sky and turned towards the strengthening wind. Fog rushed past them, fragmenting now and revealing more and more of the night sky. When they had vanished the two friends turned in unison towards the waiting portal.

'Come on then,' said Fortune.

On the mountain summit a dragon looked out from his hiding place between two closely-positioned stones. His breath was short and cold. His eyes were hard and red. He was still Shatter. Just.

His memory worked sporadically now. With a great effort he was able to piece together recent events: he had led his army through the fog and on to Covamere. How had he achieved that? Something had guided him. His own greatness, he supposed. The attack. The instant it had started he himself had fled to the rear of the advancing column, flying back and then up, and then further up and on and on, flying higher and higher until the fog dropped away beneath him and the air was thin and the mountain narrowed to a peak.

The mountain top! Of course, such a retreat as had never been known before. No boulder here to fall, but it was good enough. Here he could stay, safe and alone, without this troublesome world intruding upon his tortured senses.

Except that another dragon had intercepted him – Barker's son, the dangerous one. Had he not already killed this dragon? Or had that been another? His insanity was now a maelstrom, a whirlpool of doubt where only one speck of certainty remained.

I! I remain! I exist! Nothing else!

Still, he felt compelled to avoid the war he had precipitated, for although the outside world was only a product of his own mind, still it threatened him. This was the paradox which was most distressing to him: although he was alone he felt vulnerable nonetheless.

So, in retreat in every imaginable way, he had met Wood just short of the summit and attacked him without hesitation. The youngster's wing had broken easily enough; he would have finished the job had he not heard the voices of the two females from over the ridge. Crumbling confidence had combined with chinks in the scaly armour he had grown to keep the outside world at bay to hold him in retreat while Wood had crawled away into the sanctuary their presence seemed to offer.

And so now he watched as the females tended to him, and as he watched it all became so simple. Once he had worked to destroy the Charmed. Then, at the Fortress, he had finally seen that all creation needed to be demolished – charm, nature, dragon, even land itself.

But now, putting all that confusion aside, he saw his destiny more clearly than he ever had before. The world, this dizzying, false world, had contracted around him until now it comprised only this mountain top, this ring of stones, these three dragons. All else was void but they, they were real as was he, and only in their destruction would he find true salvation and the ultimate triumph. This was his goal; to this confrontation had his whole life been directed!

In a world shaped by his own insanity, Shatter still believed that he was Lord, and it was this unshakeable belief which made him dangerous. Perhaps invincible.

'Which one?' said Cumber.

They stood in a low, broad cave and were faced with a choice of three tunnel entrances. Neither one of them recognized this chamber; indeed, they had travelled only a short distance into the main passageway from the entrance before they had reluctantly agreed that the place was wholly changed from when they were last here.

'I think the Maze may move things around,' said Cumber mournfully.

'This "Maze" again,' replied Fortune with a groan. 'Will I ever find out what it is?'

'Probably sooner than you think, if this tunnel takes us where I think it's taking us.'

But now they had to choose, and the choice was impossible.

'Perhaps it doesn't matter which path we take,' exclaimed Cumber suddenly. 'If the Maze wants to guide us, then it doesn't matter, don't you see? If we're really meant to be here then we can go any way we want!'

'Some maze,' grumbled Fortune as they picked the middle tunnel, 'if all paths lead to the same place.'

On they trudged. The tunnels were wide and rough-hewn, cut from the same black rock of which the whole mountain was formed. As they journeyed it became hotter.

'Does she still love me?' blurted Fortune abruptly. Cumber groaned.

'Does a dragon fly?' he responded. 'Fortune, you were made for each other, can't you see that?'

'And she was all right when you left her on the mountain?'

They had already exchanged their news in brief, and Cumber had reassured Fortune that Gossamer and Velvet were probably in the safest place of all at the moment, and as far away from the battle as any dragon on the mountain. His own eyes had widened when Fortune had told him matter-of-factly about the charm he had seemed to wield at the prison, and earlier when the Deadfall had collapsed.

'And you say the power left you again?' he quizzed.

'I don't think I ever really had it. I think it was this Maze of yours working though me.'

'Fortune, you are a master of the understatement. If you knew the import of what you're suggesting, well, I just don't know . . . I mean, do you realize what you've done?'

Fortune laughed. 'Stop blustering, Cumber,' he chuckled. 'No, of course I don't – I'm only a Natural.'

'Hmm, yes, of course you are.'

Cumber seemed to float away then on a cloud of internal

thoughts. Fortune observed his distant expression with a wry smile.

'How I've missed you, Cumber,' he said. 'I can't tell you what it means to me that we're travelling this last path together.'

'Hmm? Oh, well, don't then, because you ought to save your energy for walking — and whatever may come later on.'

Fortune nodded, and was reminded by Cumber's enthusiasm how tired he himself really was. Cumber was his strength now — he really did need him or else he would surely drop where he stood.

I have so little to give, he thought helplessly.

He stumbled, the heat making him giddy, and when he rose again with Cumber's assistance he heard a rasping noise which he only gradually realized was the sound of his own breath in his throat. Swallowing hard he staggered on, his vision blurring before it steadied again.

'Talk to me, Cumber,' he croaked. 'Guide me.'

And so Cumber told him about Velvet, about how she could match him in conversation word for word, about her indomitable enthusiasm and fierce loyalty. As he spoke of her his voice softened and Fortune felt new energy trickle into him.

'Why, Cumber,' he smiled. 'A dragon might almost think you felt some affection for this Velvet.'

'Oh, well . . . hmm . . .' floundered Cumber, quite unbalanced. 'Yes, as I said, you keep quiet and save your breath, Fortune. We've a long way to go, I've no doubt about that.'

As they moved on through the Plated Mountain's deep, black tunnels the sounds of distant battle filtered through to their ears, but they were remote and muffled; they felt protected here.

'If the world were a hurricane,' whispered Fortune, 'this place would be its eye.'

'The world is a hurricane, Fortune. That's exactly what the Turning is.'

'Tell me about Mantle again,' murmured Fortune, but the tide of fatigue rose again and he found himself clinging to Cumber's voice as though to a piece of driftwood yet hearing little of what he actually said. He could no longer distinguish the sounds of battle from the humming in his own head, and although the tunnels were now unbearably hot he started to shiver.

'Something wants me,' he mumbled, 'but I'm not sure I want to go.'

Cumber eyed him uncertainly but before he could speak again the tunnel pulled them round in a tight curve and the noises of war grew abruptly louder, reaching a crescendo as they passed through a narrow section of passage. Heavy blows pummelled the walls here; flakes showered from the ceiling. For a breath or two it seemed that some mighty charm was about to break through.

But it did not. They proceeded still deeper, the noise died and a new silence slipped in to take its place, calming and reassuring. The humming in Fortune's head lessened too, and he found himself able to concentrate on Cumber's words again.

'. . . a lot like Ordinal,' he was saying, 'and an impressive dragon in his own way. It was Mantle who spurred us on when we were in danger of lingering at Aether's Cross, you see, or so he told me. In fact, I hope it's Mantle we'll find at the end of this tunnel, because you see I think Halcyon has gone beyond needing other dragons now — he may even be dead already for all I know.

'Mantle knows what's happening, Fortune. Trolls' bones moving, charm moving, moving away from the world and the Realm, and it's all to do with the Maze — I saw the entrance to that place in Mantle's chamber, you know — so if we're here to do anything at all it's to find a way to save the charm before it's destroyed forever, although I don't think even Mantle really knows how that can be achieved, or even if it's possible at all . . .'

On he spoke, filling in the spaces he had left between the facts he had already shared with his natural friend, speaking about the Turning, about how magic was leaking from the world, about the rings of stone he and Gossamer and Velvet had systematically demolished . . . and about how little he really understood.

'If charm dies,' he said, 'the cycle will end and the world will cease to turn. And when that happens it will cease to be. That's what Mantle told me — I suppose that's really all he told me when you sum it up. The world needs saving.'

'But how?' put in Fortune, listening carefully but staring hard into the gloom of the tunnel ahead. Was there light?

Cumber sighed. 'I think Mantle and Halcyon have a plan,' he said, 'but they have no real confidence in it. I was a part of it, helping them up on the mountain with Gossamer and Velvet, but . . .' Here he paused.

' "But"?' prompted Fortune, at which Cumber swung round and presented him with a sly grin.

'But they didn't reckon on you, Fortune,' he replied.

They traversed another narrow space in the passage and emerged suddenly into the light Fortune had seen shortly before – Mantle's chamber, but much changed since Cumber had been here last.

It had all but disintegrated. A monstrous glare filled the whole cave, its source a fat beam of colourless light which punched its way up from the chasm and turned the blackness of the rock to bland milk. The floor had been reduced to a broken ledge encircling the shaft of light, and the trolls' bones had vanished, every one, leaving walls and ceiling quite empty.

And one third of the way round this narrow ledge was a dark mound which both dragons took at first to be a pile of black scales, but which Cumber eventually realized was a dragon. A black dragon.

'Wraith?' whispered Fortune.

'Mantle!' cried Cumber in anguish.

Without further ceremony he hurried around the precarious ledge to where the old dragon – or his body – lay.

CHAPTER 37

The Healing

Gossamer and Velvet listened as Wood gave them a brief account of Shatter and his rise to supremacy. More painful for them all was his confession that he had fought with Fortune.

'We were growing apart even at South Point,' he said with a remote look in his eyes. 'But that is no excuse. I would never have wished us to grow this far apart. I wish I could see him again.'

Gossamer saw the pain behind his telling of this part of the tale but did not press him on it, sensing that this was neither the time nor the place.

As Wood spoke she felt herself grow angry at the unspeakable destruction these two dragons, Shatter and Wraith, had brought upon the world, of the exiles they had imposed, of the deaths in which they had rejoiced. And, looking at the sadness in Wood's eyes, she found herself mourning just as much the friendships these troubled times had ripped asunder.

At last Wood concluded his story and she appraised him, her eyes burning. 'So, what now?' she demanded brusquely, her anger and grief spilling into her words.

Wood blinked at her. 'Didn't you hear me?' he replied. 'Shatter's still up here — he must be. You must leave me here and save yourselves.'

'He killed your father,' replied Gossamer bluntly. 'He did this to you.'

But Wood only shook his head, immensely tired.

'My anger is spent,' he said.

'But mine is not!' snapped Gossamer. 'Hear me, Wood —

we're not leaving. If we go, Fortune dies, do you understand?'

The statement spilled out of her mouth before she knew it was even there and shook her to the very core.

But it's true: that is why we're here!

'You can't know . . .' began Wood.

'I can and I do know! Now, give me your wing!'

By now Gossamer was furious, more than anything furious that one dragon could have reduced another to this pitiable state. Reluctantly Wood lurched forward, wincing as the remains of his broken wing caught on the standing stone. Together, with Velvet and Gossamer both supporting the crippled Wood, they struggled from the shelter of the circle's perimeter and into the open space it contained.

'Too exposed,' grunted Wood. 'He'll see us for sure now.'

'Let him!' retorted Gossamer. Her rage warmed further and now, as they started to cross the icy ground within the confines of the ring . . . was there something else too?

'It's changed,' whispered Velvet, who up to now had remained uncharacteristically quiet. And sure enough it had.

The circle had expanded so that it seemed they were crossing a vast plain. At the same time the boulders which defined its edge had grown even further, swelling now to massive proportions and shifting with subtle motions, changing shape until bones and skulls seemed to press against their outer surfaces from the inside. They seemed alive yet dead, aware yet unconscious. Observers, but not participants.

Judges, perhaps.

The three dragons moved in a painful cluster across the new landscape, Wood protesting, Velvet resuming her customary chatter in an attempt to keep up his spirits. Gossamer plodded on with grim determination.

Her goal? The centre of the ring, simply.

Once there? She did not know, but she knew that they needed Wood if they were to succeed in their task tonight. And she knew, though it frightened her to contemplate it, that they needed Shatter too.

The land stretched before them. The ring's centre: a shallow cone raised slightly above its surroundings. The ground:

hot, the snow which lay across it beginning to vaporize, chattering upwards in sudden gouts of steam.

Their trail was stained red with Wood's blood and soon he began to drift into unconsciousness.

'Keep him awake!' ordered Gossamer to Velvet.

No sooner had she spoken than a huge cloud of steam exploded in front of her face. As it cleared she saw, way off in the distance, a dragon step out from between two of the enormous, brooding boulders on the far side of the ring. He paced towards them, his eyes burning red, penetrating her even though he was so far away.

She grimaced, suddenly aware of a growing, an expansion of space. 'He's near!' she cried. 'He's here!'

Shatter stopped, frowning at her shout, and at once they seemed to travel. The world contracted again, snapping shut, locking into place, regaining its true dimensions.

Shatter gazed at her, curious, a mere tree's length away. She looked down. They were on top of a small mound; they were already at the centre of the ring, as they had probably been for some time. Though the arena of the circle was back to its normal size, the stones at its perimeter were still huge and twisted. Gossamer snarled at them, 'Would you betray me? Would you have us deceived?'

They answered not, but her anger swelled.

All around them now the ground steamed, vapour swirling up and out of its seams in a violent dance. It gathered around Shatter then swept past him into space, leaving him dark and menacing, still staring into Gossamer's face.

'Who's first?' he said hungrily, although behind the cold anger of his glare Gossamer felt sure she could see desperation.

'You are,' she replied. She turned her back on him.

Reaching out to where Wood lay, only half-conscious, on the mound, she closed her eyes and spoke a chant which up until this very instant she had quite forgotten. A sprite chant it was, old and weak, but a charm nonetheless. Magic.

Below them a mighty groan shook the ground, as though some underground beast had turned over in its sleep. The snow cover had all but vanished now and the ground was black as the sky. Power filled Gossamer's wings as she folded them gently across Wood's broken wing. Velvet looked on, amazed and afraid.

Gossamer bent low, her entire spirit embracing the injured Wood. She felt charm – earth charm – stirring in her and beginning to flow, and whether it was hers or that of another she did not care; she cared only that it came and that it worked, and that she could help direct it on its healing course.

And then Shatter attacked. He raced up the low hillock, knocking Velvet to one side and then turning to confront Gossamer. She lay still over Wood, her wings covering his whole body, her heart beating a slow, heavy rhythm as it pulsed life through them both.

Shatter paused, his confidence ebbing. He felt the life here!

This female is so strong, he thought. *She is so real!*

She turned to him now, her face calm. Smiling? The sad smile passed briefly over Gossamer's features as she pulled away from Wood, leaving the young dragon spread-eagled before Shatter's claws. His body was twisted; his injured wing was concealed beneath him.

Now it was Shatter's turn to smile. The pause, the missed heartbeat had passed and now his prey was ready to fall at last. He closed in, leering, saliva steaming in his mouth, red fire dancing in his eyes so that the world became the colour of blood. Teeth parting, he bent down towards the sacrifice that the pitiful, ignorant female had made ready for him.

'Mantle!' shouted Cumber, heedless of his own safety. The old dragon was surely dead but he had to be certain. Close behind him came Fortune, concerned as much for his friend's safety in this inhospitable place as for the welfare of a dragon he had never met. The light flickered close at their side, hot and humid like the breath of a waking monster.

'Mantle!'

Cumber threw himself at the pile of scales and almost wept when it turned over, extending a wrinkled neck and opening small yet twinkling eyes. Flakes of blood dropped to the ground wherever Mantle flexed his broken body, but he was alive – alive!

'Wraith,' he murmured. 'He was here, but he is . . . more.'

'Don't speak,' urged Cumber. 'We must get you out of here.'

But Mantle protested as vigorously as his sad condition allowed.

'I must speak,' he began, then he saw Fortune for the first time. He looked quizzically at Cumber. 'A Natural?' he said slowly. 'Here?'

'This is Fortune,' explained Cumber defensively, for it seemed that Mantle did not approve. Fortune himself said nothing, only observed the exchange between these two charmed dragons. Something was chiming behind Mantle's cautious disapproval, something which set his heart racing.

'Hmm.' Mantle closed his eyes briefly. 'Does this Fortune know of the Turning?'

'He does,' responded Cumber, casting a nervous glance back at his friend.

'Then let him tell me of it.'

Cumber dithered, out of his depth. At last Fortune stepped forward, taking care not to lost his grip on the precipitous ledge. 'There is a cycle,' he began slowly, 'like a cycle of seasons. Take charm – it has had its summer, but now winter has come. The next summer will belong to nature, and then its winter will come. And so on: charm, nature, charm, nature, turning endlessly about each other.

'But that's not all there is to it,' he went on with growing excitement. 'That's what the turning of the world is, but it can't do it on its own. Every time a winter comes there is the threat of death for both charm and nature, for the whole cycle, the whole world. Every time a winter comes that ultimate death must be averted.

'Winter has come at last to this cycle of charm, as it has for countless cycles before, and as then a way must be found now to stop the world from turning too far, otherwise the winter will never end! All will be lost: nature, charm, the Realm, the world, perhaps even the very fabric which holds them all together. An eternal winter which we cannot conceive because we would not even exist!'

Fortune paused, panting hard. Mantle appraised him with cold, hard eyes.

'And the Maze?' he demanded.

443

'I think,' said Fortune hesitantly, 'I think the Maze is the heart of charm, perhaps even the heart of the world. When the world turns this time it will turn about the Maze, and the Maze alone has the power which is needed to avert the eternal winter.'

'Impressive,' remarked Mantle, flicking a glance at Cumber, who was listening to Fortune with his mouth hanging open. He never knew his friend had such insight — it was like hearing a different dragon! Then Mantle spoke again. 'But?' he said.

'But,' repeated Fortune, frowning into the light. 'But there is a problem. If the Maze is the heart of charm — if in fact it is charm — then it must sacrifice itself so that nature may finally prevail and the world turn true. In order that it may one day live again, it must die now.

'It must know this, and that makes it unpredictable. And very dangerous.'

'Excellent,' mused Mantle.

'Fortune!' Cumber exclaimed. 'I never knew you knew all that! I never knew it! How do you know it; how do you know it's true?'

'I don't,' answered Fortune with a faint smile. 'But it tastes true, doesn't it?'

And Cumber had to agree that it did.

'Which brings us neatly around to Wraith,' announced Mantle, still hunched over upon himself but stronger of voice now and more purposeful. 'As you have no doubt guessed, he came here and attacked me, then forced his way into the Maze. He is in there now, even as we dally here.' He nodded into the depths of the light-filled chasm. 'This Halcyon and I had long planned, but now . . . now I wonder if we were not wrong all along.' Here he looked up again.

Looked at Fortune.

'There are precedents for everything,' he continued. 'All which happens has happened before: the Turning, the fall of charm, and even the presence of a natural dragon in the chamber of the Keeper of the Maze of Covamere.'

Cumber eyes grew wide, for although he knew in outline the old story of the Natural who had dared to challenge the Maze he knew nothing of its detail, nor indeed had he ever dreamed of considering it in the context of current events.

Fortune felt his heart stop, and in doing so became painfully aware of the hole which had always existed there, a hole so familiar that it was like a wound which would never be healed. And he remembered the dream at the prison camp, when he had fainted.

'A Natural entered the Maze long ago,' explained Mantle, largely for Fortune's benefit but Cumber too listened intently. 'And though he failed the challenge he emerged unscathed, and in doing so rescued a charmed dragon who was lost in the void therein. A legend was made — although now it has faded — and the two dragons concerned moved away from Covamere. Now one of them has returned.'

'Wraith?' interjected Cumber excitedly. Mantle nodded.

'He was the lost dragon,' he confirmed.

'And the other? The Natural?'

'That name I think Fortune knows,' Mantle replied softly.

With tears in his eyes Fortune said the name. 'Welkin,' he murmured. 'My father.'

'Indeed,' Mantle breathed. 'This changes everything.'

'You met him?' quavered Fortune.

'He was a great dragon. Yes, I was proud to meet him.'

Fortune wiped away the tears from his eyes and looked out into the chasm.

'Then if it wasn't for my father Wraith would not be here.'

'Yet Wraith was our last hope,' responded Mantle, 'mine and Halcyon's. There is a task to be done within the Maze of Covamere and it seemed to us that there was only one dragon with the power to achieve it, however evil he might be.'

Fortune smiled.

'But now there's another,' he said.

'Now there is another.'

Cumber's gaze darted between the two dragons and he trembled with pent-up energy. But this was just too much!

'Excuse me!' he exploded. 'But are you suggesting that Fortune should go in there? Because if you are then you're looking at one dragon who'll . . .'

'Who'll do what?' interrupted Fortune, grabbing his wings and shaking him. 'Cumber, it's my choice to go or not — not yours, not Mantle's. If my father was here that's one thing;

445

if Wraith is here that's one thing; if I'm to go in there that's something else entirely. And only I can decide.'

He held the amazed Cumber tight for a few breaths more before embracing him hard then, no sooner had he hugged him, than he pulled away again and turned back to Mantle.

'Your decision?' asked the old dragon.

This question Fortune did not need to ponder.

'Go with Cumber!' he commanded. 'He will see you to safety but . . . but I have a feeling we will meet again.'

With a dazzling smile he slapped Cumber's flank and turned into the light. He paused briefly, flicking his eyes around the narrow ledge which encircled the entrance to the Maze. The rock was beginning to crumble, its edges turning to powder as the Maze tugged at it from far below; the whole cave was trembling.

'Find me a way out, Cumber!' he cried as he leaped into the overwhelming glare. 'And get out yourselves . . .' His voice floated away as he was swallowed up.

There was an almighty crashing sound, the light shrank and folded in impossible directions, then blinked out.

The floor was whole again, the entrance to the Maze gone.

One way in, one way out.

The Maze of Covamere was sealed.

For Wood, time had slowed to a miraculous crawl.

He watched his life's blood drain into the snow as he was carried across the summit, and watched the snow turn to air as the ground boiled away.

A young, female voice hammered at him relentlessly, preventing his escape into unconsciousness and possibly beyond. He felt endlessly, irreparably tired.

All he wanted to do was sleep. In his dreams his mother would be alive and love his father, he would still know his dear friend Fortune and Welkin – old, great Welkin – would still lie in his hollow and watch the night dragons play in the sky.

In his dreams the world would be still and safe. In his dreams he would be content. He thought the dreams had come when behind the closed lids of his eyes he suddenly saw a picture. It moved with a semblance of reality but it was rough and dark, as though seen through stone.

How could a dragon see through stone? Fortune was in the picture. He was drowning as Wood had thought him drowned in Ordinal's cave, except this time he was drowning in rock, rock made alive, liquid rock which battered and crushed him at every turn. His jaws were white as though lit from within. They screamed in agony. Light flared from Fortune's eyes, signalling the direction of his gaze – up!

But every time he looked up a fresh wave of deadly rock knocked him back. Escape was up, up was safety, yet something prevented him from fleeing – a barrier, a wall, a web . . .

Fortune howled in pain and the liquefied rock splashed out towards Wood, towards his injured wing where it struck him, burning, burning!

A surge of energy filled his body, and an ecstasy.

He flung open his eyes to see Shatter, the mad dragon, the murderer of his father, reaching over him with his jaws agape. His body came back to him, his tiredness fled and he drew up his wings. His wings!

Whole again, healed, his wings caught the air and pulled him aside as Shatter lunged. Wood's body was strong and he bore down as his sworn enemy sprawled before him. His teeth struck sparks off the heavy scales at the base of Shatter's neck and he kicked backwards off his flank, snapping one of Shatter's horns in two and cutting a deep, bloody groove across his exposed side.

He flew out in a broad circle while Shatter gathered his wits and then sped back towards the mound. Head lowered, horns tilted, Wood struck Shatter hard in the throat as the mad dragon lifted his head to sight his foe. The momentum lifted Shatter clean off the ground and flung him halfway across the breadth of the ring of stones. He struck the ground hard, blood spraying from a dozen wounds.

Wings pounding, Wood turned again and bore in, striking low, tossing Shatter high towards the waiting rocks. This time the wounded dragon fell limp, quite dazed and apparently unaware of his surroundings. The stones stood, protecting their boundary, watching the duel. Waiting.

Once more Wood thundered around, flying wide and far outside the circle. He wheeled about the summit as though

447

he owned the whole mountain, yet his aim was fixed firmly on the one target which filled his vision: Shatter.

It came to him then, as he soared in the moonlight, that where he had once sworn revenge upon the Charmed, now all his venom, all his fury was being thrust at a natural dragon. It was a revelation, and though the realization did not banish all his fears and doubts about the charmed ones, what it did was to make him ache even more to see Fortune again, to talk and to run with him. To fly with him. And maybe, if he could only find a way, to explain.

He re-entered the circle low between two twisted boulders, thumping the air as he sped across the arena for the death blow.

Only Gossamer saw the glint, the final spark of red surfacing in Shatter's eyes. 'Wood!' she cried desperately. 'Leave him! He's . . . !'

But the wind of his passage swept aside her warning and the distance between him and Shatter halved, quartered . . .

Wood thought he heard Fortune's voice cry a warning to him, but he could not be sure.

He barely had time to see Shatter rock back on his haunches and raise deadly, bloodstained claws before he struck. Shatter's talons tore out his throat even as Wood's jaws bored their way through broken ribs and closed on the mad dragon's failing heart.

The impact was massive. Gossamer watched, her breath frozen, as the two dragons careered in their fatal embrace across the rest of the circle to the far perimeter where they crashed against the tallest, narrowest boulder in the ring of guardians.

They fell together down the side of the boulder to the ground and lay there motionless.

A mighty groan issued from the standing stone and it shook. Then, gradually, it pulled shallow, root-like spurs from the ground at its base and tipped over, falling outwards with a rumble and a rush of air until it hit the rock floor with a great concussion.

Tiny pebbles and splinters of stone cascaded around it for a time and then all was calm.

The two female dragons moved hesitantly to where the warring males lay inert. Shatter was dead, his body snapped almost in two by the sheer force of Wood's final blow.

Wood eyed them from the bloody remains, his breath a damp gurgle in the ruins of his throat. 'Now you know what you have to do,' he whispered, his eyes dull lenses in the pale moonlight.

Gossamer looked through her tears at the fallen stone and nodded. Yes, now she knew.

'I think . . . I think I'll lie here for a while,' said Wood with a crooked smile. 'Time you two did some work.'

'But we must look after you first,' began Gossamer.

Then Velvet stepped up to her and whispered,

'He's right. We should go to work. Now.'

As if to reinforce what Velvet had said the ground trembled behind them and they glanced round to see a narrow crack race to the far side of the ring. Colourless, angry light filtered up from the split, staining the air with its heat.

'Tell Fortune,' croaked Wood, 'tell him I'm sorry.'

Gossamer stared at him for a long, held breath, then forced a smile across her agonized face and replied,

'Tell him yourself!'

Wood nodded weakly and drifted into what may have been sleep.

Reluctantly, knowing in their hearts that there was nothing more they could for him, Gossamer and Velvet turned to the stones of the last ring of stones and made ready to save Fortune.

CHAPTER 38

Injured Mountain

Tunnel of light.

Sheer and brilliant walls streaking to infinity. Tunnels dividing, dividing again, turning and separating, looping, stretching, multiplying, multiplying . . .

The Maze of Covamere.

Fortune crawled through tunnels within tunnels within tunnels. Wind tore at him from every direction, distances crushed him with their immensity, time laughed and fled towards eternity. The Maze was . . . The Maze *was*.

With an effort which nearly broke his back Fortune turned his head up to try and look out upon the spectacle of the labyrinth through which he made his slow, painful way. He was in a tunnel, that much was familiar, except it was a tunnel not of rock but of light, a glowing tube which flexed with a life of its own. The brilliant walls throbbed with energy; the air – if air it was – was hot and dry. Ahead and behind the tunnel divided into innumerable other, identical tunnels, so that with every step he took Fortune had to decide: which way? This or that? Here? There? The choices were impossible, the prospect of escape from this overwhelming system of tubes and channels even less likely than that of success in reaching its centre.

Is that where I need to go? The centre? Which way is it, when there are so many ways?

Lost and alone, trapped in a maze where all directions were false, Fortune cried out for help. But there was no help to be given and he could only crawl on, head bowed, heart cast down, hope all but gone.

* * *

The battle of Covamere was already raging when the storm reared and pounced on the Plated Mountain.

Dragons flinched and then fought on beneath its shadow but this storm was not one of mere cloud and thunder. Clouds boiled from the cracks and ravines which were starting to open up in every exposed mountain slope, sucking up the brutal magic of the warring Charmed and hurling it back down tenfold. Shafts of lightning dragged behind them greater shafts of charm, striking and splitting the earth further with titanic blows. The ground shook beneath the onslaught and slowly, inexorably, the mountain began to crumble.

On the ground the fighting was fierce and relentless. The initial advantage of surprise was now lost to the Naturals and they had scattered throughout Covamere, grouping and regrouping as the Charmed chased them out from the arena and up the mountain.

And with the unearthly storm pressing them hard against the soil, no dragon dared fly. What had once been fog now boiled with hot rain and exploding ash and the sky was no longer a place for dragon or indeed any creature who desired to live.

Charmed died under the weight of countless Natural attackers; Naturals perished by the score as a single charmed dragon fired a bolt of fire charm into their midst. Magic seared the darkness and the Realm seethed at the limits of vision as it poured its nightmare power into the world. A flash of lightning froze a tableau of natural dragons quartered by a slicing claw of charm; frenzied Naturals fed from a pile of Charmed corpses. The mountain shook as dreadful energies began to rip it from within.

Yet through it all wove dragons with a greater purpose. Through the mayhem, resolute and strong-hearted, the dragons of the Flight and the Hardship forged their way, dying like the rest but also begging, crying out for an end to the slaughter, for they alone guessed that here on the Plated Mountain was surely every dragon left in the world. Few dragons were now alive who were not now fighting to the death against others of their kind.

But the storm lowered further, squeezing the dragons ever tighter in its embrace with the breaking land and the message of peace was barely heard. The fighting continued at an ever faster pace.

Cumber and Mantle were blown from the collapsing tunnel like two leaves on a winter wind. They fell together against the cairn and even then had to scrabble further across the plateau to avoid both the falling rocks and cracks which were opening in the ground. The air was scorching; thunder roared in their ears; the light of battle was not far away.

No sooner had Fortune entered the Maze than Mantle's chamber had started to cave in. Their desperate flight through the gyrating tunnel had been a nightmare of landslides and slicing rocks and choking, burning soot, but escape they had, miraculously. Mantle's wounds had been less severe than Cumber had first thought and even he had managed to negotiate that murderous passageway without sustaining further injury.

Now they struggled together across the shaking ground, heads lowered against the hot rain and tumbling ash, desiring only to be away from this hell.

But where to go?

Find me a way out, Fortune had asked of Cumber, but what had he meant?

'Up!' shouted Mantle over the cacophony.

'What?! Through that?'

Cumber glanced up into the whirling, flashing cloud which hung above them. Surely Mantle didn't mean . . . ?

'Where you left your friends!' Mantle cried. 'There is work still to be done!'

'Up?' Cumber's voice trembled.

High above the storm Gossamer and Velvet laboured as they had never laboured before. Periodically Gossamer glanced at Wood; the young dragon was still barely alive, but the sound of his breathing was so tortured, so laboured, that she held little hope for him.

Arcs of lightning and even charm were reaching up from the broiling cloud bank which the fog had become, vaporizing the ice on the summit approaches and occasionally earthing on the standing stones themselves. Velvet regarded

452

these great discharges with dread, Gossamer with a combination of suspicion and awe.

'I'm tired, Gossamer,' gasped Velvet, leaning heavily against one of the stones. 'Can't we rest?'

'No, dear,' came Gossamer's reply. 'We have no time. Shut your eyes and keep moving. We can do this.'

Together they had felled half of the stones in the circle by pushing them over bodily until they collapsed outwards, pointing away from the centre. Half remained standing; both dragons were exhausted.

'I don't understand why we're . . .'

'To save Fortune,' Gossamer cut in. 'Don't ask me how – I just know that we must.'

With a groan Velvet raised herself up and wedged her upper body against the coarse surface of the rock poised above them. Gossamer flew to its peak and, grasping the top, leaned outwards on stretched wings so as to tip it off balance. Crystals of ice and rock shattered at its root and with a thick, tearing sound it rolled out of the ground and thumped on to its side.

The two dragons stood, their chests heaving, surveying their work.

'They fall easily,' said Velvet between breaths. 'But there's so many of them!'

'Come on,' panted Gossamer. 'Each time we drop one there's one less.'

They moved to the next stone in the circle and bent again to their strange task.

Quite unaware of the storm which was sinking its fangs into the mountain, quite unaware of anything but the endless elaborations of the Maze's tunnels, Fortune pressed on, his throat dry and raw. There was no sound here – even the constant wind was silent – but his own heartbeat thumped in his head.

Hopelessly disorientating, each stretch of tunnel was identical, each fork in the passage looked the same as the last. How could a dragon know where to go?

Dragons floated before him, Gossamer's face most vivid among those of all his friends. And there was . . .

'Wood!' Wood indeed, but with his body twisted and

broken. All the dragons he had ever loved, his father included, his old, kind face clear now in Fortune's deluded vision where it had never been in his waking mind. All the dragons . . . But which did he need?

It was Gossamer's face, of course, which dominated his blurred vision, but he knew that was not what he needed, not here and now. Reluctantly, feeling the tearing in his heart as he did so, he pushed it to the background. Who then?

A dragon bearing fresh, white scales. Cumber!

His familiar face wove before Fortune's streaming eyes. His mouth was moving.

'What? What are you saying, Cumber?'

The words were faint, broken by the wind.

'. . . which way you go . . .'

'What, Cumber?'

Fortune strained as he had never strained before. On these words all depended.

'. . . doesn't matter . . .'

The wind stopped abruptly. Silence, with not even the beat of his heart to be heard.

Then a glorious smile of relief across his face, and crashing with it the tunnel walls, all the tunnel walls, exploding into space as the labyrinth unwound all about him. Coils of light whipped away in all directions, shrinking into the darkness which held the complexity of the maze in its cold embrace. Space, and void, and simplicity at last.

'It doesn't matter which way you go!' shouted Fortune ecstatically. 'All paths lead the same way in the end!'

And here, at least, it was true.

Floating free, he looked down past his own wings to see the glowing network of tunnels in which he had been trapped spread out beneath him, a spider's web big enough to snare dragons. *And I have escaped it!*

He reminded himself that he had escaped only this first part, this lesser maze: still he had not escaped the Maze itself. For the moment however this did not diminish his excitement, for what dragon could have remained unmoved by the sights which were laid before Fortune now?

Over the whole world he flew. The glowing maze was

454

dimming, melting into the landscape which was spread below him. The whole world was opened out flat like the skin of a fruit, vast and wondrous. As he flew over its contours Fortune had the disconcerting impression that as well as looking down he was also looking up, seeing oceans turned to mountain ranges, mountains become craters. Across the world he soared, passing continents he had never heard of, let alone seen, awed by the scale of creation, moved by its beauty.

There was a great ocean, there a desert, there . . . there a mountain, *the* mountain! He sped towards the Plated Mountain, and it was only now that he realized how much it was that he was really seeing. Points of light blazed up the mountain slopes and he knew in an instant that each point of light was a dragon.

Across the whole world he had seen no other lights. All the dragons were here, now. The lights were winking out inexorably, one by one. Wherever he looked, another dragon died. The battle!

Then it was past, flashing behind him in a blur of speed, although not before he saw something else which pierced his mind, something in the sea beyond the land. But too soon that was gone as well, and it was then that Fortune realized that he was no longer controlling his own movement. Frantically he thrashed his wings, trying desperately to turn back so that he might help the countless dragons dying for no reason on the Plated Mountain. But he was pulled on relentlessly and forced to give in to whatever force was directing him towards his final goal. He looked up and saw the Realm.

It crouched over the world, but where the world was great and bright the Realm was a small, bleak stone. It moved about. It pulsated like an angry sore, reaching out tendrils of shadow which brushed the speeding world and immediately shrank back as though scalded. Fire belched from the cracks which ruined its surface, and displayed to Fortune creatures which his mind refused to see, lumbering through the flames in endless torture.

Below him the world, above him the Realm. He turned from them to face the darkness of the void.

* * *

'The battle's moving upslope,' said Tallow, his keen ears finding detail amid the overwhelming bombardment of sound. 'I suppose we should follow, but . . .'

They halted here, suddenly unsure of what they should do.

It had been a short, cruel flight from the lesser portal where they had left Fortune and Cumber, and they had not needed Tallow's skills to find their way: they had needed only to follow the light and noise of war.

But although they saw much devastation on the way to Covamere — pillars and dwellings overturned, burned corpses and severed limbs scattered heedlessly across ruined ground — they saw few dragons living; the centre of the fighting, it seemed, had moved on.

They came to ground in the remains of the very arena where Cumber had observed Wraith descend into the midst of his troops, indeed the very place where the battle had started.

'Such a terrible waste,' gasped Brace, casting a horrified eye over the killing field which lay all around them. Dragons both natural and charmed lay heaped in the smoke and snow, fog crawling around them as though preying upon the dead.

'No sign of Wraith's Hardship,' came Scoff's grim comment.

'Nor the Flight,' added Volley sorrowfully.

The ground beneath them heaved and twisted, hot air belching up through fresh tears in its surface. A sudden movement caught Tallow's eye, a flicker of life in a passage-way to their left. Bunching together, they approached with caution. All was dark as Tallow scanned the passage, the flash of rain blurring what little vision he had in the murk. Lightning scored the sky and reached into the narrow space. Three dragons — two Naturals and a Charmed — stood a mere wingspan away, watching them furtively.

Shadows scattered across the ground and walls and the lightning doubled its strength to send a tapestry of light over the confrontation.

'We are the Flight and the Hardship,' intoned the three dragons as one, although there was a disconsolate air to their words. 'There is no alternative to the choices we offer. You must join us. Please.'

'How many are you?' cried Scoff at once, heartened by what he had heard.

'As you see — three,' came the cautious reply.

'Now you're seven!' shouted Brace excitedly.

'We may have a chance,' added Tallow, stepping forward.

'Tallow!' exclaimed one of the Naturals, and it was Volley who recognized her.

'Werth!'

And indeed it was. Werth, who had inspired and bullied the Flight before Fortune had come and who now stood with charred scale and battered horn in the ruins of Covamere. Despite her obvious exhaustion she raised a dazzling smile.

'This is Lumny,' she said proudly, 'and this is Duce. I recruited them! They're with me now, but so many others are dead.'

'You must tell us what you know . . .' began Tallow but Werth cut him short.

'No time for that,' she snapped. 'We must take our word to the battle. It's Fortune's word and it's a good word. We can stop this battle. If we believe it we can do it.'

As she spoke the scorching rain seemed to ease a little and the clouds lifted a fraction, as though the storm had sensed their mutiny.

'The fighting has moved up the mountain,' said Duce, the charmed dragon, confirming Tallow's suspicion. He indicated a side passage with a ragged, yellow wing. 'This way will take us out of Covamere, towards the battle.'

'Then let's go!' cried Brace, leading the way with a flourish.

The thunder came down again, and then the thunder was in the ground, lifting and ripping it, tearing it open in enormous, jagged swathes. Lightning poured from underground, firing its bolts upwards into the cloud and melting the rock from which it was born.

The ground on which the seven dragons were standing danced and then collapsed altogether as a tide of liquid fire surged from deep underground and lifted high into the air. At last the subterranean heat which had once created the Injured Mountains broke through to the Plated Mountain, shattering its base and sending tendrils of fire snaking up its slopes towards the summit. It swallowed the passage, the arena which it flanked and, with titanic gulps, the whole of Covamere.

Gossamer felt the storm turn quiet. Three stones were left standing; the rest lay still around them.

A short distance away, leaning still against the first stone to fall, Wood groaned and turned over sluggishly.

'What's the matter?' asked Velvet with a quavering voice.

'I don't know,' Gossamer replied, 'but it's not good.'

Thunder struck the mountain deep at its heart and suddenly the clouds were lit from behind by a huge, red glow. The light filled and then surpassed the cloud, racing towards them like a growing sun until it disappeared briefly, only to re-emerge through the ground, splitting in two the circular plateau of the summit and filling the widening gap between the two halves with boiling, molten rock.

Gossamer and Velvet were thrown apart by the blast. Gossamer cried out in desperation as she saw Velvet crash to the ground on the opposite side of the great crack which had opened up between them. Wood too was on the other side.

Two of the three remaining stones fell, their collapse unheard in the thunderous roar of the boiling rock; the last tilted back then stopped, staying stubbornly upright, locked solid above Velvet's motionless body.

Gossamer squinted into the glare, dodging the sparks and embers which were exploding from the ever-widening lake of fire. Each breath she waited the further away the opposite shore receded.

The world and the Realm were reduced now to mere specks in the void, but as he watched them recede Fortune saw a shared motion which opened his eyes to a new pattern in the darkness. World and Realm turned together, locked in a circular embrace which sent out faint rings through the void in which he tumbled. The blackness was not featureless but etched with a pattern so fine that its radiating lines might have been spun from a whisper. The pattern formed a network, a gigantic, incomprehensible structure which casually, as if in passing, held the world and Realm – and how many countless other worlds and Realms? – in their rightful places.

It was vast. It was the fabric of everything which was real and much which was not. It was the Maze.

Fortune drank in the awesome spectacle, aware that the Maze did not really look like this, but that this web was merely his own mind's way of interpreting a structure he could not possibly comprehend.

It is so much greater than I realized, he thought, humbled.

As he tumbled he saw that the strands of the web grew dense at one particular point, and with a rush of fear and excitement he realized that it was towards this place that he was falling. His speed increased dramatically and he saw that at the centre of the coiled strands was a hard, tight nugget of light, a glowing orb which expanded rapidly until it filled his vision.

It became enormous until he felt sure it would devour him like the beast it surely was. He closed his eyes tight but it was no good; even through his closed lids he saw it looming. The heart of the Maze!

As he braced himself for the impact the orb suddenly opened petals at once vast and delicate, world-sized vanes ribbed with bands of light, each with the power to swat a star. He passed through and they closed behind him, and he knew that just as the Maze was sealed from the world so its heart was sealed upon him now.

The light whirled, he whirled and blackness descended.

CHAPTER 39

The Seed of Charm

An eyeblink later he awoke.

His own claws, gripping solid ground, or at least a semblance of it. It glowed; pale veins pressed up against it from beneath taut skin. He looked up. The floor curved upwards into walls and a domed ceiling. He was inside a sphere. It was white and radiant, woven from individual strands of light, woven in fact from the very fabric of the Maze. A prison? Or a safe place?

The heart of the Maze.

Here it was that the web of the Maze converged upon itself, wrapping itself tight and close to form a glowing bubble on to the interior skin of which Fortune now clung with fanatic strength. It was cold in here, but more than that it felt . . . sick. The bubble shivered occasionally as though some great fever had infected its weave. Sometimes the shudder was a convulsion which threatened to throw Fortune out into the empty space which the bubble contained; he clung tight and resisted the motion. In a flash he knew that it was this same sickness which had made charmed dragons mad.

Looking up, Fortune thought he could see something floating at the very centre of the heart. But before he could make it out something else appeared from behind it. Something black and huge which unfolded wings like thunderclouds. Something which moved downwards with oily precision. A black dragon. Wraith.

To a large extent it was indeed still Wraith, for the strange merged creature which he and the basilisk had become retained the individual personalities of both progenitors.

Basilisk blood was pumped by dragon heart, and dragon flesh embraced basilisk bone, but within the whole were still two . . . for the time being.

Wraith felt the tug of the basilisk's thoughts like a barb in his mind. To give in to them was a seductive notion, with their promise of immortality and memories to rival those of eternity itself, but there was a bleakness there which Wraith found utterly repulsive. This creature wanted to die!

The prospect of death was one which Wraith rejected so vehemently that he put up formidable barriers to prevent their merging from completing itself. He sensed something of the power which could be his if he let the basilisk more fully into his consciousness, but he did not trust the creature. Rather he hoped to use its charm without recourse to sharing its mind. It loitered within his body like a parasite, one with the strength to aid him in his task, but with the will to see them both destroyed were it only given the chance.

The basilisk's yearning for self-destruction was quite alien to Wraith, for though he did not yearn for immortality — the basilisk's twisted mind was warning enough against that false dream — he yearned even less for suicide.

I will not be defeated, he thought, *however glorious the end. I will prevail!*

And so he held on to that part of him which was dragon, while the rest of him sucked up basilisk magic and basilisk cunning, taking from this ancient creature which seemed content to give of itself and take nothing in return. Quietly it sat within his dragon body, neither threatening nor pleading, simply existing, and waiting, waiting . . .

The Maze Wraith had negotiated before and so it was with comparative ease that he found his way to its heart. Once there he grew doubtful, circling that which he had come to claim, uncertain of what he should do. He had been here once before, after all, and had failed. What had he done wrong?

Then, as he pondered, sifting through basilisk memories for clues as to how he should proceed, a scent came to him on an impossible breeze.

He sniffed, and then smiled, for this was the scent he had tracked across the world, which had eluded him over the years until this very moment. The scent he had long ago

461

learned to hate and which now, at the end, he would use to his own, final glory.

'See, basilisk,' he whispered. 'The Natural comes.'

He closed his eyes.

Fortune watched tensely as Wraith dropped slowly to the skin of the bubble, the outer membrane of the heart of the Maze.

He felt tired but alert — he could see clearly through the thin, cold air of the heart; he could hear its massive pumping. Weariness was within him still but he was managing to hold it in check for the moment; how long he could do this for he could not guess. He waited, conserving what little energy his body had left, and took the opportunity to observe closely the Black Dragon, this titan who had brought war to the world.

His eyes were hidden by confident black lids — Wraith felt secure in here, secure enough not to need his vision. His wings were huge sails possessed of their own terrible beauty, marbled with veins of copper and gold. They were black but they were full of colours more rich than Fortune had ever imagined. His body was a long, glossy skeleton joined with the sparest of flesh. Two pairs of clawed legs were tucked beneath his taut belly while a monstrous third pair reached up along his neck, these extra limbs like shafts of bone grafted from a corpse. Their ends faded into transparency, lost in the magic they wielded. His neck was long and narrow, his head sharp and beautiful.

And still his eyes were closed.

'Natural,' breathed Wraith as he alighted scarcely two wingspans away. 'We are together again.'

His nostrils moved, scenting the air. Fortune frowned but said nothing. There was something about this dragon, a strangeness about his already strange shape. Something on his flank? He could not quite see but it seemed to him that something wriggled there, something white . . .

'Natural,' breathed Wraith again, but this time it sounded like a curse. Steam gathered about his pointed muzzle and drifted out into the heart. Fire gleamed deep within his throat. Then, with a sudden smile, he said, 'How would you help me this time?'

When Fortune offered no reply Wraith, his eyes still firmly shut, paced to and fro, his claws sending tiny sparks into the web wherever they pierced it.

Fortune waited and Wraith opened his eyes. 'Welkin!' he roared. 'Face me for the last time . . . !'

He stopped abruptly, blinking stupidly. 'You're not Welkin,' he said dangerously. Now it was Wraith's turn to frown. His composure returned and he sniffed again the cold air of the Maze's heart.

'Smells like Welkin,' he mused. 'Doesn't look like Welkin. Well, well.'

'I am Welkin's son,' responded Fortune in a brave, false voice. 'And I have his power,' he added, hoping that it might have some meaning.

But Wraith only laughed.

'His power?' he rumbled, his laughter at once angry and humourless. 'He had no power, little dragon.'

Then something turned over in Fortune's mind and suddenly he was angry. 'He had the power to save you, lost dragon!' he snapped, and this time Wraith truly looked as though he had been struck and struck hard.

'What do you know, Natural?' he demanded savagely, his eyes like dead, yellow jewels.

'I know you, Wraith,' replied Fortune at once, balancing on the danger as he probed Wraith's fears. He was guessing at the details but he knew the greater story was true. 'I know you failed the first time you were here, just as you are bound to fail now. You can't even tell me from my father.'

Wraith tried to ignore the taunt but his fury was obvious. Something pulsated between his wings like a second heart. Fortune could not make out its shape. *What could it be? Something inside him?*

'Well,' spat Wraith, lowering his head dangerously, 'you have your father's clever tongue. Perhaps you have his stupid faith too. Do you know why you are here?'

'To save the world,' came the words from Fortune's mouth, and as he said them he felt bound to laugh. With difficulty he put down the urge, although tears still sprang to his eyes and his shoulders shook. To bring himself round he made himself look closely again at Wraith, at the

463

sharpness of his many claws, at the vain gloss of his carapace, at the evil in his eye . . . Yes, there was evil there, but Fortune saw something else too, something which made him almost pity this mighty beast.

Wraith turned slightly and he saw! A white tail projecting from his flank, lashing with a lewdness Fortune found disgusting. *There is something inside him!*

'Stupid!' shouted Wraith. 'As I thought. The world cannot be saved, little dragon. It needs no saving. But it can be owned!' He gestured upwards to the vague shape poised above them at the centre of the heart. 'There is the power to own the world. That is why you are here now, so that we may determine which of us is worthy of that power.'

Wraith's yellow eyes boiled.

'And we both know that only one dragon is worthy,' he concluded with cold venom, 'and it isn't you, Welkin's son!'

'Fortune,' came the calm response. 'My name is Fortune.'

The Plated Mountain shook from the massive, fatal blow it had been struck from deep underground. Ice sublimed, flashing to vapour as molten rock seethed out into air, and new clouds joined the storm as the mountain's winter coat boiled away in the blink of an eye.

Covamere was utterly consumed in the first pulse of the eruption and from the glowing pit where once it had stood a network of fiery channels sprinted up the mountainside, biting and separating as it went until a wedge of blazing lava had all but split the mountain in two. The split widened and slowly, with imperceptible ease, the mountain began to open.

Overhead the storm continued to rage only now it was not the fire of charm which met it from the ground but the fire of the volcano.

Dragons scattered in the face of the unfolding land, the battle disintegrating into an untidy brawl and then suddenly forgotten altogether as each dragon fled for individual sanctuary. In one breath Charmed grappled with Natural and in the next they rushed headlong side by side, urging each other on through the conflagration. In the briefest of times all the rhetoric of Shatter and Wraith was abandoned, all the anger turned to fear. Together at last, at what seemed the end of the world, dragons moved across the dying mountain.

The fires were great beyond description; the sound took dragons beyond deafness into a punishing realm of pain. The flame and the thunder crushed dragons between them.

And yet through the storm, defying all the elements he knew, flew a dragon who knew where to go. Tallow. Behind him flew the Flight and the Hardship, a blunt wedge of dragons both charmed and natural forging a path through the airborne debris, moving upslope, beating a way forward and always upward. As seven they had started, flinging themselves into the unfriendly skies as Covamere had erupted beneath them, and now they flew with numbers doubled, trebled, and growing still.

As they flew they sang. Led by Volley's own, their voices bellowed and filled what few gaps the storm had left for rational sound to be heard, but heard it was and as they battled past there were dragons on the ground who saw them – now white, now black as the fire and lightning played around them – a force with whom they might fight not against each other but against the deadly elements. A force of nature and of charm: of dragons.

One by one dragons climbed the searing air to where the Flight and the Hardship flew; one by one they cast down their differences and flew as one.

Gossamer lurched in a sudden updraught of scalding air. Her wings ached, her skin was blistered and tears flooded from her eyes, dropping away like rain until they flashed into steam and were gone.

She was hovering over the shore of the lava lake which now bisected what remained of the summit. It heaved and bubbled but, for now at least, it seemed to have stopped growing.

On the opposite shore lay Velvet, unconscious if not dead, the last standing stone leaning over her threateningly, its flanks and her body splashed red in the glow of the fire only wingspans away.

Most of the rest of the summit had vanished, consumed by the fire.

Of Wood there was no sign.

The air between Gossamer and the opposite shore was

ablaze with sparks, embers and burning missiles belched up by the lava; even here she was having to dodge the onslaught. She flew higher, seeking a quiet spot, a way through, higher and higher until she was thirty, forty, fifty trees above the summit.

Here the air was ghostly and her wings could barely grip it. Below, the mountain was a dark mass ringed with pulsating storm cloud and split across the middle by a band of fire. As she watched the band widened, spitting flame towards her; it looked like a vast eye opening for the first time in aeons and sending its lightning gaze out into the world. *Surely no troll was ever this big?*

Shaken by the thought, Gossamer gathered her resolve and struggled through the tenuous sky. Even at this great height she had to dodge the fire which the mountain was spewing forth, but dodge she did. Finally, after a short but exhausting flight she managed to tuck her wings to swoop down towards Velvet and the last standing stone.

The air grew thicker and hotter once more and the lake split still further with a clumsy lurch. Molten rock spat orange beads across her path and she ducked away, landing a short distance from Velvet, but even as she touched down on the heaving rock the shore suddenly buckled. A shock wave burst through and struck the leaning stone, tipping its root up into the air and throwing it down towards the ground.

It fell inwards. The wrong way. And beneath its falling shadow lay Velvet, helpless.

'No!' cried Gossamer.

A vibration coursed through the heart of the Maze, throwing both dragons off balance. Gradually the bubble's skin settled again, although it was still rocked by occasional concussions, but all of a sudden it seemed darker.

The light wavered as though its power were being drawn off elsewhere. A grey tint began to percolate through the air.

Fortune found himself staring at the centre of the heart, at the place which Wraith had indicated, and now that the light level had dimmed below its former, blinding intensity he could see what it was that hung there.

The lines of force, or power, or whatever the strands of the web were which made up the structure of the heart, were somehow entwined about this one, central anomaly. Fortune began to sense movement too, as though power were surging along the converging strands to be delivered into this point of focus. Beads of light pulsed along the carriageways which spiralled up to meet at this centre.

With a flash of insight he saw that all the power of the Maze was flowing in to gather at this one, tiny spot in the very centre of its own heart.

The thing which occupied this special place was now clearly visible, but a less spectacular, more inappropriate object Fortune could not imagine. It was a small, grey husk, barely half the size of his own head. It neither shone nor spun, neither pulsed nor spoke. It looked old, and dead, and utterly inconsequential.

And yet he knew it was the reason he was here, the reason he had journeyed into the mountain, the reason he had been imprisoned at Aether's Cross, seen his homeland destroyed, met Cumber, fallen in love with Gossamer ... the reason that the world was turning. The reason for it all. And, somehow, the solution to it all.

Fortune stared hard at it, and as he stared he felt drawn towards it. Dull and lifeless as it was, it captured his attention totally; its very greyness seemed seductive, its very inertness an attraction. With a start he realized that it was beautiful. It beckoned him.

He snapped his eyes away, suddenly dizzy, only to find Wraith observing him as closely as he had been observing the eerie, grey husk.

'So you want it, too,' said the Black Dragon.

In the time it took him to take another breath Fortune finally understood just how powerful Wraith really was, and the realization terrified him. This dragon had ravaged the world!

All the fear and fatigue which had dragged at him earlier flooded back and he fell to the floor, shaking. Wraith watched without emotion.

'Little Natural,' he said coldly. 'You are pitiful.'

Fortune felt angry with himself for showing his weakness but could not speak. He stared at the weave of the floor immediately before him, concentrating on calming his frantic breathing and willing his heart to slow.

'I suppose your father did not tell you what it is?' said Wraith conversationally. 'Well, I shall complete your education, little dragon. What you see up there is the centre of the Maze. It has a name: the Seed of Charm it is called, but I prefer to call it what it truly is, which is the Seed of Power. The dragon who owns that seed will see it bear the greatest fruit of all; that dragon will be leader of all, not only all dragons but possibly all worlds.'

The words echoed past Fortune as he struggled to hear them. *The Seed of Charm!* he thought. *Of course.*

And he knew that Wraith spoke the truth. But within Wraith's words was a shadow of falsehood, or rather of Wraith's own misconception. 'The Seed of Power,' he had said, and that did not seem right to Fortune. That did not seem right at all. Like the white obscenity on Wraith's flank, something in that thought was very wrong.

Slowly, painfully he brought his shaking body under control and looked back up at Wraith, but then found his gaze moving on further, upwards towards the Seed, travelling inexorably towards its rough, grey dullness. It drew his eyes as it drew his thoughts and when he saw it again he felt the tiredness drain completely away. It refreshed him more completely than he had ever known before, and again, soundlessly, it beckoned.

Wraith eyed him. Challenged him. Without a word Fortune opened his wings and stroked his way up towards the floating Seed. Wraith watched with avid interest.

As he drew near he expected a heat, or a barrier, or at least something, some force he would have to cross in order to reach the drab, oval husk. But nothing hindered him. He approached until he floated a wing's length from it, whereupon he paused and narrowed his eyes, suspicious yet attracted. It beckoned. Slowly, as he reached out his neck, the Seed took on a gentle lustre and its opaque shell became slightly, almost imperceptibly transparent. Faces flitted inside, dragons he loved. They all beckoned him in. Cumber, Gossamer, Wood, Scoff, Tallow and so many others, they all welcomed him. His father, Welkin; his mother, Clarion. *Come here and you will find your mother,* whispered the Seed.

Fortune knew it was seducing him, deceiving him, but he could not help himself. It was so beautiful, so full of love and promises it would surely keep. He felt its energy fill him until it poured out of his eyes, his ears, the ends of his claws.

He felt its power pump into him like the lifeblood of a star, soaking him in its warmth and glory. He felt himself expand to fill the infinite space it occupied. He felt its past inside his own memories, and saw that within its lifeless, grey exterior it held command over the world, over all worlds, and over their turning.

This, now, was the centre of everything. Reaching out his neck, he took it gently into his jaws. Light crackled quietly across his scales as he was enfolded with charm and the images vanished from inside the Seed. Opaque again, it gave a single, minute shrug as it cast off its connections with the million strands of the Maze web and settled into Fortune's mouth with neither light nor motion to betray the immense potential it now contained.

At once, the severed tendrils of light which had joined it to the fabric of the universe outside began to shrivel and decay, curling up like grass in the sun and whipping backwards towards the skin of the bubble from which they had originally sprung.

Slowly Fortune descended to where Wraith stood waiting. His outstretched claws contacted the trembling skin surface and a jolt of sudden power shook his body until his teeth rattled. The Seed lay quietly between his jaws.

'So you have it, little dragon,' said Wraith.

Fortune head was whirling. *I have it! The Seed, the Power!*

He knew – he knew in his very soul – that he could strike Wraith down here and now, that he could strike down the world for that matter, and still the Seed would feed him the power to strike down a million more Wraiths, a million more worlds.

'You may hold it,' said Wraith, 'but you do not own it, little dragon. No Natural can ever own the Seed. Your father knew this at the end, and that is why he failed.'

Fortune barely heard Wraith's words, so enraptured was he by the clarity of the strength which the Seed gave to him. It was like having sunlight in his veins, like the clearest air he had ever tasted, the sweetest water. Each breath he took he was nearly carried into the future which the Seed was offering him, a future where he had the Power, where he could rule wherever and whatever dragon or world he pleased . . . but a word of Wraith's filtered through and he clung to the shred of reason which remained to him.

Own. To own the Seed. No Natural would ever own it? Wraith was so near to the truth. So near, yet so fatally far!

Greedy, he thought with an internal smile which cast shadows across the Seed's promise of light and filled him simultaneously with grief and hope.

How can I give it up? This he thought with one breath, and with the next he thought, *I must give it up!*

Slowly he drew his concentration to bear on Wraith, giving up a small part of the obsession (love?) for the Seed which was dominating his entire being. Wraith too wanted the Seed, possibly more than Fortune himself did. But he wanted the Seed for more than itself – he wanted to win it from Fortune, to humiliate Fortune as Welkin had humiliated him. Only in this way could he find a way to live with his shame.

I can be yours forever, whispered the Seed to Fortune. Suddenly it moved, flexing between his jaws. Its rough surface grew smooth and warm, and it sent an aroma out to him, and a gentle, loving voice which sang and murmured. The sensation was fleetingly erotic until Fortune realized that it was Gossamer's scent and Gossamer's voice coming from this dead, grey shell of matter . . .

It was then, in that instant, that he began to believe he could find the strength to give up the Seed.

'Yield to me, Natural!' snapped Wraith savagely.

Fortune forced himself to recall how easy it had been to pluck the Seed from its place at the centre of the heart. *Going in is easy*, he thought. *It's the coming out that's hard.*

He lifted his head and the Seed screamed. And attacked.

Battling against the torrent of burning, freezing, slashing energy which tore through his mind and across his body, he leaned forward into what seemed like a tornado. Flakes of fire thrashed his scales and he felt his limbs shredded under the terrifying onslaught. He could hear nothing but an all-invading howl.

Somehow, with some strength he never imagined he possessed, he ignored it and placed the Seed of Charm gently, almost tenderly, into Wraith's waiting jaws.

The instant Wraith closed his mouth about the Seed's gyrating form, the wind stopped, silence fell and Fortune sank back to the ground. He looked down, expecting to see his body bloodied and mutilated. Not a scratch marked him. But more than that. He no longer felt exhausted; his mind, though still devastatingly aware of all that the Seed had shown him, was clear and working fast. More than he had in what seemed an aeon, he felt alive!

The strands of the web continued to whip through the air above them, burning backwards towards their roots in the skin of the heart. What would happen when they reached that skin Fortune did not dare imagine. In the flashing light they cast he saw clearly the shape on Wraith's flank. It had spread like a lump beneath the scales, a tumour which had sent pale, bulging veins into his dark body. He was repulsed.

But before he could look any closer Wraith sprang back, his eyes blazing with a new intensity.

'I'm sorry,' said Fortune as the Black Dragon appraised him.

'Sorry? You dare to be sorry?'

Wraith lifted his head high, the Seed of Charm held tight in his jaws, drinking in its power. He spoke from his mind but the words were clear and cold.

'At last it is mine! As are you, little dragon! As are you!'

He advanced on Fortune, charm cascading from his body like floodwater, his claws ripping great slashes through the trembling skin of the heart, his eyes filled with hate.

Fortune backed away, his own heart bursting, stricken at the loss of the Seed to this monster yet sure of the rightness of his decision. Sure? So he prayed.

As the stone fell the lake split again and a spur of rock sprang up into its path, deflecting it by the tiniest amount.

Not enough!

But it did slow its descent. Gossamer scrambled under the falling mass and bundled Velvet safely out of the way. A scant breath later the stone crashed to the ground in an explosion of sparks and shards of rock.

Facing the wrong way.

471

Amid the roar of quaking rock and spitting lava, Velvet opened her eyes, found Gossamer's anxious gaze and said,

'How many more to go? We must be nearly done!'

Gossamer hugged her and wondered how they could possibly swing that last, massive rock around to face out of the ring like all the others.

So many of the others have already been consumed by the fire, she thought desperately. But she knew that it had to be done. Fortune's life depended on it.

Fortune continued to back away.

'You think I will kill you, Natural,' laughed Wraith, 'but *I* will not. The Maze will see to that, after I leave. A fitting end, do you not think?'

'When you leave?' responded Fortune sharply.

'To leave is hard,' agreed Wraith. 'But I have this!' His eyes bulged as he regarded the Seed of Charm held so tight in his jaws. 'There is no way out for you, Natural!'

He flicked his head to one side and the Seed changed shape. A long, grey needle extruded itself from its dull surface, extending out as far as the web-like membrane of the bubble to which they both clung. On and through it continued, and Wraith whipped his head back so that a long, perfect gash was cut big enough for ten dragons to pass through.

The needle vanished, absorbed back into the Seed without a sound. A wind howled in through the gash, hot and dry, and a distant rumbling began to build.

'This is my triumph!' he bellowed. 'For this will I truly be worshipped.

He bent to the gash as though to leave, then stopped and turned back to face Fortune. The smile he displayed, despite the bulk of the Seed in his mouth, turned Fortune's heart to ice.

Fortune could see no escape. He thought briefly of backing away but he would surely have had no hope of defeating Wraith under normal conditions, let alone a Wraith with the power of the Seed of Charm at his disposal. He stood his ground, not daring even to breathe.

The Seed began to spin in Wraith's jaws, grey still, relentlessly grey as it hid its true strength behind its impassive face. He did not know what end Wraith planned for him now but he knew that he was defeated, and that his death would be terrible.

'Goodbye, Welkin's son,' growled Wraith as he loomed over the Natural, and there was, it was barely possible, a trace of sadness in his voice.

He must have seen the reflection in Fortune's eye, or else his own charmed senses or those of the Seed betrayed the newcomer to him. Whatever the reason, he whirled round at the instant a third dragon flew into the heart of the Maze through the very gash which Wraith had opened in order that he might escape.

There could have been no dragon whom Fortune least expected to see here, at the very heart of charm itself, than Wood.

CHAPTER 40

The Turning of the World

It was Wood, but it was a perfect Wood.

Fortune looked past Wraith at the astonishing sight of his friend of so many years, so many arguments, so much heartache, lifting into the heart of the Maze to join him in this final confrontation.

Wraith flashed his gaze between the two of them, suspicious that some trickery was unfolding.

'What is this?' he growled ominously.

'I have come for my friend,' said Wood in a quiet, rational voice. Fortune almost laughed aloud; it all seemed so normal.

'And who will come for you, Natural?' retorted Wraith.

'You will have to kill us both if you wish to leave,' said Wood, flying gracefully around the Black Dragon to land at Fortune's side. 'Hello, Fortune,' he added nonchalantly.

Fortune opened his mouth but no words emerged. He touched Wood's wing to make sure he was really here, that it was not a trick of Wraith's. *But how would I really know?*

Wood glanced over at his friend. 'I wish Welkin were here,' he said, and his eyes were brimming with tears. 'I saw the night dragons on the way; they're real, Fortune, they're real!'

For the briefest of intervals Wraith was not there, the heart, the Maze itself was not there. All that existed was a pair of natural dragons sharing a dream of their youth come true. Together they could almost feel the warm grass of South Point curling up between their claws, taste the salt in the air, feel the freedom of the wind inside their wings. Wordless apologies crossed over and over again between them as at last, at this final, great turning point, with all the world poised above them and ready to fall, they were finally, truly reunited.

'I've missed you,' said Fortune through his tears.

'I'm glad I came,' replied Wood.

Wood's journey here had been swift.

He had drifted in and out of unconsciousness while Gossamer and Velvet had proceeded with their strange labour, but when the eruptions had started he had felt his life finally beginning to slip away from him. His last memory from the mountain top was the ground on which he lay entwined with Shatter's broken corpse turning red, then white, and then a yawning emptiness which had swallowed him completely.

Then he remembered only glimpses of a journey over and beneath the world, across a web of light towards a brighter glow defaced by a long, open gash. Propelled by some unknown force he had passed through that gash and emerged here, his body whole again, his spirit soaring, his mind more calm than it had ever been before.

For the first time he felt as though he was truly Wood. And the feeling made him rejoice. What he was here for, or what he could possibly do to help Fortune against this monster he could not conceive, but here he was and here would he stay.

He was Wood, and no dragon could take that from him again.

Wraith found himself unable to move. Though he knew he held the power to sweep both these upstarts into the void, still he held back. He found himself intoxicated by the eyes of these two Naturals. In the one, Fortune, he saw Welkin. This was to be expected, of course, for they were kin; but this other dragon, this newcomer. What of him? For in his eyes too Wraith thought he saw a sparkle which was Welkin's, a ripple of humour, a glint of imagination. *Is Welkin in all these Naturals?*

The notion horrified him. Did Welkin have so much power that he could live on in all natural dragons? *He had no power!* The rational part of his mind snapped back at him but other juices were working in him now. Wraith's blood was mixed intimately with that of the inscrutable basilisk, and now the Seed of Charm was pouring its sap into his system too. Wraith, unlike Wood, had never been so detached from his own identity.

You should have killed them all while you had the chance, muttered the basilisk inside his fears. *Why did you bother to take prisoners?*

'But what dragons would there be to rule otherwise?' blurted Wraith in response. He saw the puzzlement cross the faces of Fortune and Wood and grew angry. 'Fear me still, Naturals!' he howled, taking a step nearer, but he flinched when he saw that they still stood their ground.

No prisoners, taunted the basilisk. *Only death is worthy of a true conqueror.*

'There would be no world left!' pleaded Wraith, thrashing his head about, his jaws still clamped fanatically on the Seed. 'What leader can rule without his subjects? You wish only death — at least my promise is for life!'

To prevail is not necessarily to live, have you not learned that yet?

Wraith felt his spirit being sucked up into the tornado of energy which the basilisk and the Seed shared between them, and there was nothing he could do to stop it. Piece by piece, thought by thought, he was being eroded. Nothing to stop it . . . 'There is!' he bellowed. 'I will stop it!'

He jumped forward, the two bony claws which hugged his neck extending to clutch at Fortune's throat, honed edges flashing in the ever-changing light of the decaying heart. Light crackled at their faded tips, magic growing.

He pounced.

Fortune would never have moved in time.

Wood leaped squarely into Wraith's path and took the blow full on his chest. Wraith's flailing claws lifted the Natural high and hurled him across the diameter of the heart. Dissolving strands of the web lashed at him as he tumbled, appearing to lacerate his body.

Hardly aware of what had happened, Fortune side-stepped Wraith's charging body, forcing the Black Dragon to change direction sharply. Wraith flung his head around, balanced on the very lip of the gash he had opened. The

476

basilisk's tail whipped at his flank, cutting into the black scales there and drawing rich, dark blood. He balanced there, struggling as though weighed down by a heavy load. And the Seed, Fortune knew, was heavier than life itself.

Wraith teetered on the brink, his yellow eyes bulging, flickering to silver and back again, his teeth closing on the Seed until they drew sparks across its surface. For an age he held himself there, staring blankly, incredulously into Fortune's gaze and then, as though moving in resin, he slowly, slowly began to drop through the gash and out of the heart of the Maze, out into the rumbling void which the Maze itself had become.

His expression twisted, the Seed of Charm still fast in his jaws. He reached out wordlessly towards Fortune, but whatever force was pulling him out pulled hard and relentless. His legs, his body, his wings and finally the two, long, terrible claws of charm disappeared from view and there was a sudden pause in the rumbling outside.

Fortune rushed to the edge of the gash and looked out. There was Wraith, falling out into the void with that same, dreadful slowness. All around him the web of the Maze was unravelling itself with ferocious speed, a network of deadly white strands whipping against a sullen emptiness suddenly visible behind them. The Maze writhed; it spun. It was tearing itself apart.

The rumbling had started again, but now there was a new sound, a ripping sound which grew until it became a scream. The gash split further, running right around the circumference of the heart until it met at the opposite side and the entire sphere began to separate.

Fortune clung to the half on which he had been poised and again, miraculously, Wood was at his side.

'How . . . ?' Fortune stammered.

Wood was quite unharmed, his body whole and unmarked. 'I don't know,' his friend replied. 'But I know the blow would have killed you.'

The remains of the heart disintegrated beneath their claws and they kicked off into the void. Below them Wraith swam laboriously through the sickly, flashing light, grasping frantically at the tendrils of web which the Maze offered to him, flinching as they slashed at him.

'Hear me, Wraith!' shouted Fortune as he too tumbled through space. 'The Seed of Charm it may be, but it is not the Seed of Power! It never has been. There's only one dragon who can take it out of the Maze, Wraith, and it isn't you!'

The Black Dragon looked exactly like a spider now, but a spider caught on its own web. 'I had to let them live!' he cried, his voice a dust mote in the storm whipping around him. 'How else could I have ruled? I would have been lost . . . !'

Huge energies boiled around his struggling form as the web closed its coils. His wings and claws struck out at the clutching tendrils but gradually they overwhelmed him, sucking him in, wrapping him into their embrace. Tighter and tighter they bound him until, for a flash of time, all the destructive power of the Maze was pouring through them and into the body of Wraith, the Master, the Black Dragon. Now he was the heart.

There was a brief, silent concussion, then an enormous, burning flame which flung the strands of the web apart again. Where Wraith had been a billion shreds, a mosaic of glistening particles tore through the empty space and were blown into infinity by the storm which blasted through the collapsing, dying Maze. A long, lingering scream pursued them on their billion journeys. It did not die away, simply faded as it moved beyond the void. So lonely. Lost dragon.

The Seed remained, grey and shabby against the scintillating backdrop of the fallen Maze, drifting slowly towards Fortune and Wood, free of the heart which had confined it for so long, waiting for a saviour.

Waiting for a guide.

Tallow and Werth led the Flight and the Hardship over the brow of the summit and into the maelstrom that the mountain peak had become.

Scores of dragons had died on the journey up the slopes, most during the passage through the storm clouds where lightning had torn its way through their ranks with terrible precision. Barely one hundred dragons survived to reach the clearer air above the storm. Beneath them the volcano pitched and juddered and filled the sky with fire and ash.

478

Tallow scarcely had time to register the colossal loss of life before he was faced with the sight of the fallen ring of stones, the lake of fire, and the struggle of the two young females to turn an immense boulder surely a hundred times their combined weight — and for what purpose he could not imagine. He arrowed the dragons in towards them and then, incredibly, a voice pierced the raging air.

'Velvet!' it cried, and there, swooping in over the cracked central plain came Cumber. At his flank flew a wrinkled, black dragon who looked older than time itself and yet who flew with the grace of youth. The two groups, one large and one small, converged upon the one remaining stone, crying out names and greetings and prayers as the mountain tried to blast them from the sky.

'Cumber!' shouted Brace, reaching the young Charmed first. To Cumber's amazement he flew straight to his side and butted him with a massive yet affectionate blow of his horns. 'Am I pleased to see you!'

'Are you?' replied Cumber, surprised by Brace's display of emotion.

'I am,' confirmed Brace vehemently. 'Now, where's Fortune?'

The direction of Cumber's glance said it all, but he explained all the same. 'Down there,' he said mournfully. Then a look of determination spread across his face. 'But we're up here! Come on!'

To their right the lava pit boiled; to their left what remained of the ground still supported six of the felled stones, splayed out flat in the arc of a perfect circle . . . all except one.

Velvet and Gossamer were struggling in vain to swing it around to face out of the circle along with its companions. Although the stone was obviously far too heavy they were pouring all their energy — of which they had scant reserves — into the effort. Cumber was touched and, despite the hazardous conditions, it was with gentle good humour that he alighted on the ground beside the stone. The other dragons remained airborne, awaiting his instructions, for he alone seemed to know what needed to be done.

'Velvet,' he repeated, this time with quiet affection. 'I've been so worried for you.'

'I'm all right,' she chirped. 'But we need help with this stone.'

Her face was so tired and so filthy, yet her eyes were so bright that Cumber could not help but smile back at her. The warmth of their shared smile spread to the exhausted Gossamer and they all three embraced briefly before Cumber turned and shouted up to the circling dragons.

'What are you waiting for?' he yelled. 'Let's get this stone moved!'

They coasted up to the Seed. It seemed subdued now, as if some great task had been achieved, which of course it had.

But Fortune suspected there were more and possibly greater tasks to come before it would all be over.

He turned to Wood. 'I have to leave now,' he said.

Wood nodded. 'I don't think I can come with you,' he replied sadly.

Fortune eyed the Seed of Charm, then reached out with his wing and gathered it towards him.

'You could go anywhere with this,' he offered, but Wood shook his head with a smile. 'I'd rather not, if it's all the same to you.'

'Are you really here, Wood? Is it really you?'

The Maze was breaking apart all around them and Fortune felt his heart breaking along with it. Wood had saved his life here and now there was nothing he could do for him.

'I wish Welkin were here,' said Wood suddenly. 'And Clarion too. They both ought to be here, to see the night dragons.'

As he spoke a shower of light fell behind him. Whether it was a rain of distant night dragons or a shower of sparks from the web of the Maze Fortune could not tell, but it was beautiful whichever it truly was. 'Maybe there's a way you could come with me . . .' he began.

But Wood halted him with an upraised wing. 'I think the time has come for me to go too,' he said with a gentle smile. Then he chuckled. 'We never did see the Charmed do their sacrificial dances, did we?'

'They would never have lived up to your fantasies,' replied Fortune, his eyes moist. He felt desperately sad but the moment was right now; their stories had turned and managed, however briefly, to touch again at the last, and now they both had to go. The Maze crashed close by and the sound echoed across eternity.

'Goodbye,' said Wood, turning to where the trail of the night dragons shone. 'I'm glad they're real.'

'Goodbye, Wood.'

Fortune watched, his heart splitting as his friend spread his wings and moved slowly off into the void. Though the Maze thrust fire and charm at him as he went, the energies seemed to slip past him as though he were invulnerable which perhaps, now at last, he was. Away flew Wood, never vanishing, only growing smaller until Fortune's mere dragon eyes could no longer find him.

It was a long time before Fortune turned to take up the Seed of Charm again and even when he did so it lay quiet in his jaws, as though respectful of the heartful of grief this young, natural dragon now carried within himself.

It was so simple, the secret of the Maze of Covamere: that a dragon, having entered the Maze, having taken up the Seed of Charm, must then simply give it up again before trying to leave.

This secret the basilisk had always known, but few dragons seemed ever to understand its subtlety.

One such dragon was before the basilisk now, a natural creature of all things, daring to hold the Seed itself in its feeble jaws. Such drama however was below the concern of this ancient one, and it eyed Fortune only briefly, fleetingly interested when the dragon saw it and registered first confusion, then horror. It floated on.

Some remote part of it had wondered if the symbiosis it had shared with Wraith might have rendered it mortal at last, but that shred of hope had been dashed when Wraith had finally been destroyed. The rebirth had been agonizing not just for the pain it had inflicted but for the reminder that after an eternity of life, and an eternity of seeking death, an immortal creature could actually be resurrected. As Wraith's body had disintegrated so that of the basilisk had reformed itself with dreadful precision so that now, in this strange limbo between world and Realm, between all worlds, through the tatters of the Maze it swam. Reborn though it was, still it sought oblivion.

It neared the remains of the heart of the Maze. Here it stopped and turned, lowering itself briefly to involve itself in the tiny, insignificant reality of the dragon. It searched for, and found, a word.

Fortune watched the basilisk prowl past him and approach the shattered heart of the Maze, ignorant of what it was yet in awe of its presence. There it turned.

GO!

The word blew through his head. He obeyed instantly.

The basilisk swung back to the pieces of the heart and opened a mouth as wide as the cosmos, a silver eye as broad as the void, and fell upon the heart of the Maze like a predator on creation.

Collapsing still, the Maze wrenched free every connection with reality it had ever forged and spun its final, dying web about its attacker, ripping away, among so many billions of others, its last, straggling junctions with the world and the Realm.

It was in that instant that magic left the world.

Fortune fled.

He sped away from the ball of raw, bleeding energy the Maze had become and searched in vain for some route back to his world. The Seed felt light in his mouth, seemingly devoid of power; he could gain no assistance from it now.

The remnants of the Maze, and whatever it was the basilisk had become, shrank to a point of light, and then both were gone. Alone in the one, true void, Fortune floundered lost in a maze from which he could see no means of escape.

Lightning bolted from the distant storm, sending jagged streamers into the lake of fire. Hot boulders showered across the decimated remains of the mountain top. Charmed dragons fell from the sky.

Every charmed dragon at the mountain peak felt the final, impossible wrench as the Maze was severed from the world.

The Realm fled; inside every Charmed the magic began to die; wings shaped for ornament rather than flight collapsed in the thin air, casting their owners to the heaving, boiling ground.

Only Cumber guessed what had happened and he rallied the terrified dragons to his side. 'These are the death throes of the Maze!' he shouted over the deafening contractions splitting the land all around them. 'The death throes of charm itself. Have courage, dragons – use charm while you can or we will never leave this mountain!'

He turned his face up to the sky, so calm a vista in comparison to the landscape to which they clung. In his mind he watched the threads of charm leaving the world, a billion contacts, a billion sparks of magic vanishing into the inconceivable distances between the worlds.

The death of charm. It is happening! He snatched at a fleeing thread where once he had opened whole routes through to the Realm. The magic wriggled, slippery and elusive in his grasp, but at last he fixed it and filled his muscles with its power. His wings swelled, growing wide and sleek like a Natural's. The charm died in his grasp.

'Use it while you can!' he warned as other dragons struggled to use the sparse magic too. 'It won't last!'

The charmed dragons of Wraith's Hardship worked desperate magic on themselves in those last few echoes of the Maze. As the world lost its charm so did they, and it was with the keenest urgency that they repaired themselves ready for the new world that was to come.

Then a horrifying thought suddenly occurred to Cumber. 'Scoff!' he howled, searching the sky in vain for his friend.

He has no wings at all!

All around: confusion, dragons flailing, charm sputtering fitfully, pathetically in the moonlight. No Scoff.

'Come on!' cried Gossamer, impatient despite the obvious distress of her Charmed comrades. 'There isn't much time!'

The stone had locked solid, refusing to budge.

Fortune tumbled in the emptiness, the Seed in his mouth, seeking out a direction he could not remember. The Maze had gone; the Realm had gone. Only blackness remained. The world was nowhere to be seen.

Quelling his panic, Fortune closed his eyes and focused his thoughts on the Seed. Beneath his inner gaze it was still hot and powerful and it cast reflections of ideas into his mind, whispers, seductions . . .

Power . . .

But not for me.

. . . escape . . .

Yes!

. . . to hide . . .

. . . to wait . . .

. . . to turn again . . .

To turn.

Fortune turned all his trust in towards the Seed and opened himself fully to it. *If you guide me now*, he thought, *I will not betray you. This is the way I will guide you.*

And as he turned himself inwards, at last he felt himself to be travelling, moving fast through the new emptiness of the void outside the world, speeding, speeding with the rush of centuries on his face and a point of light in the centre of his vision. The point became a dot, then expanded to show a disc and a curve and a broad belt of shadow beneath the light . . . and suddenly he was over the world and under the world, as he had been when first he had entered the Maze. It was exhilarating and exhausting and terrifying.

Approaching, always approaching, he tensed himself, for he knew that where the Maze had let him out of the world before, there was no Maze now to let him back in. One way in, no way out.

The scream of the world was loud in his ears as he fell down towards it and up beneath it. There seemed no way through. There was no escape.

'Push!'

Cumber directed a group of dragons on one side of the fallen stone while Tallow urged on those on the other.

'Can't you work your charm on this rock?' grunted Brace as he pushed shoulder to shoulder with Cumber.

'It's brute force now . . . I'm afraid,' Cumber replied between short, heavy breaths. Lava fountained around them as slowly and painfully the giant boulder began to swing around towards its correct position.

Gossamer flitted back and forth overhead for only she knew, by some deep intuition, where the stone must be.

'Hurry!' she cried, her face distraught in the cruel light of the ocean of fire. 'Please hurry!'

Landscapes slipped past Fortune as though in a dream; territories were laid out flat beneath his gaze. Yet at the same time he was inside, flashing through underworlds and inner spaces.

The world turned beneath him and above him in all its splendour, and as it turned he saw it realigning its parts, recreating itself in new shapes, according to new laws. The world was turning, and Fortune was witness to it all.

Ahead, if there could have been such a direction in this unearthly dimension, was a growing patch of light. Orange it pulsed, slowly expanding until it filled his vision, a vast lake of fire shaped like a pinched oval and flickering with sparks of light.

It looked like an eye. It was the way out. It was closed.

Too slowly the stone turned.

With a troll's groan the mountain shifted. Its entire southern half began to collapse in on itself, launching a great cloud of ash and flame high into the sky. The eruption split the storm and with a sudden, cataclysmic outburst the lightning slashed its last claws into the night. As the ash spread so it damped the fire in the storm: thunder died; rain turned to hot mud; lightning fell dark.

Moonlight and lava light joined blue and orange to send brilliant beams playing across the dragons straining at the mighty rock on what was now a tiny island of solid ground. It was only half-turned, sideways to the circumference of the broken ring.

The lava sea which surrounded them bulged like a swollen eye, its oval shape pinched at either end by what was left of the mountain's northern ramparts. As its bubbling surface rose, the island shuddered and tipped, throwing many dragons hard against the side of the boulder, but many more away from it entirely.

Dragons took to the air as the ground betrayed them at last, great splits rending its surface until it was a network of steaming, splitting vents. The stone tilted. threatening to return to its starting point.

'No!' cried Gossamer and Cumber, their voices one.

Out of control, Fortune raced towards the eye poised deadly before him.

It belched fire across his wings; it was like an ocean of living, breathing land. Troll's blood. He twisted desperately, seeking a new direction, seeking to escape the fate towards which he fell at horrific speed. Now the eye was greater than his vision – it was his whole world.

The Seed was quiet in his grasp, helping him no longer. Then, in a starburst of clarity, *Gossamer! Help me!*

Fortune!

Gossamer felt him draw near, she sensed his closeness, the incredible speed of his approach.

'Now!' she shouted into the moon.

For a breath, a heartbeat, all was still.

Here, here.

Here the world turned.

The island tilted once more.

Gossamer dived through the scattered dragons towards it.

A shaft of rock ripped through the lava sea and struck the last fallen stone which, with an unearthly moan, scraped across the rippling ground, turning, rotating . . .

Gossamer approached the turning stone, contacted it, pressed herself against its moving form. Only slightly did she deflect its path, so tiny was her strength in comparison to its massive momentum, but deflect it she did, and she knew that she had moved it from a fraction of wrongness on to the one, true course it needed, she needed . . . Fortune needed.

Every dragon – Cumber, Brace, Tallow – every dragon saw the truth of this final course, and every dragon felt the final, enormous silence as it locked into place, as everything locked into place, and all the stone rings, all the circuits of the world were joined.

Since its creation the summit ring had waited for this final configuration to be brought and now, though much of its circumference had been devoured by the lava, its place and its purpose were fixed. Much of its power was lost with its lost stones; perhaps what remained would be enough. Its lesser fellows on the mountain were gone forever; now only it and its giant sibling, the huge ring which encircled the entire mountain and of which the Deadfall was just one tiny part, existed, their power and precision combining to focus the draining magic into one point of growing light.

To a dragon the Flight and the Hardship lifted high into the air over the sea which was rising beneath them. Opening, Gossamer stared in wonder as the orange lava peeled back, revealing a perfect, dark circle at its centre, like a pupil in an eye of fire. She watched, breathless, as a dewdrop of light came into focus in the middle of that circle.

Claws of fire reached out as Fortune sped through a tunnel of flame. The eye loomed, the eye was everything, orange death everywhere he looked. It reached out to destroy him . . .

And then it opened.

Light blossomed, a tiny, fragile light.

The moon!

Dragons against the moon!

Fortune blinked, the eye of fire blinked and he was through! At last he was revealed again to the world, flying strong and true towards a sky flecked with brilliant stars and held firm by a moon full and bright. Against that moon flew dragons, back-lit blue and glowing orange with the reflections of the flame.

Already the eye had closed.

His cry of fear turned to a cry of birth and joy as he burst out into the world again, jaws ever tight on the Seed of Charm as his wings lifted him out of the lava which had slammed shut the instant he had breached it.

One blink sooner, or one blink later . . . he thought deliriously. *The world turns on the blink of an eye.*

The lava met itself and exploded, launching molten rock up into his path, but he powered through unhurt, using the rising heat to dance a joyous course up towards his waiting friends.

He had escaped the Maze, the Seed in his mouth.

Joy and friends and at the end of the tunnel the hope of peace and warmth and an end to the long, long winter.

Shadows against the moon.

Another shadow, thin and hard before the moon's disc. A dragon, a charmed dragon, flew from nowhere, blocking his path and separating him from his friends. A black dragon! Fortune felt a scream swelling inside him . . . then he realized who this old, black dragon was. *Mantle*, he thought, projecting his thoughts to a dragon he knew would hear them. *I might have known you would be here.*

CHAPTER 41

Night Dragon Guide

Fortune reviewed his headlong escape from the dying Maze and found the memories tiring and infinitely heavy. The Seed throbbed in his mouth, a dead weight which seemed to be striving to pull him back down into the maelstrom the mountain had become.

He felt tired; he wanted it all to end. Hot air buffeted his outstretched wings. The sky tasted sharp and hostile and his gaze darted in every direction, restless yet desperate for rest. For escape.

'You've already escaped, young Fortune,' said Mantle with a chuckle. 'You made it; you're here.'

Fortune struggled to reply. His mind was empty of the power he had just used to project his thoughts and now he was painfully aware of the absurd size of the Seed jammed between his jaws and preventing him from speaking. He felt ridiculous.

But despite this he was not ready to let it go again. Not yet. *Not ever . . . ?*

Mantle narrowed his eyes. 'You have one last thing to do, Fortune, and it may be the most difficult of all those you have done so far in your life. But before that,' he added quickly as Fortune again strained at his locked throat in a vain attempt to reply, 'listen to me, and listen well.

'The world has turned at last, Fortune, like a great boulder. It has fallen and it is already too late to divert it from its course, for any creature trying to stand in its path would be crushed to oblivion. This is the way of things, Fortune, the natural way, and the charmed way.

'Charm? Well, its time is done, for now. As it falls so nature will rise. But mark this, Fortune, for some day this knowledge will undoubtedly save you — charm lingers. It lingers, Fortune, a sliver here, a spell there. You may think the death of charm is a final one but its ghost will haunt the world until its flesh is made quick once more. Imagine a shore strewn with rock-pools left by a retreating tide: many will evaporate but just as many will be deep, deep enough to survive until the tide returns. Some of them will sleep, a few will be content just to remember, but some, some will grow bitter. Beware the abandoned magic, Fortune; it would yet see all dragons destroyed.

'Now, the Seed, give it to me.'

Fortune blinked, astonished. Mantle's voice grew stern and forbidding.

'It is what its name promises, Fortune — it is the only hope for the future rebirth of charm, and hence for the future of the whole world. It must be planted, and that is something you cannot do.'

Fortune's mind writhed in agony. Mantle's words burned as if igniting the air between them and he knew that he must pass the Seed over. And yet, and yet . . .

A fraction of a beast had gained a clawhold inside him and now it barked a dire warning. It promised terror and eternal torture for the betrayer of the Seed. It threatened Fortune, it tried to seduce him, it pleaded with him not to liberate the Seed.

Fortune's will shrank in the devastating presence of the basilisk.

Still it survived, still it yearned for oblivion, still it sought a way that the world, and perhaps therefore its own eternal, unbearable life, might be brought to an end.

Fortune's jaws tightened, slaves to an impulse not his own, and a crack raced across the dull, grey surface of the Seed. Light spilled out, trembling with fear, scintillating with rage. For the first time, in the murk of the whirlpool his thoughts had become, Fortune realized that the Seed was fragile. If he closed his jaws he would crush it like an egg.

Mantle saw the conflict, saw Fortune pulled further and further away. Fortune's eyes closed then opened again silver and Mantle found himself staring into the face of the basilisk.

He recognized it at once; after all, had he not stood over it once, many years ago, pleading with Halcyon not to weave it into the mountain defences? It had been sleeping then, and Halcyon had been confident that he could draw upon its powers without ever waking it.

Mantle had not been so sure. Now he knew he had been right. Its breath billowed around Fortune's bobbing head, tainting the air he was breathing and he sensed that here, now, was the turning point for which he himself had waited for so long.

The waiting he was used to. The dead time between Cumber's first visit to his chamber and the cataclysmic events of the last few days he had passed in quiet meditation, talking long nights with his memories and with the small number of charmed faeries still left in the mountain. Like Halcyon he had waited, although unlike Halcyon he had survived the wrath of the Black Dragon. *Halcyon, I mourn you.*

Now his own turning had arrived. Would it crush him as it rolled? If it did, it would crush the world too.

Fortune was battling, that much he could see. But he was losing.

'You wish to destroy the world, beast,' said Mantle urgently, 'but you would still live on. You know that truth. That is your fate. In one form or another you will prevail. Let the world live – it is beneath you.'

Fortune's eyes bulged as though a new volcano were building inside of him. His face was contorted, in every sense he hovered, airborne, trapped between desires both native and alien.

Mantle shut his eyes again, and inside he wept, for he knew they were bound to lose.

Gossamer watched the motionless drama play itself out below.

Fortune and the strange, black dragon were tiny shapes set hard against the livid, crimson fire. Already the summit had consumed itself, what remained of the ring of stones swallowed by a final surge of lava, and now a pall of ash rose to devour its remains, blotting out the fire in its black folds. To devour them all?

She yearned to cry out, to dive down and embrace her

491

love again, but she knew she could not, should not. At least . . .

Something was terribly wrong. Her heart, thundering in the presence of the one dragon for whom she lived and from whom she had been separated for so long, skipped several beats. She looked past the black dragon into Fortune's face and, despite the distance, into his eyes. What she saw there was not Fortune; it was not even dragon.

'Give me the Seed,' intoned Mantle hopelessly, desperate now as the future narrowed to a spare choice of lifeless finales.

The basilisk exhaled, Fortune's jaws clenched and the Seed cracked further, its power pressing at the membrane which stretched tight inside its wounded shell.

'If you hear me at all, Fortune,' repeated Mantle, 'give me the Seed.'

Charm was among them despite the turned world, knotted about the two dragons in taut threads. Much of it was the charm of the basilisk, infinitely weak yet devastatingly accurate, but some was Mantle's own, spare, captured magic he had been weaving about himself in preparation for the journey he was now convinced he would never make. Charm sparked, charm flashed; for a brief time, charm lived.

Into the knot flew Gossamer, the magic of the earth guiding her, the language of the sprites whispering a course through treacherous currents of charm. She pulled her wings around and reached a dead halt between Fortune and Mantle as they faced each other in the hot sky. The ash cloud licked at them, hungry.

She said nothing, and for a long, painful breath they dipped together, riding the waves of heat thumping off the cloud rising below. Then, so gently, her neck extended, she nuzzled at Fortune's flank, then touched the tip of his muzzle with hers. Words came to her and she spoke them, clear and strong. 'Defeat it, Fortune. It is so weak, so sad. You've done it all now. This part is so easy.'

She reached out and tipped her head to the side. With a delicate touch she stretched her own mouth wide open and around Fortune's. Slowly, intimately, she clasped the Seed, steadying it with her tongue as she did so.

They held the Seed of Charm together, sharing its burden. Just as he had been launched from the maw of the volcano so now he leaped free of the basilisk's old, dry clutch. In that instant Fortune found himself again and returned with violent joy to the now, to the here. *Gossamer!*

He relaxed his jaws and watched as with a single, elegant motion Gossamer lifted the Seed from his grasp and into Mantle's waiting claws.

It was so easy.

The cloud boiled up around them and then retreated, and when it retreated the basilisk had gone.

'Gone,' said Mantle, voicing their collective thought, 'but not forgotten. And it will never forget. It too is abandoned charm now, Fortune — be cautious.'

Though the lightning of the storm was swamped now by the looming ash, new static flashed inside the blue, moonlit clouds. One such flash seemed to illuminate Fortune's mind and sent him reeling from the shock, as though he had been slammed back into his body from some tremendous distance. And by his side was Gossamer.

He lurched in the air beside her, grinning stupidly. She gave him a soft, quizzical look, then grinned herself, but before either of them could speak Mantle broke in again.

'Time enough has been wasted now,' he said. 'Tell Cumber this for me, Fortune: tell him he made a difference — it's important to him.'

'I will,' replied Fortune, the grin on his face subsiding as he grew solemn again.

'And you?' asked Gossamer.

'Now it's my turn to make a difference,' responded Mantle with a dazzling smile which lit up both his companions' faces once more. 'Now I am the guide!'

Fortune flexed his wings as though to move forward but Gossamer glided in front of him.

'Goodbye, Mantle,' she said, with a sideways glance at her lover.

'You're right to rush me,' chuckled Mantle. 'Old dragons

493

have a tendency to talk too much and I've a long journey ahead of me.'

'Where . . . ?' began Fortune, but Mantle silenced him with a shake of his head.

'Best you don't know,' he said. 'Best no dragon knows. The Seed will take me there.'

'Will you come back?'

'Goodbye,' said Mantle firmly. 'And good luck.'

'You too,' replied Gossamer and Fortune together.

The old dragon turned his wings and rose speedily up into the night sky. Up he flew and further still until he was a minute speck against the moon.

Then the Seed grew hot and white and a light burned brighter than the moon, brighter even than the sun, a blazing star which spun and caught and then raced across the sky in a soaring arc which began in this world and ended no dragon knew where. The trail it left glittered long and sharp, drifting behind and beyond the stars as Mantle, new dragon of the night, guided the Seed of Charm to its place of rest. Its place of waiting. Its haven.

Now, at last, Fortune turned to Gossamer. Above them lingered their dragon companions but for now only the two of them mattered.

For a time they hovered together in the hot, thin air, heads close, breath mingling, eyes closed in rapture. All the time they had spent apart retreated into memory and a new future expanded before them, one filled with brilliant clarity and the sound of hope.

Fortune opened his eyes, for he heard the sound of more than just hope.

'The sound of the sea!' he blurted.

Sure enough, there it was, the rhythmic wash of wave upon shore, light and lilting and aching of home. But where was home? Fortune looked down into the swirling ash and seemed to see an ocean. Islands rotated about a fragile reef and a voice – his mother's – whispered a single word, 'Haven.'

'Haven,' echoed Fortune. 'Home.'

'Can you take us there?' murmured Gossamer.

'I don't know,' he said in wonder. 'I think . . . I think perhaps I can!' Then he looked at her, closely now, intimately, and with widening eyes exclaimed, 'You're white!'

'It's a long story!' laughed Gossamer.

They embraced, a clumsy, airborne flurry which raised a cheer from their friends who were spiralling down to take them up into their wings, and then the cheer came again and the sound of the sea grew stronger, beating and rushing until it became the sound of wings and there below them, rising from the billowing ash, came a dragon borne on huge and colourful sails which pressed down the air with vigour and pride.

It was Scoff.

'Made an entrance once before,' he grunted as he struggled into the warm and welcoming flock. 'Might as well do it again.'

Cheers and laughter, and wonder that he had found enough magic to grow such splendid wings in the midst of such a disaster. Up they all flew, comrades and friends, Flight and Hardship, dragons all, into air so sheer it scarcely existed. But air mattered not, only dragons mattered now and theirs was the sky. Moonlight played on a field of moving wings and Fortune moved to the head of the column and struck out west, for he alone knew where they should go.

He alone could guide them home.

Winds blew in through the night, pressing the ash cloud down over the land and forcing it west towards the sea. The Plated Mountain fell beneath the shadow of the cloud, its dignity protected as it was split and sundered by inner turmoil. Its roaring was muffled by the shroud of black ash.

For tens of days the ash lingered, brooding over the remnants of the trolls' birthplace. Then finally it lifted, carried high around the world to turn sunsets blood red for years to come. When the ash settled the land was grey with its fallout instead of white with snow. No new snow fell there for a very long time.

Long before the ash finally left the dragons were gone. They flew the night the mountain died and the Maze of Covamere lost its grip on the world, and like the snow they stayed away.

One creature remained, however, floating on a shard of

charm in a world which had abandoned magic, pale and infinitely sad. Through eternity it had grown but now it shrank, living still yet without the heart to endure any season but the final winter which these frail, absurd dragons had succeeded in averting.

Wraith had brought it new power which it had had no desire to use, and it had consumed the collapsing Maze when that dragon had died, in the hope of bringing an end to all creation. Almost too late it had seen that at the heart of the Turning had not been the Maze at all but the Seed of Charm, but in the end even that knowledge had not been enough. The dragon Mantle had been right: even had it destroyed the Seed and thus the world, still it would have survived.

It was its doom. It struck out across the wasteland of its existence, while inside it the remains of the Maze splintered. Away from the mountain, from the Heartland, from the world itself it sped, moving out past the moon until it was gone from the place which had been its home for so long. Time yawned ahead and it needed a place to sleep. This time forever.

CHAPTER 42

The Empty Sky

The wind carried them on, filling their wings from behind and making light of the effort it took to rouse their exhausted bodies. For a whole day and night the sea shimmered beneath them, blue and brilliant, rolling past with a calm which itself brought calm to the spirits of the dragons who travelled far above it. Occasionally they saw white foam and dark shadow as mighty creatures breached the surface, travelling too, but otherwise they journeyed alone in the empty sky. None of them had flown this way before and so the way ahead was a mystery, but all trusted the one dragon who led them on with the promise he swore he would keep, to lead them to a new home.

Despite their hope it was in silence that they flew, for what had they lived through if not the destruction of all their homes? Although their bodies were buoyed by the wind their hearts were cast down; only Fortune's determination kept their heads raised, and their wings moving. They dared, just, to hope that somewhere ahead was a place they could live in peace.

A broken band of green and gold appeared on the horizon. None spoke, but as they neared land some dragons began to enjoy the tranquillity of the air and the warm, sympathetic breeze which carried them on, on . . . Slowly the islands grew larger. Fortune watched them approach with a strange detachment, for had he not seen them before?

He had flown here not so long ago. Then the Maze had been around him and the world had been flattened like an opened fruit and the islands had slipped past beneath him almost unseen, so captivated had he been by the spectacle of the Plated Mountain. But he had seen them, floating in the serene blue of the ocean, a perfect chain in a perfect sea.

Haven.

Reefs rose from the waves, mosaics of coral splintered with a thousand colours and caressed by loops of foam. The beaches rose into lush green forests and then fell again into golden sand. Island after island after island, each unique, each beautiful, each a tiny link in the circular chain which was the archipelago of Haven.

One hundred islands or more curving into the haze, and above them a straggling group of tired dragons falling now from the sky, choosing a beach at random and descending to rest at last on the fine gold of the sand. Waves chasing up the shore, sunlight in the trees.

Haven.

Fortune and Gossamer watched their friends and comrades descend to the first island, but together they flew on a little further until they reached the centre of the circle, where they found a broad coral reef with no proper land of its own.

Much of the reef lay secretly beneath the water but parts of it rose clear and it was on one of these delicate structures that they alighted and lay together and talked and found that their fears were gone and their love was stronger than it ever had been. Into the night they talked and laughed and shared this precious new time. Perhaps that night they truly sensed the meaning of the turning of the world; perhaps they simply responded to their desire for each other. But whichever it was, for that short, precious time alone together on the reef, soothed by the rhythms of the ocean and the steady breath of the wind, it was true security they experienced. And if as the time passed the feeling did too, then at least they were able to remember its strength, that it might be with them again in the future.

'The sea is my friend,' murmured Fortune in the perfect, starlit night. 'I hope I never have to leave it again.'

A night dragon raced the dawn above them and Fortune thought about Wood, who at the last had seen the night dragons and known that they were real, as Welkin had said. And then too, he thought of his father.

* * *

The reef was theirs and it was with comfortable reluctance that they left it the next morning to revisit the others on what turned out to be the largest of the islands in the circular chain.

A patchy welcoming party was stretched lazily on the island's grassy eastern slopes. The morning was cold but with a promise of early sunshine; the winter had not merely passed — it had fled.

Cumber was first to welcome them. Like the other Charmed who had survived the eruption of the Plated Mountain he was different, a leaner, large-winged dragon, the changes forced by the retreat of charm from the world. Magic was hard to find now, even harder to wield, and most of the charmed dragons had given up altogether. One thing which he had retained was the white camouflage he had taken on, and if he missed anything it was the former gold of his scales.

'Never mind,' laughed Fortune. 'Every dragon will know you and Gossamer and Velvet, whether you like it or not!'

So now the hundred or so dragons who had escaped the wrath of Shatter, of Wraith, and of the Maze itself, were all Naturals.

The constant companionship Cumber now enjoyed with Velvet seemed to reinforce this fact: one Natural, one ex-Charmed, both dragons.

'You suit each other,' smiled Fortune in a rare moment of privacy with his old friend.

'Oh, yes, well,' replied Cumber, embarrassed as usual at the suggestion that he might be experiencing any kind of emotion, 'you know she's terribly good company, and I suppose we do get along quite well really and I suppose the more time we spend together the more we find we have in common, despite our different backgrounds and, well . . .'

'So you love her then?'

But at that Cumber would only smile bashfully and twist his claws in the grass, leaving Fortune to guess at what he already knew.

The day began as a day of greeting, of re-acquaintance, then of storytelling and finally, as night drew in, of celebration and feast. Tales whirled around the banquet of fish and

499

fruit as dragons who had flown tired and wordless to Haven finally woke up again to their friends and to the future.

'. . . when Shatter first spoke to us I knew he was trouble. Mark my words – that dragon was rotten to the core . . .'

'. . . then Scoff, he came out of nowhere. Took his head right off . . .'

'. . . so much sadness. So many deaths . . .'

'. . . sorry? For the Black Dragon? Believe me, no fate was too terrible for that one . . .'

On through the night they shared their histories, and perhaps it was only fair that the stories became larger and more exaggerated as stars turned overhead, for horrors grew alongside triumphs, and confusions only served to heighten the dramas. Fortune told and heard and laughed and cried along with his friends, and in doing so it seemed he told and heard the entire story a thousand times.

The story of Wood in the Maze of Covamere was told by Fortune more than once.

'Wood was a hero,' Gossamer would say. 'He saved me and Velvet, and by killing Shatter he saved you, Fortune. But he surely died there on the mountain; no dragon could have survived it.'

'Maybe not,' Fortune would reply, 'but I saw him all the same. He saved me in the Maze too; in that world and in this he saved my life. He truly made a difference.'

'We all made a difference,' Cumber would say proudly, and then Tallow or Scoff or some other beaming dragon would bowl into their little group and sweep one or other of them away into the party to hear some tale told taller and richer than before.

The night swept on and the celebration died into smaller and smaller groups. Stomachs were filled, legends were exhausted, and sleep, put off for so long, began slowly to steal across the island.

As dawn rose Fortune and Gossamer, nestled together in a quiet hollow, were met by Brace, Scoff, Volley, Tallow and Werth, who seemed to be becoming inseparable from the big navigator.

At once he and Gossamer knew that they were leaving,

and they embraced their friends warmly before a word was said.

'They're still alive,' blurted Brace, clearly uncomfortable with the emotion of the occasion.

'Maybe,' added Scoff with gentle caution.

'The dragons of Aether's Cross.' Fortune nodded. 'Could they have survived?'

Scoff shook his head.

'Don't know,' he replied. 'Wraith worked hard to keep them alive. Maybe.'

'Wraith wanted slaves,' said Brace bitterly.

Fortune considered for a moment and then said,

'I think Wraith just wanted dragons to follow him. What good is a sovereign without his subjects?'

It was clear from his expression that Brace could find no sympathy for the Black Dragon but fortunately Gossamer intervened.

'I believe that Mantle sent the earthquake which destroyed Aether's Cross,' she said firmly. 'He would not have seen so many dragons killed, even with the stakes as high as they were.'

'I believe it too,' stated Fortune with conviction. Gossamer held his wing tight. 'Those dragons — and I hope your parents are among them — are alive, I'm sure of it. But is there enough charm left in the world to get them out?'

'That we can't know,' replied Brace sadly. 'But we must try.'

Then he looked at Gossamer and smiled the smile of a devoted brother.

'I promised to protect you,' he said, 'but Fortune has taken up that promise now. I made another promise too, Gossamer — that I would save the rest of my family. That promise no dragon can take from me. Wish me luck.'

'No need for luck,' interjected Werth, nudging Tallow. 'We've got the greatest navigator in the world!'

'Navigation doesn't conquer magic,' replied Tallow. 'But it will be an adventure, that's for certain.'

'We're going for Weft,' explained Volley to Fortune, who smiled through the puzzlement of Brace and the others and nodded.

'I understand,' he said warmly.

'I don't,' commented Scoff. 'But Tallow's right. Don't need luck.'

'No?' laughed Fortune.

'No. Need an army!'

So it was in laughter that they parted, and it was with hope that Gossamer watched her brother lead his companions up into the blue and out towards the rising sun.

Cumber and Velvet joined them then, and as they watched the retreating dragons dwindle until at last they were lost in the brilliant haze, it was Velvet who spoke to the empty skies the question they had all asked themselves but none had dared to share.

'Does the Turning stop here?'

And watching Brace and his band depart, Fortune could not help but remind himself that all the dragons around him now looked just like him — Naturals; charmed dragon had become natural dragon, but would the turning go on? The question frightened him because, deep inside, he believed it would, which led to an answerable question.

As if she had heard him Gossamer whispered, 'What will become of us?' Perhaps of all dragons she knew most intimately the delicate junction between the natural creature and the charmed.

But Fortune's question was more true, though he could not yet know it.

'No,' he corrected. 'What will we become?'

He gazed, searching, into the high, empty sky.

Epilogue

A beach of coral, lit by distant stars.

On the coral a dragon, motionless, straddling the gap which separates dream from reality, alone between a brace of worlds. There Fortune lay, dozing, waiting, remembering . . .

They had found the abandoned nest high on the central reef a few days after arriving at Haven. Fortune and Gossamer felt an affinity with this place of coral, for here they felt in touch with the deeper places of the world, places which might be reached through the countless pores of the reef, the reef itself a structure, a maze even, which extended down into the ocean and ended they could not guess where.

On the reef they had found it, and upon seeing it Fortune had wept.

Its shape he had seen before, indeed he had known it since his birth. It was a shape from far away, from Torr, from South Point. From home. Only one dragon could have built this nest, and that was the dragon who had first whispered the name of Haven to Fortune in a distant dream. Clarion.

They had searched in vain for her. The nest showed signs of recent occupation but neither the reef nor the surrounding islands showed any sign of his mother. She had moved on, Fortune believed, and would return.

Now time had moved on, the moon had spun three times through its cycle and returned again to fullness. Wavelets stirred the foam though no breeze blew and the stars glistened like frost. The night was warm and somewhere in the heart of the reef Gossamer began to feel the heat of new life glowing against her flank.

Fortune drifted in and out of sleep as the stars moved in their heavenly round, and later he could not have said whether he had passed more of the night in dream or in reality, nor which state it was which embraced him when he lifted his eyes to see the falling star.

At first it seemed to be an ordinary night dragon cutting a shining arc through the darkness. But then, when it was directly above him, it stopped and grew large, larger still, until it finally began to descend. Soon it floated before him and as he gazed into the blinding whiteness he saw that inside there was a dragon, a stranger with a familiar face held in an aura of flawless light.

'Father,' he breathed.

'My son,' replied Welkin.

The second star raced in low over the sea, lifting a trail of silver ripples from the water as it approached the reef and then halted before him, framed with the same aura which embraced old, smiling Welkin. In it was his mother.

'Go to her, Fortune,' said Clarion in a voice as clear as spring. 'The time is yours now, for a while at least.'

'Don't go,' he pleaded, but already the two dragons were accelerating upwards together, joining to form a single point of light which fused and then expanded briefly to fill the heavens and then shrank to a barely perceptible glimmer.

And then it flared one last time and Fortune watched it ride the sky on a trail of fire, vanishing beyond the darkness behind the stars, perhaps going to the places where Mantle had gone, perhaps beyond even those. Perhaps they would never stop.

Fortune woke then, or perhaps he fell asleep, and as he did so a distant, joyful cry shook him free of whatever magic it was which had held him in its spell. Opening his wings he kicked away from the shore, hugged the air and turned inland to answer the call of his new-born infant.